C000255572

The Apocaly...

War of the Undead

A Zombie Tale by Peter Meredith

Forward

This is the story of the second day of the apocalypse as seen from the perspective of those who fought on the front lines of the quarantine zone and by those who were trapped within. Although there are easily ten-thousand stories from that time, few give us as full an understanding of the dire nature of the emergency as those depicted within these pages.

I have assembled a short list of the pertinent individuals mentioned within and they are as follows:

Benjamin Olski—A resident of Poughkeepsie, New York. One of the few to survive the destruction of that city.

Dr. Thuy Lee—Lead researcher at the R & K Pharmaceuticals Walton facility. Using the innovative and inadequately tested Combination Cell Therapy, she had discovered a cure for cancer, however her work was sabotaged resulting in the subsequent apocalypse.

Ryan Deckard—One time security chief at the Walton facility.

Chuck Singleton—A cancer patient and one of the few people to leave the Walton facility alive. He was late for the beginning of human trials and thus was not infected by the deadly Com-cells.

Stephanie Glowitz—A cancer patient and one of the few people to leave the Walton facility alive. She was also late for the beginning of human trials and thus was not infected by the deadly Com-cells.

Dr. Samuel Wilson—Oncologist at the Walton facility. One of eight people to survive the destruction of the Walton facility.

Anna Holloway—Anna was a research assistant at Walton as well as a spy for a competing pharmaceutical company. She is in possession of a stolen vial of Com-cells.

Lieutenant Eng of the People's Republic of China—Eng is a spy and saboteur. In his undercover role as a research assistant, he made changes to the Com-cells which had worldwide repercussions.

John Burke—A cancer patient who received only sterile water during the trial. He thinks that he is immune to the deadly effects of the Com-cells.

Courtney Shaw—A state trooper dispatcher who oversaw the initial quarantine zone around Walton.

General Horace Collins—Commanding officer of the 42nd Infantry Division, a National Guard division with its headquarters in Troy, New York.

PFC Max Fowler—Soldier in the 42nd Infantry Division.

Marty Aleman—Chief of Staff of the President of the United States.

Jaimee Lynn Burke—Aged eight, she is the daughter of John Burke and the first person to escape the quarantine zone. She is thought to be partially immune to the Com-cells

Eric Von Braun—Even though he died at the end of the first day of the apocalypse, Von Braun is mentioned a number of times within these pages. While he was injected with the Com-cells, he was able to partially fight the effects of the disease through the heavy use of narcotics. This lessened the rage within him, allowing him to retain a modicum of mental acuity, making him far more danger-ous than the average infected person.

Chapter 1

A First Kill

March 27, 2015

4:01 a.m.

For one man in Poughkeepsie, the screams and the frequent gunshots meant a dream come true. For Benjamin Olski, the zombies that were running amok outside his apartment window represented a chance of a lifetime, but only if he could rein in his fear.

Terror had been growing in his mind ever since he peered through his quarter-inch thick spectacles and watched the first man die on the street. It had been just some dude, looking stupidly preppie with his collar up-turned and his khakis neatly creased. As though he were part of a morbid opera, he'd been surrounded by three of *them* in a wheel of golden light thrown down from a high streetlamp. With the dark all about, the scene was vague in its details and grainy like an old home movie.

The beasts were black-eyed and had hands that were hooked into claws. Their mouths, dark pits smeared with old blood, gaped wide, looking way bigger than normal mouths; they were like the jaws of a lion. Because they moved so well and with such deliberation, Benjamin initially mistook them for ghouls, but they were too well dressed for ghouls and too clean to have crawled out of a coffin. No, these weren't creatures from the grave; they were zombies, *fast zombies*, the very worst kind.

The soon-to-be dead preppie had looked like a fool, putting up his fists as though he was going to box with them, as if that was even a possibility. Benjamin, crouching his lanky frame behind his bedroom curtain shook his head, saying, "What an idiot."

A second later, they attacked. The preppie fool punched one and then was ripped apart by their teeth and their claws. Benjamin watched, gripping his .38 caliber pistol in two sweaty hands. He could've gone down there and killed a few of the zombies, but even as he told himself that the man was a goner anyway, he knew that it was just an excuse.

The truth was the zombies struck cold terror in his heart. They were vicious and strong, and so much faster than he'd been led to believe by all the movies he'd seen and the stacks of comic books in his closet which he had read over and over again.

When the three zombies in the street lifted their heads from the feast, they wore glistening beards of dark blood and Benjamin had whimpered.

But now was his time to shine…hopefully.

Across the hall from him lived Cheryl O'Neil. She had long, long legs; a deep year-round tan and tits only money could buy. For a year now, she had starred in his dreams and not just in his increasingly perverted fantasies. She also took center stage in his daydreams, the ones in which he was a hero, the ones straight out of a comic book.

He had lived so much of his lonely life in those books because what choice did he have? He was greasy, scrawny, and his pale skin sported perennial zits that bloomed in every season. Because his mother had told him they would scar him if he touched them, he left them to bead into sickening pustules. Since he seldom bathed, he stank of old sweat.

At twenty-eight, he was a nerd, a sad, socially inept nerd who could only dream about a girl like Cheryl, except now was his chance to impress her!

There was a man in the hall screaming vulgarities and pounding on her door. Benjamin stuck his eye to the peephole and saw it was one of her many ex-boyfriends. Just another no-name jock. Cheryl's boyfriends all came and went quickly and all were tall with lantern jaws and perfect hair and none bothered to introduce themselves to Benjamin. They never even seemed to notice him when they passed in the hall, almost as if he wasn't fully human in their eyes.

But now the tables had turned. The ex-boyfriend didn't look right. Sweat streamed from his thick, wavy hair and his normally handsome face was twisted into an angry mask. But it was in his eyes where the biggest change lay. They were wet and dark like pits of tar.

"Open up, bitch!" the Ex yelled at the top of his lungs. "I know you're in there. I can smell you. You're behind this. You did this to me!" His fists were bloody from all the pounding; he didn't seem to notice or care. He was driven by his need; wanting to get at Cheryl and hurt her and probably eat her as well.

Benjamin knew what he had to do. He'd read a thousand comic books and they all agreed there was only one thing a hero could do in this situation: he had to save the girl. After living a lifetime unseen in a societal shadow, he had to step up and prove himself…but the Ex seemed so big and so violent and the sound of his fists splintering the wood had Benjamin cringing even with the gun in his unsteady, damp hands.

Strangely, the gun seemed both heavy and small. It felt like it weighed fifty pounds in his soft hands and yet he was afraid that it wasn't big enough to do the job, and he was afraid that he would miss and he was afraid that if he did hit the Ex it wouldn't kill him and he was afraid… just afraid.

He had lived his entire life in fear. It was why he had always retreated into the world of daydreams and comic books. "But not now," Benjamin whispered. "Okay, okay. Here I go. Here I go." He couldn't seem to bring himself to move. He just stood there, hyperventilating, as Cheryl's screams, which had been muffled, were growing louder with the disintegration of her door. The Ex was practically through.

"I can do this," he hissed, gathering together the filmy shreds of his courage and stepping into the hallway. The man was right there not five feet away. Benjamin raised the pistol. It was like holding a living thing. It was hot and all the shaking in his right arm seemed to come from it. Benjamin took hold of it with his left hand as well, mostly to try to tame it but partially to control the embarrassing trembling. Oh, how badly he wanted to pull the trigger right then. It would be so much easier to shoot the man in the back; much easier than actually confronting him, but would a hero do that? Would *Batman* or *Wolverine*?

"No," he said, under his breath.

Benjamin steeled himself, puckering his ass, taking a firmer grip on the gun and swallowing loudly. He then yelled in a reedy voice that was nearly as high-pitched as Cheryl's: "Stop! Leave her alone."

Although Benjamin had the pistol out and had it pointed with all the menace his shaking hands could generate, the Ex didn't seem to be too concerned by it. He turned from the door, snarling like a dog, showing black gums. His hands were bleeding and the blood wasn't right, it was too dark. It came out a deep maroon, looking almost congealed. Just like the rest of him, it was wrong. Benjamin knew it. Fresh blood should've been brighter, almost cherry in color.

"You're a zombie," Benjamin said, voicing his accusation.

The Ex's snarl turned into one of the hated sneers, the kind that jocks had always used to dismiss nerds like Benjamin. "Who the fuck are you calling a zombie? You little pig, shit, fuck!"

He took two steps forward and Benjamin took two steps back, hitting the wall next to his apartment door with his back foot. It was unexpected and he guessed wrongly, that his door had closed behind him. He thought he had trapped himself in the short hallway with a very big man-eater and, in a rash of panic, he pulled hard on the trigger.

The gun bucked in his hands, again so much like a live thing. It was like trying to hold onto a small, violent animal that wanted to jump out of his hands. The bullet went over the Ex's right shoulder, cutting the air with the hiss of a snake until it struck the chandelier over Cheryl's dining room sending glass raining down.

Benjamin didn't hear the sound of breaking bulbs and shattering glass. He was in a panic zone where nothing registered on his senses except the half-formed zombie in front of him. His hands were spazzing in fear and when he shot a second time, he did so with the same jerking motion, missing a second time, again high and to the right.

"Fuck!" Benjamin screamed, pressing his back against the wall. He was trying to aim for the head because, as everyone knew, that's where you had to hit to kill a zombie and this was most certainly a zombie. It had barely paused after the first shot and didn't at all after the second. It was now so close that Benjamin's third shot traveled exactly two feet before it crashed through the upper teeth of the zombie and blasted out the back of its throat.

The Ex was staggered but didn't fall. It said something in a horrible, wet gurgle before it again tried to rush forward. Benjamin fired twice more taking out chunks of flesh and bone before he managed to bring the Ex down. He then stood there for a few seconds against the wall, hyperventilating and shaking.

"What did you do?" Cheryl asked in an airy voice. She stood in a state of contortion, her arms bent and crooked, one leg twisted so that she looked to be protecting her privates with one knee. Her back was hunched forward and her neck was extended, stork-like so she could see out into the hall without taking a step.

"I saved you," Benjamin answered in the same breathless manner.

"You killed him." Cheryl pointed briefly at the dead Ex before pulling her hand back. "You killed Andy."

He nodded and then couldn't stop. An uncontrollable shaking gripped his entire body; he was practically convulsing. The shakes became so bad that he thought they would rattle the gun right out of his hands. This was a real fear because he'd seen enough movies to know the gun would discharge when it hit the ground. And where would the bullet go? Half the time it would plunk someone straight in the forehead.

The smart thing would be to put it down, but he was afraid to; he was afraid there would be others like the Ex... and maybe worse. That dreadful thought had him considering the idea of reloading the six-shooter.

Cheryl derailed his train of thought by asking: "Why?"

Benjamin had been fiddling with the .38, trying to remember how to pop open the cylinder, but stopped and looked at her, wondering if he had heard her correctly. "Why? Why what? Why did I kill him? You're asking me why? It was self-defense...your self-defense. You should be thanking me, that's what you should be doing. He was going to kill you."

"You don't know that," she said, still in that same awkward bent position.

"Are you retarded? Of course he was. Look at his hands." Benjamin used the pistol to point at the Ex, but Cheryl didn't look at the Ex; she just stared at the quivering gun. Embarrassed that his fear was showing, Benjamin stuck it down the front of his jeans so that the grip hung out for a quick-draw. He thought he looked cool.

"He was breaking all the bones in his hands just to get at you," he went on to say. "Do you think he was doing that just because he wanted to talk? No way. He was one of *them*. He was a zombie. That's why I went for the head shot. It's the only way to kill them...but it can be tricky in battle situations."

"Oh," she said.

Benjamin looked confused. That was it? He saved her life and all she could say was *Oh*? He couldn't remember a single comic book he'd ever read where the damsel gets rescued and all she has to say is: *Oh.*

"I think you're in shock, Cheryl. Maybe you should come over to my place and have a drink. I have some beer. It's Rolling Rock. That's good, right?" He had no idea. The beer had been sitting under an ancient pizza box in the kitchen closet when he had moved in eighteen months before. He had since chucked out the pizza box but had kept the beer, thinking that one day he would try it.

This seemed like the perfect day.

"Come on. You'll be safer over here. Your door won't hold them back."

"Them?" she asked coming forward, timidly. Her big blues went unblinking as she stared at her Ex and all the holes in his deformed head. "He...I...I...How do you know they're zombies?"

Benjamin helped her over the body and then hurried her into his apartment, locking the door behind them. "I'm somewhat of an expert on these sorts of things. I've been studying zombie lore for years." This was actually true in its way. As a zombie fanatic, he knew everything there was to know on the subject, and now he could honestly say he was one of the few people on the planet who'd come up against one and defeated it single-handedly.

Feeling manly, despite the shakes that wouldn't leave, he went right for the beer. It was warm, smelled like skunk, and tasted like ass. He said, "Ahhh," and tried not to grimace.

Cheryl took one sip, frowned and put hers down without touching it again. "They're zombies," she stated, her eyes still wide and unblinking. "Ok, alright. I can...I can see that, I guess. I mean I heard screams and I saw people. They were getting attacked."

"They were getting eaten," Benjamin corrected, remembering the stupid preppie jock who had bought it right in front of his window. He was absently fingering the rounded head of a tremendous zit on his chin. Cheryl had trouble looking at him.

"Ok, ok, eaten. They w-were getting eaten. Eaten alive, right?"

"Yeah," Benjamin answered and then took another swig of the awful beer. Again, a grimace twisted his features, but he accepted it this time, he even took another swallow as soon as he could set his face to rights again. The beer helped with the shaking.

"And you kill them with head shots. Do you have another gun?" She looked hopeful until he shook his head. Crestfallen, she asked, "So what do we do? I tried the police but all I get is an answering machine."

"Have you tried seeing what they're saying on TV?"

"No, I was afraid the light and the noise would draw attention. I mean, did you see all of them out there? They were breaking into people's houses and cars and dragging them out and..." For a few seconds, her mouth continued to form words but the sound had stopped.

Benjamin took a huge pull of his sewer-tasting beer, coughed, spluttered weakly, and said, "Yeah, I saw. Maybe we should try to find out the extent of this. What we do will depend on if this is nationwide or if it's just us, together, alone."

It was just after four in the morning and more than a hundred calls had been made to the local CBS affiliate, but not many of them had been answered and none since the lone technician had stepped out to see whether he was the butt end of a seriously huge practical joke. His name was Arnold Ness, and the sound-reducing headset he wore had made him oblivious to the frequent gunshots that had been going on for half the night.

He had taken less than twenty steps into the parking lot before he was attacked. Now Channel Two was running unattended and the feed coming in from New York hinted that nothing in particular was amiss.

Benjamin and Cheryl squatted in front of the TV. He had a hand on her back; she wasn't wearing a bra. They watched until there came an explosion from somewhere north of them. Cheryl ran to the window and stared out. "I think it's the hospital," she said and again there was that airiness to her that made it seem as though she was made of helium, like some sort of balloon, and that a stiff breeze might send her floating away.

"Get down!" Benjamin hissed, pulling her to the floor and getting in a good feel in the process. She didn't seem to notice. "If you're seen they'll come for us," he said directly into her ear. He then pulled his gun, theatrically—the only way he knew how—and went to the edge of the window and peaked out. "It's the hospital alright. It's on fire. Ho-lee-shit the flames are all the way to the top of the building."

"So what do we do?" Cheryl asked again, pulling him down into a squat. When Benjamin started to shrug she snapped, "You're the expert. That's what you said. So what do we do?"

She was right, he was the expert. He wanted to stay put. Hiding in the apartment with her had a lot of possibilities. Then he remembered the Ex saying: *I can smell you.* Benjamin didn't think a person could hide from their own smell. "We make a break for it," he said, feeling the shakes threaten to come back. He put his hand on her back again. "There may be other survivors."

He stood, went to his kitchen table and finished off the first beer of his life. Next, he went to his bedroom and grabbed a box of shells. Behind him, Cheryl watched on tippy-toes as he used his thumbnail to dig out the spent shells from the cylinder. They bounced on the hardwood floor and rolled away under his bed. He reloaded and stuffed the remaining shells into his backpack.

"What should I bring?" she asked.

He considered for a moment trying to weigh all his fears. He desperately wanted to get out of the city as fast as possible, but all his reading told him to expect the worst: a full on calamity that would stretch from coast-to-coast, meaning they should be packing every last can of beans.

He compromised. "I think we should bring only one bag each, like a backpack. Take only one change of clothes and fill the rest of it with food and water. But be quick! I want to go in five."

She was ready in three; in jeans and a leather jacket, she minced her way around the corpse of her Ex and together they slunk down to the lobby where they stood just inside the doorway, afraid to go any further. There were "people" on the street, moving restlessly. But they weren't people, they were zombies of course, just like the dead Ex. They would stare up at the streetlights as if they'd never seen them before or they'd rush at moving cars, throwing themselves across the hood or beneath the tires. Sometimes Benjamin caught a good look at them when the light was right and their black eyes were like deep holes in their faces.

At the sight of them, Cheryl froze with her face to the cracked lobby door, but Benjamin had the gun and was feeling the beer. "Follow me," he said, heroically, and then like a mouse, he crept out into the night, his eyes darting all about. He reached for her hand but she refused him, holding her purse in both hands, keeping it close to her bosom.

In seconds, they were in the parking lot hunched down between the cars. He led her to his '97 Tercel; she took one look at the rust and the flame decals on the hood and turned up her nose. "We'll take mine, it's way better." She had a 2012 Nissan Juke, an odd little two-door vehicle that was in fact better in every way. For one, there wasn't duct tape holding the driver's side mirror in place.

He put his hand out for the key to which she only snorted, "No way. It's my car, I'll drive."

"What the hell?" he hissed. He didn't care for this new, assertive Cheryl. First not holding his hand and now this? She seemed too full of herself. "Are you forgetting I saved your life?"

With the night air damp on her cheek, all the airiness seemed to have leaked out of her. She looked down her narrow nose at him and said, "Yes…maybe. We don't know that for certain, but…but it doesn't matter. This is my car. I drive my own car and if you don't like it, well, you can leave."

Benjamin was outraged. He had put his life on the line for her! He had killed for her. "Maybe I will leave," he hissed, turning for his Tercel. He stuck the gun under one arm and was digging for his keys when her fear got the best of her.

"Wait, I didn't mean that. Don't go. We should go together, right? It'll be safer, right?" Fear didn't sit well on her features like it did for the leading ladies in Hollywood. She looked contorted again: lips askew, her forehead lined like a rake had been run across it, her eyebrows all cock-eyed. Even her hair, normally a golden run of honey-blonde that flowed like a river, was plastered down looking as dirty as his always did. He didn't like it. This wasn't how his fantasy was supposed to be.

"Alright, I'll come with you, but only if you do what I tell you and you let me drive. I know how to drive in these situations. It takes skill and precision. It's not like going to the store."

"Then I should hold the gun, right?" she asked. "You know, just in case we get attacked. You drive and I shoot."

"No...wait. What?" he answered. "I...I...maybe you're right about driving." He knew he was, at best, an average driver and he had already proved that he was a piss-poor shot. How much worse would he be at both if he tried them at the same time? "You can drive. A gun like this is a bit much for a girl to handle. It's got a kick to it like a mule."

She didn't argue or say anything concerning his chauvinism, she just jumped into the Juke and gunned the engine into life. He was barely in his seat before she was peeling out of the lot.

"Take it easy," he admonished in his superior manner and then not a second later cried, "Floor it!" as two zombies came rushing from around the building.

Cheryl leapt a curb, ripped up some grass, and made it to Parker Avenue and then, two turns later, they were on I-44, buzzing east. There were zombies in the road and many more on the side streets and in the lawns of people's homes. Wherever they went there were screams and gunshots, fire and smoke…and bodies. There were so many bodies, scattered about like discarded trash, littering the city of Poughkeepsie. They were everywhere.

Benjamin kept a firm grip on his gun until they cleared the first police roadblock just outside the city limits. Here there were more bodies and more zombies, many in the blood stained uniforms of state troopers.

"Don't stop!" Benjamin ordered. "Don't even slow down!" There was a car in front of them that was being attacked by a dozen or more zombie-cops. They were bashing in the windows and dragging the people out. The screams went right to Benjamin's soul, freezing it.

Cheryl glanced at him and his gun and he took the look as a challenge to his manhood. "They're already goners, damn it! You don't understand about zombies, they're infected and everyone they bite gets it too. You see? It doesn't matter what we do, they're gonna die."

"Why are you getting so mad? I didn't say anything."

The screams were so loud and shrill, they were like drills in his ears. "Just keep driving," he moaned.

She drove along the shoulder, hitting something that felt like a downed telephone pole. It could only have been a person. Benjamin cringed and Cheryl made a mewling noise in her throat—then they were back on the road and it was clear.

"We made it," Cheryl said, giving him a sour, sick grin.

"Yeah," he replied. For a time, the car was quiet as the road hummed under them, until an idea came to him. "We should probably find, like, a police station or some…" He paused as a car came speeding around the bend in their direction. It flashed its headlights and Cheryl flashed hers right back. "Slow down," Benjamin suggested.

She did, however the other driver swished right past without stopping. "What do you think that was about?" she asked.

He knew it meant trouble. Everything meant trouble. "Maybe we aren't out of this yet." Ten miles further on, he was proved right. They crested a low hill and saw before them four police cruisers blocking the road, their lights whipping the night. In front of the cruisers on the two-lane highway were thirty or forty cars and trucks lined up.

Cheryl pulled up behind the last one and then looked at Benjamin expectantly. She wanted him to get out of the Juke and find out what was going on. He wanted to stay put and double lock the doors if possible. But he was the hero and the expert.

With a shaky breath he stepped out of the car. The night was chill and he blamed that for the case of the shivers that struck him. He had his gun, which he held out in front of him and it was little wonder that the people in the truck just ahead of the Juke refused to talk to him. No one would. The people in the cars were of two frames of mind: hysterical and weeping or panicked and dangerous.

Most pointed their own guns his way and the rest either hid beneath coats and blankets or sat, staring at him in horror.

Feeling alone and vulnerable, he made his way to the front of the line where there was shouting and more guns being pointed in every direction. A small mob was gathered on the road in front of the police cars. It was impossible to tell how many there were because the police had spotlights trained in their faces. The glare was so bad that Benjamin moved to the shoulder of the road so that he could see properly.

"Stop right there!" a policeman with a loudspeaker yelled. The order was directed at Benjamin; he had been pinned beneath the powerful strobe of one of the spotlights.

Benjamin froze in place. Even the features of his unpleasant face seized up, causing someone to mutter: "Is that one of *them*?"

"Get back with the rest!" the policeman with the loudspeaker demanded. "No one leaves the road or you will be shot. You are in a quarantined area and cannot leave. Turn your vehicles around and go home."

A man in a yellow sweater yelled back, "You have no right to hold us here against our will! This is a free country, damn it."

The loudspeaker blared in response: "Under sections 1169 and 1170 of the Greater New York Charter we have the authority to uphold this quarantine. You are being asked to return to your homes until it is safe. Disperse now!"

"Or what?" Yellow-sweater demanded. "You'll shoot us? We have you outgunned." He waved his arm to indicate the men around him.

The beam of light on Benjamin was like something out of a sci-fi book. It seemed to have powers beyond illumination—Benjamin felt immobilized by it as though it were a freeze ray. He wanted to drop his gun and hightail it out of there but he couldn't budge.

"I say we get these pigs," the man in the yellow sweater said to the others on the road. "What do you say?" When he turned to look for agreement he did so with eyes that were ugly and dark just like the dead Ex's had been.

Benjamin was afraid to say no to him and more afraid to say yes. Thankfully, being frozen as he was he couldn't do either.

Two of the men were equally jazzed up to rush the police, a few others were conflicted and only stared around in confusion and the rest were backing away. Benjamin wanted to back away as well, only the light held him in place like a tractor-beam. It wasn't until the man in the yellow sweater charged and guns began to bang and roar that the light pivoted away.

Then there was blood spurting and screams and muzzle flashes blinking in the night like huge and angry fireflies.

The man in the yellow sweater was hit by a hail of bullets and yet he kept going, charging the police cars while dragging what looked like a Gordian Knot of intestines on the ground seven feet behind him. Benjamin

flung himself into the ditch on the side of the road and began to crawl and whimper back toward where he had left
Cheryl and her long legs, hiding in the Juke.

When the shooting died down and there was nothing
but awful gurgles and ugly growls, and a single man crying, Benjamin jumped up and raced for the car. Behind
him came a monster. He heard the slap of feet and harsh
breathing. Fear had Benjamin by the throat and when he
turned, his face was drawn back in a rictus of fear and his
hands were taut claws.

It was a man after him…or what had been a man
once. Its face was covered in blood and its teeth looked
long and white and very sharp.

Without thinking, Benjamin shot him the chest.

The man stumbled into Benjamin's arms and suddenly gone was any sign of the monster—the man's eyes were
very blue and the gums of his mouth nice and pink. He had
been covered in someone else's blood but now there was a
hole in him and his own red blood was coursing out.

"Why?" he asked in a soft, confused voice.

"I…I…" Benjamin couldn't spit anything else out,
and it didn't matter. The man died right there. His head fell
back to hang loose and long as if a lynch mob had gotten
him and not the cowardly bullet shot by a cowardly man.

"Oh, jeeze!" Benjamin moaned and then dropped the
corpse onto the street where its head smacked against the
pavement sounding like a fallen coconut. "Oh jeeze!" Benjamin said again, this time feeling his dinner rise up into
the back of his throat.

He thought for sure he'd throw up, but when he bent
at the waist he saw movement off the side of the road.
There were real zombies coming out of a grove of hem-
lock. Further back were others, mere silhouettes but they
were zombies, Benjamin knew.

There were so many.

Forgetting the man he'd just murdered and the acid of
vomit in his mouth, Benjamin ran for the Juke, making it
just ahead of the first creature.

"Go! Get out of here," he yelled, his voice creeping over the edge of hysteria. Cheryl started to head down the road toward the police cars, but he grabbed her wrist. "No, not that way. Just…just turn around. We can't get out this way."

When she made the turn, she drove over the leg of the man Benjamin had shot. He could hear bones break like snapping twigs. This time he did throw up and because of the zombies all around them, he didn't dare roll down the window. He puked in Cheryl's backseat.

Chapter 2

A Disappointing Meeting

4:41 a.m.

General Collins of the 42nd hated to be kept waiting, and this was especially so when the fate of the country had been thrust into his lap. The last thing he needed was to be cooling his heels in the Governor's mansion while the night went to shit and the zombies multiplied and swarmed like locusts.

According to his watch, he began his meeting with Governor Stimpson at 03:41. It wasn't a long meeting. They were in the same room for all of six seconds, just long enough to shake hands.

Stimpson was the living embodiment of a politician: he wore a beautifully tailored, dark blue suit, was soft-skinned, tanned, smooth and glib, full of empty but pretty sounding words; he had a wide toothy grin and was a good hand-shaker—in other words, a complete fake.

He had breezed into the room with that phony smile cemented in place, gave the general a firm shake of the hand and said: "I'll be right with you, General. I have some things to take care of." He started to walk away but turned swiftly, catching Collins wiping his hand on his BDUs; there had been something decidedly slimy about touching the politician. Stimpson pretended as though he hadn't seen. "Make yourself at home. The kitchens are open if you're hungry."

Kitchens? How many were there? "No, thank you."

"Suit yourself," Stimpson said, giving a second, even brighter, professional smile and hurrying away.

General Collins stood for a moment wondering what could be more important than a city the size of Poughkeepsie being destroyed. With a weary shake of his head, he settled himself down on the plush leather couch and took out the smart phone he barely understood. The logistics of calling up a division sprawled over six states was daunting; there were plans in place, however they read like a repair manual for the space station. He had a tiny PDF version on his phone; it was a thousand pages long and the wording was hell on his aging blue eyes.

An hour later, he was still seated on the couch and still staring at the phone. He yawned for the hundredth time and there were tears dripping from the corner of those tired eyes when the Governor re-emerged, still sporting the slick-as-oil smile despite the hour. He offered a second, over-warm handshake and started walking the general back the way he'd come.

"I'm frankly a little surprised you're here," the Governor said. "Why aren't you—what's the word—marshaling your men?"

"I have people for that," Collins assured, not realizing the division call-chains were riddled with old and unused numbers and that the entire process was well behind schedule. "My job entails a broader spectrum. I have to oversee the entire situation, from the lines of battle to logistics. I also have to deal with politicians."

The Governor gave him a new smile, he seemed to have a hundred of them in his back pocket that he could whip out at a moment's notice. He pointed the general to a chair opposite his desk. It was a magnificent beast of a desk, a vast expanse of Honduran hardwood, but far too big for one man, even a man with the ego of Stimpson.

"Ahh, yes," he said around the smile. "I bet you dread the politicians."

"I dread the waste of time," Collins answered, curtly. "In battle, and let me be perfectly clear here, we are in a battle, minutes or seconds can be pivotal."

"And yet isn't the motto of the army hurry up and wait?"

Governor Stimpson's smile was now at its widest; Collins wanted to rip it off his face and stomp it under his boot heel. "I don't have time to wait and neither do my men. I need *shoot on sight* orders," he said bluntly. Stimpson's smile began to unravel. Collins went on: "These… these infected persons are far too contagious and more deadly than I realized. They're like something out of a movie or a nightmare. I've seen them, Governor; I've seen them up close. You have no idea what they're like. We need to kill them and we need to kill them at a distance."

The Governor's smile had warped into a grimace and even that was crumbling. He stood abruptly. "I have to see…I mean I have a, uh, another meeting. Can you wait here for a moment?"

Collins leaned back, his face a mixture of shock and anger. "Hold on. You can't possibly have another meeting as important as this one. I have men preparing…"

"I'll be just a moment." He left the general spluttering to go stand in the hallway. It was an important hallway, all stiff and dark with mahogany walls. It was too dark in his opinion. It was heavy, and gloomy and very foreboding. It was an important hallway that led to his important office where all the important decisions were made.

"Fuck," Stimpson said in a whisper, before fleeing from the hall and the office and the important decisions. He didn't want to be anywhere near the damned place.

Making important decisions wasn't the reason he'd run for the position of governor. He wasn't governor because of some puritanical calling. He wasn't there because of the "public good", either. He was governor because it had been a way for him to fulfill his potential. He was, after all, better and greater than everyone else—the title and the position proved it. He was governor because he was important. People deferred to him; some practically bowed to him, and they all came crawling on their hands and knees, begging when they wanted something.

All except that damned general. No, he was all stiff and righteous and… "There's no way this is happening," Stimpson said, as the general's request echoed in his ears. *Shoot on sight.* "What the fuck is that? Who asks that?"

It was one thing when some freaked-out police dispatcher made ridiculous claims of zombies in their midst —regardless of whether the claims were at least partially corroborated by the superintendent of the State Police— but now a general as well? Had the lot of them been sniffing glue together?

Yes, he was sure *something* had happened out at the Walton facility, something horrific. Airborne PCP, or that crazy new drug: bathsalts; someone had probably poisoned the water with it, or maybe they had put heroin in the hash browns. It had to be something that made sense. But zombies? No way! It wasn't possible. In fact, a part of him had agreed to call up the 42nd just to prove, if only to himself, that it was impossible.

General Collins wasn't supposed to side with the crazies. He was supposed to be the adult in the room. But that was out the window now. *Shoot on sight…*the words kept on whispering in his ear like a skipping record.

In a patter of patent leather, Stimpson fled to a sitting room where his staff had waited in an uncomfortable silence. The Governor burst in, throwing his hands in the air. "He wants *shoot on sight* orders. Can you believe that?"

The six staffers and two guests were silent, each glancing around to see who would speak first. Offering opinions was the quickest way to having one's career ruined—bad advice was remembered long after good advice had been appropriated by the Governor as his own.

Eventually, Jennifer Gilmore, Stimpson's chief of staff, said in a quiet voice: "Don't do it. These are your constituents, Bob. If you start killing them…I don't know if they'll forgive you."

"You mean when they're dead?" Andy Rizz, the Superintendent of the New York State Troopers asked. He laughed at his own joke; it was a dry, humorless sound. When no one joined in, he cleared his throat, making the knuckle of cartilage in his neck leap.

Jennifer gave him a scathing look. "I mean their relatives and their friends and everyone who sees the Governor on TV giving the execution orders."

"And if he doesn't give the orders?" Rizz demanded. "My troopers are dying like flies out there and it'll be the same with the army!"

The man from Health and Human Services, Jerome something, Stimpson could never remember what, shook his head. "The army has much better guns. They have tanks. As far as I know, zombies can't take down a tank."

"He can't authorize tanks," Jennifer replied, talking about Stimpson as if he wasn't there. "And for the same reason. Tanks and rockets and machine guns all kill indiscriminately. We can't let this catastrophe be used an excuse to feed the military industrial complex. Remember, Bob, your voters are not big on the army and they voted you in to help put a stop to all this military spending."

"You'll look weak," Rizz countered. "And if this gets out of control, you'll be blamed."

"No, the army will be," Jennifer countered. "We'll be able to spin it so you won't be touched, Bob, but just as long as you aren't seen as the trigger man."

Rizz leapt to his feet. "This is ridiculous! If half the state gets eaten alive no one can spin you out of that."

Jennifer, looking completely unruffled, folded her hands in her lap and said, "I can. You forget I was working for the mayor during Hurricane Katrina. Practically that whole stinking city was destroyed, but because of me, he came away smelling like roses. The trick is to pin it on someone else and just keep hammering it home. You see, Bob, it's all about the optics and if you give these fascist orders to shoot on sight, it'll be you who gets pinned."

That was the winning argument.

They had gone on for a while longer. Jerome something had stuttered out a bunch of scientific sounding poppy-cock about the virility of the disease and its communicability and some nobody from the Department of Transportation had blah-blahed on about something called a panic-jam that could grip the entire state, but what Stimpson only really cared about were the optics.

How was he going to be perceived? That's what mattered.

He nodded wisely as the conversation progressed and smiled when appropriate, his tanned face showing easy laugh lines that always had the voters thinking he was such an amiable, likable fellow. A guy you could have a beer with, that is if he actually drank beer, which he did only at county fairs when he needed to be seen as a 'man of the people'.

He couldn't be seen as the guy who murdered his own citizens.

"Thank you for your input," he said, still showing that winning, confident smile as a hundred miles south of him a housewife named Janice Tate barricaded herself in her bathroom.

Janice was done screaming. When her husband had torn out their son's throat with his teeth something in her voice-box had just plain ripped in mid-scream.

Since then she couldn't even talk, not that there was anything to say. Joe had turned into one of the things…one of the demons roaming the streets in the town of Pleasant Valley, New York, a ten-minute drive from Poughkeepsie. Joe was a monster.

Janice threw her weight against the bathroom door just as Joe attacked it. The wood shuddered with the violence and all Janice could think about was Joe's teeth. They were white in his dark mouth and so long and so sharp. She hadn't had time to count them but now there seemed to be so many more than he once had.

Teeth, teeth, teeth.

She was going to be eaten alive. Janice Tate stretched out one arm for the medicine cabinet, hoping to God there were enough pills to kill her before the teeth got her.

The door thudded again and again. It was shaking; she was shaking. There was a sharp *crack* from it just as she grabbed the first bottle—Joe's statin meds for his cholesterol. She flicked off the lid and chugged the twenty remaining pills, chewing them and, in her fear, not tasting the bitter medicine. The next bottle she grabbed was a half-finished bottle of Tylenol with codeine.

"Yes," she whispered and then down the hatch went sixteen pills. Now a huge fracture split the door. Joe put an eye to the crack and it was just as black as the ace of spades. "No, no, no!" she said reaching for the next bottle.

Janice didn't want to die like Mrs. Donner from across the street. She had gone on and on, wailing in horrendous pain as she was eaten. Two doors down, the Olson's son, Freddy, had let out blood-curdling screams for twenty long minutes. His problem was he kept escaping, jumping up and running for his life, but he was always dragged down again. It was a problem because he wouldn't die. Janice knew what was best.

A white bottle of aspirin went down her gullet next and, as Joe smashed through a panel of the door, she washed it down with nearly a half a cup of cough syrup. She wanted to overdose. She wanted to go out quietly, however fate wasn't so kind. Joe got through the door when she was two fisting bottles of who knew what.

He went for the soft skin of her stomach, his teeth slicing in as though she was made of cream cheese. She vomited an ugly goop of purple mess onto the top of his head and then she found her voice again and let out a reedy scream. She cried for help and she cried out to die.

A hundred miles away Governor Stimpson was oblivious. He sat back down behind his desk and looked at the general and secretly disliked him, although he didn't know why.

General Collins was stiff in his chair. *Like a fucking board*, Stimpson thought. And when he nodded, the Governor was sure he heard the metallic creak of stiff-ass metal. He was like a robot and should be treated like one. "Your request to shoot on sight is denied," Stimpson said, picking the tiniest piece of lint off of his suit coat. "Your men will fire their weapons if they are attacked by someone with a gun. Do you understand? Do not fire unless fired upon. That strategy worked in Iraq, it damned better work in America."

Collins could see the dislike in the Governor's eyes; he couldn't care less. All he cared about was his men, his mission, and his country. "And if my men are attacked with some other deadly weapon? A knife, a club, what-have-you?" When the Governor paused to consider this, Collins added, "My men are not trained as law enforcement officers. You'd be endangering their lives if they aren't allowed to fight back."

But what about the optics? Stimpson wanted to ask, however the general was clearly a man who didn't understand about the bigger picture. He was too short-sighted.

"I have to look at the bigger picture, General. Remember Kent State? I won't subject my people to another Kent State, especially not on this scale. That reminds me, you are expressly forbidden to use any planes, bombs, tanks, mortars or machine guns. Oh, and no flame throwers, either."

A hundred miles away Janice Tate was beating on her husband's head with all her might. Joe had gotten to her liver and the pain was so exquisite that her bladder had let go in a hot rush.

Governor Stimpson picked another piece of almost invisible lint from his suit and said, "Really, this isn't much of an issue. By their very presence, your men will deter anyone seeking to break the quarantine. And if someone tries, then I expect your men to use proper judgment and restraint. We both know how things can get out of hand. Perhaps we should consider bodycams. So the men will…"

"Bodycams?" Collins demanded, letting out a crazed cackle. "Yeah, let's do that, and while we're at it maybe we should read the zombies their fucking rights!" Collins found himself on his feet with the knuckles of both hands planted firmly on the ridiculously huge desk. "You have no clue what's going on, do you?"

Janice went stiff, immobilized by the worst pain yet. Joe had chewed his way into the hepatic artery; she could feel her pulse like thunder. She could feel it right to the tips of her ears. Her arms shot out and her fingers were splayed. Then through the pain she thought she could hear her pulse and it was a miracle! The lub-dub grew fainter with each beat. She was dying. Finally she was dying.

"What I know, General, is that there are conflicting reports from a few hysterical eye witnesses. Yes, I know something bad is happening in and around Poughkeepsie, but so far no one has proved to me that it's bad enough for us to turn the guns of our armed forces around on the very people they were sworn to protect. Your job is to contain this, nothing more."

Janice breathed her last, a hitching, bubbling sound that never seemed to end. It just got quieter by degrees until it disappeared beneath the sound of Joe's lips smacking as he rooted around in her guts like a pig at a trough.

Collins kept his fists on the desk because he knew if they came off he would punch the Governor right in that smarmy smile. Through gritted teeth he said: "Containment isn't going to be enough."

Stimpson let out a practiced air of sadness as though he wished there was something more he could do in the situation. "Get me some hard proof, General, that I can bring to the people. Until then I want anyone caught trying to break the quarantine detained only. Think about how they must be feeling, in their minds they've done nothing illegal, certainly nothing that would warrant execution. They will be detained only. Is that clear?"

"Yes Sir," Collins replied, feeling a pain in his guts. His men were going to pay with their lives. "I have one question. Why did you bother calling us up if you aren't going to use us properly?"

Because that's what the optics called for, wasn't an answer Stimpson could give to this narrow-minded general. As Governor, he had to be seen as doing something, but what he couldn't be seen doing was killing his own people. "Like I said, you were called up to enforce a quarantine, not to kill people. Really, General, you're embarrassing yourself with this shoot first attitude. Have you considered that this *issue* might burn out naturally? Have you stopped to think that these infected persons might just die on their own? Or get better on their own? You see? We just don't have enough information yet to just go around killing people and until we do you will carry out your orders with the minimum amount of bloodshed."

The general pictured the one and only zombie he had faced: it had taken three rounds to the chest and hadn't even slowed. These things weren't going to die on their own, of that he was certain. "You need to see for yourself what's going on."

"I plan on it," the Governor replied. He would tour the front, eventually…but only when the camera crews arrived and the situation was more controlled. Going without the cameras would be like not going at all. "Until then, you have your orders. Oh, and General, find out who did this. We need to bring them to justice." By this he meant he needed to be able to point a finger somewhere else just in case fingers started pointing at him.

At that moment, the zombie, Joe Tate, lost interest in the corpse of his wife. The body was growing cold and the maddeningly erotic thump of its heart had ceased. In somewhat of a lethargic stupor, it left the house and stumbled uncertainly for a few hundred yards. His hunger had been satiated, however it came roaring back an instant later. He'd heard the scream of another human and that was all it took.

Chapter 3

A Choice of Socks

6:30 a.m.

At exactly half past six, the President's Chief of Staff, Marty Aleman, received the daily security briefing, just as he had for the previous six months and, as always, he marked the President as "in attendance" though the old man was still snoozing away. It was a little white lie that hurt no one. Hearing the endlessly dire reports straight from the mouth of the experts about the Russians and the Chinese and Iranians and the seemingly endless number of terrorists, had given the President an ulcer in his first year in office. That was another little secret no one talked about; no one could know that the great man had any weaknesses. He felt he had to appear perfect from his shining, helmet-like hair down to his perfectly manicured toenails.

Marty would normally give him a watered down version of the threats facing the country right after the President ate breakfast. A servant would bring tea and coffee, the official photographer would snap pictures of him nodding sagely, and they would be interrupted a dozen times, but in the end, the President would get the knowledge he would need to face the reporters and he would get the advice he would need to get re-elected.

The advice was always the same: do nothing.

Who really cared if the Russians were gobbling up chunks of the Ukraine? What business was it of ours if the Chinese took over the South Pacific? And who were we to tell the Mullahs in Iran that they couldn't have a nuclear bomb? Sure, these were issues that would have to be dealt with, but that didn't mean they had to be dealt with now.

The American people had spoken in three straight elections: they weren't going to put out any effort to nip things in the bud if it didn't affect them right at that moment.

This morning was different.

With his mirror-shined shoes snap-snapping urgently across the glossy, wood floors, Marty hurried from the West Wing to the Executive Residence. Normally, he gave the security briefing in the Yellow Oval Room, a spacious open room that was also used as a reception area prior to state dinners. That morning he bypassed it, heading through the West Sitting Hall and right to the President's Bedroom.

A pair of Secret Service agents gave him a quizzical look, but said nothing as Marty began tapping on the door, lightly—the President didn't care for loud, incessant knocking, even if it was an emergency. It made him high-strung and snappish.

Emanuel Geometti, the President's butler, answered, again with little more than an inquisitive look—the President also didn't care for whispering, it made him paranoid and he didn't like it when people within earshot spoke to each other in a normal tone either—it interfered with his concentration, even if he was just picking out socks.

"It's important," was all Marty said as way of explanation to the butler.

"What's important?" the President asked. He was seated on the end of the bed holding two pairs of socks: red for a touch of whimsy, or black for a serious day. He had been considering going with the red, but the early knock had him thinking otherwise.

"Emanuel, can you give us a minute?" Marty asked. When the butler stepped out into the hall, Marty explained the situation, and then when the President just stood there with his mouth hanging open, he went over it again. The word "zombie" hadn't been uttered by Governor Stimpson and yet the concept was right there front and center. Marty did his best to downplay that side of the situation occurring in New York, but the President wasn't a complete fool.

"What you're describing is a zombie outbreak," he said.

Marty nodded and shook his head, simultaneously so that he just sort of bobbled from the neck up. "Yes, but there is no way we can use that word. We're going with *infected persons*."

"Do we have proof of any of this? I mean real proof? A video or something?"

"We have a bunch of eye-witness accounts, including a National Guard general who did a personal reconnaissance in Poughkeepsie, but we don't have a video beyond a few grainy and fleeting ATM camera shots that we can't use. I've seen the pictures. They look somewhat like that *Bigfoot* hoax from a few years back."

The President looked down at his socks, unable to come to a decision on which to wear. He needed his butler, just like he needed Marty. "So, what do we do?" That was the usual question he would ask after Marty's daily briefing. The usual answer was "nothing." The President was always "looking into it" or "conferring with world leaders" or "waiting on a comprehensive study." And the people were always reassured that the President was ready to "tackle" the issue, whatever it might be, just as soon as he could.

Doing nothing would not work, not this time. The President had punted on Social Security reform, and welfare reform, and tax reform and pretty much everything of importance, but this wasn't something he could leave for the next administration to clean up.

"We jump on it early," Marty suggested. "We contain the situation and we find those responsible and hold them accountable."

A pinched look collapsed the President's face. The situation, if true, was unnerving, however the idea of "jumping on it" was even more so. There were so many consequences to actual action that it was mind-boggling, especially to someone who couldn't make up his mind which socks to wear.

"Do you mean we should send in the Army?" the President asked. "Because I-I don't know about that. Is it even legal?"

Marty smiled in that benign way he had when speaking to the President, or to his four-year-old granddaughter. "Well, Sir, the Posse Comitatus Act basically keeps the military from performing any duties domestically that are normally assigned to local law enforcement. As an example, our armed forced wouldn't be able to arrest any citizen attempting to break the quarantine. However, the National Guard can, as long as it's not under the command of the regular Army."

"So…so what does that mean? Do we use the army or not?"

"We should, but not yet. We can't be too eager, especially since this is still New York's problem." Marty paused as he saw the President's blank look. "It's their problem because of the Stafford Act? You know, the act that authorizes the use of the military for disaster relief operations but only at the request of the state governor, which, as of yet, we have not been given. That being said, we should prepare for that contingency. With your permission, I would like to ready FEMA crews."

"FEMA?" the President asked with some hesitation. The Federal Emergency Management Agency was still a bit of a bugaboo around the capitol. After the fiasco of hurricane Katrina everyone was wary to invoke the agency beyond the occasional tornado or flood. It was true that FEMA's emergency plans had been updated and the training that its members received was more thorough and detailed, but there was a specter of failure hanging over the agency.

"Yes, FEMA," Marty said. "It's our best tool at the moment."

"But what if…" the President couldn't finish the question.

"What if they screw up again? This is an entirely different situation. For one, the press is on your side and for two, we'll put them under the jurisdiction of General

Collins of the 42nd. That was one of the issues in New Orleans; too many agencies going in too many directions. In this way, you are seen acting confidently, like a true leader but you won't be on the hook for any issues that might arise. It'll be on Collins or Governor Stimpson."

"I like that."

Marty knew he would. The President's inability to make decisions had been well established. Even as a state senator he had voted "present" on almost every vote that didn't concern naming a bridge. It had always been up to Marty to steer him to the proper conclusions. In some ways the President was like a talking doll; you had to pull his string to get him to dance. This was why Marty always made sure to get to him first thing in the morning before anyone else could get to him and muddle up his thinking.

The Chief of Staff went on pulling the string: "Now, we should call a full cabinet meeting on this, of course, but don't let the Sec-Def drag you into this. If he brings up the Insurrection Act you just tell him that any authority the office of the President has was nullified by the 2008 repeal."

"2008 repeal, got it."

"And don't be surprised if Milt in Homeland Security gets his panties in a bunch. FEMA is technically under his jurisdiction. Just remind him that *everything* is under your jurisdiction."

"I never liked that guy," the President muttered. And that too was Marty's doing. He was personally repelled by the idea of an entire department dedicated to "Homeland Security." That was what the FBI and the CIA were for, not that he cared for those agencies either.

"Well, if things go to pot, he'll be the first we hang out to dry," Marty said. At first the President smiled at this but then a frown of worry swept his face like a rain cloud threatening to darken a picnic. Marty patted his shoulder. "Don't worry, Sir, this will not get out of hand, I promise you that. The 42nd is being called up even as we speak. It's a ten-thousand man force, equipped with the finest weapons money can buy. We have to start looking at this as an opportunity. Remember what that old Chicago guy from the last administration said: never let a crisis go to waste."

"Meaning what?"

"Meaning we let our enemies on the other side of the aisle hang themselves on their rhetoric. They're always going on about de-regulating everything under the sun. They have even wanted fewer regulations on big pharmaceutical companies and this was an R &K screw up."

"Did they break the law in some way? You said it was an accident."

Marty was within a whisker of rolling his eyes. "Sure. Probably. But it doesn't matter, either way. Now's our chance to rein in *Big Pharma*. They've made their last penny of profit off the sick."

"Good," the President said, with little enthusiasm. In the last election, he had raked in a ton of dough from R & K—perfectly legal campaign contributions, of course, all except a few hundred thousand that had been funneled back door into an overseas account that not even the First Lady knew about.

He wanted to mention something concerning the legit campaign donations, but Marty was already out the door with his cell phone kissing his ear. He wasn't calling about the state of readiness of the 42nd, nor was he talking to Milt Grodin who headed up FEMA, no, he was on the phone with the FBI. There were culprits involved in this disaster and he wanted to make sure the right people were blamed.

"Emanuel!" the President bellowed. "I need you, immediately. You have to help me choose." In the right hand was the whimsical red and in the left was the serious black. The butler knew all about job security and thus made a show out of deliberating the choices, as if this was to be the hardest decision facing the leader of the free world that morning.

Red was chosen, while eight hundred miles north, within the slowly expanding quarantine zone, terror built on terror and the stench of fear grew to become a physical thing that coated people like crusts of ice, causing them to shiver in their hiding places. They trembled beneath their beds like children, or in closets under piles of clothes or in the back seats of cars in garages, slumped down low beneath the edges of the windows.

One little six-year-old, named Helena, frightened by the screams coming from her parent's room, climbed up into her chimney where the soot turned her into shadow and the ash covered her scent. She was safe for three hours until she couldn't hold her pee-pee for a second longer. She squirmed down and left little black footprints in the beige carpet. Helena shouldn't have flushed the toilet when she was done, but out of habit she did. Her mother ate her minutes later.

For the most part, hiding was pointless, the zombies could sniff people out easily. Only those who were armed and who turned their homes into fortresses and, most importantly, fought back, had a chance at survival. Even then, the odds weren't good. Few people were equipped with enough ammo to fight off the growing hordes or they were using weapons unsuited for the killing of zombies.

Knives put a person in arm's reach of death; bats and axes spread the deadly Com-cells around, infecting everyone. Fire was clumsy and tended to kill friend and foe alike. Sometimes even guns were practically useless. With the dark, people found themselves shooting scoped rifles from distances of ten feet or less. In these cases, the scope made the rifle *less* accurate. Others found out the hard way that although shotguns could blast the heads right off a zombie, they also filled the air with deadly spores.

A family might survive an attack, only to *turn* a couple of hours later.

Interestingly, the best weapon of the night was the .38 Smith &Wesson. In the dark, it was as accurate as any other gun and because of its manageable recoil, it remained a steady weapon to fire even by smaller individuals; women and children used it as effectively as men did. Its greatest asset was the fact that it was considerably under-powered compared to most of the weapons in the quarantine zone. There were a mere handful of weapons of a smaller caliber, simply because men liked guns more than women did and men liked them big.

Excessive stopping power was a useless characteristic against zombies, as they simply did not stop no matter what sized weapon was used against them. Only a head shot had any chance at killing them and the .38 was the least likely round to cause an exit wound.

The people in the quarantined zone fought or hid and in some desperate cases they ran. The streets were deadly. Cars seemed to attract the creatures, drawing them out of every nook and cranny in town. Cars were swarmed and people were dragged out into the streets and eaten alive. A few, like Benjamin Olski, were lucky to get out of Pough-keepsie without actually hitting a zombie. Many who made it out were forced to plow through the undead, crushing them under their tires and covering their vehicles in black blood and spores. The drivers and their families all suc-cumbed, eventually. The disease turned most of them, but a few held on only to be riddled by bullets from law en-forcement officers on the verge of full-blown panic.

All night, state troopers had trickled into the area and were directed by dispatcher Courtney Shaw to fill the holes in the perimeter. The main roads were her first prior-ity and she was stretched thin just to cover those. At 5 a.m., when her eyes were rimmed red, her task force of eight women were yawning and slumping over their key-boards, Courtney had only managed to reach 70% con-tainment. There were simply too many firebreaks and log-ging roads and fishing trails that spider-webbed outward from the epicenter at Walton.

Fearing the spread of the disease, Governor Stimpson, had used the arbitrary distance of twenty miles as the ra-dius of the quarantine zone and General Collins had tasked her with putting a cork in every road out of the area. Courtney had to use a calculator to figure the circumfer-ence of the circle she was expected to cover. "Holy shit," she had whispered, seeing the number. "A hundred and twenty miles? Are you sure?" she had asked the general. "There's no way we have enough troopers."

By her count she had approximately two hundred and forty-one men in and around the area, not realizing that twenty-three of them had already been infected or killed in the staging area just outside of Poughkeepsie and another fifteen had been killed or wounded in desperate shootouts with frightened and sometimes diseased citizens.

Collins sighed into the phone. He hadn't needed a calculator to realize they were likely screwed. "You'll find a way to do this because you don't have any other choice. Button it up tight until I get the guardsmen in place."

"But…"

"Just do it," he growled, before hanging up on her.

She had done her best but she knew it wasn't good enough. Having grown up in Pleasant Valley, she was familiar with a good chunk of the land. Her father and brothers had hunted there, her uncle grazed sixty Holsteins on 20 acres there and she had tromped along half the dirt roads as a kid going to and from friends' houses or to school. She knew there were more ways in and out of the area than that she could count.

There was only one way to button an area that big and that was simply not to. She straight up lied to Pemberton and told him they were guarding a seven mile radius. This cut in half the number of places that needed to be guarded, allowing her to double the number of men at each, and yet the line still did not hold.

The men guarding the road into Titusville stopped answering their calls at just after one in the morning. It was a scramble to replace them. Hell, it was a constant scramble all night long. When the six men holding the main highway south, ran out of ammo in the face of a colossal horde of undead, they fled, leaving the five thousand people of Wappinger Falls to fend for themselves. Unfortunately, they were almost all fast asleep and the first inkling that there was something dreadfully wrong, was when they heard the screams; screams so loud that some people thought they were storm warning sirens.

For Courtney, it was hours of work without let up, directing men here and there, hoping to God they were plugging every hole.

Her little crew worked the phones and they worked them in fear. Courtney spent a good chunk of her time listening to a dozen police nets simultaneously. She was deathly afraid that there would be a suspicious call in Albany or Hartford or White Plains, somewhere outside the circle that represented the quarantined area, somewhere so far outside the circle that she would find herself stuck in a new and ever widening quarantine zone, unable to get out.

Although they didn't have time for it, Courtney wasn't the only one listening to these far-flung police calls. The entire staff was listening and second-guessing every domestic violence call, every drunk pulled over for crossing a yellow line, and every false alarm called in by overwrought housewives when their men were out trucking the big rigs back and forth across the state. They listened to those calls and were afraid.

"We should get out of here," Renee Bilton whispered.

"And abandon our troopers?" Courtney shot back. "No, we stay until the National Guard shows up." Had Courtney known the state of readiness in the 42nd Infantry Division she might have changed her mind. She had begun the call-chain for the 27th, the 50th, and the 86th infantry brigades, however without her focusing squarely on it, things had ground to a halt. The commanders of the 50th from New Jersey and the 86th from Vermont called their governors instead of instituting the call chain. With both governors completely ignorant of the situation, neither was given authorization to proceed.

The 27^{th,} from New York had proper authorization from the governor, however three key personnel in the chain never picked up their phones; one was Lieutenant Colonel Guy Lawler, commanding officer of the 1st Battalion, which just happened to be the closest infantry battalion to Walton. He was vacationing in the Bahamas and sleeping off three too many pina coladas from the night before. His executive officer, Major Renwald had let his phone's battery die and slept through the night like a baby, and the battalion's operation's officer, the "S-3", Captain Mason had simply left his phone in the car. He didn't see the message until after five that morning when he was about to drive to work.

The 1st Battalion was the closest unit to Walton and they were one of the last to get their call-chain functioning, which meant the thin blue line was all that stood between the zombie horde exploding in size and engulfing America.

In desperation, Courtney found herself calling police stations hundreds of miles away, but what she really needed was the damned army to show up. She assumed things would get better when they finally made it, and she assumed they had been trained to handle situations like this, and she assumed they had better weapons. These assumptions weren't based in reality.

Chapter 4

Her Need Fulfilled

6:41 a.m.

Anna Holloway, spread-eagle and naked as the day she was born was lashed to the bed. She had to piss like a mother, her hands were purple and numb, and she had an itch on her belly where Eng's semen had dried, but did she complain? Hell no.

Her watchword was compliance, and it had been all night long. For two long, miserable hours she had been used in the most sexually demeaning ways imaginable by Eng. The perv had flipped her like a pancake, bent her over chairs and stuck his ridiculous thing in her in every conceivable manner and yet it was hard to call it abuse, especially since she had more than asked for it, she had begged loudly for more.

A shiver went up her spine at the memory, causing her to discover another itch in the small of her back. She tried to wriggle it away and as her only triumph of the night beyond not being killed, the itch left her.

"Hoo-fucking-ray," she whispered. Even though she had insisted it wasn't necessary, and that she wouldn't try to run away, or stab him in his sleep, or take his gun and shoot him in the face, Eng had shredded up one of the sheets and had tied her in place because, of course, given the opportunity she was going to do one or all of those things. And why? She knew he would probably kill her... No, he would definitely kill her. It was just a matter of when. After all, she was a loose end. As far as she knew, she was the only person left alive who could point the finger of blame at him.

Her worries ate at her, but he seemed just fine. When he had finished living out every one of his sick fantasies with her, he fell asleep on the floor with just a pillow and blanket. It was strange and creepy as hell. For five hours he had slept, and in all that time he hadn't moved once. Worse, for Anna, who was desperate to escape, his eyes had remained cracked. Here was a guy who couldn't open his eyes wide enough to fit a quarter in sideways when he was awake but in sleep she could see his damned pupils.

It made an escape attempt dicey as hell. Slowly, ever so fucking slowly, she twisted at her bindings. She strained in agonizing silence, pulling as hard as she could until her limbs shook. Eventually, after an hour of stifled grunts, she felt one of the sheets start to give away. It was the one clamped around her left ankle.

Fuck!! she screamed in silent rage. What good would a loose foot do her? Sweating harder than she had during Eng's pathetic rutting, she laid-back to stare at the ceiling. Tears wanted to come. Now that she wasn't fighting the sheet, fear over her terrible situation had her close to blub-bering. The cold reality was that by letting the damned *Chink* go to town on her, all she had done was hold off her death by a few hours.

There was no question, he would kill her. He would need to move and fast. He'd need to get out of the country. And he didn't need her. He was an actual spy with the complete backing of his government, while she was just one woman who was now too petrified to go near an ATM for fear that her bank accounts were even then being moni-tored by the FBI. And who could *she* turn to? Certainly not Rhonofis, the French pharmaceutical company she had been spying for. They weren't stupid, they would disavow all knowledge of her. She would bet her life on it.

So where did that leave her? In all likelihood she was even then being hunted by the police or the FBI, which meant there was no way she could go back to her apart-ment. And her car was back at Walton surrounded by zom-bies. She couldn't go to her bank or to her mother's or anywhere.

The only thing of real value that she possessed, the only bargaining chip left to her was the vial of Com-cells. It still sat in her lab coat. Eng had torn the coat off of her and had thrown it haphazardly to the side, not batting an eye when it made a "clunk" sound. Anna had nearly choked. How quickly would she have died if the vial had broken? Or would she have died at all? Another shudder ran down her back as she remembered the walking horrors around Walton.

Now, with the dark beginning to turn, she still didn't know why she had kept the damned vial. It was, after all, direct and irrefutable evidence of her guilt.

She fell asleep and dreamed about a prison where all the other inmates were zombies. She found herself outside her cell with a chance to run away but there were more zombies out in the real world and so she ran back to the one place she was safe, her cell.

For his part, Eng slept like a baby. He couldn't have been happier. Although it had been touch and go for a while there, he had accomplished every one of his goals: Thuy was dead, the Com-cells were now a catastrophic failure, and his supervisor in China was about to disgrace himself. Eng had heard through the grapevine that his superior was about to begin testing a version of the Com-cells that could only end in a fiasco.

Even the fire had worked to his advantage. It had destroyed every scrap of evidence that linked Eng to whatever was happening around Walton. Really, the only evidence left was right there in the hotel room tied to the bed. Yes, things were looking rosy for Eng, and man if his balls weren't aching in all the right ways.

He had dreamed about Anna. First about fucking her and then about killing her and, in his dreams, it had been easy. He had taken her lab coat, wrapped it around her throat and pulled until her face was purple and her eyes bulging black.

Eng came awake with the gray dishwater of morning light in the air. He gave the girl on the bed a look and thought about fire. One more blaze should do the trick. It would take away, not just fingerprints, but also fingers and every drop of Eng's DNA he had left either on or in Anna. The one thing a fire wouldn't take care of however, were dental records and Eng figured a chair leg applied thoroughly and ruthlessly would confound any dental expert.

These were the happy thoughts that had him smiling. He saw Anna pretending to sleep and that was just fine—in fact it was better than fine, it was perfect. Who needed to hear her whine and beg for her life? That sort of thing became annoying, fast.

He flicked on the TV, expecting to see the fire at Walton leading the news and he wasn't disappointed. A few hundred deaths, a building going up like a bomb, a respected pharmaceutical company at the bottom of it all; this was what made for good television. But what was being displayed was more than he figured, a lot more.

This was Defcon 2. This was the National Guard being called out. This was a possible terrorist attack on American soil. This was the airports being closed and roadblocks thrown up over half the state. This was the President being briefed. There was even a shot of the old geezer stepping off *Marine One*, looking "concerned."

It was a moment before Eng realized that it was canned footage. It was full light around the President in the shot and yet Washington DC was in the same time zone as the dinky motel where the sun was still twenty minutes from cracking the furthest horizon. Eng breathed a sigh of relief but it caught in his throat as he saw the crawl at the bottom of the screen: *Travel restrictions are in place in the following counties: Putnam, Duchess, Orange, Ulster…*

Eng had no idea what county the cheap roadside motel was in but he had a sinking feeling in his gut. Thinking that there was no way anyone would be looking for him for at least a week, and feeling his dick throb every time he had looked over at Anna, he had pulled over, the night before, at a motel ten minutes from Walton.

Now, he yanked out his smart phone, and gritted his teeth as he looked up a map of New York only to find… A second later, he spat out, "*Cao ni ma!*"

"What is it?" Anna asked, coyly, from the bed. She wasn't stupid. She could read the scrolling words at the bottom of the television screen and knew what was happening. For her this was a golden opportunity. They were surrounded.

She envisioned searchlights and sirens, and barbed wire across every road with police cruisers sitting nose-to-nose as a secondary barrier. She pictured men in camo skulking in the tree line carrying big guns, and barking dogs going through the bushes, sniffing out anything with a pulse. There was little chance that Eng could get past any of that, but she could. If there was anyone on the face of the earth who could sweet-talk their way out of a bad situation it was Anna Holloway.

Eng needed her still, but neither of them knew just how much.

A world away at the Siangou Research and Development facility in Shanghai, China, the very place to which Eng was hoping to flee, a disaster was brewing on an epic scale.

From all outward appearances, the Tiesu Research Facility of Shanghai was state of the art. It boasted the finest western-made equipment money could buy and all the top researchers had either been trained overseas or at the Tsinghua University in Beijing, easily China's top college.

Tiesu was a tall building and new; less than five years old. It gleamed wherever there was the least bit of glass or metal, and was a brilliant, stark white practically everywhere else. Its security rivaled the Pentagon's both in depth and breadth, with checkpoints and armed guards on every floor. It seemed like the least likely place for a plague to originate and yet within six weeks, three billion zombies would be able to trace the source of their affliction back to one person.

Jiang Xiao, the facilities third highest ranking researcher strode through his labs with a blue mask held to his face. He wore latex gloves but nothing else in the way of protective gear, not even a lab coat. Ergot Alkaloids weren't harmful in the tiny amounts being used in the preparation of *his* Com-cells. Just as Eng had predicted, Jiang had been stealing all the information that Eng had stolen from Dr. Riggs.

"Let me see the results," he snapped, in sharp Mandarin, at one of the junior researchers the moment he came through the heavy steel doors of the number "9" room.

The labs were numbered with the most important projects quartered in the first three labs. There was a reason he'd stuck the Com-cell research so far in the back where only the newer scientists worked. As the chief scientific liaison, he had done his own manipulation of Eng's findings, adding nitrogen and a tiny amount of sodium borohydride—a reducing agent in the bleach family—to the mixture. He inserted just enough to ruin it and he wanted the researchers who were too new to question a thing.

And really, who would question a thing? Any negative issues would be blamed on Eng or the Americans, or one of the many underlings that were constantly under foot, and any positive outcome would be claimed by Jiang.

The junior researcher, one of the meek little ones he liked to brow beat, but which one it was he couldn't tell behind her mask, smiled at him with her eyes in a way that made it seem as though she was in pain, and then pointed Jiang toward her station where she had the latest stats already on screen. The tenth round of testing showed results that were as dreadful as the first nine had been. Basically, nothing was happening.

"May I recommend changing one of the variables within the Com-cell, Dr. Xiao?" the junior researcher dared to ask. "It makes no sense to continue replicating the trial, endlessly."

She was wrong, there was one perfectly good reason and that was to thoroughly discredit Eng and the American Com-cells. Jiang looked down at her, his face held in rigid lines that came to a sharp part in his neat black hair. "I don't remember asking your opinion," he said. His tone was haughty and his eyes hard. As always, he was snappish and exceedingly quick to offer harsh criticisms; at best it could be said that he treated his underlings as though they were his personal chattel and yet, if asked, he would describe his leadership as "fatherly."

Dismissing the girl with the Ph.D., he clicked the mouse, bringing up the lab results of the unofficial research project, what he had told everyone was his own personal concept, when in truth it was the exact formula Eng had sent him—Riggs' formula, the one that turned people into monsters. Behind the mask, a smile cracked Xiao's generally humorless face. The tumors in the test rats had shrunk forty percent in three days.

"Excellent," he whispered.

The junior assistant cleared her throat and he shot her a look from his coal-black eyes. She blanched at the look but steadied herself before saying: "There may be a problem with this project. I am so sorry, sir, but the anti-social behavior that we noted two days ago has increased."

"And what did I say then?" he demanded.

"Uh…uh, you explained that the neurotropic activities of the ergot alkaloids may cause temporary hallucinations and attendant irrational behavior, but that the end result is worth the risk. That's what you said, Dr. Xiao, however this is worse than that."

"Show me," he ordered, striding toward the kennels so quickly that the tiny junior researcher had to jog to keep up. As he waited for the researcher to punch in her door code, he fitted his mask on properly over his face. If there was a problem he was sure that it was the fault of one the young idiots working for him and there was no telling what they might have done.

The door opened and the girl stepped back, drawing her lab coat closer about her thin shoulders. She was afraid and for good reason. The noise in the room was surprising; there shouldn't have been more than the occasional low squeak of the caged rats but it sounded, instead, as though there were a hundred snakes hissing in anger.

Xiao followed the noise past the official test subjects, who squirmed about in rat-fear, but otherwise looked fine. The problem was in the cages beyond them where his rats were. His rats had been injected with the same formula Dr. Lee's had used in her project at Walton, the same formula that had been sabotaged by Eng, the same one that Eng had assured him would work miracles.

"What is this?" he demanded. "What did you do?"

His rats looked awful. Their usually glossy coats were clotted and nasty. Even though each enjoyed a cage to themselves they were patchy and mutilated as if they'd been fighting. The wounds wept a black substance and the same fluid dripped from their eyes.

His proximity to the cages riled them up to a higher degree. They hissed even louder and flung themselves against the thin metal bars to get at him. Some even tore at the bars with their jagged teeth; one somehow managed to break the metal.

Xiao turned to the girl in outrage. "Explain this!"

She hadn't budged from the doorway and now she cringed back another step. "We believe this is a side effect of the Com-cells. We did not stray from your instructions."

"I want to see the access logs. I want to know who fed them and what they fed them. Someone will pay for this…and you…"

"Doctor Yaoh."

"Doctor Yaoh? You call yourself a doctor? If you're a doctor why don't you tell me what is coming from their eyes. Hmm?"

"We don't know. You were in meetings all yesterday and you told us not to bother you at home and you said to run only the prescribed tests. You were very clear on that, sir."

She was right but that didn't absolve her in his eyes. "Do you not understand the first thing about taking initiative?" She kept her eyes on her clunky, sensible shoes. "I guess not. You have a lot to learn about science, Yaoh. We'll start today. I want you to find out what that black fluid is. Run cultures and do a full blood panel on them.

And then…then move them to the number three lab and increase their bio-status to Category B. Just in case."

Category B required a much more stringent level of personal security: hoods with face-shields, gowns, and heavier rubber gloves and boots.

As per his instructions, the infected rats were moved, and in accordance with their training, all precautions were taken. The staff was glad to see the rats moved, especially Yaoh. These particular test subjects gave her the freaks and she had stepped back, allowing the other scientists to wrangle the hissing and squirming little demons into smaller transport cages.

Given the choice between touching the fiends and cleaning up after them, she happily chose the latter, right up until a piece of jagged metal punctured her glove and slid beneath her skin. The "9" laboratory hadn't had its bio-safety level increased and all she had on was latex. She didn't panic, not entirely, but she was afraid and disgusted nearly to the point of being nauseous. The rats had been revolting, filthy things, and the black goo had smelled of a toilet in one of the city slums where the water only ran every other day.

Cleaning the tiny pin-prick was her first concern. As she hurried to the sinks, she tore off the gloves and went through the ten-step procedure to clean a puncture wound, leaving off the final three steps: present one's self to the building medical personnel, fill out an incident report, and present one's self to one's immediate supervisor.

Yaoh wasn't about to put her neck right into the noose over such a small scratch. Jiang had a reputation for firing first and asking questions later and she needed the job. For five minutes, she scrubbed the wound until her flesh was red and raw. Satisfied that no germ could have survived, she reached for the paper towels and that was when she realized that in her haste she'd stuck her gloves in the front pocket of her lab coat instead of disposing of them properly in one of the bio receptacles.

She glanced around quickly to see if anyone caught the mistake and then slipped the soiled gloves out of her pocket and into the proper trash. She didn't see that in the bottom of her pocket was a small drop of black goo.

It was just one mistake; one small breach of protocol—but it wouldn't be the last.

Within thirty minutes Yaoh was wincing from a headache. In another thirty it was practicably unbearable and yet in the People's Republic of China you couldn't simply beg off work so easily, not if you wanted to keep your job. There was always the option of going to see the medical personnel, however Yaoh was suddenly feeling suspicious of them and their needles and their bright lights.

"I have a meeting," Yaoh suddenly declared to the other scientists. "With a representative." This stopped the friendly banter, which had been going around the room. Everyone's mood had lightened now that the black-eyed rats had been moved much further down the hall; now they went thin lipped and their smiles took on a preformed appearance. Sudden meetings with a *People's Representative* were usually an unpleasant harbinger of things to come.

"It's about my cousin," Yaoh said, trying to assure them. "She's…they think she's a subversive but she isn't."

That helped, but only a little. Everyone in China had heard stories where investigations blossomed and grew deadly roots that reached out to strangle the guilty and the innocent alike.

One of the scientists, a man named Veng who had unruly, spiked hair, and wore glasses two centimeters thick, and who had a serious crush on the meek Yaoh, asked: "Do you need a character witness? I am more than willing to…"

"No," Yaoh said, practically running out of the lab. With her head throbbing, she headed for the lady's room, but at the door she heard voices on the other side. They would be loud as a roomful of hens, she just knew it. She knew they would cluck maddeningly and the sound would pound into her head making her grow crazy, making her want to hurt them. She already wanted to hurt them.

Barely holding herself together, she went for the elevators and rode one deep underground where it would be quiet and cool, and where there'd be fewer people to hear her moan. The basement was a labyrinth of storerooms and machinery and dark shadows if one knew where to look.

Yaoh searched out the dark to hide in. She found a room in which the lights had burned out. It was perfect. Not only was it properly gloomy, it was also piled to the ceiling with boxes of lab equipment, all of which clinked with the sound of glass on glass as she barricaded herself in.

Her mind was going—the pain was great and so too was the hate. It was awful and all she could think was that she had to hide, she had to burrow as far from people as she could get or she would hurt them. As fast as she could, she moved the boxes against the door, and all the while the sound of the lab equipment breaking went right along her nerves like someone dragging a needle across her brain.

Still she worked and she took the pain, knowing that it would be a blessing when all the boxes had been shipped to one side of the room and there was only quiet and dark.

Finally, it was over and all that there was left to her was the pain etching along the neurons in her brain. There was a sound that accompanied the Com-cells multiplying: it was a crackle, like fire. It started small much like the pain had, but soon the crackle became a roar, again just like the pain.

Long, hard minutes passed and both the pain and the sound grew huge in her head. The pain thrummed and the sound of it was enraging, building and building within her until she couldn't take it anymore. With a shriek, she charged the boxes and began throwing them aside in great heaps. Something drove her to get out of the room but her eyes were growing ever dimmer and the room seemed to grow darker with each box she flung. The boxes crashed as she heaved them but where the door was she couldn't tell. There were always more boxes and more pain.

She was in the far corner of the room with a box high over her head when the door was shoved open behind her and a stab of light had her cringing.

"What's going on?" a man asked. He was short and thin with olive skin and black eyes. These generalities were the most Yaoh could make out, that and the fact he looked so clean. And he smelled clean, cleaner than she felt at least. From thirty feet away, she caught his scent, an intriguing mixture of old sweat, cheap cologne, and yesterday's fried dumplings. It awakened something primal inside of her.

Yaoh was suddenly ravenous. It was a wicked, greedy hunger that knew no bounds. It was a hunger that neither morals or laws could restrain. By now, her brain was black with the Com-cells, she was simply beyond thinking. She leapt over piles of fallen boxes to get at the man.

His eyes bugged to the full extent his epicanthal folds would allow and, too late, he tried to slam the door in Yaoh's face, only she was far too fast. She was strong, as well.

Her ninety-four pounds felt like a hundred and fifty to Xun Long Bao. He was a maintenance worker and was used to hefting large boxes and crates around all day long and yet this tiny woman pulled the door out of his grip and was on him before he could even think about screaming.

When they went down, struggling together and her teeth tore into his left bicep, he certainly screamed then. It wasn't the bite of a rape victim using her last defense or even a lunatic under the spell of some mental aberration, it was the bite of a monster. She latched on and then pulled up with her whole body, tearing out a hunk of meat that dribbled blood all down her face.

She tried to swallow it without chewing and nearly choked. At first Xun could do nothing but scream but as she tried to retch up his flesh he pushed her off of him, finding her surprisingly light. Then he was on his feet and racing down the hall with Yaoh right on his heels. She was cheetah fast, but had terrible vision and wasn't good at abrupt turns. This was the only thing that allowed him to make it to the stairs ahead of her. He ran up four flights and burst out into the lobby of the Siangou Building.

"Call the police!" he wailed, running for the main doors. "Call the police!"

Yaoh came out of the stairs filled with an all-consuming hunger. It was a predatory hunger. Even though there were people all around her, she oriented on the fleeing man. She could smell his fear, it was invigorating. She could smell his blood, it was intoxicating.

She raced after him as he left building, running into the heart of Shanghai, the most heavily populated city in the most heavily populated country in the world. The streets teemed with humanity. The roads were like endless rivers of people. They crowded the heavens, living one on top of another in skyscrapers that reached a hundred stories into the air.

Their smell was overpowering, taking over the last remnant of Yaoh's mind. She went mad because of it and her hunger was only equaled by the sudden rage that engulfed her. She wanted to kill them all.

People shied away from the tiny woman with the black eyes and the mouth that was runny-red with blood. She looked like a demon and that was appropriate; within a day, she would create hell on earth.

When she tore through the crowd, fighting to get to the wounded maintenance worker, she infected nine people. When the police tugged her off his limp body she infected six more and left spores lingering in the air. She was taken to the fourth busiest police station in the city and within three hours, there were over two hundred people infected in the building. They roared and spat and bit and slowly the Com-cells spread.

The 7AM to 3PM shift raced out of there as soon as they could. Some went home to infect their families. Others went to the market and infected scores more there. Many, with headaches growing behind their eyes, went to one of the fifty bars between the station and their homes. In all, they took fourteen different busses and six different train cars, coming in close contact with over a thousand people. On average, those thousand took two hours and six minutes to become contagious and by eight that night, the city's police force had responded to over three-thousand Com-cell related attacks.

It might seem like a drop in the bucket in a city with twenty four million people, and yet those attacks would decimate practically the entire police force by eleven that night, leaving the city completely defenseless. China has no second amendment. People were forced to defend themselves with knives and clubs, bricks and sticks, all of which were practically useless.

The numbers of zombies in such an environment swelled exponentially, doubling every hour. At nine, there were six thousand zombies roaming the streets attacking everyone in sight. At ten, that number was twelve thousand; at eleven, that number was twenty five thousand.

The sun rose on a city in flames. Bodies and body parts littered the streets. Zombies, now numbering over a million, surged in teaming packs toward anything that was even vaguely human. Brick and steel would keep them at bay, however the majority of the city lived in densely packed slums; a perfect breeding ground for a zombie army that would, before the day was out, rival the size of all the armies in the world combined.

And that was just the first day.

Chapter 5

The Outlaw

6:55 a.m.

A fundamental shift had occurred in Dr. Thuy Lee. It announced itself civilly; in a manner no one else would've ever noticed.

She slept in.

Not that six in the morning was sleeping in for a normal person, but for her it was and, regardless, she never slept in. Never. Thuy Lee always had too much to do.

In middle school, on top of her regular studies, there had been violin practice two hours a day, and her language tutor. In high school there was her 5.0 grade point average that she maintained from the first day right up until she gave the valedictorian speech—and there was also piano and early placement college courses.

At the university there had been the shock that it wasn't the temple of knowledge she had expected. She had discovered there were three categories of students: the first were the partiers, who eked their way through classes, coming in with red eyes and smelling of dirty laundry. The second were the pseudo-intellectuals who went around all day using the very largest words in their vocabulary, spitting them out as though they were bullets of the gun. Later in life they were the ones most likely to mention their degree within the first two minutes of meeting someone new. The last category was made up of people who were genuinely excited at the idea of learning something new—like Thuy.

Thuy carried twenty-six credit hours a semester and wished she could sleep even less than the six hours a night that she did. She had burned through her classes one after another, ingesting every new fact she could get her hands on.

After that were her postgraduate studies and then there was her first real job: R&K Pharmaceuticals had grabbed her up as fast as they could. Even before she had tossed her mortar board in the air they had her signed on like a left-handed pitcher with a 98 mile an hour fastball. Even then she had not let up. For the last ten years she had worked eighteen hours a day trying to unravel the mystery of cancer.

All her life she had been working her hardest, striving to be perfect and now she was clearly not. She had failed and failed huge.

Strangely, it brought about not a sense of melancholy but a sense of relief. This was the first day of her life she had nothing to do. She had no job—or so she suspected. Her research, regardless that it had been sabotaged had been responsible for mass death. Her career was over. No one would touch her after this. And this meant that she had nothing to do with her morning.

The authorities would want to talk to her, she was sure, but what could she say that would be at all helpful? Aim for the head?

Next to her, Ryan Deckard was breathing lightly. He smelled of her shampoo and was bursting the seams of her pink silk robe. The night before, after each had showered, they kissed gently, neither had the strength to do more, then each fell so quickly into sleep that they slipped into unconsciousness intertwined like lovers. He had rolled over in the night and she had awakened wishing he would come back and then, she wished she had the courage to roll over and cuddle him.

Her dreams had been of Von Braun and Riggs. Their faces kept crumbling off and they had chased her, relentlessly, first through a burning building and then out into woods that were deep and endless. When she woke in a sweat, she had wanted Deckard to hold her, to rescue her.

She knew what most of her colleagues would say about that. They would cluck for sure. There were many feminists in the science community and, for the most part, Thuy had no need of them. To her the real feminists were the giants of the past who had freed women from what was, for all intents and purposes, cultural slavery. Those women were people to admire. The whiners of today who became offended when a man held a door open for them were shadow-puppets in comparison.

Besides, Thuy was too busy outdistancing men in every way to be coddled by perpetual complainers. In fact, she liked to think she was the ideal feminist having made her own way in the world while demanding and receiving the respect of both men and women alike. Yet, and here she winced a little at the thought, she was wishing that Deckard would hold her and chase the terrors of the night away. Of course, Thuy had an excuse, she had seen things of such horror it was a wonder she didn't have her thumb permanently corked in her mouth.

Through slitted eyes, she gave Deckard a peek. He seemed younger in sleep. The hard lines of his face were more relaxed and the normally grim set of his lips was gone; he seemed softer somehow, but worn at the same time. Part of this was due to the fact that he sported little scabbed-over cuts all over his face and hands courtesy of the explosion set by Anna Holloway. Thuy still didn't quite understand why the young woman had tried to burn the Walton facility down. Was it to hide evidence? Weren't the zombies roaming around killing people evidence enough? And what part did Eng play? Had there been two saboteurs involved? Or was Eng merely a spy? Or was Anna the spy and not a saboteur after all?

Thuy didn't think she would ever know. And really did it matter now? Years of her hard work had been destroyed, utterly; there would be no going forward no matter what happened. There would only be the endless investigations and finger-pointing and lawsuits and the testifying—assuming of course that the authorities could get the infected patients rounded up and controlled without spreading the disease further.

This was something that the efficient-minded Thuy would have thought had been completed by now. Yes, there had been a lapse in security…or a few of them she supposed, but she was sure that by now Walton had been surrounded and that the majority of the infected people had been killed in the fire or had been captured by the police.

She was clueless about the terror and the slaughter that was occurring in Poughkeepsie or that the little stream that coursed through nearby Pleasant Valley ran red for miles down to the Manchester Bridge, or that the town of Highland, across the Hudson, was so devastated that out of a population of 4720 people, less than a tenth could still be counted as human. A sleepy toll-taker, wearing a bland expression and a neon-yellow vest over a set of proverbial watermelon sized breasts, became the first to die in Highland as a band of black-eyed zombies followed a car up the incline.

"You can't be walking in the middle of the damned road," she yelled out to the group from her seat in the toll booth on the eastern end of the Mid-Hudson Bridge. "And please! Don't think you can come up on me like I'm scared of you sorry-ass punks." Her name was Yvonne Tillers; she was two-hundred pounds of sass. She had grown up in the Bronx and none of the skinny white boys with their patchy beards and their hipster glasses who attended one of the colleges in the area threw the least amount of fear into her.

Before the boys could make it into the light of the toll station, she was out of her booth, the many gold rings on her fingers flashing. Yvonne was a sight to see when she got angry. It was a true fact, no one messed with her when she was angry. "Get your sorry asses over on that side walk before I call the po…" It was then she saw their faces. In that second her anger straight up disappeared. The heat of it was just gone, replaced by a sudden cold terror. She tried to run back to her toll booth but her two-hundred pounds of sass wasn't made for sprinting. They caught her in the door of her booth and she screamed and screamed. Her screams echoed over the Hudson for what seemed like ages. Twenty minutes went by and still she screamed, a heart rending sound. The beasts had to gorge their way through rolls of belly fat just to get at her vitals.

Yvonne died a very slow death.

Others heard her screams. The birds and animals that heard it shivered in their nests and their burrows. The humans cowered in their homes doing nothing but locking the doors and calling the sheriff. A hundred calls were made; after three rings they went to a pre-recorded message because the sheriff had died hours before at Saint Francis Hospital where the zombies outnumbered the living by ten to one. He had died screaming much the way Yvonne had screamed: high and girlish.

And Thuy knew none of this. Her night had been one of basic survival. She had fought to stay alive before fleeing through a gap in the quarantine. Then she had slept, unaware of the chaos she had left behind. Unaware that Highland had been overrun by horrible creatures that were somewhere in limbo between the living and the dead, or that in the town of Lloyd people hid in basements and attics, under cars and in trash bins, and, in the case of three ten-year-old boys who'd been having a sleepover, in a tree house.

The zombies had sniffed them out, but the wooden planks nailed to the trunk of the cottonwood had been an obstacle they could not overcome, but this didn't save the children in the long run. After hours of waiting to be rescued, one of them, Jared Cooper, went mad from fear and worry and decided to chance making a dash for home where his parents were supposedly waiting, just up the street. There were four zombies beneath their tree and the other two boys pleaded with him not to go.

"I'm fast. I'm fast. I'm fast," he repeated over and over as he looked down the plank ladder. Even for a ten-year-old, Jared was athletic. He played basketball and football and he was fast and agile even with fear contorting his limbs, making him want to shrivel into a ball. He fought the feeling and went down the ladder like a monkey. At the bottom, he zigged around the zombies and their long arms. One hooked the collar of his wind-breaker and tried to reel him in but Jared was able to pull away, leaving his jacket behind.

He ran up the block, past the Dern's house, noticing that the front door was smeared with blood and flung wide. He ran past the Albertson's which was brightly lit but abandoned. He ran past the McDonald's and stared with wide unblinking eyes at the body on the front porch. It was Lisa McDonald, the only girl he had ever seen naked. He had seen her in the flesh on a dare. A month before, he had shimmied up the birch that grew outside her window and stared in at her as she got ready for bed. She had dropped her shorts like it was no big deal and walked around her room in only her tank top. He saw her butt and everything. Then she took her top off. She had been eleven and flat as a board. He would later tell his friends that she was "skinny" and "there was nothing there," and yet he had stared, entranced, growing a funny twig of a little boy boner.

Now she was lying on the porch, face down and one of her arms had been torn off. It was lying in the grass making no sense to Jared. It looked pale and still service-able as though someone could stick it back into its slot and it would be good to go.

Jared ran with his head swiveled like an owls. The bare arm, the same one he had seen attached to that beauti-ful, scrawny girl, wouldn't leave his mind. It was the first thing he planned on telling his mom about when he got home.

Three doors down was the house he grew up in. He hammered on the door but couldn't yell; his lips were numb from his fear. His throat felt terribly scratchy like bark rubbing on burlap. He could only bam on the door until his hand hurt. When he looked back, he saw that the zombies were coming for him. They started appearing in doorways and through the slats of fences. Jared began cry-ing and with his lips against the heavy wood door he croaked out a single word: "Mom."

His mom was home but Karen was too dreadfully afraid to even think about moving. She was afraid in a way that no twenty-first century woman could fathom. It wasn't a fear of missing a car payment or getting too tipsy at a fourth of July barbecue. It wasn't even the vague, nebulous fear of American crime which always seemed to happen to someone else.

It was fear unimaginable.

She had seen her husband Gary being eaten. The last time she had seen him he was crawling across the kitchen linoleum with their neighbor, Libby Keats riding him, tearing at his shoulder meat with bloodied teeth. He had been hamstrung by Libby's twins, one of whom had been in the corner chewing on Gary's left foot. The other twin had been under Gary with his head half buried in his round belly burrowing his way through Gary's intestines.

Gary had come to a shuddering halt next to the marble-topped island where the family normally took their breakfast and where Libby would come over sometimes to sit and crab about her life. Like a water buffalo being eviscerated by a pack of lions, Gary had toppled over on his side and was tugged here and there as mother and sons ate their fill. Above him on the wall was a cuckoo clock; it cheeped pleasantly every time the second hand began a new revolution. It cheeped pleasantly twenty-six times before Gary let out a last sad, wet noise and died.

It was twenty-six minutes of hell for Jared's mom who had been hiding beneath the sink. Now, she was sitting in her bed holding the pistol she had always detested. She had been "afraid" of it back before she understood what real fear was. It was pleasantly heavy. The weight made the gun feel real when nothing else did. She cuddled it, waiting for the perfect moment to put it against her temple and pull the trigger, and yet the perfect moment never seemed to arise. She figured she would know when it came.

Jared ran from the zombies, his legs going in barely controlled wheels as he sped around the house for the back door. It was open! He dashed through, shut it behind him, and then stopped. His ten-year-old body locked rigidly in place by the transformation that had occurred in his kitchen. There was a great pool of drying blood that had made a literal island of the marble topped island, and there were smears of red, lumpy stuff and a partially eaten foot beside the cabinet where the cereal was kept. The body of his father was long gone. Gary had come back to life an hour before and had literally stomped away.

This terrible scene was the opposite of what Jared had expected to find. His home was supposed to have been a sanctuary—his mom and dad were supposed to have been untouchable Gods into whose bosom he could always crawl for help. Jared, his expression frozen in a cardboard cutout of terror, went straight away to his mom's room. Whenever he had a nightmare or was picked on at school that was where he would go.

He found the door unlocked, just as the kitchen door had been, and for the same reason: his mom was courting death, looking for an excuse to use the gun. Jared was just that excuse. He was a mess; his eyes bugged out, his hair was going everywhere, his clothes were torn, and there was a wild, almost unnatural look to him. He could barely speak.

"Mom," he wheezed, when he saw her.

Karen put a bullet in his chest. Jared fell back to stare at the ceiling with a horrified look of puzzlement on his face. He lived long enough to hear a second gunshot. But for Jared, death was only temporary. Somewhere along the path from the treehouse to his mother's bedroom door he had breathed in Com-cells which were multiplying like mad. When the night was deep he opened his eyes and, a few hours later, when the sun was beaming through the slats onto Thuy as she was lying next to Deckard and wondering about the future, Jared was strong enough to stand.

He ate briefly from the corpse in his parent's bed, but the lack of hot blood bothered him as did the fact that his mother's face was crooked. In fact, that angered him. He smacked her, bit her cheek, and then stood up chewing. He couldn't understand the concept of 'why' but he wanted to. Just then there was a reason to all his hazy memories beyond the anger. There was a purpose to the hole in his chest and to the furious hunger in his gut. He strained hard to figure it out but his brain was mush and his only thought was: revenge.

Someone had done this to him and he was going to find out who and he was going to eat whoever it was. He longed to in an ugly perverse manner. He had an uncontrollable urge to drink from a spurting artery like it was a crazy straw. He wanted to suck the blood's origin straight from the bone and he wanted to roll in the open chest cavity of a man whose heart was still beating. These desires were demanding, overpowering. He didn't even try to fight them—what was the point? Revenge and thirst were the only points he understood.

And, lying in the sun in her bed, Thuy had no idea.

She had escaped certain death and figured she deserved these few minutes to herself, relaxing, perhaps for the first time in her life. She was even considering the idea of 'brunch' a meal that was quite foreign to her, when the phone rang.

Deckard's dark eyes were open and staring at her, stopping her hand as it reached for the phone. "There is no law saying you have to answer that," he said. There wasn't a hint of sleep to him. He had gone from full on REM sleep to completely cognizant in half of a phone's ring. "Think before you pick that up."

The urgent ring meant only one thing and it wasn't a call from her mother looking to discuss her love life for the umpteenth time, it wasn't a telemarketer looking to sign her up for a chance to win a timeshare. No, the phone call had to do with the Com-cells and Walton. It meant an end to the ten minutes of 'me' time she had allowed herself.

Was it Doctor Kipling demanding an explanation? Was it the police...also demanding an explanation? Or was it the media with an already formed explanation looking for a sound bite? Or worst of all, was it one of the forty family members looking to assign guilt?

She picked up the phone, hoping for the first time to speak to a telemarketer, hoping to hear all about the timeshare opportunity that wouldn't last much longer. "Doctor Lee?" It was a man's voice and it was heavily mixed with authority and accusation.

"Yes?" she answered evenly.

"You and the others are to remain indoors until we arrive. Do not attempt to flee and…"

"Who is this?" she interrupted.

"As far as you're concerned, this is the fucking government," the man said. "You will comply with all instructions or risk a charge of treason on top of everything else. Do I need to tell you what the penalty is for treason?"

Thuy knew it was death…or at least that's what it was the last time anyone had ever been charged with treason. It seemed that nowadays a person could commit all sorts of 'treasonous' activities and receive little more than a movie contract and maybe a slap on the wrist.

But things might have changed overnight. How many people had died at Walton? How many state troopers? How many CDC agents? She had no idea of the full scale of the calamity. If she had known, she would have run.

"I will comply," she said.

Chapter 6

Formation

7:15 a.m.

The phone rang for Max Fowler at 5:47 in the morning. He cracked an eye for a fraction of a second and then shut it, somehow falling back to sleep before the phone rang again. "Shit," he groaned.

The bleary, lump of pale flesh and wild bleached blonde hair next to him, muttered, "You aren't going in this early. They always screw you on your overtime. Let it go to voicemail."

"Yeah." His wife was right. Max had worked for *Winston and Sons* long enough to know they were big when it came to the promise of extra pay for extra hours but very short when it came time for the checks to be written. Max was asleep two seconds after he hit the 'ignore call' button.

He was deep into REM sleep when the next call dragged him slowly into consciousness. The bleary lump that was his wife, Charlene, made an angry sound and said, "Just turn off your phone."

"No shit," he said, angry that his work was being so persistent, but when he picked up his phone it was oddly dark. It took a second ring from the cordless house phone to wake him to the fact that something was wrong. "It's not mine," he said, a sudden worry in his gut.

Charlene had a strange new fear as well. No one called the house phone at that time of the morning unless it was an emergency. With her body still coming awake, Charlene slapped around on the nightstand next to her side of the bed until she found her glasses. Because her hair was so long she had to swing her head back before she stuck the glasses to her face; she stared at the phone. "I don't know who this is. 738-4161? Does that sound familiar?"

Max sat up. "4161? I don't...no, I don't think so. What's the area code?"

Even with her glasses, she had to squint. "518. Where's 518?"

"Albany, I think," he said, relaxing. Neither of them had family in Albany. He reached out his hand for the phone but didn't answer it. Just as his wife had, he squinted at the numbers. "You know what? It's probably your brother Joe calling from a police station. He told me yesterday that he was heading upstate and you know what a lead-foot he is. If you want me to bail him out, it's going to have to wait until morning. Real morning, I mean."

The phone stopped ringing and went dark in his hand. The two of them waited in silence to see if there would be a message. When the little light started blinking, indicating someone had left a voicemail, Max made a face and thought to himself: *this had better be important.*

The voice in his ear spoke sharply: "PFC Fowler, you are instructed to report to your unit by zero-five-thirty hours. This is an emergency call up of the National Guard, authorized by Governor Stimpson. Failure to report for duty will result in disciplinary action."

For a few seconds Max stared at the phone, that nervous feeling returning. "It wasn't work," he said to his wife. "That was my guard unit. They're calling me up and," he glanced over at the clock, "And I'm already late. That's fucked. How can they expect me to be at the base at 5:30 when they don't call me until 5:47?" He felt confused and with his brown hair going in every direction he looked it as well.

"Maybe it's Joe, pulling a prank on you," Charlene said, hopefully. She didn't want to think what was happening if the call up was for real. Being married to a military man, even a part-time military man meant she lived with certain fears, and a call-up staged before the first light of day could only mean the shit had hit the fan and in a big way. The only thing that would justify it was a new war or maybe a natural disaster. Her mind went immediately to the Indian Point nuclear power plant in Buchanan; it wasn't that far away. If it had melted down…

On the nightstand was the remote control for the TV; she flicked on CNN and the two of them stared at the screen. Two grim-faced reporters were taking turns making wild guesses concerning the call up of the New York State National Guard and what it had to do with a series of road closures in and around the town of Poughkeepsie, New York. They were in possession of very few facts but that didn't stop them from shooting their mouths off; it didn't even slow them down.

With great seriousness, they not only kicked around the idea of a terrorist attack, but also the more humdrum catastrophes that were possible: a chemical leak like the one that had killed three thousand people in Bhopal, India. Or a biological incident like the Ebola outbreak that was even then continuing, adding to the eleven thousand deaths currently reported, or a nuclear accident, like Chernobyl.

The talking heads went on and on in this serious manner before suddenly turning their frowns upside down as they switched topics to some celebrity who was acting as though she was the first person ever to be pregnant.

"Maybe it's a flood," Max suggested, hoping to calm his wife. He could see the 'look' gelling on her face. It was the look that came when she was just about to forbid him from doing something she didn't approve of. "I have to go. If this is real and I don't show up I could be looking at jail time."

"You're already late. Maybe you could say you didn't get the call. At least wait until there's some news."

He couldn't do that. He had made commitments and was a proud member of the National Guard, and yet he dragged his feet getting dressed in his BDUs, and made a full breakfast of eggs, toast, and coffee instead of slurping down a bowl of Cheerios, he also stopped on the way to Cortlandt to get gas even though he had three-quarters of a tank in his Nissan Sentra.

Smelling the fuel had him thinking: *I hope it's a chemical spill*. A chemical spill would mean a day spent sweating in his mask and MOPP 4 gear, but, as an infantryman, he wouldn't likely be doing much more than handling crowd control or directing traffic or standing around bull-shitting. When it came to a chemical spill he wasn't trained for much else.

It was close on seven before he finally reported for duty, and he wasn't the only one dragging ass. Only half the company was there, lingering in front of the battalion headquarters. Most were puffing away on cheap Camels and looking up at the building, nervously. Max found the trio of men he usually hung with during drill weekends. One of them, Private Johnny Osgood, had his hacky-sack out and was toeing it into the air with little thumps.

"Did I miss formation?" Max asked.

Max's best friend in the company, Will Pierce, had been chewing at the end of his thumb nail. He spat a crescent moon out into the dirt and shook his head. "Naw. It's the usual, hurry up and wait."

"It ain't the usual," Johnny said, bending to retrieve the fallen sack after he had bipped it off the side of his foot. "You saw Captain Ganes same as me. He wasn't like his normal self. He was all twitchy like he had friggin bedbugs. Here you go, Max," he added, tossing the sack in Max's direction.

Max bounced it once on his knee and then grabbed it in midair. It was chilly so early in the morning and he wasn't in the mood. "So what's going on? The news was all over the place guessing this and that."

"Terrorist attack," Specialist Frank Maguire answered. "Fucking ragheads."

"Yeah, fucking ragheads," Johnny echoed. "Some guys were saying it's an Anthrax attack or maybe like Ebola. Whatever it is, you know it's got to be big otherwise why get our asses out here, right? Normal terrorism is for the FBI or the CIA, right? So this has to be big."

"I'd say so," Will agreed. "I just knew it was going to happen someday. I just knew they'd come back and start killing Americans again. If there was one thing about Iraq that was good, it was that we were killing them over there instead of them killing us over here. No one ever thinks about that. Man if I had a dime for every time one of them…" The appearance of Captain Ganes and First Sergeant Brad Coker shut Will's mouth. The two men, both veterans who'd fought in Iraq, wore matching frowns as if they were concentrating on not shitting themselves.

"Fall in!" Coker barked.

The sergeants, what few were there, began growling out orders: "Move your asses" and "Forget the smokes!" and "Quit your bullshitting and form up." and "Williams, stop being a shitheel and dress right for God's sake." As the four under-manned platoons formed ranks, Captain Ganes stood there shaking his head. His orders were crap, possibly the worst orders an officer could ever hear. What was being asked of him had him in a sweat, especially seeing how few men had responded to the emergency call-tree.

When the men had formed ranks and the platoon sergeants had received their reports, Coker turned to the captain and he too was shaking his head slightly. "Report," Ganes said.

Coker snapped up a salute. "Ninety-six unaccounted for," he replied, his voice, usually that of a giant's was barely a whisper.

Captain Ganes, who was also the manager of the local Shop-Rite fifty weeks out of the year, swore, "Fuck." It wasn't even close to being the proper reply of an officer. After a deep breath, he returned the salute and said: "Post." At this order, the sergeants filed to the rear and the platoon leaders: three second lieutenants and a first lieutenant came to stand in front of their perspective platoons.

For three minutes the captain kept the men of Delta Company, 1st Battalion of the 69th Infantry Regiment locked up at full attention. He simply didn't know how to start. He had led men in battle; he'd been personally targeted by snipers; he'd felt the fantastic heat of an IED exploding thirty feet from him and had the scars and the Purple Heart to show for it. All that seemed like a walk in the park compared to explaining to his men that very soon they'd be killing their own countrymen, perhaps even their own relatives.

It wasn't just a possibility, it was, sure-as-shit, going to happen and, when it did happen, what group of Americans was going to sit back and passively allow themselves to be trapped in a death circle with a rampaging horde of zombies banging down the door?

The term 'zombie' had been used by Colonel Merrell in his briefing simply because no other term fit. The official term was "Infected Persons" but everyone knew they were fucking zombies. The word *zombie* had popped right into Captain Ganes' mind the second Merrell described them as persons afflicted with a virus that renders them into unthinking, cannibalistic, monsters that were impervious to pain, and damned near impossible to kill.

In the conference call, Merrell had gone on and on about them, but Ganes hadn't paid much attention. He was trying to come to grips with the very notion of zombies walking around the fields and farms of rural New York. When the actual concept embedded itself in his psyche, he mulled over the problem as an Army officer should. His rifle company was the closest unit to Poughkeepsie and it would be up to him to maintain the current quarantine zone until more help arrived. His current command of a hundred and three men would be trying to hold back close to 50,000 men, women, and zombies.

The zombies, if that's what they really were, would be the least of his problems. He'd seen enough movies to know they'd come on dumb and slow—it would be like target practice for his men. No, it would be the real people that would be a nightmare to deal with. These weren't soft city folk. The people around these parts were not only heavily armed, they were also the direct descendants of the men who had given George the III so many problems. And it was going to be Delta Company playing the part of the Redcoats, denying the rights of a frightened and angry citizenry. His men, manning check points and firebreaks were going to be right out in the open; they'd be sitting ducks, again just as the Redcoats had been.

How many men with scoped hunting rifles were in the quarantine zone? Five thousand? Six? How many had grown up shooting deer and rabbit every season? How many could hit a man-sized target at three hundred yards? Too many for his tiny force to do much against, especially with the rules of engagement handed down from on high.

Captain Ganes sighed and said, "At ease," again in a manner that wasn't fully military in nature. He was a pale, thin-lipped man and looked like the grocer he was, especially when he bobbed up and down, going heel to toe as he talked. "Gentlemen, there has been an incident and now, your country and your state needs you. They need that same courage you have demonstrated time and again. They need that same devotion to duty and, now more than ever, they need that strict adherence to orders which has been drilled into every one of us, whether it was at Fort Benning or West Point."

He paused for a breath that lingered as the men began to glance around. This was the first time they'd ever been lectured on the importance of obeying orders and they rightly interpreted their captain's meaning: something extremely distasteful was coming.

"I'm sorry to say that there has been a rather large accident involving a highly contagious biological pathogen." Again, he paused as the men began to groan and grumble.

"At ease that shit," the First Sergeant snapped from the back of the formation.

"No, it's alright," Captain Ganes said. "The men have a right to be pissed off. Hell, I'm pissed off. I'd rather be back home in bed with my wife."

"That makes two of us," Specialist Will Pierce joked just loud enough so that the entire company heard. There was a burst of nervous laughter, again not proper for men in a military formation—and yet it served its purpose. They relaxed by the slightest degree. These men weren't like regular Army soldiers who were accustomed to taking orders, not only on a daily basis, but on an hourly one as well. Ganes had to make sure they were in the right frame of mind for what he was going to ask of them.

"Sorry, Pierce," Ganes said, when the laughter died down. "But the missus doesn't stray for anyone inferior in both *rank* and *length of service* if you get my meaning. And that's you on both counts." Will Pierce grunted out a laugh and, next to him, Max Fowler nudged him with his elbow. First Sergeant Coker, a man with twenty-three years in the regular army, wanted to lash out again and get the men "under control" but Captain Ganes caught his eye.

When the chuckling died down, and it did quicker than it normally would have, Ganes cleared his throat. "Back to the subject at hand. As I said, there has been a biological incident. Someone has released either a bacterium or a virus in and around Poughkeepsie. It is highly contagious, but, as far as we know, it isn't deadly. The virus causes certain changes in a person's mental state, causing them to lash out in a hyper-aggressive manner. They will be violent and may…and they may…and they might, uh try to eat you."

A few men laughed. The rest began to whisper. PFC Max Fowler only shook his head as he realized what they were going to have to deal with. "Are you trying to say they're zombies?"

The whispering stopped immediately. "Yes," Captain Ganes said. Again, there was a tittering of laughter from a few, while the rest leaned in, waiting for the punch line that they were sure was coming. "This isn't a joke," Ganes told them. "The official term for them is *Infected Persons*. Use that in every communiqué. Do not use the word zombie. Colonel Merrell made that very clear."

"Zombies," Will Pierce said in bewilderment. "This is crazy.

"*Infected Persons*," Ganes snapped.

Max raised a hand, not caring that he was breaking more protocol. "We're going to be given live rounds, right? We'll have a full combat load?"

"Not exactly," the captain answered. "The operations orders are still being drawn up, however I've been told to issue only M16s. No grenades, no mortars, no M240s. All of you in fourth platoon will be acting as riflemen."

"And the rules of engagement?" Max asked. Technically, since it was a domestic situation, ROEs weren't used, instead there were guidelines called *Rules for the Use of Force,* but since that was what the men called: *Brass Babble*, Ganes didn't bother to correct him, at least on that matter.

"I'd get to them if you would just shut your mouth," Ganes barked in growing frustration. It was time to rein things in again. "I want silence in my formation, damn it!" He paused to see if anyone was going to challenge him. "Good. Currently, we can only fire if fired upon or if we are physically attacked. Because of the contagious nature of the virus, we have asked for the orders to be amended to allow for weapons discharge against any individual coming within thirty feet, but that hasn't been approved yet. And that brings me to the bad news."

Max almost cried out: *contagious zombies wasn't the bad news?* He held back, barely.

Ganes read the look. "Yes, that wasn't the bad news. We will be enforcing a quarantine zone with a circumference of one-hundred and twenty-two miles." This caused the formation to collectively gasp. They all began looking around and most started counting how many of them were present, easily calculating that there wasn't even one man per mile.

"This is crazy," Max said, again speaking out of line. "There's got to be like, twenty thousand people in Poughkeepsie. We're supposed to hold them all back? Alone?"

"No. There is already a sizable police presence around the town. We will be supplementing them until reinforcements arrive. The good news is that the entire 42nd is being mobilized."

There came a collective sigh of relief, but not from Max. "Sir, with all due respect, but the entire 42nd has got only like, 10,000 men and they're scattered in six states. It wouldn't be enough even if they were all here right now. It would be something like seventy men per mile of perimeter. That's not enough, especially if there's a panic and everyone tries to leave the town at once." Every single man in the unit was, for just two seconds, suddenly stone quiet as they realized how dangerously thin their lines would be under the best of conditions. The whispering began again.

Ganes had to nip it in the bud. "Fowler, you sound like a chicken-shit. You sound like a whining bitch. This is the situation. Yes, it sucks but we don't have a choice in the matter. There is a virus spreading in that town and it's our job to keep it from running over the entire country. So, are you going whine like a baby or are you going to step up and do something about it?"

"I'm going to step up, Sir."

"Hooah! That's what I want to hear," Ganes said, grinning. There was a touch of worry showing in that grin. Everything Fowler had said was true but their situation was worse than he knew. The closest reinforcements to them was the 42nd Infantry Division marching band and a headquarters company that was composed of medics and cooks and typists with asses that could barely fit into the largest BDUs...and they were two hours away! And to make matter worse, Delta Company would have to carry out their mission covered head to toe in their MOPP 4 protective gear, and that included their gas masks. Their ability to see targets beyond a hundred yards would be severely compromised. Who knew if they were going to be able to hit a thing?

And it was a given that they were going to be tested. Already the police had been involved with two fire-fights and, with the sun up, Ganes was sure there would be more as the people of Poughkeepsie tried to make a break for safety.

Chapter 7

Soldiers On the Line

7:36 a.m.

With his headquarters company straggling in from all over the state, General Collins was still relying on Courtney Shaw and her small team of dispatchers to place the first of his men on scene. He could read a map the same as Captain Ganes and both knew the men weren't heading anywhere near the twenty mile mark as described by the governor—and neither cared. Courtney's placement made sense when little else did.

Collins put the fate of his soldiers in her hands. She was competent, smart and clearly tough as nails.

The first convoy of rumbling five-tons out of Cortlandt, New York split up at the junction of I-9 and Interstate 84. Three went west, three east, and three north. No one knew which way was best, and by best they meant safest. The soldiers in the backs of the trucks didn't have a clue exactly where they were or where they were going. For the most part they were stone-faced and quiet, except when they whispered questions that no one could answer:

"Is the disease airborne?"

"Will these masks even work against it?"

"Why did we leave the Strykers and the 50 cals back at the base?"

"This sucks, man. Why us?"

"When's chow time?" Will Pierce asked, determined to be cool about the entire affair. He was pretty sure he could deal with the zombies when the time came, in fact, he was looking forward to it. Half his life was spent on his Xbox, living in the land of Make-Believe where blasting the slow, stumbling hordes of undead was a daily occurrence. His only gripe with the situation was the MOPP4 gear. It was hot as fuck and in the heavy black gloves, his hands felt fat and slow. The gloves would be the first thing to go when the shit hit the fan.

Despite the heat and the sweat crawling down his body, PFC Max Fowler was trembling. He was having trouble coming to grips with the loaded gun that sat upright between his knees. First off, one simply did not travel with a loaded gun. Every hunter knew that and every recruit straight out of basic training knew it as well. The only reason a person would travel with a loaded gun was if he expected to use it soon after exiting the vehicle.

Every time the truck slowed, Max would stare out and grip the weapon tighter. He had made the mistake of dragging his feet all morning and now he was going to pay the price. He had been the last into the truck and now he was going to be first out, first to confront whatever it was that had the entire 42nd Infantry Division scurrying like ants.

"It'll be cool," Will told him, slipping him a wink. "You'll be with me and I ain't gonna let no..." The truck lurched, suddenly and there was a grinding of gears. The ride became rough; they were driving on the shoulder now, passing the lines of cars and semi-trucks that were being kept from entering the quarantine zone. There was a mile of ugly traffic to pass beyond. It was a loud, messy affair. People blared their horns and cussed. Some rode on the shoulder or on the grassy strip between the north and south bound lanes, while others tried to get in among the army trucks so they could pass through the barricade.

"Don't they watch the fucking news?" Max asked. The news stations had been pretty crystal clear about the road closures. The mess of cars made no sense to him. "Why on earth would anyone want to go *into* a quarantined zone? Jackasses."

"You never know. Maybe they got family inside *The Zone*," Will suggested, unofficially setting the slang that would be used by every soldier before the week was out.

After practically plowing cars out of their way, the convoy came to a shuddering halt just shy of a state trooper barricade. Immediately, Lieutenant Warren, one of the platoon leaders, was out of the cab bawling: "Three men! I need three men!"

Max went stiff on the bench. As he and Will occupied the last two bench seats, they were the logical choices to exit the truck, however, from his position Max could see the hundreds of vehicles they had just passed and he could see the hundreds of angry faces in those vehicles. In front of them, on the other side of a flimsy looking barricade, was another mass of cars even greater in number, and the people in them were both angry and very afraid. They were screaming to be let out of The Zone. It sounded as though a riot was seconds from erupting.

There were six cops manning the barricade and Max couldn't see how three soldiers were going to make much of a difference.

"Let's go!" Lieutenant Warren demanded as he came around to the back of the truck.

Max was scared shitless by the crowd and clung to the bench. Across from him, Will Pierce had a lip curled in disgust at seeing the mob. He shook his head at the lieutenant. "We'll get the next one. I didn't sign up to play traffic cop."

Warren's eyes blazed. "Since when do you say 'no' to an officer? This is a direct fucking order: get your fucking ass off this truck right now or so..."

Just then a Specialist named Starling stepped over the crates of ammo stacked on the floor of the bed and climbed out of the truck. "I'll do it. Shit, I'll take normal people over the diseased ones any day." Two more soldiers followed right after.

The lieutenant promptly forgot all about Will's insubordination. He started rattling off instructions, talking like an auctioneer, spitting words out one over another. The drivers of the three trucks didn't wait for him to finish; they ground the vehicles into gear and in a belch of smoke took a turn veering east. Warren was forced to run to catch up.

They drove for a half mile, skirting The Zone, going up and down the idyllic, rolling hills the area was known for. It was green and lovely and, seemingly, peaceful. The trucks were an ugly blot, passing through. Along a ridge-line they slowed to a crawl.

The man next to Max was his friend Johnny Osgood. He tried to stretch his skinny neck to see why they had stopped. "What is it?" he asked. "Is it another barricade?"

Max stood on the tailgate and stared over the top of the truck. There was nothing in the road, however off to the north he saw two SUVs pushing their way through the thin forest, making a trail where none existed. "No. It's some civilians trying to break the quarantine. Fuck, they act like they don't even see us."

"Maybe they think we're here to rescue them," Will said. "Poor saps."

There was some shouting from the lead five-ton and a good deal of waving of arms, however the SUVs continued to trundle along. Finally, Lt Warren climbed out of the cab and broke a cardinal rule: he fired three warning shots, kicking up dirt directly in front of the lead vehicle. The drivers of the SUVs panicked and both tore the bark off trees and ripped up the sides of their vehicles as they maneuvered desperately to turn around.

"This is going to be impossible," someone muttered.

"I don't know about that," Will said, giving the men in the truck a cheery smile. "That looked simple enough."

"It looked to me like the L.T. broke the rules of engagement," Max whispered to his friend. He too had been encouraged by the minor event. The civilians had turned tail at the first sign of resistance.

"That's what I would call leading by example," Will replied. "If someone gives us any shit we'll put a couple of rounds across his bow and if anyone complains we'll just say that's what LT Warren did."

The two were still grinning when the convoy entered the town of Myer's Corner which was nestled, practically out of sight of all civilization, among the green hills. It was quaint and picturesque, but its main street was hardly more than a wide spot in the road and it was hard to tell what on earth supported the town.

It was eerily deserted. No one was on the street and the buildings were cold and silent. Most doors hung with "Closed Until Further Notice" signs. After the unimpressive business district they passed a number of homes and the few remaining inhabitants gawked, timidly at the trucks from behind window curtains or doors cracked a bare few inches. Max waved once and received only a glare in reply.

At the far end of the town, where the hills and forest recommenced were two police cruisers parked nose-to-nose with two state troopers holding shotguns in their sweaty hands, squatting behind them. The trucks rumbled right up, stopping only a few feet away.

"Pierce! Fowler! Osgood! Get your asses down here right this instant," Warren commanded. There was no second guessing the order and Max didn't want to. The spot seemed ideal. No one was clamoring to get in or out of The Zone, and the only evidence of zombies was the crackling of gunfire the origins of which couldn't be pinpointed. Because of the maze of hills, it seemed to be coming from every direction. Max jumped out of the vehicle before anyone could push past him and volunteer for the plum location.

A roll of concertina wire was rolled out of the truck and then a 900 round ammo can was lugged to the edge; Johnny Osgood hauled it to the side of the road. Again, the lead vehicle began to motor away, forcing Lieutenant Warren to speak quickly. "No one crosses in either direction," he said, pointing north and south, just in case the three soldiers were completely clueless. "I want two up and one back at all times. Remember masks are to be worn by the up men at all times so rotate every twenty minutes. Good luck."

He didn't pause to see if there were any questions; the last truck was leaving without him once more and, again, he had to jog to catch up.

When the trucks were lost among the hills, the silence was heavy and thick. Sure, there was the distant rifle fire, but up close it seemed as though even the birds and squirrels had been struck dumb. The five men, two state troopers and the three soldiers stood staring awkwardly at one another until one of the troopers said, "Well, it looks like you boys got this."

"Got what?" Max asked.

"Got things under control." He nodded to his partner and the pair climbed into their cruisers, K-turned, kicking up a good deal of dust in their eagerness to get away, and left the soldiers.

"What the hell was that about?" Max asked, sticking a finger up under his helmet and scratching his head.

Sounding like an angry rooster, Johnny Osgood yelled after them: "Chicken shits!" Unnerving echoes followed the screech, bouncing off the hills and trees. The echoes made them feel even more alone than they were. They felt suddenly abandoned.

When the echoes died, there was a whistle to their left. All three jumped and pointed their M16s, but it was only a sparrow in a tree jumping from branch to branch. The bird broke the gloom and the normal sounds of the forest perked up. Will declared the spot "perfect." The first thing he did was take off his Kevlar helmet and chuck it to the side of the road. He then pulled off the heavy rubber gloves. Johnny followed suit and even unbuttoned the protective outer coat of his MOPP gear.

Max wasn't ready to relax so quickly. He liked the extra protection and actually pulled his gloves up, tighter.

Will snorted laughter at him before saying, "Help me with the wire." The razor-sharp wire stretched for thirty feet, not enough to cover the road and the shoulders on either side. They supplemented their meager barricade by pulling down branches and hefting fallen logs from the forest. "That'll stop a Prius," Will joked. Johnny laughed, cawing like a crow. The sound was unnervingly loud. It seemed hollow and out of place and it felt to hang in the air supported by the cries of the cicadas and the buzz of flies; there were a lot of flies about.

"We could build a moat," Johnny suggested. "You know, like a ditch."

Because of their BDUs and their heavy MOPP gear they were already sweating. "You go right ahead and knock yourself out," Will said. Johnny put away the entrenching tool that he had pulled from his pack.

"So two up," Max said, pulling out his protective mask. "You want to do the first stretch with me, Will?"

"What? Are you kidding?" Will asked. He settled himself down in the shade of a tree that sat just off the road. He put his back to the bark and opened his MOPP overcoat wider. "Only when…if we see a zombie, I'll put on the mask. Until then, no thank you. It's too hot."

It wasn't exactly hot; the morning was new and the clouds that had dumped so much rain the day before were threatening, banking thick and dark in the west. Now that they weren't actively working, the MOPP gear was comfortable. Johnny, with a great deal of sighing, eased himself down as well.

Max shrugged, giving into the "if you can't beat 'em, join 'em philosophy."

Instead of digging foxholes and clearing brush for fields of fire, they sat and chatted about everything under the sun: zombies, of course, but girls and movies as well. They also bitched as only soldiers could bitch.

At about 10 AM some of the locals began to creep down the road like shy mice. For the most part they were advanced in years and for sure they were a timid lot, but they were armed. Most carried rifles or shotguns, while a few had pistols. They smiled and nodded and stayed back a ways until one woman in a tracksuit and sunglasses, got up the courage to ask what was going on. "Zombies," Will told her matter-of-factly. "I know it sounds crazy but listen to all that shooting." The sound of gunfire had never let up. The shots came, one, two at a time with rarely more than ten minutes between them.

"You should pull up stakes," Johnny suggested, loudly enough for them all to hear. "I'd get clear out of here for the time being."

The advice was taken much to Max's anger. The locals had been frail and nervous, but at least they had been armed. The town emptied quickly and then the silence was like a weight. It was ominous, threatening a coming doom. Max checked his M16, re-checked his extra magazines, and then double re-checked his mask and gloves, keeping them near, just in case.

Will tried to scoff at this, however at 8:58 by Max's watch, a gun battle flared east of them. The sound of guns banging away drifted along the still air and the three soldiers held their breath as they listened. The crackle of M4s and M16s was mixing it up with the heavier boom of 30-06s, 308s, and 30-30s, bores that every hunter was accustomed to hear, but only in late autumn when the leaves were red and gold and the deer rutted and the squirrels frantically stored for winter.

They were out of place now.

"You think it's zombies?" Johnny asked. "Or are the people really fighting the army?"

The firing quieted down and because the thin crackle of the M4s died away first, Max had the feeling it was an actual battle. "That sounded like it came from that first stop we made," he said. "You know the one Starling, Mick, and Boyd got out at?"

"The one we were supposed to get out at," Will reminded them. "Maybe we should, uh…" He pointed to where his and Johnny's helmet sat in the dirt on the road's shoulder.

"Yeah," Max agreed, strapping his helmet on his head and zipping up his MOPP overcoat. Once they were geared up properly they each pulled out their entrenching tools and began to dig proper foxholes. Max's was barely three feet deep when the first zombie came slouching down the road.

"Shit," Johnny whispered. "Is that…?" It was thirty yards away. A slight bend in the road had hidden it until that moment.

Max scrambled for his mask as the thing charged in a gimpy stuttering run. It had been a man, and it had been fed upon. Its face, looking like black-moldy hamburger, was nearly gone however its teeth were all present and accounted for. They were stark white in black gums and looked big enough to be tusks.

Johnny ripped his mask out of its carrier, hissing: "Shit, shit, shit," as he did.

The masks were hot and tight, and with the hood, it made Johnny feel claustrophobic and more than a bit para-noid. He couldn't see Will and Max though they were right next to him on either side, and what was coming up behind them he could only guess. There could be zombies there, as well. He spun in place, wagging his head from side-to-side. They were alone…alone with the zombie.

He spun back around, nearly smacking Max with the business end of his M16. Max didn't notice. He was just thinking they had spazzed out for nothing. The zombie had managed to get hung up in the concertina wire and was flaying its own skin off trying to get at them.

"Maybe we should…" Will started to say. He was interrupted when Johnny started firing, ignoring complete-ly the Rules of Engagement. He was simply too keyed up. His heart was going so hard in his chest that he could feel it in his hands. The M16 was set for three round burst, but he was pulling the trigger so quickly that he might as well have been going full auto. His aim was atrocious; half his shots struck sparks off the road's surface and the other half thudded into the thing's arms and shoulders.

"The head!" Max cried. "Shoot it in the head! Damn, what kind of shooting is that?"

Johnny was hunched over his rifle in the strangest manner. "It's the mask," he whined. "It got in my way so I couldn't hardly see. But look. I got him." With his chest heaving, he pointed with the M16. The zombie was an ugly hunk of shredded meat that oozed black goo from a dozen holes.

"I was going to suggest that we wait until it got through the wire before we killed it," Will said, wearily. "Now, we're going to have to untangle it."

"We could just leave it," Johnny replied. "It's not going anywhere."

Will shook his head. Even with the mask covering his face and the plastic hood that draped down to his shoulders, he managed to look annoyed. "And let the flies land on it? What do you think will happen then? They'll get all germed up, and the next thing you know they'll be landing on your MRE or drinking the sweat out of your helmet. You want to end up like that guy?" He pointed with his rifle at the zombie.

"No," Johnny whispered so low that the mask held back most of the sound.

"Yeah, me neither." Will picked the entrenching tool that had fallen in his half-dug foxhole. "Let's do this."

It was a horrible task, made slightly better due to the bulky MOPP gear. The mask made the body difficult to see, which was a positive, and it kept back the awful stench, which was an absolute blessing. They hauled the body to the side of the road and buried it in a low trench. Will then insisted they clean the bloody concertina wire and no one complained over the extra work involved.

They shouldered in the door of the nearest house and then went back and forth with pots of water until the wire was again shiny. The three soldiers then cleaned themselves and their gear. Max was glad for the work. It kept his mind from dwelling on the fact that the zombie had been real. Completely and utterly real. Every time the thought entered his head, he got the shakes and would pause to look around, afraid that more of them would come storming down the road, or that the one they had killed would suddenly crawl out from beneath the thin layer of dirt.

"We killed it," he said, to reassure himself. "They are killable."

After they were clean, the three stood well back from the concertina wire, staring down at the bend in the road, waiting for the next zombie. It wasn't a long wait. One came bipping right down the dotted yellow line as if he owned the road. "Don't let it get in the wire!" Will cried and began shooting.

As he'd been trained, Max turned his gun slightly to the side and took careful aim down the barrel. His first shot went off into the woods and scared a bird into flight. His next took the thing's left ear off its ugly head. The third went high, hitting a tree, and a fourth wasn't needed.

"I got it!" Will yelled as black brains went flying and the zombie fell to the side, its body stiff and rigid, looking like a tree going down.

"Nice shot," Max said and gave his friend an awkward high-five. Feeling content with themselves they again went to work burying the body.

It had taken fourteen bullets to bring down the one zombie and they didn't give it a thought. None of them considered for a second how many rounds it would take to kill a dozen zombies, or fifty. They figured they'd be re-supplied eventually. After all, there was a constant stream of helicopters buzzing all over the place. Some were stuffed with equipment, ammo mostly, while others had men hanging out of them. None of the three remarked how many of those birds flew east with men in them and re-turned empty. There wasn't supposed to be anything east of them that needed so many men.

Chapter 8

Jailed

8:33 a.m.

From an upper story window in Thuy's townhouse, Deckard watched the government men pull up. They had to be Feds. He could tell by their matching black suits and ties. Normally, they looked stiff, but dapper. Now, with the heavy gasmasks strapped to their faces they looked ludicrous.

There were four all told. Three arrived in a Humvee and one came in a local ambulance that had been commandeered and modified for the occasion: what looked to Deckard like white bathroom caulking had been run along every glass edge and metal joint.

Stephanie Glowitz, who, along with Chuck Singleton, had been staring out from the next window over, asked in a whisper, "Dr. Lee, will we be able to breathe in there?"

Thuy didn't answer. Resigned to her fate, she continued to watch the men, her face wooden. They were coming to arrest her. The reality of that fact was just hitting her. It was one thing to conjecture over the possibility of incarceration, it was another to see the agents of the government coming for you.

Stephanie reached a long arm over and tapped Thuy. "Dr. Lee? Hey? What do you think? Will we be able to breathe in there?"

"I don't know," Thuy answered without giving the question so much as a thought. She could've been asked if she liked cherry pie and would've given the same answer. The government men walked down her walk and disappeared from the view of the window. They would knock any second and then they'd arrest her and put her in prison and take away the sun forever.

"You ok?" Deckard asked, giving her a concerned look. She liked the look. He cared for her. His feelings radiated out from him.

They would take that from her too. "Yeah…I'm just." Thuy tried to shake her head to show that she was feeling slightly disoriented, but her head shake became a confused motion as her shoulders twitched and her hands came up and trembled for everyone to see.

Thuy retreated into science, giving Stephanie an answer. "How long we can breathe, depends on a number of variables, the most important being the permeability of the seals. If they are airtight, then it depends on the length of time we're in…"

The government men knocked on her door. They had done so, *importantly*. Three heavy knocks that couldn't be denied.

No one moved. Around them the townhouse felt dead as though the knocking had transformed it into an ancient, dusty, mausoleum. Even the air seemed thick and stale as if it had gone unbreathed for centuries.

Stephanie was the first to speak. "They won't arrest me and Chuck, will they? We didn't do anything wrong. We didn't even get the IV."

"You broke the quarantine," Deckard said. "That's all the justification they'll need."

"I just want to know how they knew we was here." Chuck said in that slow, calm cowboy drawl of his.

"I'm sure we'll find out soon enough," Deckard replied. "Look, if you two want, you can hide and if they ask, we can say you left, but they'll likely go after your families if you do."

"No, I can't do that," Stephanie said, picturing her plump, little mother being dragged from her home in shackles.

Another series of knocks came to them; these were *important* and *demanding*. Wordlessly, Thuy started for the stairs and behind her came the others. She tried to smile when she answered the door. "Y-yes?" Her voice broke and the smile, which had been warped to begin with, trembled into a frown at the sight of the men. In their masks, they were tall, angry, boggle-eyed aliens. Each held a gun in their gloved hands as if their presence wasn't threatening enough.

The leader of the alien band looked Thuy up and down, before turning his head toward the others, he seemed unsurprised at their number and unimpressed by their appearance; only Thuy was wearing anything different from the day before. She had put on a white blouse over black slacks. Deckard wore his clean but wrinkled black suit, Stephanie had cover her thin frame with jeans and a heavy cream-colored sweater, and Chuck wore the oldest and most faded pair of blue jeans that Thuy had ever seen. Above that he had on a blue work shirt, rolled at the sleeves and scuffed with soot.

They were a ragged lot compared to the suited-up agent.

In the agent's free hand he held a white note card which he brought up to eye level before reading, "Dr. Thuy Lee, Charles Singleton, Stephanie Glowitz, and Ryan Deckard, you are hereby legally detained under executive order R-3. Please, face the wall and put your hands in the air."

Chuck turned slowly, his eyes going flinty. Thuy and Stephanie turned quickly, fearfully. Deckard's lip curled. "R-3? Who do you think you're fooling? Executive orders are numbered in…"

He stopped as one of the Fed-aliens brought his pistol up. He was wearing purple latex gloves which looked almost clownish but the gun looked very real. "Shut up and turn around," he said. Although his voice was muffled, there was unmistakable anger in his words.

Deckard turned and, as he had expected, they were each expertly searched—he had left his Sig Sauer under the couch cushion a few feet away for this very reason.

The search uncovered nothing but a pen in Thuy's pocket and Chuck's house keys that he had carted with him from Oklahoma to California, to New York City, and then to Walton. They were taken from him and he counted it no great loss. The clapboard little cottage with the slanted shutters and the squeaky porch boards felt a world away. No, it weren't no great loss, not compared to the woman at his side. He would give up a hell of a lot more for Stephanie Glowitz.

With much glaring from the boggle-eyes, the four of them were herded out to the street and then shut up into the back of the ambulance. Much to Stephanie's great fear, she could hear the sound of the feds caulking up the joints around the door.

Quickly, the air inside grew stale and heavy. Stephanie held back another question about how much oxygen they had left; she was sure Dr. Lee would start off with *It depends*, and Stephanie knew that would only make matters worse. She would end up fixating on every little variable. It was better just to…

The ambulance started up with a hum that was soon superseded by the urgent wail of its siren. The four of them began to rock and each pictured them flying along at a ludicrous speed, but there was no way of knowing how fast they were actually going. No one spoke.

Stephanie laid her head on Chuck's lap. She blinked the sweat from her eyes and tried not think about how the air felt old and used. She tried to force the word *suffocation* from her mind. She tried not to think about how it was more and more of a struggle to take a deep breath.

It was odd, she thought, that no one else looked like they were on the verge of panic like she was. Dr. Lee was pensive, her normally exquisite features drawn down. Deckard was scowling; he seemed more angry than afraid. Chuck was leaned back and relaxed. He had an arm thrown out casually along the back seat every bit as though he were lounging at a bus stop, waiting on the 3:01.

Stephanie had her hands clasped tightly together and her knees were pinched. To her, it felt as though the ambulance was under water, as though the government had decided to get rid of the loose ends of the Walton fiasco by driving them right into the Hudson.

"Jeeze," she whispered. Chuck laid his broad palm on her forehead and brushed her hair back. His hand was rough and dry, the calluses on it, like the knots of an oak tree, looked old and she thought he must have been born with them. She kissed the hand and then laid it across her eyes. That was better. That was love.

That was what?

Slowly, so as not to startle Chuck, she pulled his hand back. She tried to be calm and cool as she stared at him. Above all else she didn't want him asking, *What's wrong*, in that sleepy drawl of his. No way did she want that, because then she'd have to lie. She'd say *nothing*, when she would really want to say *everything*. Everything was wrong. She was dying of suffocation. Cancer was eating her body from the inside out. The government had put her under arrest. She had been a part of death and destruction and she had seen things that would have had her running for a hit of any drug she could get her hands on not too many days back.

Everything was wrong…and one thing was right, and for some reason that one thing threw a greater fear into her than all the rest combined. What if she screwed it up? There was no denying that she had screwed up everything else in her life. A college scholarship had gone up in the smoke of a thousand bong hits. A plum job for a fashion magazine that her friend Amanda Dockins had got for her, had come to nothing because she missed so much work due to sickness. In the early days of her cancer, she had fooled herself into thinking she was just dealing with a bad case of bronchitis. The friendship with Amanda had disappeared along with all her other friendships. Few friendships can stand the pain, the anger, the self-pity, and the wasting away of a cancer victim. Sure they were all there at the beginning, but the daily, depressing grind of the disease turned friends into acquaintances who assured her that, "We'll do lunch, next week, I swear."

She had screwed up a lot, and now, with what felt like so little time left to her, here was the greatest thing she could possibly screw up. She had never been in love before and yet, right there in the rocking ambulance, she was sure this was it. In the last three weeks, she hadn't gone five minutes without thinking of Chuck Singleton. There was an ache in her breast for him that put the cancer to shame. She was in love.

"Y'all ok?" he asked.

That was something she could answer. "Yes." Stephanie smiled and he smiled back.

The smile made the rest of the hour-long ride tolerable. What became intolerable was when the ambulance came to a standstill. The engine was shut off but no one came to retrieve them. The air grew stifling and a choking sensation came to wrap itself around Stephanie's neck like a Ball Python. She tried her best to be brave, to hold back any useless complaints. She didn't want to be seen as a whiner, however she couldn't help but breathe as though she were gasping in the last of the oxygen.

"One sec," Chuck said, easing her head out of his lap. He squatted in the low interior next to the wall dividing the cab from the back. With a meaty thump of his hand, he banged the wall. "Get us some damned air back here!" he bellowed.

The request was ignored.

Thuy glanced around as if the yell had woken her. She'd been awake, but was apathetic to her fate, however she did care for the others. Two had been her patients, people who had looked to her for help and the other was the man who had saved her life.

"Try hitting the back door. I doubt it was constructed to withstand blows from this direction."

She was incorrect. The door withstood the hammer-like blows Chuck dealt it with his size 13 "shit-kickers." When he lay back, dripping sweat, and panting the smothering air in and out, she appraised the situation, coolly. "Try the windows." Each door had a small square of wire-

crossed safety glass set in its middle. They crumpled outward, each taking three blows only.

Like a dog, Stephanie stuck her head out into the
world and chugged the air as though she'd been holding
her breath for the entire ride. Thuy had a little more deco-
rum. She knelt a few feet back, sharing the left hand one
with Deckard. The cool morning air didn't seem to lift either of their spirits. She kept her face turned down and he
scowled.

Chuck grinned, easily. "Looks like it's gonna be a
beauty of a day."

"If we get to see it," Deckard said, jutting his chin
toward the one tent that stood apart from the rest. The ambulance was parked well away from where a large number
of soldiers were toiling away, stringing rolls of concertina
wire, digging foxholes, and setting up very large army
tents. One of the latter sat all by itself fifty yards away
from the rest. Just like the ambulance, it had an extra layer
of protection to ward it from the Com-cells; its edges were
grey with duct tape. A guard with an M16A2 stood outside
of it—he was the only one, besides the feds who wore a
protective mask.

"Quarantine tent," Deckard explained.

"What is everyone wearing?" Stephanie asked. The
soldiers worked in uniforms that weren't the usual swirled,
camouflaged green, but were olive drab in color and
seemed extra thick, and on their hands were heavy rubber
gloves.

"That's MOPP4 gear," Deckard said. "It's supposed
to protect against chemical and biological attacks. These
guys must be National Guard by the looks of it. That gear
is a little out of date."

"It looks hot," Stephanie said.

"Oh, yeah, it's a bitch to do anything in, especially to
fight in. Once, when I was…" Deckard stopped as the
Feds came back. They were still masked and brandished
the same pistols.

"Move to the back of the vehicle," one of the men
said in a hoarse shout. "And don't try anything stupid."

94

When they were as far back as possible, one of the government men opened the ambulance doors and used his gun to indicate they were to get out.

"Mighty fine of you," Chuck said, as he unfolded his long frame, stepping out into the morning. He acted as if the pistols weren't even there, as he held his hand out to help Stephanie step down, he looked to Deckard, as though he was out on a date.

Deckard matched his cool demeanor, but his was a charade. Most federal agents he'd run into had been A1 assholes and that had been under normal circumstances. Who knows what kind of power-trips they'd be on now that they were acting under a true emergency?

Worse than the agents were the National Guard boys. Just a glance told him they weren't infantry. The soldiers working on the rolls of concertina wire looked to be having fits, as the razor-sharp wire tangled on everything, including their clothes; most had ruined the integrity of the MOPP4 gear and didn't seem to realize it. The men putting up the tents acted as though they were attempting some sort of alien architectural puzzle; they bitched and snapped at each other in frustration. The men unloading crates of ammo from five-ton trucks were intermingling them with boxes of MREs.

Worst of all were the men on the line, a hundred yards away. They smoked cigarette after cigarette in nervous anticipation of what was to come. Quite a few held their M4s as though they were holding a stranger's baby—awkwardly and afraid to drop them. Even from this distance, Deckard knew they were not 11Bravos. These were cooks and dental technicians, clerks and laundry specialists; there were even members of the 42nd marching band who had been pressed into service on the line where the pucker factor would peg at its highest reading.

That they were here at all told the four of them that things around Walton had escalated into nightmare status. None of them had the first inkling that things had gotten so bad and yet there was gunfire in the distance and of course the, quarantine tent. The Feds gestured with their guns for the four of them to go to it.

Stephanie eyed the duct tape, nervously. "Will that hold back the germs?"

"Ah think it's suppose-ta hold *in* the germs," Chuck said in his slow Oklahoma drawl. He spoke as though his day held thirty hours instead of the usual twenty-four. "Ah just hope it's empty. Ain't no way they'll get me in there if it's all germed up."

That had also been Deckard's big worry and now that it had been spoken aloud, it was all of theirs as well. Stephanie actually glanced back at the once hated ambulance, looking as though she wanted to climb back in and shut the door behind her.

"Get moving," one of the feds demanded when the four came to a stop a few feet from the zippered tent door. "We have orders to shoot anyone resisting arrest."

"We aren't resisting arrest," Dr. Lee stated. "We are resisting the possibility of spreading the pathogens further. Are there infected persons in that tent?"

"There wasn't the last time I checked."

It was, at least, an honest answer. One of the feds pulled off a strip of duct tape to expose the zipper. "Go on!" he growled. At first, no one moved. Chuck looked ready to fight and Deckard's insides were spooling up. Thuy was calm. With a sigh of defeat, she went to the zipper and drew it down.

Inside the gloom, sitting on a wood bench that had once belonged with a picnic table, were two men she recognized.

"Doctor Wilson, Mister Burke, it's good to see you alive. Is it safe to come in?"

Both men were red-eyed and bleary. Burke's hair stuck up at sharp angles and Wilson's afro was indented on one side. There was a strange pattern to it as though someone had used his head as a step stool. They blinked against the sudden infusion of bright sunshine. Wilson brought his soft, brown hand up to shade his eyes and said: "We are not infected, if that's what you mean. Who are you?"

"Doctor Lee."

"Ah, sum-bitch," Burke said, shaking his head.

Seeing as the tent wasn't infected, Thuy stepped in, followed by the others. "I'm not here in a medical capacity, Mr. Burke. I'm no longer in the business of cures or diseases, so you have little to fear from me."

"I don't think he was worried about that," Wilson said, after clearing his throat. Like Burke, he had trouble looking her in the eye. "Tell her, John."

"Oh hell! I didn't think nothing would happen to you, but when we was captured, they asked who else made it out alive. We's tole them y'all's names. I never did think they'd go and hunt y'all down."

Thuy was actually relieved by the explanation. "You couldn't have known, Mister Burke. Your ignorance is forgiven."

John Burke frowned at the word "ignorance", not liking the sound of it at all. In his mind, he equated it with stupid, which he sure he was compared to the other people in the tent, all save Chuck Singleton. Because of his accent, John assumed a sort of kinship with him that extended to a mental equivalence.

As the others spoke, Deckard walked the perimeter of the twenty-by-twelve foot tent. It was well sealed and staked, and yet, it was still just a tent. Escape would be simple…if it wasn't for the guard out front and the place crawling with soldiers.

"Has anyone been in to talk to you?" he asked Dr. Wilson.

"An FBI agent named Meeks. He acted as though we were criminals."

"And do you know where we are?"

Wilson sighed, his shoulders drooping. "About twenty miles from Walton, so we're safe. Out there is the command post for the army or the National Guard or whoever it is in charge. It seemed like they started building it around us about an hour ago."

"How did you get caught?" Deckard asked. "Were there a lot of road blocks?"

"I don't know if there's a lot. We only ran into the one. I tried to talk our way around it but," he paused to sigh again, "but they wouldn't listen, so I tried to get past them on the shoulder of the road."

Burke, who had been absently scratching his head, became animated at the memory and grunted out a laugh. "Y'all shoulda seen the ol' Doc. A gangster he is not! He tries to go around the poh-lice all nice like so they don't arrest his ass. He even put on his blinker all nice and tidy like."

"So what happened?' Stephanie asked.

Wilson made a face as if he were sucking on a lemon. "They shot out my tires and they were new, too!"

Another laugh came from Burke. He nudged Chuck who was sitting beside him with an arm around Stephanie, and said, "When they shot, he yelped like a dog what had his tail stomped on. I swear to gawd he did!" Burke continued to chuckle for a few seconds but when no one joined him he sighed as if the memory had been a pleasant one for him.

Thuy was the furthest from laughter than any of them; she felt the weight of guilt on her like a thousand gravestones piled on her shoulders. She couldn't take a full breath because of it and she couldn't think. All she could do was picture Dr. Riggs lying in the haze of smoke on the fourth floor while the elevator struck his ankles over and over again.

Stephanie was in the same boat in that she couldn't think straight, either. Questions went round and round: why had she and Chuck been arrested when they had done nothing wrong? And what would happen to them? Would they go to jail? Or would they be forced to sit there until someone truly infected was shoved through the zippered flap? What would they do then?

Deckard had the same question, only he had an answer. The one thing that made sense to him was to kill anyone who came through the door with even a hint of black to their eyes. Kill them and then throw them back out through the tent flap. There seemed to be some sort of incubation time before the victims became the monsters and he didn't think they could wait for that to happen, even if it felt like murder.

Chuck was the only one there who didn't worry much for the future. He had a bit of a headache and his many cuts zinged irritably when he moved and his lungs made gurglily noises when he breathed. Whether that was from all the smoke he'd sucked down, or from the cancer eating him alive, didn't much matter to him. He was content to just sit in silence, holding Stephanie and listening to the army do its thing.

Outside the tent, the sounds were many and confusing: the blatt of trucks was constant, the bark of sergeants yelling orders was like the scream of gulls, the distant rifle fire kept up a fine tempo. All this made it seem like *something* was being done to fix the problem.

The sounds and the growing heat of the morning lulled them almost into sleep until a helicopter's rotors could be heard beating the air. Each of them was sure that it was there for them in one capacity or another. The zipper coming down a few minutes later confirmed this.

Soldiers in MOPP4 gear came in first; their guns were leveled. Behind them came a man named Major Haskins; his name was taped to the outside of a voluminous plastic biohazard suit. His eyes were blue and angry but beyond that, he was a nondescript entity because of the heavy mask he wore. There were two others with him dressed in the same manner and both were equally angry.

"Dr. Thuy, I'm Colonel Jeffery Haskins Ph.D. I am the facility director of the US Army's bio-weapons response team. This is Dr. Tanis of the CDC, and Special Agent Meeks of the FBI."

"Hello," Thuy said, not getting up. Suddenly, there was a spark to her, as bright and hard as one struck from steel and flint. Despite everything that had occurred, in her mind, there was no need for the FBI to be there. It was almost offensive, especially when he was brought by two Ph.Ds. "Is there something I can do for you?" she asked, with an eyebrow raised.

"Yes," Agent Meeks said. "You can explain yourself. You can start by telling us what the hell you did. And know this, you are already culpable for the deaths of thousands, any dissembling on your part will be considered obstruction of justice."

"In that case, I think I will need a lawyer."

Behind his mask, the agent's eyes went to squints. "Oh, Dr. Thuy, there'll be no lawyers for you. Count on it."

Chapter 9

A Hungry Child

8:39 a.m.

Compared to what was happening in and around Poughkeepsie, the outbreak in Hartford took place in slow motion. It was two days before anyone even knew there were zombies in their midst.

The day after Walton went up in flames, six-year-old Jaimee Lynn Burke woke up in an old Lincoln Continental. Its roomy back seat had been ripped or torn a dozen times over in its long life and now the duct tape holding it together was splitting and in need of being repaired itself.

Stuffed under the driver's seat were the remains of a McDonald's fillet-o-fish sandwich. It let off an eye-watering stink, only the little girl couldn't smell anything but the human. It was close. It was a man, she knew because to her their privates had a different odor, like warmed over spam.

Jaimee Lee sat up, feeling a spike of hunger in her guts. It was a need akin to lust and yet it was beyond any normal human desire. It drove her to fumble for the door before her eyes were even opened. They were gummed shut and she raked at the black goo covering them with one hand, smearing a three-fingered streak across her pale face. Now she was able to see the handle.

"There's the darned..." she started to say, but stopped at the sound of her own voice. She sounded phlegmy and growly, like a tubercular truck driver with a two-pack a day habit.

She coughed and swallowed, wondering what was wrong with her however, the question was dismissed in a flash as the door came open and the full smell of the man struck her. Just like that, nothing else mattered to her but her hunger; not the rain running in a slant, or the cold that tented up her skin with a million goosebumps, nor the fact that she was shoeless.

Her hunger was everything. Even the strange anger roiling inside her was a distant second to the hunger. She splashed out into the rain, making a bee-line for the man. He was tall and broad with a back the size of a billboard. He wore a hard hat, a coat, and heavy boots; across his waist was a belt of tools. Jaimee categorized him as a "worker" but did not bother to narrow the description down beyond that. What did it matter? Only hunger mattered, and eating. She went right for the man and only paused long enough to find the flesh.

Beneath the helmet and above the collar of the coat was a strip of hot meat. The man had his back to her and had no idea she was even there. His first indication of trouble was when he felt something on his back— and then there came the wicked teeth.

The pain was sharp. "Ho—fuck! What the fuck?" he cried, twisting and doing an odd, spinning dance as he tried to dislodge the creature on him. He was sure it was a rat and his belly crawled in disgust. But it wasn't a rat. He caught hold of one of Jaimee Lynn's scrawny arms and threw her off of him, still cursing.

"Fuck," he said, in a breathy whisper when he saw what had attacked him: it was a little girl with mud in her eyes and red on her lips. "What the fuck do you…"

She scrambled up, stopping him in midsentence. She hadn't heard a word he was saying; her eyes were focused entirely on the soft skin beneath his stubbly jaw line. That was where the good blood was, and the tender meat. Her body quivered in anticipation.

"Back off!" the man yelled. His name was McMillan and he was having trouble piecing things together. Who was this girl? She was feral and looked like she had crawled out of a cave or perhaps had crawled out of a distant time when humans were mere savages. She was like a wild animal, a wild rabid animal. She was panting and licking her red lips, savoring the blood.

He had never seen anything like Jaimee Lynn and, although her appearance was unnerving, he certainly wasn't scared in the least. McMillan stood two feet taller and outweighed the girl by two hundred pounds. He could crush her like a bug with one of his size thirteen, steel-toed work boots. If he had a worry it was the fact that it looked like he would have to use force to restrain her.

"Hey, look, settle down," he urged, putting his callused hands out to the tiny slip of a thing. It was a waste of breath. He could see her gather her legs beneath her, preparing to spring at him again, and yet, despite being forewarned, he was almost bitten a second time. She was fearsomely fast and her aggression wasn't animalistic, it was demonic.

She flew at him, hands like claws and her mouth open to bite. Just before her teeth latched onto his neck, he managed to catch her by her pale yellow hair and held her out at arms-length like a bedraggled cat and, like one, she hissed, spat, and tried to claw at his arm. "Relax, damn it!" he yelled. "Now, tell me where you live."

The blood lust was too strong for her to understand a single word; all she cared about was getting to that throat and chewing through the salty skin. She could see blood pulse beneath that soft covering of flesh. It made her stomach feel like an empty fifty-gallon drum.

"Can you hear me?" McMillan asked, giving her another shake. When all he got was the same inhuman growling, he decided that the police would have to deal with the little psycho. He turned Jaimee Lynn around and tried to walk her to his truck. It was impossible. The girl acted as though she would rather rip her own hair out by the roots than get in the truck. He was compelled to take her by the back of the filmy hospital gown she wore and lift her bodily in. The girl spazzed like a demon-possessed cat, making McMillan curse, spittle flying from his lips as he forced her into his truck.

In order to shut the door behind him, he had to let go of her with one of his hands. Wet and sleek and adder-like, she spun in his grip and sunk her teeth into his wrist. It hurt like bloody-hell, making his lips twist. He tried to pry her off only she had latched on and began to make dreadful sucking noises as she drank his blood. This, more than the pain, overcame what little compassion he had for the waif.

In order to get her off of him, he punched her twice in the temple. He pulled the first blow because she was so small and frail, but when that didn't work to get her teeth out of his flesh, he gave her a proper thump using all his strength. Her eyes went in two different directions and her jaw went slack.

She looked at him dully.

"I'm sorry," he said defensively. All he could think about was that no one would believe that he had to hit her. What would his wife have to say about it? Or his friends? Shit, what would the police think? "I'm sorry, but you made me hit you. It's your fault."

Jaimee Lynn began blinking as if waking from a deep dream. The punches had shaken her and for some reason it made her hunger less, which allowed her to think with a little clarity. This was a man next to her and a big one at that. She could never eat him because he was too strong.

"I need a small one," she said, in a raspy voice, picturing a child in her mind. It was a girl child with yellow hair, a gap-toothed smile, and a pointy chin. She was familiar, only Jaimee Lynn couldn't put a name to the girl, not realizing that she was picturing herself—the Jaimee Lynn she was used to seeing in the mirror.

"You can talk?" McMillan asked, surprised. "Well, good. You can explain to the police why you bit me."

"Because I'm hungry, very hungry," she said, rubbing her stomach. She began to feel the hunger start to override her thinking again. It was his blood, she realized. She couldn't be that near so much clean blood without it overcoming her.

McMillan leaned away from the girl, disgusted by her answer. It had been a frightfully honest answer. "You should tell that to the police. Say it just like that." He reached into his pocket for his keys just as she reached for the door handle.

"Bye," she said, as she pushed the passenger door open and fled into the rain.

"Hey!" McMillan yelled after her. He jumped out of the truck but she was running like a rabbit and he didn't even take a step. "Fuck," he grumbled, standing in the slanting rain, feeling it wash away the blood that leaked from his wounds. They ached, dully. A check of the side mirror showed him that he would probably need stitches in his neck. "What a pain in the ass," he mumbled, knowing that his day was shot.

Once he had called his boss and explained that he'd been attacked by some drugged-up "guy"—there wasn't any way he was going to say it had been a little girl—he went to the emergency room where he waited, along with thirty others, to be seen by a doctor. Soon a headache began to throb behind his eyes, which wasn't helped by the fact that the hospital staff seemed to be moving in slow motion.

After an hour, the pain was so bad that he was rolling on the floor, practically in tears. This bumped him up in priority and very soon, he found himself on a gurney with a sheet drawn around it as its only privacy. Everything was too bright and too loud. It made him want to puke.

The Com-cells were replicating with unbelievable quickness, making his nerves feel like there were live wires attached to each. When he started to scream, an IV was hooked into his arm. In a minute, the fire in his mind was doused so that it was only a pile of smoking embers. "Ah, better," he sighed.

"It's better for us, too," someone on the other side of the sheet muttered just loud enough to be heard.

"What's that supposed to mean?" McMillan growled. He wasn't in any mood to take crap from anyone.

"Nothing," a second voice answered. This one was female. She began whispering. The nearly inaudible hissing bothered McMillan. What was she saying? Was she saying something about him? Something about why his head was pounding and his eyes were going blurry? What did she know and why didn't she speak up? Was that on purpose? Was she trying to tease him with her secret knowledge?

The very questions bothered him as well. He was very confused and he wasn't one who was normally confused about anything. Generally, he was sure of his facts. For instance, he knew he was supposed to be here for some stitches, yes, that was a real fact, but where had the headache come from? Were they releasing something into the hospital air? Some sort of poisonous gas? But if so, why was he the only one affected? No one else had complained about headaches. Maybe it was something they fed him or it maybe it was in…"

McMillan eyed the IV bag with sudden fear. It was half-empty. How did it get so empty, so quickly? How long had it been in his arm? Certainly minutes only.

His watch would verify that, only the numbers were twisted tick marks, and the hands jumped about on the face, appearing here and there without rhyme or reason. Tapping it didn't help either; everything blurred so that it didn't look as though he was even wearing a watch; it looked like a leather strap that would hold him down and keep him there forever.

"They drugged me," he whispered, in dread.

The IV came out with a firm tug and blood oozed from the wound—it was darker than it should have been but not yet black. Next, the blood pressure cuff made a sound like a roar in his ears as he tore away the Velcro and, finally, the monitors let out piercing tones when he pulled off all the wires that had been attached to him at some point.

McMillan tore aside the curtain to face his enemies. There were many of them, dressed in blue or green. One came up to him. "What are you doing out of bed?" She had the creaky voice of a witch and the cruel glint to her eyes to match it. McMillan knew her. She was the one who had stuck the IV in his arm. She was the chief poisoner.

He answered her question by punching her flush in the face. There was a hue and cry as she fell to the ground, her nose bent and gushing blood. For all of a second, McMillan stared at the blood; it was so cherry-red that he had to wonder if it was sweet.

Then men were charging him. McMillan was a big man and just then, against his enemies, he felt bigger still. And stronger, too. He flung people about as if they were made of paper. They were powerless against him, and the Emergency Room ran red with blood as he swung his heavy fists as though they were sledgehammers. People screamed in terror and their fear goaded him to more violence. Mercilessly, he stomped the ones who fell until their features were mush. Quickly, the ER emptied of people— all save for one individual. This one wore a shiny badge that sent shards of light burning into McMillan's eyes and in his hands was a gun.

The gun fired three times before McMillan fell.

He had devastated the Emergency Room, leaving three dead in his wake, and yet it could have been worse. McMillan wasn't yet contagious. The Com-cells had been fast getting to that stage, but now, as if directed by some unseen force they began to heal their carrier. For two hours, McMillan laid there as investigators took statements and wrote reports and photographed the chaos. Had it taken them two hours and ten minutes they would have been in for a rude surprise when McMillan opened his eyes.

Luckily, for them, the coroner had bagged the body before that could happen. McMillan was put on a slab and then slid into one of the "chillers" as the morgue technicians called the refrigeration units. This didn't kill the Com-cells. No, they were far from dead. The only effect the below freezing temperatures had on the disease was that it multiplied at a more leisurely rate instead of the frantic pace that was usual.

Still, when the coroner slid open the slab the next day he was in for of a hell of a surprise. McMillan was covered in what looked like moss that was the color of ink as black as night. It was so dark that when he opened his black eyes the coroner didn't even notice.

Three hours after running from McMillan, Jaimee Lynn had forgotten all about him. She was too busy eating the third child she had caught. The small humans were so much easier to catch than the big ones, and they were tastier, too. But they didn't have much blood to them which meant they died quick and came back just as quick.

Jaimee Lynn was in an abandoned building sucking the blood right from the carotid of a third grader. She frequently smacked her lips, and her breathing was hot and quick. Behind her, Misty pawed at her back.

"Mine," Misty said. "Mine."

"In a minute," Jaimee Lynn answered, shrugging off the hand. She bent again and slurped noisily, uncaring of the effect it was having on the "girl."

Misty had stopped being a real girl an hour after Jaimee Lynn had left McMillan. Jaimee had caught her on the way to school and had throttled her with hands that were like mechanized steel. When Misty stopped kicking, Jaimee Lynn had drunk until her belly sloshed. She then dragged the little girl corpse off to the abandoned building and buried her under rusting iron, thinking she would make a nice treat for later, but then Misty came alive.

For the most part she just laid there looking up at the partially stove-in roof, listening to the rain creep all through the building. When she could talk, she didn't have much to say beyond her name.

Jaimee Lynn thought she was stupid and guessed that she was that way because she had died. But she did have her uses. She did whatever Jaimee Lynn told her. No questions asked. She was like a robot slave. The next girl was the same way and Jaimee Lynn figured this last one would be as well. It meant they could eat one of the big people pretty soon.

Even while she was eating, Jaimee Lynn's belly growled at the thought.

Chapter 10

Middlebush Massacre

8:58 a.m.

Chaos vied with confusion as operational adjectives. As every military operations officer knows, both are, at least to some extent, built into military plans since neither can ever be fully weeded out. What was occurring around Poughkeepsie was an exaggeration on par with madness. Bluntly, it was being described as an exceptional cluster-fuck, and it was no wonder: there was no plan in place to call up an entire division in six hours. It was simply an impossibility.

When Governor Stimpson started growing anxious at the slow speed in which the call-up was progressing, General Collins had to remind him that during Hurricane Katrina, it had taken three days to put a single brigade in place, and they didn't have zombies to worry about on that occasion.

One issue they were having was that a disconcerting number of guardsmen had failed to show up mostly due to CNN running the unfounded story that a massive Ebola outbreak was occurring in the Mid-Hudson area of upstate New York. Another issue that Collins was having difficulty overcoming was that the only major north/south highway in that part of the state ran right through the quarantine zone and thus was unusable. Traffic jams grew like tentacles to entangle most of the northeast. The logjam of cars ran a hundred miles or more in every direction. Logistics had broken down, reinforcements were stranded, half-formed companies sat idle on the side of the road and orders were being given by officers sitting in cars fifty miles from The Zone, and those orders were based on hours-old information, assumptions or just plain guesses instead of cold facts.

And yet, things were progressing, albeit erratically. Squads of soldiers were straggling in and were being sent straight through to the lines. Sometimes, they came loaded down with equipment, sometimes with just their empty weapons. One squad showed up in their dress uniforms thinking there was a surprise inspection underway.

Officers began to find their rhythm as their minds shifted out of the civilian mode and into the military, and right up until 8:58 a.m., the situation was at least somewhat manageable. The number of zombies was being described as "light" and, except for a few tragic incidents, the citizens were afraid and angry, but not violent. At 8:58, at the junction of Albany Post Road and Middlebush, just south of the town of Wappinger Falls, where a barrier of barbed wire had been erected to delineate the 'zone' from the free area, an incident occurred, making things a hundred times worse.

The "Middlebush Massacre" as it would become known, was started by accident. Tensions were wire-tight and the fear on both sides of the barricade was like an easily communicable disease, spreading from person to person until both sides were on a hair trigger. An incident was bound to happen and a teenaged boy named Cody Cullin was determined to record it. His desire was for YouTube fame and already he had recorded a dozen zombie sightings, though he was the first to admit that, so far, his videos were dark and grainy and not very good. However, what he uploaded at 9:07 a.m. would be seen by thirty million people by the end of the day.

The video was amateurish and very narrow in its scope. What it didn't show were the hundreds of angry civilians pushing to get out of The Zone, edging, closer and closer to the flimsy and lightly manned barricade. The people screamed obscenities, they revved their engines, menacingly, and those with guns held them at the ready. They riled themselves into a fevered pitch so that they were practically frothing at the mouth and yet all the video showed was one man yell: "You can't legally stop us." The man held a cellphone in his hand and, as he yelled, he gestured at the soldiers with it. Tempers had been on the knife's edge all morning with fear causing the mundane to appear monstrous.

One of the soldiers, sweat stinging his eyes and his protective mask clouding his vision, panicked at the sight of the man pointing what he thought was a gun and fired his weapon pointblank into the man's chest. Guns came up from every direction, however because of the angle of the recording it looked as though the three soldiers and the two state troopers were firing unprovoked into a small group of unarmed people.

The gun battle that followed was brief. The troopers with their shotguns and the soldiers in their heavy MOPP gear got off a few shots and then went down in a blaze of blood and screams; of course, this aspect of the one-sided fight never made it onto YouTube. All anyone saw was the first twenty seconds, and it was enough to make Cody Cullin an internet star.

For the rest of America, the shit had hit the fan.

Over the course of the next three hours, the video would trigger a dozen gun battles between citizens and soldiers. Sometimes the people won and were able to surge out of The Zone. Sometimes the soldiers were forced to shoot into a mass of humanity until the mobs broke and fled back into The Zone.

The first Courtney Shaw heard about the shoot-out she was sitting in her chair, eyeing her map of the area, as a state trooper bleated uselessly in her ear. The chair felt welded to her ass. In fact, her ass was so numb from sitting for so many hours on end that she couldn't tell where it ended and the chair began. The same went for the headset that was molded to Courtney's skull. It felt like some sort of vestigial horn that had grown in upside down, curving down her cheek instead of rising into the air. She was tired but determined to make every effort to help the very weird situation. She had lied—necessary, white lies, she told herself. She had manipulated those in power—another necessity. Now, adrenaline was keeping her going when her body just wanted to lied down.

"I honestly don't care how long you've been on duty," she said, tiredly to the trooper out of Peekskill. "You will turn your cruiser around and get to Milton or you will be brought up on dereliction of duty charges. Those orders come from the Superintendent." She paused and covered over the mike so she could speak with her partner. "Renee, have you heard anything from the Superintendent yet?" Courtney figured the man would have said something similar to the trooper, but wanted to cover her ass all the same.

Renee barely looked up from her board. "Not a freakin' peep."

Superintendent Ritz, on orders from the Governor himself, was supposed to be getting video proof of the zombies. He had left Albany at seven that morning and hadn't been heard from since. He wouldn't answer either his radio or his cell phone—it was more than a bit unnerving. In his absence and with the First Deputy Superintendent not up to speed, and the Assistant Deputy Superintendent a known jackass, Courtney was running the four thousand-man department. She was pulling troopers from every corner of the state to deal with the traffic and the zombies and the crazy quarantine zone and a thousand other things, including directing soldiers, many of whom were out in the middle of nowhere, too far for their radios to reach and without cell service for their phones.

Courtney's mind was zipping along at a pace she didn't think possible.

In a way, it was her Zone. Its shape was nothing like Governor Stimpson envisioned. He pictured a perfect circle with the Walton Facility as the epicenter. The real shape was somewhat like a paint-splatter. With the dwindling manpower she had to work with, it was far more economical *and* realistic to concentrate on certain areas that she deemed crucial to hold. In order to stop the spread of the zombies across the Hudson she had thrown in as many men as she could to hold the area around Highland. North of Poughkeepsie she had men spread out over miles of pretty farmland to keep Albany from being reached, but the most important area of all was to the south where three highways fed straight into New York City. The YouTube video was shot at the barricade at Interstate Nine, the central of the three highways.

"Holy shit!" cried Renee, suddenly. "Courtney you got to see this." She shoved her Smart phone into Courtney's face.

Twelve seconds later Courtney's brown eyes flew open wide. "Where is this? We gotta find out where this is."

They couldn't tell by the video and so Courtney's eight-woman task force had to drop everything and begin calling the one-hundred and forty cruisers in the area. They had only just begun when General Collins called demanding, "Have you seen the video?"

He understood the implications better than anyone. It was one thing for the National Guard to tell a frightened populace to stay indoors and that everything was going to be alright, it was another thing for them to be seen gunning down what looked like unarmed civilians. His adjutant had been given the video and he hadn't wasted a second barging in on the General in the middle of a meeting with his brigade and battalion commanders.

"I'll find out," Courtney assured him. In her other ear, the state trooper was still there and still complaining. "I have a wife and children who live in Stone Creek," the trooper whined. "They're too close. I need to get to them before…."

"It's eight miles beyond The Zone," Courtney replied, tapping the map. Her own family had moved out to Buffalo a few years before and she had already sent out messages to her friends who lived nearby to get the hell out of Dodge. Really, if she had anyone to worry about it was herself. The trooper headquarters was on the Taconic State Parkway, only ten miles southwest of Poughkeepsie and only a mile from the Hillside Lake barricade—it was a little too close for comfort. And yet she couldn't tell this unknown trooper that everything would be hunky-dory and then run herself.

"Listen, I'll keep an ear out for anything weird going on around Stone Creek. In the meantime, get your ass to Milton. The troopers there have a hundred or so civilians trying to slip past."

She cut the link and then groaned—it was all the rest she allowed herself before she joined the others and began calling the individual cruisers. Things were falling apart. People saw the video and now they feared the government as much as they did the zombies that were pressing from behind. When word of it spread, they took matters into their own hands. Fourteen troopers didn't answer their radios when the dispatchers made their calls and others began to scream that they were under attack.

Courtney stood up and shouted to the women in the room: "Send me the coordinates of every trooper who doesn't answer. We have to plug every hole." It took thirty-six minutes to figure out they were screwed.

"I need more men," she said, again tapping her computer screen, hoping that by some miracle more soldiers or troopers would get through the building traffic jams. She expanded the map hoping to see a river she could pull the men back to in order to strengthen their lines. When she did, she saw something peculiar. "Who are these guys at Poughquag?" On the map, twelve miles east of them was a marker indicating an army unit was loitering just south of the little town. "What's M.B?"

Tanya Miller covered her mike and said: "You don't want them. It's just the army marching band and some cooks."

"Do they have guns?" Courtney asked. She didn't wait for an answer. She went on the army net and found the frequency for the 27th Brigade Support Battalion who were hunkered down far from the fight.

"I need to speak to the C.O. right now," she demanded in clipped tones. So far, this new authoritative voice of hers had worked like a charm. This time it hit a snag and worse she was about to discover an entirely new problem.

The person who answered was quiet for a moment and said: "I'm Colonel Winthrop, I'm the officer in charge, and you are?"

"I'm General Collins' assistant. I am going to appropriate some of your men. We have situations developing that require reinforcements."

Winthrop was quiet again, before saying, "I don't know who you are, but you're not the General's adjunct and you won't be appropriating any of my men."

Courtney tried clearing her throat as if she were startled that anyone would question her. "These are orders straight from the General. I am tasked with forming the quarantine perimeter. There is no higher priority than that. Now, I need to know how many soldiers you have available. I'll even take the marching band."

"Who are you again? You didn't mention a name or a rank."

"I'm with the office of the Governor of the State of New York. My name is Courtney Shaw."

"You're Ms Shaw? Finally! I've been cleaning up your messes for the last two hours."

"My messes? What messes are you referring to?"

Colonel Winthrop laughed. "You have been sending the general's soldiers all over the place, turning the perimeter into a mess. I'm still trying to find out who is where. I need you to know that this is going to stop right now. From here on, you are not to direct a single soldier. Do you understand?"

"Yes, I suppose, but I…you still need to move those men from Poughquag up to the line. They're just sitting there doing nothing."

The Colonel scoffed: "Wrong. They're manning the line right now."

Courtney made a face as though she was talking to a wayward three-year-old and asked, "How can that be? They're twelve miles behind the furthest perimeter. I have the state police, in conjunction with men from Delta Company of the 1st Battalion holding a line stretching north to south on highway 82."

"Highway 82? That can't be right. That would mean they are technically in The Zone." There was a pause and Courtney heard fingers tapping at a keyboard and then Winthrop came back on, seething: "Do you realize what you've done? Those men are in the infected area and must remain there. The perimeter is supposed to be twenty miles from Walton in every direction, those were the orders I received, and I'm sure you received the same ones."

"Yes, but…" Courtney began but then a little dot caught her eye. It represented the trooper station she was seated in. It looked exceptionally isolated, sitting in the middle of nowhere—sitting in the middle of The Zone. "This is crazy," she hissed. "You have a line outside a line. It makes no sense and neither does the Governor's idea of the perimeter. Are you looking at a map? Your perimeter includes Kingston! There are fifty thousand people in and around that city. And it also contains Newburg. That's another twenty nine thousand people. They aren't going to sit still and let you cage them up. Have you heard what happened at the barricade south of Wappinger?"

"Yes, and we are working on contingencies in case that sort of thing comes up again. Now, if you don't mind I have work to do."

"You call what you're doing work?" Courtney demanded. "Haven't you noticed a complete lack of zombies or refugees coming your way? It's because we're already doing the job, damn it! Move your men up so we can contain this properly."

"I can't," the colonel replied. "And besides we have had incidences, so whatever you think you're doing it isn't a hundred percent effective."

"That's because I need more men, damn it!"

Winthrop was quiet for a moment and seemed sad when he replied. "I can't. I have my orders."

"They're going to change," Courtney began, "Mark my word, I'm going to see…to…that…what the hell?" The map on her screen suddenly clicked off.

She shook her mouse as Winthrop said, "Like I said, I have to go." He hung up, but she wasn't really paying attention. Her stomach was going suddenly squirrely. First, she was told by the army that she's *in* The Zone and now her internet goes on the fritz? She didn't think it was a co-incidence.

"My internet is down," Renee said, wearing a look that Courtney was sure was matched by her own puzzled features. The other women all nodded along: a choir to the preacher. Renee tried her Smart phone next and her eyes went huge. "And my phone, it ain't working!"

The station phone lines were out as well. *We're officially in The Zone*, Courtney thought to herself and then shivered, feeling suddenly abandoned by the world. "Just calm down," she said as the women looked ready to bolt. "Let me contact the general. It's almost for sure nothing."

Easier said than done. The radio call was picked up by some colonel who let her know that the general was in another meeting and that all calls from the governor's office were to be handled by the division communication officer, Colonel Herald Winthrop. "Hold on, Ma'am, I'll get that frequency."

"Never mind," she whispered and thumbed off the radio. "What the hell's going on?" The only answer she could come up with was that the army was gearing up, putting its pieces in place, meaning that Courtney's ability to make a difference was over. She felt useless, and worse, trapped. She looked out the window at the gloomy day and felt hedged in as if there was nowhere to run. The one question was: did she tell the others what was happening? Not just the other dispatchers, but did she tell the troopers who were putting their lives on the line for nothing? What about that trooper's family in Milton? Or the entire city of Kingston. They were all fucked.

"Wait...uh, wait here," she said to the now quiet room. "I'm going to go talk to Pemberton. Maybe every-one should take a break." She left the call center and stopped just outside the door, feeling her heart pound and her breath like a rabbit's, speeding in and out so quickly that it didn't feel as though any of the oxygen was catching in her lungs. It was as though she were breathing out faster than she was breathing in, or that perhaps there was a fire of fear eating the air inside her. She couldn't seem to catch her breath.

She was beyond afraid. She was straight-up petrified. She was trapped. Death on one hand from the guns of the military. Death on the other from the diseased teeth of the zombies. Standing in the hallway seemed the best thing she could do. It was the safest thing to do, that was for sure, and it was the easiest. She was running on fumes.

A huge yawn gaped her mouth but a sudden roar caused her to gulp it back. A squadron of Blackhawks cruised overhead, each crammed with soldiers and supplies. From the direction of the sound, she knew that they were going to Poughquag. They were adding men to the wrong perimeter. The trap was closing.

"Pemberton!" she shouted as she marched down the hall to his office. She found him clicking his keyboard and wearing a look of complete befuddlement. "We're trapped," she told him. It just came blurting out and she had to fight her eyes to keep tears from doing the same. "The army has a new line twelve miles east of here. It's… it's crazy! They act like they don't care about us or the troopers or even their own men. Hell, they're not even using natural barriers. They've given up the Hudson! I can't...Pemberton? Are you listening?"

"My computer…the internet's not working at all," he said, still with his face squinched and his eyes blinking slowly in a dull manner. He looked as though ten years had been splashed across his face in the last day.

"It was the video, I bet," Courtney said. "The one on YouTube; that thing is poison. It's going to turn people against everyone in uniform. It was that or all the news people shooting off their mouths about stuff they don't know…not that the truth is any better."

"Did you say we're trapped?" he asked.

He pulled out a Rand McNally Road Atlas and flipped its wide pages to New York. She pointed out Poughquag to the east, halfway to the Connecticut state line. "They're setting up the new line here and if I had a guess they're running it up highway 55."

The lieutenant stared at the map long after Courtney lost interest. He looked as though he were trying to find meaning in it. "We should try to get out of here," Courtney said. The lieutenant's staring continued for another minute as another flight of helicopters thumped overhead. Courtney tried again, "I mean we're not doing anyone any good here, and if we stay, they'll get us eventually, the zombies I mean. That or we'll run out of food. I say we gather up as many troopers as we can and get out of here before the Army's perimeter is fully closed. I know a few ways out of…"

Pemberton interrupted: "No." He wiped gently at the map as if clearing away nonexistent crumbs; he smoothed it at the edges. "No," he repeated. "Our duty is to the people we helped trap. We should stay and fight."

"We can fight once we get clear of the edge of The Zone!" she cried.

"And who would we fight? Our troopers on the other side of the line? Our soldiers? Don't you see we'll be just like all those other people? They killed to get out and just made things worse. We know better, Courtney."

She wanted to pull her hair out. "Staying means dying. You know you can't fight all the zombies; even if we could get all the troopers in The Zone here, it still wouldn't be enough. We will die!"

Pemberton pushed the map away and then went to the window. He knocked it hard with his knuckle. "We'll fortify the station. The walls are brick and the glass is thick. I don't think zombies can get in here. We can hold out a long time here, maybe long enough for the government to straighten things out." He went to his desk and pulled out a short-barreled Glock, and checked the load.

"I think I want to leave," she said. "Now, before it's too late."

He grinned in a fashion that suggested mental instability rather than mirth. "All morning I was thinking the same thing, but about a half hour back I saw that." He pointed across the parking lot where a run of woods was shading the edge of the asphalt. A zombie stood there, swaying. Because of the shade, Courtney couldn't make out its features beyond the fact that one of its arms looked to be dangling longer than the other, but she knew it was one of them.

She shrank back from the glass and now Pemberton's smile was a bit more lively. "She can't see you because of the glass. You want to know something strange? I know her. She was a waitress over at the Roadside Inn off of Vassar Road. I used to think she was so cute and now I should go over there and shoot her in the head."

"You'd be doing her a favor," Courtney said, and then repeated, "I think I want to leave."

Pemberton checked the load of the Glock a second time. "I won't stop you, just do me a favor first, call back the boys. What they're doing is a waste of…of everything." He left to kill the waitress and Courtney ran back to the call center where she explained the situation. A single gunshot was the exclamation to her story.

"Don't worry, it was just a zombie. Now, recall everyone! Pemberton wants to make a stand here. He thinks the doors will hold." She didn't leave yet, she joined the others working the radios and telling the troopers the bad news. When she had gone through her list, she tried to locate General Collins, reaching him in the Governor's office. She lied her ass off in order to speak to him.

"General? This is Courtney Shaw, I need your help."

"Courtney, you are out of line!" he snapped. "I'm in a meeting with the…"

She interrupted: "I-I know but I think I'm trapped. I think we're all trapped. Someone authorized a shift in the lines and no one told us."

Collins heard the fear in her voice and despite the fact he had a host of dignitaries staring at him, including the Governor, he asked: "Where are you, exactly?" When she told him, his eyes went to the map on the wall and he felt his heart sink. "I'm sorry, Courtney, I didn't know. If I had…" What? What would he have done? Zombies had gotten through the porous initial line on the eastern edge of The Zone—the line had to be shifted. It was pure, painful logic and there had been nothing he could have or would have done to change it. War was hell and a war against zombies was even worse than that. There was no way he could help her. He didn't have the time or the man power. "Try to hold on as long as you can, we'll figure out something."

He hung up and Courtney sat staring at the satellite phone much as Pemberton had stared at the map. Finally, she decided not to bet on the army. She whispered to Renee: "I'm taking off, now before it's too late. I think I can get through the new lines. Will you come with me? You're the only one I trust here." Renee was thirty—the same age as Courtney, and both went to the gym, sometimes together and chatted as they walked a few imaginary miles on the treadmill; the other six ladies were older and most were shaped like soft bowling pins.

"Ok, but not yet," Renee said. "Let's wait until some of the troopers get back. You know some will want to take off. We'll go with them."

Courtney glanced around quickly before saying: "If a trooper is going to go AWOL they aren't coming back here first. The ones that comeback are the ones who are going to stay." Renee took one look outside at the parking lot where Lieutenant Pemberton stood a few feet from the body of the waitress, and quailed. She wouldn't go no matter how much Courtney pleaded.

With Renee huddled at her desk, Courtney asked the other women if they wanted to chance going out and was turned down by everyone. "Then I'll go alone," she said, to the quiet room. No one said a word.

Before leaving, Courtney went to the armory; all the shotguns were gone and the three M16A1s were as well. She picked out a Glock, much like Pemberton's and added four full clips. She would've taken more but the lieutenant stood watching her.

"This is a mistake," he told her. "We can hold out."

Her gut told her they wouldn't be able to. Maybe there was a chance they could live for a day or two, but what would happen when the food ran out or the water? What would happen if there was the tiniest mistake? What if they let in someone with the disease? It had happened at Walton and she was sure it would happen again.

"Sorry," she said. "When I find the army, I'll let them know you're still here and alive, Ok?" She scurried out of the station with a scarf wrapped around her face to keep out any stray germs, the Glock in her left hand and the keys to her Volkswagen Beetle in the other. The bright red Beetle may have been the worst car ever to attempt to take through the hills and forests on the edge of the Catskills. In fact, it barely made it out of the zombie engulfed town of Hillside Lake.

The undead were everywhere, in numbers which shook Courtney to her core. And they were faster and stronger than she had anticipated. She was forced, over and over again, to turn away from the direction she wanted to go and was soon lost in a thick forest that seemed to go on forever in every direction. Without thinking, she pulled out her Smart phone to Google her position, however the screen was blank.

"This might have been a mistake," she whispered.

Chapter 11

Scorpions in a Bottle

9:51 a.m.

Escaping The Zone was practically an impossibility for everyone. At first, Eng drove the Nissan one handed while he kept his other sweaty hand on the blue/black handle of his .38. Driving this way was fine in the motel parking lot and on the side street, but things in The Zone were deteriorating fast and, eventually, he gave Anna a hard look and stuffed the gun in his pocket. "Don't try anything," he hissed. "Or I swear you'll go down with me."

"What would I try?" she asked, innocently. They both knew she would try *something*; that something being wholly dependent on the timing and the circumstance they found themselves in. That something would also depend on how she could benefit from the situation. As Eng drove, she kept her eyes open for the least chance. Soon she found that escaping from Eng wouldn't increase her chance of living.

The morning was filled with the undead. They came out of the fog, lurching and moaning in obvious hunger. Some were like Von Braun had been, black-eyed and hating everything, even the very air they breathed, and some were brain dead but otherwise whole. These were very fast, like sprinters. Most however were bloody and missing chunks of their body, sometimes very large chunks. It didn't seem to weaken them in the least but it did slow them down.

They attacked cars on sight.

It was all Eng could do to keep them off the Nissan. He swerved all over the highway and sometimes drove on the shoulder or the median. There were other cars on the road but not many and they drove in the same wild manner Eng did. They flashed their lights and honked but what they were trying to get across wasn't obvious until Eng came to the first roadblock.

It was mobbed by hundreds of cars. They were crushed in so close to the barricade that no one could move. "Stay back. Don't get too close," Anna said, laying a hand gently on his arm. She pulled the rear-view mirror around to check her face. A sigh escaped her at what she saw; she was scratched and bruised and the circles under her eyes were pronounced. She tried on a winning smile. Hoped it would be enough and then she ran her fingers through her hair.

"What are you doing?" Eng asked.

"You want to get through the road block? This may be the only way." With her hair done as well as it could be, she reached for the door handle but Eng stopped her.

His eyes were slitted but the suspicion shone right through. "This may be the only way you get through but how do you plan on getting me through? Are you going to tell them I'm your adopted brother? Or your servant?"

The truth was neither. She had actually planned on using tears and a declaration: "That man raped me!" She would show her scabs and the rope burns on her wrists. She would also tell about his gun and he would either pull it out and get shot by real warriors or he would skulk back into the crowd, while she would use her looks and a faked timid persona to get in close. She was sure, that given time, she would be able to sweet talk her way across. "I'll think of something," she assured Eng. "Don't worry."

"No. I want a plan," he replied. They were two scorpions in a bottle and neither was going to trust the other. "We cannot take a chance on you winging it. Look." He pointed toward her window. Zombies were crossing a field of wild grass coming toward the cars. For now, their numbers were manageable, below a dozen, and people were already taking aim with rifles. "We passed hundreds on the road. They're going to hear the guns and they'll come running."

"Son of a bitch," Anna said. In order to run her sweet talking mouth, she needed time. "Turn the car around." Guns were already popping off as he swung around and turned back east.

Both of them were without their cellphones, having lost them back at Walton, and so they drove in a meandering path, looking for one of the hidden ways out of The Zone. As far as Anna could tell, there weren't any and, to make matters worse, the number of zombies continued to grow as the morning progressed. Three hours passed under the running tires. Sometimes they trundled along at walking speed hoping that a thin parting of the trees would mean they were coming up on an old logging road, other times they raced among the forest trails or on narrow roads with zombies converging on them from all sides.

During all this, Anna watched Eng, looking for the perfect opportunity to escape. All she needed was a moment where he grew tired and let his attention lapse. It never came and finally she slumped in the passenger seat. "So what do we do?" she asked. "You're the super spy. What does your training say we do?"

"My training never covered zombies," Eng replied; there was a pause and then he smiled; it wasn't something he was all that good at. It made him look ill. "We never covered any of this."

"Then what do we do?" she asked again. "We can't just drive around in circles until we run out of gas." When Eng shrugged, she almost rolled her eyes, but only just remembered the gun and the fact the man was a lunatic, an ass and a sociopath. She almost discounted him as she was mentally ticking off her very dubious assets: her looks, one vial of deadly serum, a car with half a tank of fuel, and a Chinese spy. His potential was limited since he really didn't understand Americans—but then again neither did the vial of Com-cells or the Nissan, she realized. They were just tools.

So far, they had counted on getting lucky to find a way out, now she analyzed the problem from a purely scientific point of view. First was to formulate a hypothesis, a guess based on her understanding of the variables before her. The variables being tens of thousands of zombies, a few thousand survivors clamoring to get out of The Zone and some hundreds of soldiers and law enforcement officers tasked with keeping the other two in.

She understood zombies perhaps better than anyone. By using a combination of drugs and channeled hate, they could be controlled to an extent. She had proved that with Von Braun, however he was, in all likelihood, dead, and she was out of drugs. The cops and the soldiers could be controlled as well, again to an extent, but she was limited with this variable as well because of the urgency of time. This left the survivors, the citizens.

She smirked. "They aren't normal citizens, they're Americans." Just as many academics did, Anna felt herself above concepts of nationalism and she tended to look down her nose at Americans, and at the same time, she somehow found honor or purity in cultures other than her own no matter their level of abject poverty, or their lack of freedom or the societal rot that had them fleeing to America. She saw Americans as fear-filled, gun-toting hicks, and had, among their other lesser qualities, a deep-seated phobia of the very government they voted for year after year. She could use that just like any other tool.

Cody Cullin, the YouTube star, had guessed about the accidental circumstances that led to bloodshed, Anna was planning a purposeful massacre. "Let's go back to the road block at I-55. I have a plan." She wasn't about to get eaten alive, even if she had to cross out of The Zone tramping over a thousand bodies.

She chose the roadblock at I-55 for one specific reason. Yes, it had looked like all the rest: cars squished together with barely any room to open a car door. And of course, there was also a slew of angry citizens, guns, cops and zombies. The lucky difference was the deep brook on The Zone side of the barricade. This strip of water thirty feet wide more or less held back the zombies. For her plan to work Anna was going to have mingle with the people and there was no way she was getting out of the Nissan with zombies about.

"Wait until I scream," she said to Eng, after explaining her plan.

"Yes," he said curtly. She was glad to see his face was set and she hoped she looked as cool and calm. Out of habit, she checked her look in the glass of the passenger side window and then started picking her way through the cars. Most were jammed with either people or belongings as though entire homes had been condensed and crushed down to fit through a car door. The people inside, with their laps overflowing with useless electronics or dogs or even other people, stared as Anna strode past.

Men stood outside the cars. All were armed, many chain-smoked. They too stared at Anna. No one seemed to notice Eng following after with his right hand stuffed into his jacket pocket.

"The army doesn't have a plan for us," Anna said to a group of men who stood behind an SUV thirty feet from the wire and the felled trees across the road. They'd been talking in quiet voices, casting hard looks at the handful of soldiers blocking their path. They raised their eyebrows at the woman in the stained lab coat. "There is no cure," she added and then moved on to the next group.

"I just came from Albany. The Governor just agreed to fire-bomb Poughkeepsie and we're next," she said to them.

One of the men said: "They said they're working on a cure."

"I'm sure they are but it won't come in time to save us. These things take years."

"How do you know?"

She flapped her singed white lapel at the man. He had a faded cap on his head and wore a checkered shirt stuffed into dirty jeans. In his hand was a gleaming rifle that had obviously been better cared for than any of his other possessions, likely even better than his wife and kids. If he had graduated high school, she would've been surprised. "I have a doctorate in microbiology. I worked on the project that started this. Take it from me, you and everyone here will die if we don't get through that barricade."

Another man pushed through the group. With his suit shiny at the knees and his shoes scuffed, he looked to Anna like an insurance agent and perhaps it was his white-collar garb that allowed him to command the others. "No. Don't listen to her. They said the army is on the way."

"They are, but not to rescue us. Listen. We're in a status A quarantine. No one gets out. Period!" The group began to grow angry, but Anna knew it would take more than words to stir these people to violence. They were moronic patriots who put God and country over the value of their own lives. "If you don't believe me maybe you'll believe this." She pulled the sleeves back on her lab coat showing the ugly red marks where Eng had tied her to the bed.

"What is it?" the man with the checkered shirt asked.

The insurance agent knew. "She's been tied up," he said with a growing realization in his eyes.

"They tried to keep me from getting out to warn you," she said. "But now that you know, your lives are in even greater danger. They won't let you live no matter…Oh my God!" It wasn't exactly a scream, however Eng caught on that now was the time. He fired the pistol from inside his coat.

The stubby .38 was a dreadfully inaccurate weapon at ranges beyond fifteen feet and only three of his bullets hit anything other than air. Luckily, for Anna a bullet went through one of the cruiser's windows, shattering it. In a second, the soldiers and the troopers returned fire and, keyed up as they were, the citizens began shooting as well. Many were killed, but their rifles were deadly and there were so many more of them.

Four of the six soldiers guarding the barricade died in the first flash of gunfire, another was holed through the neck and would slowly bleed to death over the course of the afternoon. The last fell on his face and cowered as lead flew all around; glass flew like shrapnel and tires blew.

Then there was silence. The citizens came out from behind their cars to see what they had done. It wasn't pretty, death never was. A few looked at Anna, none did so with blame in their eyes. They blamed themselves or tried to believe they had missed, that the expensive scopes on their rifles were lying, deceiving their eyes.

"I'm getting out of here," the man with the checkered shirt said. He hurried for his truck, bringing on an exodus that bordered on panic. Barricades were plowed over and at least two of the corpses were mangled to a point where recognition was impossible.

Anna started scanning the vehicles, looking for one which might have room for her, but most looked to be filled to over-flowing, and the few that appeared to have room shied away from her and her lab coat. Everyone knew lab coats meant germs.

Eng wouldn't have let her go anyway. He came sidling up to her, his hand coming out of his pocket with the hunk of hot metal. "Let's go," he said, threatening with the pistol.

"Aren't you going to thank me?" she asked, unable to take her eyes from the weapon.

"No. You did what you did to save yourself, not to save me. Come on." He started escorting her to the Nissan parked at the back of the mass of cars, only the rush to leave made it too dangerous. Cars were thumping into each other and scraping paint in their owner's haste to get out of there. Anna and Eng were forced to wait on the side of the road until the last few cars shot by before they could get to their Nissan. Eng didn't zip out of there like the others. He drove slowly until he came up near to the barricade.

He's going for the guns, Anna thought. On his side, there was a black assault rifle sticking out from underneath one of the sagging cruisers. On her side, still in the grip of a dead trooper was a 9mm Glock. She decided she would go for it if he stopped the car.

I'll be quick. I'll be quick. I'll be quicker than he is,
she thought to herself, trying to psyche herself up. It was a
life or death decision. She would dive for the gun and
come up firing and he would die because the rifle was long
and would be slow to bring to bear on her. He would die
and her problems would be….mostly over.

Her hand was on the door handle when movement
caught her eye. The one soldier still alive was on his knees
and reaching for his own weapon. "Eng!" she screamed,
grabbing his arm. The soldier's gun was coming up in
what felt like slow motion, its bore looking like a black
eye searching for her.

Eng was more than willing to let the soldier kill Anna,
however he didn't like his own chances against a man
armed with an assault rifle while he only had the .38. He
stomped the gas and the Nissan leapt forward. It was a
nimble and quick car, but it could not outrun a bullet. The
back windshield blew inwards and then there was thudding
sound, as though someone was smacking the car with a
hammer. Next, there was a "bang" and the car started
shuddering as it drove.

Anna crawled down into the footwell and hugged herself until they were out of sight and the awful thunder of
the gun had ceased. She sat up and stared out the back.
The Nissan was in a poor state: the upholstery was shredded, there were holes big enough for her to put her thumb
through all over its hide, and there wasn't a single window
left intact. The back tire on the passenger side had been
struck and now they were shedding vulcanized rubber at a
rate that couldn't be maintained. Soon it became a lurch
and then there came the squeal of metal grinding on pavement. Only then did Eng stop.

He brought out the .38. For the moment it hung at the
end of his arm, pointing at the ground. "Let's see how
good you are with a jack."

"Me? That soldier is just down the road. He could be
here in a few minutes."

"Then you better hurry," Eng said, icily.

She didn't like the sudden quiet of the nearby forest. It made her feel very much alone with a psychopath. "You still need me."

"Yes, I need you to change the tire. Now let's go!"

She wasn't weak or ineffectual in any way; she had changed tires before but the tire would remain forever unchanged. Going to the rear of the vehicle, the biting odor of gasoline struck her nostrils. "Aw, shit," she said in a whisper. The tank had caught a bullet as well and beneath the car was a growing puddle.

"You still need me," she reminded Eng. He had grown uncomfortably still and quiet, much like the forest around them. He glanced back the way they had come and then brought up the pistol, pointing it her way.

Chapter 12

Reunion of the Damned

10:32 a.m.

Ryan Deckard sighed for the thirtieth time and when he did, he made sure that it was loud enough not just to be overheard but to piss some people off as well.

"Do you have something to say," Special Agent Meeks asked. He wore a smarmy smile but with the blue biohazard suit and the mask, it wasn't seen. Deckard didn't need to see it, he felt the arrogance of it come right through the plastic.

"I sure do," Deckard said. He'd been leaning against one of the tent supports, but now he stepped close so that Meeks had to tilt his head up to see the taller man. "Why don't you stop being a dick? This isn't an interrogation. This is you preening for the camera." A bagged camera had been brought into the tent to record Thuy as she explained at length what had happened at Walton. She was constantly being interrupted by the sanctimonious Meeks.

Thuy had stood firm during it all and really didn't need a protector, especially when the bullying was scientific in nature, however Deckard could only take so much.

"I will get to you and your so-called 'security arrangements' soon enough," Special Agent Meeks sneered.

Deckard snorted both figuratively and literally. "Here's all you'll get out of me." He hocked up a ball of snot and shot it in a gob to splash against Meeks's face shield. The agent did a herky-jerky dance and, backing away from Deckard, he tripped over Chuck Singleton's long legs. The Okie had done nothing to keep it from happening.

John Burke grinned, showing the gaps in his grill. "That was a bit of alright for a city-boy. Now, iffin, y'all wanna see how we spit out in the sticks, I'll show you a thing or two. I can shoot a line of skoal twenty feet and smack a bull-finch right 'tween the eyes."

"That won't be necessary, Mr. Burke," Thuy said, gently. She turned to the visibly angry, FBI agent. "Though I don't agree with Mr. Deckard's method of handling this situation, I concur that we have strayed beyond anything resembling a debriefing. You are clearly trying to trip me up in some fashion, perhaps in order to assist in some future criminal proceeding. Sorry, but I will not 'play' along. Despite what you've hinted at, I have rights."

"Are you saying you are no longer cooperating?" Meeks asked, quietly.

"I won't be cooperating with a kangaroo court, whose sole purpose is to find a scapegoat. I will cooperate scientifically. I will answer your questions honestly and to the best of my ability, however if you insist on asking the same questions over and over again, then I'm sorry, I will not answer. If you've forgotten a previous answer you should refer to the recording." She indicated the camcorder held by one of the soldiers in the room. The other two held guns.

"She's answered all of my preliminary questions," the army Bio-weapons expert, Colonel Haskins stated. He hadn't liked the answers to his questions, especially the probable incubation period. He had felt his stomach drop when Thuy had said: *A person exposed to the Com-cells will, depending on body weight and metabolism, become infectious within approximately two hours.* The idea was sickening. They started with forty patients and half a day later, Poughkeepsie with its fifty thousand people was a ghost town. Reconnaissance flights had shown only the undead left roaming the streets.

Haskins knew that the official jargon was "Infected Person" but the Air Force recon planes had amazing photo capability. All it took were a few close-up stills of the zombies eating people for him to forever throw the words

"Infected Person" out the window. These weren't people anymore. These were things that had to be exterminated.

Dr. Tanis of the CDC was also quiet. He had no need for scapegoats, and he was sure he wasn't going to have time for them either. He had been privy to the official projections of different outbreaks since he had come to the CDC fourteen years earlier. For three straight years, he had been in charge of writing MMRs: Morbidity and Mortality Reports. It had been a wearing three years churning out documents entitled: *Estimating the Future Number of Cases in the Ebola Epidemic—Liberia and Sierra Leone, 2014-2015.*

With its thirty-one charts, and ninety-eight pages that one had been a best seller. Thankfully, the projection had been off. CDC projections frequently discount the idea of changing human reactions to a deadly pathogen in their midst and they have a long history of instilling that prejudice within their reports. Ebola was a fine example. What caused the outbreak to flourish was the way the bodies were ritualistically cleaned before burial. Relatives handled the corpses at a point when they were carrying their highest pathogen load, covered in blood and feces. It wasn't until this was pointed out, repeatedly, that the death tolls began to level off.

Tanis didn't think they would be so lucky this time. There wasn't a behavioral component to the spread of the Com-cells, there was just a mindless, insatiable hunger driving the infected. The virus was definitely blood-borne and yet, because of the elements of the fungi within it they had to take precautions against it being airborne as well. He went to rub his weary eyes forgetting the plastic hood and just ended up smearing his face screen. "I will need more specific information on the Com-cells," he said.

"The original?" Thuy asked. "I have more information about that, based on memory, granted. Let's see they're approximately 143,000 nucleotides in length. It encodes seven structural proteins including nucleoprotein, polymerase cofactor, VP35, and VP40. There's also, GP, transcription activator, VP30, VP24, and RNA-dependent

RNA polymerase." She saw his eyes begin to glaze and realized that he'd been too long compiling data on other people's work rather doing anything original. In her experience, it tended to dull the mind. "Unfortunately the specifics, the uh written specifics were kept under pretty tight lock and key at Walton. They were undoubtedly destroyed in the fire."

"Well, whatever you can remember might well be helpful," Tanis replied.

Special Agent Meeks, still with his face shield smeared with spittle, said, "She's going to be more than helpful. She's going to jump through every hoop I can think of or I'll have her on obstruction of justice and this isn't a normal obstruction charge. It'll be a life sentence for you young lady. I'll fucking see to it."

"She's answered your questions," Deckard growled, stepping between them.

"Back off!" Meeks snapped. "You're on the same hook as she is. That goes for all of you."

"We didn't do nothin' wrong," Burke said. "Me and Chuck and Stephanie didn't do nothin'. No offense, Doctor Lee, but you could say we was the victims here."

Thuy was surprised how much that hurt. "I'm sorry," she whispered.

"Sorry?" Meeks demanded. "You've killed 50,000 people and sorry is all you have to say? And you three," he said pointing at Chuck, Burke, and Stephanie. "We are talking about the destruction of America! You may not love this country but I do and I will do anything to keep her safe. You will comply or else."

Stephanie laughed suddenly. She really laughed. It was all belly and it was loud. It didn't go with their surroundings and the others worried for her, but she didn't need their worry. "Don't get me wrong, I love my country, but do you really think you can threaten me or Chuck? Haha! We're dying of cancer you stupid douchebag. You don't scare me in the least…and those guys with the guns? Nope, not afraid of them either. So why don't you take your threats and shove them up your ass?"

Both Burke and Chuck started grinning but in seconds, they were rolling on the ground laughing, tears springing from their eyes. Even Deckard joined in, though his laughter was mostly out of spite. There were still many punishments that the FBI could mete out to him and Thuy. Wilson was in the same boat as Deckard, and he was actively worried about his practice being taken from him. He smiled but it was without strength.

"So you have nothing more to say?" Meeks asked Thuy. She shook her head. He then turned to the others. "And you think you have nothing to fear? I think we'll put that to the test. People have been slipping out of the quarantine zone and we have to put them somewhere. Be sure to make them comfortable when they arrive."

That quieted the tent. They all feared becoming zombies, all except for Burke who thought he was immune. "Don't be a dick," Burke rumbled. "No one here did anythin' wrong."

"I have my orders," Meeks replied. "All escapees are to be housed in a quarantine tent. This is the only tent available." By the crinkling around his eyes, they could tell he was smiling malevolently. "Now do you have anything more to say, Dr. Lee?"

In truth, she didn't. She hadn't held back in the least. "I have told you everything, honestly."

"Then I have even less regret," Meeks said. He gestured for the others to leave with him. The two doctors left with downcast eyes and soon the six were alone again.

John flipped him the bird as he zipped up the tent. He then got up, scowling as the others remained seated looking shocked. "It'll be ok," he told them. "Y'all can jes sit over at the far end of the tent and if there does happen to be sumptin wrong with anyone they bring in here, I'll do him up good."

"The spores maybe airborne," Thuy said. "Do you understand what that means, Mr. Burke?"

"It means they goes in the air I reckon."

"But we don't know that for sure," Deckard said. "I think John's plan is the best we have."

Thuy hated the idea and wouldn't be a part of it and yet she was in no position to stop it either. She was dreadfully afraid of coming to come face-to-face with whoever they brought in. Would they realize she had been at the heart of everything? Would they blame her? Of course they would. There was no question of that.

It was such a horrible idea that when the zipper started to come down a few minutes later she hid her face in her hands and only peeked through her fingers. A teenage boy: small and thin with a bush of brown hair on his head, and a nose and feet that he was still growing into, was hustled through the opening and stood looking as if he was going to vomit on his tennis shoes. Like a gang of highway robbers, first Stephanie and then the others, lifted the front collars of their shirts to cover their faces.

"Sit right there," Burke growled, pointing at a corner near the door. The boy looked too shell-shocked to even think about disobeying. Burke looked him up and down. "Y'all get bit or scratched?"

"No I didn't I was…"

"Jes nod yo head, boy!" Burke snapped. "There ain't no need to be runnin' y'all's gums."

"Mr. Burke!" Thuy hissed. "Have some compassion. I'm sure this young man has done nothing wrong. We should treat him with respect, and it would be appropriate to explain to him what is going on around here. The reason we're here is because there was an accident and some, for want of a better word, germs were released."

"I know, they make people into zombies," the boy said, his teeth worrying at his lip.

Thuy swallowed hard at that. She held up a finger, wanting to argue the point because, after all, what he had said wasn't scientifically accurate. Deckard nudged her in the ribs and shook his head slightly. She bit back a proper explanation. "Yes, in a sense the victims become *zombies*." She put special emphasis on the word since she had to choke it out. "And once they have metamorphosed they become contagious. We're worried that you might have been exposed to one of the, uh, zombies."

"No...no I ran," the boy said. "I...I, put my little brother in my tuba c-case and I-I ran."

"Tuba case?" Thuy said, feeling pain score her heart. How desperate does a person have to be to put a child in a tuba case? "How long ago was that?"

"I don't know. Like around sunrise."

The words made her head go light. If Thuy hadn't been seated, she would've fallen over. Parts of her were completely without feeling and in other parts all she felt was a deep pain. "Sunrise?" she asked breathlessly. "That was hours ago. We...we should try to get help for your brother. Where do you live? Where did this happen?"

"Thuy," Deckard said, gently.

"No!" she cried and pushed his hands away. "I did this! We...I have an obligation to help him and his brother." She tried to get up but Deckard held her down. His hands were like iron and his arms, steel. She fought him, but he was too strong and too big. "I d-did this!" she wailed. She cried in great retching sobs and the tent was quiet but for her. The boy cried as well. In silence, tears dripped from his eyes. His brother was dead, he was sure of it...he only hoped he died of asphyxiation in the tuba case and not from the zombies.

"Ever-one hush," John Burke said, holding out his hands and cocking his head. "I hear them comin' back."

Thuy began shaking her head, afraid to see more children being herded into the tent. She didn't think she'd be able to handle any more children. Tears streamed down her face and her breath began to hitch, sounding like a bad case of hiccups, but when she saw the people who came in, her body slipped back into her control, mostly. She couldn't stop herself from flying at the pair, her hand out stretched to rake their eyes out.

Deckard stopped her, barely. "No, they may be infected."

"All the more reason they should die!" Thuy screamed.

Anna Holloway had been expecting to denounce Eng the second they entered the tent, now she hid behind him as Thuy fought like a beast to get at her. "I didn't do anything," she said. "I was a spy, but that was all. I didn't sabotage anything. It was Eng who did it. Ask him. He speaks English better than you and me."

The Chinese operative shrugged, glanced around and then planted himself wordlessly next to the teenager who drew into himself even more.

Chuck took hold of one of Thuy's arms and Deckard the other. "Just calm down, Doc," Chuck said, easily. "They'll get theirs, you can bet on it. When that Meeks guy comes back, he'll rip into them and that's for darned sure. Until then we should keep away, just in case they got the zombie bug."

After glaring fiercely for a second, she turned cold. "That's a sound plan, Mr. Singleton," Thuy said, quietly. She would have her revenge, one way or the other. Never in her life had she ever contemplated the word revenge seriously, but now it took over her mind, filling her with a white-hot hate. "We should keep our distance for an hour or two, and I agree we should turn them over to the authorities, eventually, but I want them to suffer. I want revenge." Her words were so cold Anna felt the chill of them wash over her.

"You've already had your revenge on me, Dr. Lee. Look at me! Look at my hand. You did that when you left me dangling in that elevator shaft. Remember that? And look at my wrists and ankles. Eng held me hostage and raped me for hours last night. Don't try to pin this on me. I've been punished enough…and all I did was take some pictures and send some emails. It was Eng who sabotaged the Com-cells. It was Eng who made all of this happen."

"What about the fire?" Thuy asked in a voice as soft as silk and as deadly as an adder. Anna's face turned the color of old cheese. "You set the fire that ended up killing Riggs and Milner. Remember that?"

"You have no proof," Anna answered, too quickly. It was only a guess. She didn't know what sort of evidence Thuy possessed.

Thuy laughed softly. It was an evil sound. "Proof is for the courts. You are guilty in my eyes and I swear there will be a just punishment for you. Something more than a few lacerations on a pinky. Something closer to true justice. An eye for an eye, perhaps. Something that would make Hammurabi smile."

Anna began to deny everything, one last time: "But I didn't do…" It faltered under the hard glare. She looked away from Thuy. The others were just as cold. Only Eng and the boy next to him were different. The boy looked as though he'd been hit over the head with a shovel and Eng was smiling, gloating.

"Now who's fucked?" he asked.

An hour before, just after they had made it beyond the barrier, Eng had turned his .38 on her. "I'm sure you understand. I can't have you telling anyone that I'm alive." Her mouth had come open to beg for her life and to promise she'd never mention him to anyone—she didn't get a chance to speak this lie. Eng had cocked the pistol causing her heart to leap into her throat.

He would have shot her right then, but at that moment, four Humvees had come bustling into view from the east. Just as quick, the .38 was out of sight and Eng had her by the shoulders. "I will shoot you, I swear," he said. "Be smart or else."

She nodded, but that too was a lie. The Humvees stopped in front of them and men in masks had hopped out with guns pointed. They were all pointed Eng's way. "You're fucked," she whispered and then stepped away from him and went into her performance. "Thank God you came! He raped me and held me at gunpoint. He's got a pistol in his pocket."

Eng's hand had strayed to his pocket causing one of the soldiers to step forward aggressively, his finger drawing back on the trigger. "Hands up, you fuck!" he ordered. Eng's face went flat, expressionless, and very slowly his hands went to head height. The soldier's gun then swung toward Anna. "You too!"

"Me? I didn't do anything. Look at my wrists. He tied me up and raped me!" In spite of the hoods and masks, she could see their moment of hesitation. It was a moment only. They had their orders and so they came forward to frisk the two, only Anna couldn't allow herself to be frisked. In her pocket was a vial of the deadly Com-cells. Its presence would raise questions she couldn't answer.

"I didn't do anything," she said, backing away, clutching herself. Her hand had stolen to her pocket and now the vial was in her palm. She considered dropping it but they would see. She turned away as though she had a thought of running.

"Stop!" one of the soldiers demanded. She could hear the hyped-up fear in his voice; it was raw as a wound. He would shoot if he had too. With her back to him, she stuffed the vial into her bra.

"Don't touch me," she whimpered, mentally preparing the soldiers to accept the idea that she was fragile and damaged. She cried some good fat tears and when they frisked her, they kept well away from her breasts. Then she and Eng had been forced to sit in the grass, under guard until an ambulance arrived. "You zip your lip, I'll zip mine," she had whispered to Eng, hoping to come to a truce. Neither of them would benefit if it became known they were associated with Walton in any way.

He had given her the tiniest of nods.

The truce had lasted longer than either expected and now, with mutual enemies staring hate their way it would have to continue. "We're both fucked," she whispered. "Unless we can get out of here." Both were realists: she didn't trust him and he didn't trust her, but they needed each other. They were also opportunists and each looked for the right moment, the right set of circumstances they could benefit from.

It turned out the opportunity to escape was right next to them. After thirty minutes of silence in the tent, the teenage boy suddenly whispered to himself: "This is fucked." It was a snarl, but a low one.

"Look at me," Anna said to him.

"What?" he spat out. His eyes were dark. They had been the color of a summer's sky, but now they were a deeper, navy blue. They would slip into the color of midnight soon. After that...

"I know who did this to you," Anna whispered.

Chapter 13

A Fight Against Odds

11:00 a.m.

At eleven that morning PFC Fowler killed his forty-third zombie of the morning. He was in the back position fifty yards behind Johnny Osgood and Will Pierce. They had discovered that as far as accuracy was concerned it was better to shoot from further away without wearing a mask than it was to shoot from right up close with the mask on.

The trio also found that Max was the best shot of the three, something that had been argued over for the last two years, but had never been proven. All three had qualified as expert over the years, but it was one thing to hit a stationary man-sized target at three hundred meters, it was quite another to hit a target that was three inches high and five wide—the size of the average forehead. They had wasted many bullets blowing out teeth, cheeks, and lower jaws; the forehead was the only true kill shot.

The forty-third had been easy compared to the rest. It had come strolling right up the road as if on parade. Except for the missing arm, it seemed very human. Max had pushed the thought out of his mind as he leaned into the M16A1, breathed out gently, and caressed the trigger. The gun bucked mildly, as it always did, and the zombie lost the top of its head, though it didn't seem to notice for a few more steps. When it pitched forward in midstride, Johnny gave the thumbs up sign and then pointed forward.

He was on burial duty for the next twenty minutes. He climbed out of his foxhole swinging his shovel—they had gone into town and had "liberated" a few items of need: shovels, soda, chips, bleach, scrub brushes, thirteen

144

hoses they linked together, and a bottle of Jack Daniels. They were supposed to take a swig every time they manned the back position, however the bottle was practically ready for its own burial. Someone, Max strongly suspected Will, was drinking more than their fair share. His mood had been strangely cheery for the predicament they found themselves in: they had done in seventy or so zombies so far and hadn't heard dick from anyone in the unit.

As Osgood slung the shovel onto his padded shoulder and started off for the body, Max eyed the bottle of Jack. The honest truth was that he really, really wanted another swig, but he'd had his one shot already and it wasn't fair. Just then, Osgood yelled something, causing Max to jump in alarm. For some reason Osgood lifted the shovel over his head and then to Max's surprise he did a sort of primitive tribal dance around the corpse brandishing the shovel like it was a spear. He went around twice before he slammed the shovel down onto the body with a sickly thump that could be heard all the way back to the crap town of Myers Corner.

A second strike and a second ugly thump made by the shovel decided things for him. "Fuck it," Max said and took a pull of the amber whiskey. "Ahh that burns." But it was a good burn. He blew out a contented breath and looked up to see Osgood just standing there holding the thing's stiffening legs. He was supposed to drag the body from the road and cover it over with dirt to keep the flies from spreading the germs, but he was just standing there staring off around the bend in the road.

"What the fuck is he waiting for?" Max asked. He screwed on the top of the whiskey and set it aside. Then on a hunch, he picked up the M16 resting against his knee. The barrel was warm to the touch as he lifted it to his shoulder and because of the extra padding of the MOPP gear, he had to snuggle it good into the pocket of his shoulder to keep it steady. There were more zombies coming.

Johnny Osgood dropped the legs of the corpse and with one hand holding his mask in place, he ran back, waving his free arm and yelling.

"It's alright, Johnny, I'm not blind," Max whispered and pulled the trigger. At a hundred and fifty meters, there wasn't a discernible drop in the bullet's trajectory, the cross breeze was practically nonexistent, and the motion of the target: steadily forward, meant any miss was operator error. The bullet went through the thing's right eye. One leg shot straight out, it did a pirouette and then fell, twitching. Max was already onto the next target.

There were many targets, too many targets, in fact the road was suddenly full of them, and yet, just as he lined up his shot, the zombie jerked as it was struck by a three round burst. Half its face was torn off and yet it continued to plod forward. Max switched to a new target, thinking that Johnny or Will would have to clean up their own mess. He swiveled to his right slightly, blew out a light breath and fired—his bullet parted the hair, scalp, and skull of the beast and despite the horrible groove running right down the middle of its hairline, it kept coming.

"Shit!" Max tried to calm his breathing and fired again. Now it went down. How it fell or where it was hit, he didn't care. There were far too many zombies to care. The number of the beasts was thirty-five, but he would have sworn it was a hundred. Still thirty-five was a frightful number, especially for the two men in the foxholes on either side of the road. The zombies fell one after another, but very quickly, the rest were at the concertina wire. The first of them, an old farmer from the looks of his bib overalls, fell across it and got caught up in the barbed coils; the next eleven stumbled over the others and kept coming.

Johnny Osgood, twenty yards away, clambered out of his foxhole and ran. Will Pierce kept shooting and so did Max. Knowing Will would go for the closest ones, Max concentrated on the second closest one at any one time. At sixty yards he couldn't miss...just as long as he didn't rush his shots. He rushed four of them and his heart was in his throat as his gun went dry with three of the beasts, a family still in their PJs, practically in Will's foxhole.

With trained hands he dropped the empty mag, slapped home a fresh one, sprang the bolt forward and shot again in the span of a second. His thumb slipped the gun into three round burst and, four pulls of the trigger later, the last zombie fell forward onto Will, spouting black blood.

"Holy fuck!" Will cried. His words were muffled due to his mask, but there was no denying the emotion: wild, angry, panicked relief.

"You're welcome," Max said, quietly before returning the selector to single shot. There was still killing to be done. The zombies in the wire were tearing their own flesh off in order to get at the hyperventilating Will Pierce. As Max shot them through the head, needing twelve bullets to kill nine of the beasts, Will came stomping up, and was actually reaching for the whiskey before Max leapt away.

"Hey! Dumbass, you're covered in blood! Get away from me."

Will's chest was huffing hugely, trying to suck in all the oxygen he could through the filters. "Sorry. I'm sorry. Man, that was too freaking close. Oh, God, they were right on top of me for fuck's sake."

"It was close," Max agreed. "Now, go and bleach yourself. I hate you being so near when you got all that blood on you."

"Will you scrub me?" he asked pitifully.

"What would your boyfriend say?" Max asked with a smile. Will didn't laugh. He turned away but not before Max thought he saw tears in the man's eyes. "Hey Johnny! Make sure all them zombies are dead." Johnny had come back to his foxhole, lowered himself down and tried to pretend he hadn't just run off screaming.

Max thrust his head into his mask, zipped his coat, and pulled on his gloves. The usual fog of claustrophobia engulfed him. Breathing became a chore as he brought air up through the filters. After sucking in a big breath he said, "Alright, let's get you cleaned up."

Their clean station consisted of three gallons of bleach, two long-handled scrub brushes and the end of thirteen hoses stretching from the nearest spigot three hundred feet away. The pressure was surprisingly strong. He soaked his friend and then doused him with the bleach. A part of him wondered if this was the proper method to kill the germs in the blood. He didn't trust it, that was for sure, and he made sure to stand as far back as he could as he scrubbed down Will.

"Where are they?" Will asked when Max smacked him on the back. He tore off his hood, angrily. "The lieutenant said he'd be back. It's been four hours, Max. It's been four fucking hours. I don't think he's coming back."

A sigh escaped Max. He was starting to think the same thing. "So what? Are you thinking we should leave?"

Will lifted a single shoulder and refused to look him in the eye. His normal jovial self had completely withered. He was hunched, shooting his nervous glances everywhere. "Yeah," Will said through gritted teeth. "They've abandoned us. They fucking left us out here all by our fucking selves. That is treasonous. They have an obligation to us, you know what I mean?"

Max didn't remember any mention of an obligation when he had taken the oath, joining the Guard. "I'm staying. You can leave, but I'm staying. I have a wife, man. She's thirty miles that way," he said, pointing south, "and that's way too close. I can't leave, I have my own obligations. I hope you can understand."

"So we're just going to sit here killing those things?" Will said. He raised a gloved hand and was within an inch of running it through his short blonde hair, but he stopped and looked at the black rubber. "I don't think I can, Max. It's like shooting people. It's like…" He broke off suddenly and hurried to the back position. Max grabbed the bleach and came after. Will had been wet with black blood when he had come stomping up; if there were any drops, Max planned on drowning the germs in bleach. Will went straight for the whiskey and downed the remainder, probably four shots worth.

148

He stared at the empty bottle for a moment and then tossed it aside. "It's like murder, Max. It feels like murder every time I pull the trigger."

"Then go," Max replied. "Johnny and I will hold out here."

Will didn't leave. Max allowed him to stay in the back position while he and Johnny geared up and, after clearing the wire, they settled down to wait for more zombies. They weren't slow in coming. Thankfully, they came in twos and threes and made easy marks—but they did drain their ammo. The three of them had come to Myers Corner with a full combat load: 210 rounds a piece, plus they had the ammo crate, another 900 rounds. It went fast. By one p.m. the crate was empty.

"Now do we leave?" Will asked, after he had topped off the last of his magazines; he was three rounds short.

"No."

"No? You're going to say no to me? I'm a fucking specialist, Max. I outrank you. What do you have to say to that?" Max had nothing to say, especially since they had already been given orders by an officer. Will couldn't countermand them no matter what he thought. Will stood staring, sweating in his MOPP gear, until some internal frustration switch clicked on and he kicked the empty ammo crate. "Fine. We stay until we run out of ammo. Then I say fuck 'em."

He started to walk to the back position and said over his shoulder: "I thought you were cool, Max. I didn't know you were some tight-ass, gung-ho senator's son. When did that happen?"

Max was taken back by the venom in his friend's voice. "Will, I'm the same guy." For most of his life Max had been the guy who sat at the back of class making off-color comments under his breath. He was never mean about it, in fact he was a nice guy. He had an easy way about him and every one he knew considered him a friend. That easy way about him extended to everything in his life. School had been easy, but dull. Three semesters at college had been the same. At twenty, and already bored with life he had joined the National Guard, hoping to see a little adventure, but the wars had wound down at that point and he became the soldier in the back of the formation who made barely audible jokes and whose uniform was just barely acceptable and whose hair was just barely above his ears. He always knew he could do better but there never seemed a reason to try. Except now there was.

"I became gung-ho about the time the shit hit the fan. This is real, Will. Look at all those bodies. You saw how they are. They may look like normal people, but they're monsters. Someone has to stop them. Someone has to draw a line in the sand. Someone has to stay and fight."

Will glared for a moment, then grunted out a bemused laugh. "Nice speech, Captain America…shit."

Johnny swung his head from Will to Max and back again. His forehead was all done up in lines of worry and confusion. "So what's that mean? Are we staying or going?"

"Our fearless leader says we're staying, so we stay," Will said. "What are your commands, oh Great Captain?"

Max ignored the sarcastic tone. "Since there are too many bodies to bury, we'll stack them in front of the wire as another barrier. Next, I want to change the rotation. I want only one up at a time."

"Why do we need any one up by the wire?" Will asked. "All three of us should stay here. It'll save ammo. Johnny can't shoot for shit with his mask on."

"Fuck off," Johnny answered right back. "You ain't no Audie Murphy yourself, Will. But, yeah, let's all stay back from now on."

They zipped up their MOPP gear and made their "line in the sand" using corpses. It was a hundred feet long, stretching across the road and right up to the forest on either side. The wall of bodies dribbled a ghastly black fluid, like thinned oil. The flies couldn't seem to get enough of the stuff. Max and Will were staring at the insects constantly running their hairy legs through it when Johnny nudged them.

"There's more coming." Eleven of them came stumbling up the road. They were mowed down before they got to the wall. A minute later fourteen came round the bend. Three of these made it past the wall of corpses only to die in the wire.

Max was just getting up to head down to the wire when Will pulled him down. There were more coming. Twenty-three this time. They fired their guns hot and empty brass casings, blistering and smelling of spent powder littered their foxhole. The wire was covered in the beasts and no longer useful in holding them back. It was nothing but a speed bump.

They were getting desperate. Johnny was spraying bullets everywhere and Will was cursing with each shot that he missed. He was cursing a lot. They were going through their magazines too quickly.

"Johnny single shots, damn it!" Max ordered. "You're wasting ammo. And don't go for the head shots; just aim for center mass. It'll slow them down at least."

Compared to the other two, Max had a calm about him that was surreal. It almost felt as if he was born to do this, that it was natural he was fighting, not zombies exactly, but "enemies" in general, and for the first time in his life he was at one with his nature. Technology had outstripped evolution so quickly that a man was somewhat lost in society. Women were no longer dependent on him and so his primary roles of provider and defender were essentially discarded leaving him with little but cultural inertia to keep him heading off to a dreary job day after day.

Why Will and Johnny weren't feeling it, he didn't know. One guess was that they weren't married, however, he hadn't really thought too much about his wife that day —she fell into that easy part of his life. She had been easy, love had been easy, and it had been easier to get married than to not to. But, Max didn't know if that was the reason and he didn't have a second to spare to analyze why.

He fired with precision and kept up a steady pace of one bullet every three seconds: to go faster meant he would begin to miss, to go slower meant he would die. Next to him, Johnny dropped one of his magazines and when he looked up, he made a choking noise. Max turned with a jolt to see that there were zombies behind them in the town and more coming out of the forest on either side.

"Shit! Shit!" Johnny screamed. "What are they doing there?"

"They're following the sound of the shooting," Max said and fired at the nearest zombie; it pitched forward onto its face, fifteen feet away. That was too close. Max could feel his breathing begin to ramp up.

Johnny was turning a slow circle, staring all around him with his jaw hanging loose and his eyes huge and dry in his head. "I mean what are they doing back there at all? Remember the line in the sand? The zombies are supposed to be all in front of us. You know what that means, don't you? The line hasn't held. The company must have retreated and left us out here to die." He was babbling but he was right.

"Masks on!" Max cried.

"But…" Will started to say.

"Masks on now!" Max ordered as if he were a general instead of a private first-class. "They're too close and I don't want to end up like them if we can get out of this."

"How the hell are we going to get out of this?" Johnny practically screamed as he pulled on his mask.

First things first, Max thought as he too struggled the mask over his ears. "We'll fight our way back to the town. I'll take the rear." They barely made it thirty yards before the zombies were pressing too close. Will and Johnny fired from point blank range, dropping corpses almost at their feet; Max began to stumble over them as he walked backwards, firing faster now, no longer going for headshots.

"On the left!" Will yelled.

A quick glance showed that they were hemmed in now. A wall of living corpses closed from every side and the three men put their backs to each other, forming a triangle. The blasts from their M16s were constant thunder in their ears and yet, strangely, over it Max could hear Johnny sobbing. He could also hear his own breath come faster and faster. What was stranger still was that he didn't hear the Blackhawk helicopter that was right above them. With his heavy MOPP gear, he didn't even notice the down wash it was generating as its four blades cut the air with their tips flashing by at the speed of sound.

Like magic, it was just suddenly there.

Salvation was within reach not twenty feet overhead. Johnny started waving; he dropped his weapon and began swinging his arms, oblivious to the danger all around him. The only reply he received was when a door gunner opened up with an electrically powered minigun. It could fire two-thousand rounds a minute—to Max it looked like it was shooting fire instead of bullets. Zombies all around them began disintegrating right before their eyes. They would stand, transfixed for a fraction of a second, and then they just appeared to explode outward as chunks of flesh flew off of them, coating the ground in black blood.

The minigun showered the road with bullets, striking a thousand sparks and sweeping the zombies back. It was an amazing sight and to Johnny, the helicopter was a straight up miracle from God. He clasped his hands and shook them toward the great machine as if he were praying…and his prayers seemed to be answered. The Blackhawk dropped suddenly until was it was just about head height. Johnny made straight for it but with his mask tunneling his vision he tripped and Will stumbled over him.

He didn't see as the minigun turned straight on them. Max stood, paralyzed with a sudden fear: were they going to be killed as well? Did the man firing the weapon not realize they were the good guys? The heat and fire belching from the gun washed over him and Max let out a frightened sound: "Huh-ah!" In the next few seconds, hundreds of 7.62mm rounds blazed all around him and he dared not move a muscle for fear of getting killed.

Finally, a thought managed to get beyond the fear that had him paralyzed: Get your ass down!

Max dropped into a squat and looked back to see what was happening to the zombies. Everywhere they were falling, mowed down by the endless stream of bullets. Even far back into the trees they were dying. Max stared until the same voice yelled through the noise pounding his eardrums: Get your ass up!

Right. The Blackhawk wouldn't stay forever. He pushed himself to his feet, grabbed Will by the back of his outer MOPP coat and heaved him toward the beckoning door of the chopper. They were within an arm's reach when the machine suddenly rose into the sky. It went straight up like an elevator.

"Wait!" Johnny screamed. The Blackhawk paused as if it had heard Johnny. As though confused as to where it was, it slowly spun in place and, as it did so, the minigun continued to spit lead in a ceaseless stream.

"They're simply clearing the area of zombies before they land," Max said to himself. That made perfect sense. Only, the copter began to lift higher and then the angle of the blades shifted slightly and it began to move forward, slow at first, but then with gaining speed.

"What the fuck?" Will said.

"Come back!" screeched Johnny at the top of his lungs.

It didn't come back. It flew until it was just a spec in the sky and Max had to squint to see it. When he blinked, the speck was gone and they were all alone. Nearly all alone. They were surrounded by hundreds of bodies, some of which still moved. Some crawled, dragging ropes of intestines after them. Some pulled themselves along, their legs shot away or their bones turned to crumbs by the bullets. More of them laid there in a hot tangled mess, their bodies no more than punctured and torn bags of flesh, draining the black essence of their hated lives. But they did not die. They stared with an unholy longing at the three soldiers.

And some still walked on two legs.

From deeper in the forest more zombies came to discover what all the noise was about. "Come on," Max said. "We have to get out of this place."

"They left us," Johnny blubbered. "They just fucking left us."

"They saved us," Max said. "Now, come on! There are more zombies coming. Look at the forest." Johnny swayed in place, staring in disbelief. Max took him by the arm and started to drag him toward the town, but Will stopped him.

"Not that way," he said. He stretched out a thickly padded arm; dozens of zombies were lurching down Main Street. "We're trapped."

"Ammo check!" Max snapped and started to pull out his magazines. They were all empty. The only rounds he had were in the mag in his gun. How many were there? Ten? Eleven?

"I don't want to die," Johnny whispered.

Max shook his head and lied: "You're not going to die. No one's going to die."

Chapter 14

The Skin of a Balloon

12:19 p.m.

General Collins looked down from the helicopter at a battle in progress. Kingston was in flames. It was chaos. At the north end of the town, citizens were fighting three hundred soldiers, reinforced by sixty state troopers. They were fighting to get out. At the southern end, Collins guessed there were close on three thousand zombies trying, not to get into the town, but to feed on those fleeing. The people stuck in the middle weren't going down without a fight.

"I could use some artillery," Collins muttered, forgetting he was on a hot mike.

He was overheard by the pilot. "Sir, we have a dozen Apaches back at the base getting rusty. Their chain guns would do a number on those zom…I mean those op-fors. Maybe we should consider dusting those birds off."

"Shut up," the general snarled. He didn't need to be reminded that his best weapons platforms: M1A1 Abrams main battle tank, AH64 Apaches, A10 Thunderbolt, M109A6 Paladin, and the M270 multiple launch rocket system, which could drop six-thousand "grenades" in an area slightly larger than a football field, were all off limits to his troops. Hell, they couldn't even use their light machine guns! They were going toe-to toe with the civilians and barely holding their own.

Collins put his field glasses to his eyes and scanned the fight to the north. Only half his men were wearing their masks. "Son of a bitch!" He didn't care if they threw out the ROE concerning shoot on sight, especially when it came to the zombies, but the masks were a must. He flicked on his radio and then glanced at his cheat sheet for company commander frequencies before remembering that the men had been thrown into the fight piecemeal and that it was impossible to know what parts of which companies were down there.

As a remedy, he began bitching out everyone who was listening. Were they clueless about what they were dealing with? Sure, the civvies might look healthy but there was no way of knowing that for sure without a prolonged stay in a quarantine facility.

"They're not wearing their masks because men can't see what they're supposed to be shooting at with their masks on," someone said over the radio.

"Who is this?" Collins demanded.

There was a pause and then the man said: "A concerned soldier. Listen sir, there's not much danger from the germs. We are engaging at ranges well over sixty yards and the wind is at our backs. We are…"

"Shut your trap!" Collins shouted. "You have been trained…" He was interrupted as there was a thump on the frame of the helicopter, as though someone had hit it a golf ball at it. Next, the windshield suddenly cracked in the shape of a small star. Collins stared around, his mind slowly gaining understanding. They were being shot at! The question was, by whom? By which side? He was sure that some of his men weren't exactly happy with him at the moment. No one liked to fight in MOPP gear and no one sure as hell liked to fight their own countrymen.

"We're taking some incoming fire, sir," the pilot said, casually. "I didn't mean to interrupt but I thought you'd like to know."

The general clicked off the radio. There was no sense arguing with each individual soldier. "I've seen enough," he said into his mike. "Get us back to the command post."

As they flew, he opened his map and penciled a question mark over Kingston. There were four other question marks on the map—all places he didn't think would hold. But he needed Kingston. Well, really he needed the bridge that crossed the Hudson just north of the town. He had given up New Burg and the bridge that went with it. That had been a mistake. He should've listened to Courtney Shaw. Now, he was in danger of losing another bridge. If it fell and became a part of the quarantined zone, his growing logistics nightmare would be that much worse. His convoys would have to battle through roads congested with traffic forty miles out of their way.

He could still chopper men and equipment around but that was a tremendous strain on his fuel resources. At the moment, there were only so many Blackhawks available and only so much fuel. He had a third of his squadrons simply ferrying fuel so the other two thirds could pluck half-formed companies stranded by the traffic that stretched southward into New York City, and east all the way into Hartford Connecticut. Westward he had lines of cars from Binghamton and Scranton. With most of his men coming from the western part of the state, things were progressing at a snail's pace.

Of the thousand men he had managed to get to The Zone, he only knew the whereabouts of approximately seven hundred and these were constantly demanding more ammo, more water, and more men! Of the three-hundred missing men, most had simply vanished back into the civilian world when confronted with the reality of the situation. Collins was sure it wasn't the zombies that were the issue. It was pointing guns at women and children.

It was impossible to ask anyone to do it. They had to be *ordered* to do it and Collins had to be the man doing it. He would be hated, he was sure. He would go down in history as a butcher, but that was a price he was willing to pay. It was a heavy price. He had felt sick to his stomach ever since he had flown over the barricade at Salt Point northeast of Poughkeepsie. His men had done their duty. They had made sure the disease hadn't spread. The bodies of ninety-three women and children attested to it. They looked like they had been ground up in some sort of industrial accident. The civilians had counted on the fact that the soldiers wouldn't shoot women and children.

They had bet their lives on it. They had lost.

158

A number of them had been battling a late spring flu, while more than a handful were struck by allergies. One too many coughs, one too many sneezes doomed them. Once the panicked men started firing it was as though they couldn't stop. The Salt Point civvies fought back, but the soldiers were out of their minds with grief and mad with anger for being put in such a horrible predicament. They fought like demons, killing everything than moved. Of the three soldiers who survived, one shot himself five minutes after the battle, another just wandered away, and the third stayed at his post and wouldn't leave even when a rifle squad came to relieve him.

Collins knew he wouldn't bring charges against any AWOL soldier. That would be like charging someone with the crime of sanity.

"Excuse me, Sir," the pilot broke in on his thoughts, which was just as well, they were turning uselessly morbid. "We have friendlies on the ground involved in a fight."

"Huh? What?" The general looked out the window at some no-named little burg. A hundred feet down three soldiers were surrounded, fighting off waves of undead. The first thing the general noted was that they were masked properly. "Where are we?" he asked.

"Myers Corner. Permission to interface with targets."

Interface? Who talks like that? "No. The rules of engagement are clear. Maybe we can scare up some reinforcements." He started to scan his map for Myers Corner. "Where are we?" he asked again.

"We're over The Zone. Permission to engage targets with our miniguns." The general looked up from his map and found the pilot staring hard at him. Before the general could tell him no a second time, the pilot yelled: "Permission to save *your* fucking men."

A huge part of him wanted to rip into this mere captain for yelling at a general, however the man was right to speak to him that way. Those were his men down there doing exactly what he had ordered them to do. Collins closed his eyes as indecision swept him. He'd been obeying orders for most of his life. It was ingrained in him. The bad orders, the stupid orders, the blind orders all had to be obeyed. But his time would be over soon. The video of his men gunning down unarmed civilians would see to that. Fingers would be pointed, charges would be brought, the heat would come down on someone's head and it wouldn't be Governor Stimpson's head or the President's.

Just this once, he said to himself. Obeying was so instilled in him that he couldn't force himself to countermand a direct order orally. He nodded to the pilot.

The pilot gave a thumbs up to the door gunners and then lowered the copter down to about forty feet above the treetops. The gunners let loose with the minis, spinning the six barrels in a blur and firing a thousand rounds each in the course of a minute. The 7.62 millimeter rounds cut a swath through the zombies, ripping limbs off and sending chunks flying in a storm of black blood. Still, they came on dumb, ignoring the fire of death coming from the helicopter.

"Lower! Go lower!" cried one of the door gunners over the fury of his gun.

The Blackhawk dropped with a lurch, as if the rug had been slipped out from beneath it. "Sorry," the pilot said in a high voice. "It's just tight here for an extraction."

"Extraction?" Collins demanded. "No! No extraction. They're in The Zone and they're staying there. Kill the zombies but the men stay."

They were six feet off the ground at that point and the soldiers were running for the open bay door as the gunner fired all around them. He was good with the minigun, painting a silhouette of lead around the three. Collins ripped his pistol out of its holster and pointed it at the pilot. "Pull up now. That is a direct order. No one gets out of The Zone, damn it!" The general would pull the trigger if he had to. He wouldn't let anyone out of The Zone, no matter what. It was the one order that had to remain sacrosanct if the country had any chance of surviving. "Get this Blackhawk in the air, now." He turned to one of the gaping door gunners. "Fire your weapon, soldier, or get out."

The gunner turned back to the bloody work of butchering the zombies as they came out of the woods. His weapon was hot as a furnace and he was lathered in a sweat. The general turned back to the pilot. "Now."

The pilot pulled back on the collective and the helicopter lifted away from the stunned soldiers. They began screaming however, the wash from the rotors swept away their voices. The pilot hovered, turning slowly, allowing his gunners the full leeway with their guns. They chopped down zombies, killing with rage in their hearts. Only when the last of the beasts was cut straight in two did the pilot throttle up and point the Blackhawk northeast.

The silence was uncomfortable and the hard looks given the general by the crew didn't help. Collins didn't care. Leaving the three soldiers behind had been one of the least despicable orders he had given that day. When they landed at the field command post just behind the lines on the eastern perimeter where things were quietest, he waited until the crew had unmiked before looking at the pilot. "If anyone asks, I authorized some target practice and if you take anyone out of The Zone I'll have you shot."

"Yes sir."

He held the pilot with a steely gaze until the man dropped his eyes. Only then did he step out of the Blackhawk to see men scurrying around. In his eyes, they were men and not soldiers. Civilians still. Infantryman always reverted back to their soldier status quickly, however the cooks and the clerks and the, God forbid, marching band, always remained civilians at heart. They put on the uniform once a month, saluted when they had to, fired their weapons once a year and collected their pay. They did this with their minds on their "real" job or their family, or their football team.

It showed.

The command post was a disorganized mess. The officers who knew better were scrambling like mad to make heads or tails of the perimeter situation and the NCOs were out trying to instill a fighting spirit in men who were shocked to their core at what was being asked of them.

"It's early yet," Collins reminded himself. It was barely eight hours into the deployment, after all. Even regular army troops would've been hard pressed to have done better under these same circumstances.

The division S-3, Colonel Hall, came hurrying up, bent at the waist as the Blackhawks' blades were still whipping overhead. "General, the operations tent is this way." He pointed at one of the dozens of tents that had been erected. Someone had tried to form them in a grid, but it held its shape as well as a Dali painting. It bothered Collins and it bothered him that it bothered him. He had the heart of a warrior and the fuss and nuisance that went with the military's predilection for perfection where perfection wasn't necessary, got under his skin. In battle, who would care if the line of tents wasn't true on the cardinal points of the compass and exactly linear as the straight edge of a ruler?

What he cared for was a perfect fighting machine… and he had one before the rules of engagement had stripped him of his fighting machines. Yes, he had fighting men. He had artillerymen carting rifles, tank drivers blinking at the sun and wondering how deep to dig their foxholes and he had infantrymen playing traffic cop. It was pathetic.

Collins tilted his chin at the one lone tent set up sixty yards away. It was the only one under guard. "Is that the quarantine tent? Why's there only one?"

"The tents weren't considered a priority. The men have been burning through ammunition so fast that every truck in the division is being repurposed to carry munitions and reinforcements."

"Let me see what you have going on in Operations," Collins said, heading for the operations tent. When he entered someone cried, "Ah-ten shun!" and the men leapt to their feet. "At ease," Collins said, heading for the "Big Map", a computer screen larger than his flat-screen back home. It showed the area around Poughkeepsie—friendlies were marked in blue, while the "Op-for" was in its traditional red. The seven hundred men were spread in the thinnest of lines around a vast perimeter.

"How was the Governor?" Colonel Hall asked. "Did he cave at all on the use of force guidelines?"

Collins shook his head and then sighed. "No. It was that damned video. It's being aired every five minutes on CNN...or at least it was. The governor asked me what would've happened if the men had machine guns."

"What did you say?"

"I told them we would've held that check point and not let two-hundred possibly infected people escape. He didn't seem to care about that. The only good news is that the President is taking this more seriously. He's already authorized an emissions blackout for The Zone and the surrounding area."

"We know," Hall said, shaking his head. "It's making our job difficult to say the least. Many of these units either weren't issued the proper communications devices or they were left behind in their hurry. The men were keeping in touch with their NCOs via cellphones. Now they're in the dark and so are we. See these units with the asterisks? We have no way of contacting them other than to send men around in Humvees."

The general shrugged. "Then that's what we do until we can get them all linked up."

"We would but we don't have the man power yet. The traffic jams..."

"I know about the traffic jams," Collins said, interrupting. He had never seen such traffic jams in his life. Flying south from Albany, the roads were like still rivers of metal and glass. "What about our cavalry support?"

"We have fifty-two Blackhawks and six Chinooks at our disposal. We need more and we need more fuel. They're flying all over the state bringing in ten men per bird. It's too slow for what we're up against."

What we're up against...the words hung between the two men. Collins was almost afraid to ask. "What sort of numbers are we looking at?"

Hall switched to a new view on the computer screen. It was an aerial view of Poughkeepsie. It looked completely unremarkable. "Before," Hall said, and then switched screens again. "And after."

Collins grimaced. "Son of a bitch." Smoke blotted out half the shot, but what could be seen was ugly. Buildings were crumbled, bodies lay in the streets and cars were strewn about with glass like glitter all around them. Hall switched to a close up. It brought the carnage into focus. The bodies were mutilated beyond recognition and the blood streaks that ran from the cars were fine and red.

"This is what Newburg looked like; before and after. This is Pleasant Valley. Note the road out of town. The infected persons tend to travel on roads. We don't know why, although Major Kim thinks…"

"Show me Kingston," the general interrupted. The first shot was of a before of Kingston which the general waved away. The next showed the same picture, but with a small gathering of men and cars at the northern end of the town. There was no active fighting. "How old are these?"

"Two hours," Hall answered. "There is a fire-fight going on now. Our best estimates have the op-for numbering about a hundred. Against them we have parts of Charlie Company, 2nd Battalion and elements of the 427th Support Battalion, along with some local law enforcement."

"Support battalion?" Collins said with another grimace, this one even deeper than the first. "Oh, God! What sort of reinforcements are available?" At Hall's surprised look, Collins said, "The intel is wrong. I just flew over Kingston. Our men are fighting opposition forces that are at least equal in number." He didn't add that they were also fighting at a huge disadvantage by wearing the masks. They had to wear them so there was no sense whining. Nor did he say that his men were fighting at a disadvantage in weaponry either. At two-hundred yards a 30-30 with a hunting scope was more than a match for the M4 carbine, especially in the hands of the hunters they had in the Catskills who were famed for their marksmanship. "From the air it looks like a zit about to blow. We need men there five minutes ago."

"I'm sorry, Sir, but we don't have any reinforcements. We've been feeding men into the line just as fast as we get them on scene. We can order a retreat to this town: Saugerties. I think Esopus creek is deeper than it looks on this screen. That can be the southern flank and this highway here the western flank."

The general's eyes strayed to the dim figure of the bridge in the picture north of Kingston. "What about the men here? I saw at least fifty."

Hall shrugged. They were what the other soldiers called REMFs: rear echelon mother-fuckers. Mostly this was due to jealousy. The headquarters units rarely went into the field, their physical training usually involved games of softball, and their motto was: if you can't truck it —fuck it, meaning that road marches were kept at an absolute minimum. They rarely fired their weapons because that meant cleaning them to the army's exacting science, something that was a giant pain in the ass. They did their jobs like professionals, but their jobs usually didn't entail a shootout with a heavily armed populace of fellow Americans.

"I need two for guarding the prisoners," Colonel Hall said. "And at least another twenty or so for manning the com-gear, and the aviation guys need to stay, but the rest are available. I'll have them grab their gear."

Collins looked around the tent before adding: "And any officer who is not absolutely necessary. Sometimes it's like I could carpet the tent in lieutenants. And direct all incoming choppers to drop their men off in Kingston. You see that bridge? I need it at all costs."

The colonel looked at the map. He saw the bridge and he knew the need. He also saw that there were parts of the perimeter that were thin as the skin on a balloon. "But sir, the eastern border of The Zone is dangerously, perilously thin."

Collins tapped the screen at Kingston. "That's where I want them, at least for now. We have three main hotspots:

Kingston in the north, the southern zone above the academy and Middleton in the western zone. The other lines will have to hold for now."

Hall made a face as if the words hurt him. "Yes sir... but Middleton? With all due respect we should be reinforcing this entire eastern line. Hartford is thirty miles away. A million people live there. There is nothing beyond Middleton."

"There is the rest of the state of New York and Governor Stimpson thinks it's important. Look, John, I said the same thing to him and you want to know what he said? Let Connecticut look after Connecticut."

Hall gave him a sickly smile

Twenty minutes later, a diverted squadron of Blackhawks unceremoniously dumped their payload of ammo and fuel, and then lifted off with seventy ill-at-ease soldiers and headed for Kingston. When they were gone, the land was eerily silent. In the tents, thirty-eight men, doing the job of a hundred, worked to keep seven hundred fed, watered, reinforced and supplied with enough ammo to kill the hundred thousand men, women, children, and zombies in The Zone.

Three hundred yards away from the tents was the eastern edge of The Zone. Its line had been stripped of men and now there was only one man for every two-hundred and fifty feet. In the areas with forest, the men felt virtually alone, but so far it had been quiet.

So far.

Chapter 15

Into the Quagmire

12:26 p.m.

The red Volkswagen Beetle bogged down on an unpaved and brambly logging road. The rains from the day before had made a swamp out of a low point and Courtney Shaw, with her mind on more immediate fears had driven right into it. The forest on either side of the road had been thick and close, and she had been afraid of zombies coming at her from under the shadowy trees. Her head had been swinging side to side and she hadn't been paying attention to what was right in front of her and didn't see the bog until she was halfway to getting stuck.

As quietly as she could, she revved the engine, only to have the rear of the car slew around to the left and settle lower into the mud. "Oh, please, no," she whispered, the lines of her face so twisted that she was practically unrecognizable in the extremes of her fear.

Shifting into reverse and trying to back out of her predicament only sunk her even lower into the morass. Next, she tried rocking the car back and forth; shifting into drive for a second, then into reverse and back again. Other than spraying mud in an arc and digging a rut so deep that her axles were buried, it didn't accomplish a thing. She was stuck, completely and utterly stuck.

And she was afraid, completely and utterly afraid.

She killed the engine and sat listening with her head cocked. The engine ticked as it cooled and somewhere a crow made an angry sound. Nothing stirred in the forest and yet her fear mounted, threatening to overwhelm her.

Her grip on the steering wheel was such that she had to will her fingers off.

"Ok. I can't stay here," she said to herself, hoping to goad her body into action; she could feel it stiffen, almost as if her insides were collapsing in on themselves. With a creaking of her joints, she picked up the Glock that sat on the seat next to her and for a second time checked the load; she even pulled the slide back part way to make sure there was a round in the chamber. The copper winked a dull eye at her and she covered it over again, hiding it as though it was a secret that she didn't want anyone to know about.

Still she didn't move. As an excuse to stay in the relatively safe confines of the Bug, she glanced around the interior. The car was her most prized possession. It was the most expensive thing she owned—three-quarters owned actually. There were still fifteen payments left before it was fully hers...and now she was going to have to leave it half-buried in the mud, deep in zombie country. The thought made her ill.

She finished her inspection and it had been a waste of time, as she secretly knew it would be. The Bug was spotless, the inside at least, and there was nothing in it except an emergency kit. It held little of immediate use: a set of jumper cables, some glow sticks, a tiny first aid kit that would do nothing for her if she came in contact with a zombie, a space blanket that was as brightly silvered as aluminum foil and two road flares. All useless, except to call attention to herself, which was the last thing she wanted to do.

Taking just the gun, she climbed out and immediately sank calf-deep into the bog, nearly losing one of her comfortable pumps in the process. The sludge sucked at it and she had to flare her toes to keep it on as she grunted and strained to pull her foot out. To get one foot out she had to sink the next just as deep and she was quickly trembling with the effort of walking and with the fear that a zombie would come along when she was stuck and vulnerable.

On two different occasions, she half-fell, covering herself in slime. The slips were made all the worse because

168

she went to great lengths to keep the Glock out of the mud. Although she had fired guns on occasion, she was no expert; still, she knew that the shit-thick mud would jam up the works if she wasn't careful. For that reason she carried the gun as if it were the Crown Jewels and she allowed herself to be mucked head to toe rather than let even a speck of dirt get anywhere on it.

Finally, making it to the edge of the forest where the roots snaking out of the earth provided a firm base, she stood, shaking in her pumps, her navy blue pant suit now an ugly brown. She was close to panic; she could feel it in her every fiber. Her breath came in short, quiet gasps, her grey eyes were wide and spooked, and her ears twitched, overly attuned to the smallest sound. She was as skittish as a mare straight out of her pasture for the first time; she was within a whisker of bolting and if she had known of a safe place to bolt to she might have been running already.

Holding the Glock close to her chest made her feel a slight bit better. She didn't have her wits, or her bearings, or any idea where she was, but she had the gun. It was reassuringly heavy in her hands. It was solid and real when everything else felt like a nightmare.

With the Glock as her spiritual totem held up to her face, she fought to control her breathing—in and out, in and out, slowly. It was just a forest around her, an empty forest, in and out. A minute passed before she could accomplish the minor feat of not passing out from hyperventilation.

Minor though it was, it helped to calm her and she was able to look around the forest, not as a girl about to go screaming off in a panic, but as a woman who was lost, but would not remain so. She had become turned around somewhere east of where she was. The Beetle had been creeping down the oddly named Jack Elbow Road when she had come across a pair of zombies standing just beyond an intersection. They had charged and she had taken a turn without looking at the name of the road.

There had been more zombies and more turns. It all became a haze of black-eyed monsters and dirt roads that all looked the same. She had managed to lose the zombies, but also lost herself in the process. Now, she was stuck with only two options: forward or back on the boggy road. Taking to the zombie-filled forest was simply not an option. Against all reason, she found the strip of dirt that cut through the woods safer than the woods themselves. Of course, this made no sense, and she knew she was being foolish. She tried to tell herself that the road had been built by man, and that it would eventually lead to man.

The only question was forward or back. As the sun was just off center high above her, making a squat toad of her shadow beneath her feet, it was of no help clueing her to the direction of the road. Before she became lost, she had been on the southeast corner of the quarantine zone; she had no idea how many miles ago that was, she only knew that she was probably near the edge of The Zone, unless the people in charge had expanded it again.

It had been a colossal mistake to expand it the one time, and because of that mistake, she knew that The Zone would have to be expanded again and again. Without enough men to cover the outrageously long perimeter there would be leaks, which would need to be encapsulated. This would lead to a further expansion of The Zone and a need for more men. It would be a vicious cycle until something gave on one side or the other.

There, alone on the road, Courtney shuddered to think what that something would be. On the zombie side, it would mean a breakout of immense proportions: Hartford invaded or New York City, or maybe The Zone would simply continue to expand north and west, taking over enough of the country towns and hamlets to build an unstoppable momentum of zombies that would be able to wash over any barrier.

On the human side, it meant enough media coverage and enough collective fear to force the President into doing something stupid: perhaps he'd allow the use of napalm or he'd call for carpet-bombing half the state, or when things really got out of control, nuclear weapons. It wasn't out of the realm of possibility, in fact she was sure there was some military guy right then drawing up plans, just in case.

"Which means, I have to get my sweet ass out of here," Courtney whispered. Again, she was struck by indecision: forward or back.

A gun shot down the road in front of her decided the issue. Guns meant people. Perhaps they were people in trouble. Perhaps they were people about to be submerged under a mound of zombies. She didn't care. She needed to be around people just then, even if it meant danger, or even if it was the army looking to keep her locked up in The Zone. That was understandable. It was sane and at that moment she needed a touch of sanity in her life.

With the Glock held in both hands, she swiveled it back and forth, pointing it at every leaf dropping from the sky, every bird chirping, and every cricket jumping. She made her slow way down the sunken road until the forest drew back like a curtain to reveal the open world. Above, the clouds had returned heavy and thick, while in front, the road flowed down a hill, cutting through acres of newly sown carrots.

Everything was very exact. The road was a line as straight as the edge of ruler. The trees that bordered the perfect rectangular fields were abreast of one another like continental soldiers. Even the carrots were plotted just so. It was all so flawless that the jumble of cars at the end of the road was unsettling. They seemed carelessly thrown together, abandoned and forgotten, as if a giant boy had been playing with them and had just been called home for supper, leaving them a higgledy-piggledy mess.

The glass windshields winked and the metal shone, but the cars were dead quiet. Nothing moved among them. At the far end of the field, just beyond the hundreds of cars, the forest began again. At first, nothing moved there either. Then came another gunshot and she saw the flash of its barrel among the trees. Someone was there. It was a moment before she saw what it was they were shooting at: a zombie or she hoped it was a zombie, was pulling itself along through the carrots.

From that distance, she couldn't see what was wrong with it. Not that she cared, really. All she cared about was that it was a zombie and not a human. No one should shoot a human like it was a dog. Another shot finished the zombie, however the sound of the gun had attracted more. Six more came out of the woods. They didn't come out all at once or in a neat row. They straggled and the gunfire that greeted them was ragged, a shot here, two there.

Courtney was once again struck by indecision. Should she head down the road and risk getting shot? Or did she sneak back into the forest and hope to find only trees and friendly chipmunks? The forest frankly scared her to no end. It seemed endless and hidden and she was sure that every step would bring her closer to a waiting zombie. Just look how they came from every direction! It would be like that and worse in the deep wood.

Here she had a road at least and soldiers who might be persuaded to help her. In a crouch, she kept low on the sunken road, crimping along. A hundred yards the road went before she came to the first of the abandoned cars: a Subaru Outback, piled with someone's belongings. The car was cold. The next: a Jeep Laredo was the same. Three cars down the line she finally found life. In the driver's seat of a full-sized truck was a German Shepherd. It barked crazily, spraying the window with saliva as Courtney edged past.

The dog frightened her worse than the zombies; not its barking, but the fact that it was there alone. A person could be convinced into leaving their car but not their dog. The window wasn't even cracked! A chill ran up her back.

Ahead, the cars disappeared as the road dropped down toward the forest. She resisted the temptation to stand higher to see what was to come. With a weird fear crawling in her belly, she walked hunched over until she came closer to the slope. At first, all she saw were the tops of abandoned cars, then she saw their doors and their tires and next to the tires in heaps were bodies. These hadn't been zombies. Their skin was pale and their eyes were clear and glassy, as they stared up to the clouds forever unblinking. The bodies hadn't been feasted on in any way, except by the flies. Courtney could hear the flies even if she couldn't see them. They hummed hungrily.

It took a moment for the scene to filter from a picture in her mind to understanding: these people had been massacred. Quickly, she slunk back, hiding behind the bumper of a car. She felt like she was about to get sick all over the gleaming bumper; people had been massacred! Real humans. She could imagine the screams and the confusion, the flying blood, and the explosions of machine guns as they were mowed down. It was a horrible noise in her mind and yet it could not block out the horrible rational word that drowned it all out: *So?*

That was followed by: *So freaking what? What did you expect would happen?*

She hated that voice, even though it made sense. If people, possibly infected people got past the military, there was no knowing what would happen. She knew the disease spread quickly and easily. The day before, it had burned through the CDC men in no time and they were trained to deal in germs. If one person got out, the entire country could succumb to the disease in weeks or months.

The voice again: *But you think you should be able to leave?*

"I'm not sick," she reasoned. She felt fine. She felt perfectly healthy except for the pain around her heart. It was fear and self-loathing. If she had known the night before, what was going to happen, she would've told her troopers to kill everyone at the Walton Facility, and if she had been in charge of the barricade right down the hill, she would've been the first to shoot.

It was sad and it was sick, but it was the right thing to do. And yes, she was going to try to get through to the other side of The Zone.

To get there she would need a sturdy truck…and a dog. She practically crawled back to the truck, stopping once at an Audi, which had a cooler on its front seat. Inside she found sandwich fixings: sliced turkey meat, cheese, mayo. She grabbed the turkey.

The shepherd again went nuts, right up until she stuck the turkey up to the window and then out came a tongue that looked a foot long. It licked the glass, turning it into a bleary mess. "Here you go," she crooned softly, opening the door a crack and holding out some of the meat. She almost lost a finger as the dog snapped up the food. He then wagged his head all around. The scent of turkey was strong; there was more meat but he couldn't see it.

"Move," Courtney said, trying to shove the big dog back. He was too strong and she had to resort to tossing a piece of meat past him. Once in the driver's seat, she said, "Please God," and reached for the ignition. The keys weren't there. A groan escaped her. Hotwiring a car fell into the category of theoretical knowledge and she wasn't about to try it fifty yards away from a roadblock, guarded over by trigger happy soldiers.

She tried another prayer and opened the glove box; it was empty except for the usual stash of papers. She did happen to see the dog's leash on the floor in front of the passenger seat. The dog went crazy at the sight of it in her hands. He was all over her, barking and licking her face and hands.

"Shut up! You have to stop, please." The dog was making so much racket that she was sure they were going to be heard. For some reason that scared her badly even though, at the moment she wasn't trying to escape The Zone—the voice in her head said: *You know the reason why*.

Yes, she did. The massacre couldn't have been a legal shooting. The orders handed down were very clear: fire only if fired upon. There had been women, children and unarmed men among the dead. That had been murder, perhaps necessary murder, but murder nonetheless. She might be looked upon as a witness and if they were willing to kill who knew how many defenseless people, they'd be willing to kill her as well.

"Sit!" she hissed in a final attempt to corral the dog's excitement. He stopped his frenzy immediately and sat in the passenger seat with his tongue hanging out, panting.

174

Courtney hooked the leash to his collar and read the tag: *Sundance*. "Good boy, Sundance." He whined in agreement and with joy that was almost beyond his ability to contain.

Now for the tough part. She gripped the leash in one hand and slid out—Sundance stayed in place, though he trembled in anticipation. Giving the leash a tug, Courtney said, "Heel." Sundance came out of the truck in a bound and stuck his right shoulder against her thigh, ready to go anywhere with her as he had been trained. "Good boy," she said scratching around the base of his pointy ears.

Keeping low, she and Sundance went from car to car looking for one with keys. She had hope. This was still rural America where crime was a rarity; people were more apt to leave their keys in the car. The Audi she had stolen the turkey meat from had keys in the ignition, but she hesitated, remembering the bog and her marooned Bug. Fearing to get stuck again, she left the Audi but five minutes later came back. The other cars and trucks were all locked or were otherwise keyless, at least the ones further back in the mess. The ones closer to the edge of the slope were simply too near the barricade for her liking.

After pushing the cooler down to the floorboard, she snapped her fingers and pointed into the car. Sundance leapt in easily. He sat so tall that his ears bent on the roof. His nose worked overtime and he gave extra sniffs to both the cooler and to the window before giving Courtney a look full of meaning. *I would like more food and please open the window so I can stick my head out*, the look said.

"Not yet," she told him. "Not until we are well away from here and then we'll see. Wish us luck, Sundance." She turned the engine over, stuck it in gear, and peeled the car around, keeping her foot hard on the gas. The Audi fishtailed on the grassy shoulder before catching its grip and then they were flying back up the road. She had five seconds to marvel at their speed—the Audi was so much faster than her four-year-old Bug—and then she saw something that made no sense: clods of dirt began leaping up on the side of the sunken road. It was a moment before the reports of the gun firing at her caught up and she was able to put the two together.

Instinctively, she threw an arm over Sundance and pulled him onto her lap as she cringed down. A second later, what sounded like someone banging on the trunk came to her and then the driver's side mirror exploded. By some miracle, she didn't scream, and by a greater miracle, they made it into the tree line without getting hit anymore.

She didn't slow. It was with dread that she stared in the rearview mirror as the trees flashed by on either side of the car and dust billowed up behind. The army had to be coming for her. She had seen what they had done and she was sure they would try to silence her, and there was only one sure way to do that, they would put a bullet in her brain...or maybe two.

Suddenly she lurched forward, straining against the harness of her seatbelt. Beneath her, the wheels began to chug and rumble. At first, she thought one of her tires had been punctured by a bullet, but then she remembered the bog! Water splashed high, obliterating the view of the trees, and then she and Sundance were thrown forward as the mud seized their momentum. This time she didn't let up on the gas. What's more, she aimed the Audi at the side of the sunken road where the ground had been a touch more firm.

They started to slew and the revving of the engine was a roar in the silent forest as the wheels spun in a blur. With agonizing slowness, she passed her pitiful little Bug and then, just as she thought she was going to strand the Audi as well, the wheels caught on a root and the car lurched, gaining a touch of momentum, enough to keep it going, then there was a stone the size of a football that gave them a little more oomph, and then there was a log just under the mud, and then suddenly they were on the other side of the bog.

"Oh, thank you, God!" she cried. Sundance turned from the window to give her a quick look and a bark at her excitement. "We're not free of The Zone yet," she scolded him, trying to hide her smile. "So keep quiet and, I'm sorry, but we should keep the windows up for a little while longer. Just in case."

She sped the Audi in a straight line up the logging road until, after fifteen minutes, they came, quite unexpectedly to a two-lane road; she cut the wheel hard left and suddenly the ride was smooth and quiet. It was almost as though she had driven back in time to a point where there were no such things as zombies. She even reached for the radio.

There was nothing but static. That chilled her to her soul and brought her back to her senses and she hit the gas harder, wishing to be free of The Zone as fast as she could. When they broached a hill and she felt the car leap a little under her, she glanced down at the speedometer: 104MPH.

She grinned and didn't know why. Then she saw the water tower at Myers Corner and just like that, she knew where she was. Her speed dropped as she felt a wave of relief wilt her muscles. "Ok, now that I know where..." Her words dribbled to a halt. There was an army helicopter hovering over Myers Corner not half a mile away and as she watched, it started to descend.

The soldiers in the copter probably didn't have a clue about the massacre she had just left behind. In fact, they were probably rescuing people; why else would it be landing? Her foot slammed back down on the gas; she wasn't going to be left behind again. She would drop General Collins' name, or lie, or do anything to get out of The Zone. The Audi leapt forward like a gazelle, but not five seconds later, she slowed as the helicopter started shooting from guns that hung out the doors. The firing was terrifying to her. She had never seen anything like it; the sides of the helicopter looked to be on fire. It lit up the sky despite that it was daytime.

Then the helicopter dropped even lower and she hardened her heart against her fear and tromped again on the gas, determined to get to it. Even though the Audi was a speed demon, there was no getting to the copter in time. When she was a quarter mile away, it lifted straight up into the air, and then flew off, heading east. The sight was a stab in her heart.

Courtney slowed, bringing herself and the car back under control, wondering: *Now where was she going to go?* There was no answer to that.

Someone was shooting down the road from her; it seemed to be coming from the vicinity where the chopper had been hovering. "What could've lived through that?" she asked, remembering the amazing guns and the way she had blinked at the intensity of the fire. She drove up to see that the helicopter had left too early. There were hundreds of dead zombies and parts of zombies all over the place, but there were also live ones attacking three soldiers who were huddled together firing outwards.

The zombies weren't thick on them yet, crowding in so close that they couldn't move, but they soon would be. Courtney darted the nimble Audi between the ugly beasts and rushed forward honking her horn. The soldiers, seeing her coming, concentrated all of their fire at the zombies between them and the car. When it was clear, they came stumbling up, moving dreadfully slow due to their cumbersome protective gear.

Seeing the gear, Courtney felt a stab of fear. Were they contaminated? Was she? Was Sundance? The dog was barking like mad, showing huge, white teeth. Those teeth kept the men at bay long enough for Courtney to come to a decision. She would need to take chances to get out of The Zone, and letting in these soldiers was one of those chances.

"Sundance! Heel!" She pulled the huge dog as far onto her lap as she could and the men scrambled in. With their guns and their bulky outfits, they were so terribly slow and the car so dreadfully cramped that she actually started driving away before the last one was fully in. He was trying to share a seat with Sundance who was growling and again showing teeth. The man was saying something but his mask and his heavy breathing made him incomprehensible.

Courtney soothed the dog as well as she could and when he settled down, she smiled at the strange men in their strange, bug-eyed costumes. "My name is Courtney Shaw and I'm not sick or anything," she said, suddenly aware of how she looked, covered as she was in drying brown mud. "This is just mud from a ditch."

The man in the passenger seat held up his arms, turning them in exaggerated movements. He then disturbed Sundance, who was perched uncomfortably on the console, by looking back at his friends. "I think we're clean, too," he said and then pulled off his mask. "My name's Max."

His brown hair was wet with sweat and stuck up in every way. His brown eyes were rimmed red, which matched the blotches on his face where the mask had gripped his flesh. He was somewhat of a mess, but both Sundance and Courtney were very glad he was there.

He jerked a black thumb toward the back seat. "That's Will and Johnny. Tell me, Courtney do you know this area? We're looking for any road out of here."

"I've tried them all and they're all barricaded. And… and they've been shooting people. A lot of people." The men stiffened at this; Courtney hoped that it was just an automatic defensive response and not a guilty one. The car was silent for a few seconds as she decided that, guilty or not, she was going to have to trust the men. "Can you get us past the barricades?"

Next to her, Max's eyes shifted away quickly. "Probably."

Courtney slowed the Audi. "What do you mean by that? Are you saying that I won't be able to get through, or all of us?"

Max was quiet for a few seconds and his face gradually took on a pained expression. "I think I'm saying they won't let any of us out. Those were our orders. No one is to leave under any circumstances. Everyone was to be looked upon as a potential carrier of the disease."

Will snorted. "But that was before they fucking just left us. Maybe it's different now. Maybe during all that time we were fighting off the zombies, the line broke. If so we can get out of here."

"No," Courtney said. "The line didn't break. It was shifted outward to a radius of twenty miles. I'm with the state police and even we didn't know. We were like you, trying to maintain a line that was all in our heads."

"So what do we do?" Johnny asked.

Courtney shrugged with just her right shoulder; it was always the same old question. She'd been hoping the soldiers would have answers. "Some of the state troopers are going to make a stand at the station. You can do that, if you want. I'll drop you off."

Max shot her a look over Sundance's head. "You don't think it's a good idea?"

"No, especially after seeing all those zombies you guys were fighting. I'm going to find a way out of The Zone, one way or another."

All four of them, five if Sundance were counted, looked around at the countryside. It was normally pretty quiet among the rolling hills and the green forests, but this was an unnatural stillness. As far as the eye could see, nothing human moved but them.

"I think we'll take our chances with you," Max said. "Now that I've seen them up close, I know that nothing will hold against the zombies."

Chapter 16

Tyler's Escape

1:44 p.m.

"What's your name?" Anna whispered.

The boy shot his distrustful, darkening eyes her way. Anna consciously thrust her bosom out further and hid her bandaged left hand. She made sure that her smile was small and friendly and that her blue eyes remained locked on his. Her experience with Von Braun had taught her that an infected person was prone to look upon anything more than a neutral countenance with deep suspicion.

He said: "Tyler," in an equally quiet voice. It was a good sign; he still had some wits about him or he'd been born with a greater than average share. "Do you know who did this to me?" he asked, moving closer.

Anna's smile faltered at his proximity. He was not in a contagious stage, that only came when his eyes became black and leaked fluids and his mind was just about beyond the least reason, when the intense demand to feed and the even greater desire to kill was all that he could comprehend. But the boy could still be covered in Com-cells. As of yet no one knew how they were passed from victim to victim. The boy could be coated in spores that were even then being sucked into her respiratory system where they would spread and multiply, building up by the billions along her neurons, slowly taking over her mind. If so, having him shift over a few feet wouldn't make a hill of beans worth of difference. The tent was shut up tight and the air felt stagnant and heavy—a perfect breeding ground for the fungus used in the Com-cells.

Then again, he could be clean. There was no way to know and for that reason, she should've been taking universal precautions. She should've covered her face with layers of cloth; she should've moved further away and made sure that he didn't speak directly into her face. And she damned well shouldn't let him touch her.

He grabbed her white coat and she steeled herself not to react beyond a slight shiver that went up her back. To react visibly could set him off on a rampage. "Who did it? You have to tell me."

Before she answered, she gave a significant look to the others on the other side of the long tent, and then she turned her face toward him, conspiratorially. "If I tell, you have to promise that you'll do exactly what I tell you to do. It's the only way to cure you. Ok?"

"Yeah," he said, nodding eagerly.

"We can't seem too friendly." Again, she gave a look to where Thuy and Deckard and the others sat. Tyler also looked their way and shifted to his right a few inches; still too close in Anna's opinion, however he had to be played just right and she feared letting him get too far away. Now came the question: who was she going to unleash this human shaped weapon on? Dr. Lee came immediately to mind: she had left her hanging in an elevator shaft and she was a know-it-all condescending bitch who needed to be brought down a peg or two. Then there was the man sitting a few feet away: Eng.

She would love to kill Eng. Nobody deserved to die like that dumb-ass chink. He had started all of this, and despite committing mass murder on a tremendous scale, he was turned on his side, sleeping with his damned chink-eyes partially open just as they had been the night before after he had raped her. If Anna had a knife, and if she could have gotten away with it, she would've happily cut his balls off right there in the tent.

And yet, she felt Eng might still come in handy. As much as she wanted him dead, he was a criminal, just like her, and he would be properly 'cutthroat' if the situation called for it, while she was sure the others would hesitate at the wrong moments, overcome by morals or goodness, or whatever.

She wouldn't turn Tyler loose on Eng, nor would she bother with the others: Deckard was an embarrassment, mooning over Dr. Lee. Even then, he was holding her hand, caressing her wrist with the ball of his thumb, tracing the blue lines that twined there. It was pathetic. Dr. Wilson was even more pathetic. He was in his fifties and pudgy in the middle. If they could even get out of the tent, he looked so exhausted that he'd be the first to become a snack for the zombies. Chuck Singleton was as cow-eyed as Deckard but far less of a threat. Stephanie Glowitz was playing up the 'damsel in distress' role and had her head in Chuck's lap. Anna dismissed her without a glance.

This left John Burke and Anna would never kill him. Burke had been riled when they had first come in, but he too was drowsing. He looked thin and drawn, close to being done in by the cancer consuming him. Despite that, he was more useful than the rest, combined. The poor sap thought he was immune to the Com-cells. His ignorance, combined with his bravado and the fact that he was an idiot, would make him an ideal tool in the right hands, her hands.

"Who?" Tyler repeated, slightly louder now.

"He's not here right now," Anna told him. "You have to be patient. Any excitement or anger is going to make things worse and speed up the disease, so please close your eyes and rest until I tell you. There you go. No. Keep them closed. Now, the man who did this to you also has the cure. When the time comes you're going to have to hold him hostage, but don't kill him."

Tyler's eyes popped open and he glared. "But he deserves to die. It's not just me. It's my whole family and the Holden's from across the street. They got it too. I saw them and their eyes…it was horrible. It was fucking horrible!"

"Shh," she whispered. "Not so loud, Tyler. You'll be able to kill him but first we need to get the cure. Now, you have to calm down for your own good. I can't help you if the disease gets you, too."

"Okay. Thanks. You're the nicest person I've met since all this started."

She smiled a lie and said, "Close your eyes." Now, by her estimation, she had thirty minutes to come up with a plan. Thirty minutes until Tyler went ballistic, beyond her ability to control. She went over everything she knew about their location: the edge of a rinky-dink town that was bordered on three sides by tree-covered hills and on a fourth by fields where Holsteins grazed placidly behind a simple post and rail fence. She considered her assets: the ticking time bomb that was Tyler, a shaky alliance with Eng that would turn sour the second he got the upper hand and, lastly, the fact Burke could be counted on to do something "heroic" because he thought he was immune.

Oh, and she couldn't forget the vial of Com-cells lodged in her bra. She had never been more aware of her tits since they started coming in back in the seventh grade. Back then, she hadn't gone five minutes without giving herself a feel, now she was afraid to move. If the vial slipped out and broke? She didn't want to think about that.

The thirty minute window she had given herself evaporated in what felt like a blink and twenty-nine minutes later she had yet to think of anything more than pointing Tyler out the front door of the tent and hoping he caused a big enough distraction to allow Anna to slip away.

Tyler grimaced and said, "My head is really killing me. Is it time yet?"

"Can you hold on a little while longer? I haven't heard his jeep yet and you don't want to ruin your chances at getting the cure."

Tyler endured the pain for another three minutes and then he groaned loudly. Thuy's black eyes were instantly upon him. "Are you ok?" she asked him.

"He strained his back when he was captured," Anna answered, quickly. "I don't suppose any of you have any Tylenol?"

Heads shook all around, all except Thuy's. "Maybe Dr. Wilson should take a look at him," she suggested. "He

184

is a medical doctor, after all." Anna could tell that Thuy hadn't been fooled by the excuse.

Anna smiled as though she thought the suggestion was full of merit. "Tyler, it's time to get up," she said loud enough for everyone to hear. Quieter, she added, "The man who did this to you is here. He's in one of the other tents. His name is General, uh, General MacArthur. Run and grab his gun. He won't…"

"Ms Holloway!" Thuy suddenly demanded. "What are you saying to him?"

"Don't listen to anyone but me," Anna continued in a whisper. "They can't be trusted. Just run to the other tents and don't let the guards get you." She reached out to help him up, but at the last second drew her hands back. He didn't notice. His boyish face had turned mean: his lip was now a snarl and the innocent eyes were visibly darker. He was staring with a building hate at Thuy.

"Anna, is that boy infected?" Thuy was on her feet now as well, with Deckard standing a half-second later. The others remained seated, staring with eyes that bulged wide and fearful.

"He is infected," Anna answered. She then turned to Tyler and hissed, "Go!"

"No! Don't touch that zipper!" Thuy commanded with such authority that Tyler hesitated with his hand on the zipper. "He can't be allowed to leave. He will spread the Com-cells outside the perimeter of the quarantined zone."

"Ignore her," Anna hissed.

Curiously, no one added a thing, nor did anyone but Eng jump up when Tyler started to unzip the tent door. He raised his eyebrows toward Anna and asked: "Breakout?" She nodded.

Thuy started forward, but Deckard held her back. "Don't. He's infected," he said.

"Exactly!" Thuy said. "That's why he can't be allowed to leave. Why am I the only one who sees this? Every one of you knows what's at stake. You know what will happen if this gets out. It'll destroy the entire country."

Tyler had turned at all the shouting and wavered. His mind was crawling with the black Com-cells and his soul was beginning to burn with desires that were too vile to even consider and yet he was still free enough to try to make sense out of what he was hearing. Were they thinking he was going to destroy America? Was that real or was that more of their games? He was beginning to think that they were playing at something. Like this was a cruel practical joke. He wavered, fighting to right his thinking so he could understand. As he stood there, John Burke ambled to his feet and with a sigh, he started toward the boy.

"I'll keep him penned up iffin that's what y'all want."

Anna was shocked to see that it was Deckard of all people who pulled Burke back by the collar. "You're not thinking straight, Thuy," he said as he hauled Burke back, easily. This sentence upset the entire apple cart. Anna was sure that no one had ever accused Dr. Lee of not thinking straight. Everyone stared at Deckard in disbelief and that included Thuy who could only splutter.

Deckard went on: "You're not thinking. Your guilt is blinding you to reason. This tent can't hold one of *them*. Pretty soon, he'll tear it to pieces and if we stop him then we'll only get infected as well and in another couple of hours, we'll be the ones who tear it apart. And when we do, we'll escape and spread the germs from here to Hartford."

"Then what do we do?" Thuy asked in a soft, powerless voice. She felt faint like some belle out of the old south with a case of the vapors.

Deckard put a hand around her waist to steady her. "The only thing we can do is hope the guard shoots him. Either that or we kill him ourselves and throw his body out the front."

Now Thuy's legs buckled under the weight of her guilt, because once again this was her fault. Even with Anna and Eng right there, she couldn't see it any other way. "I can't do that," she said, sagging to the floor of the tent. "It's not right. None of this is right."

"I wouldn't worry, none. He's a dead already," Burke remarked. "He jes don't know it yet." He made a sudden leap for the door and both Eng and Anna rushed to get between him and Tyler.

"Go Tyler!" Anna yelled, grabbing Burke's stained chambray work shirt. "Run! Get to the general."

Tyler had been a step behind during the entire conversation, but he heard the order and it made sense. Action was what was needed. Action and killing and…eating. He rushed out of the tent with a sudden hunger that was like a cold railroad spike right in the pit of his stomach.

He ran, and Anna went to the front of the tent to watch. Behind her Eng urged her to run as well: "Go! Now!" But she held him back. The guard, in his heavy mask, was slow to recognize the blur that suddenly leapt out of the tent. "Hey!" he cried. Tyler wasn't stopping for anything, especially a useless scream. The guard gave chase, hampered by the thick protective suit and clinging mask.

Only then did Anna take off running. Eng rushed after her leaving the others standing there staring, wondering what to do. Chuck was first to jump to his feet. "Come on," he drawled, helping Stephanie up. "This is our chance."

"They might could shoot y'all," Burke said. As he thought of himself as both immune and special, he wasn't looking to go rushing off half-cocked.

"I'll take gettin' shot over bein' eaten alive any day," Chuck said and left through the front opening, dragging Stephanie behind him. She didn't relish either option.

"You heard him," Wilson said to Burke, "He does have a point. Being immune won't save you if I turn and get a hankering for hill-billy." They also left and now it was just Deckard and Thuy.

"We're going," Deckard told Thuy. She thought she could stand but just then, there came three loud gunshots, her body flinching with each one. There was a long pause and then came two more shots. "We're out of time. Please get up." When she refused to look up, he calmly bent down and hefted her hundred pounds up onto his shoulder. She didn't fight it. He was too strong and she didn't care whether she lived or died.

Deckard stepped out into the gloomy afternoon where everything was chaos. Soldiers were running every which way and Humvees were being gunned into life. He didn't think he would get far with Thuy on his shoulder but was disappointed that he only made it seventy yards into the light forest before a Humvee came slashing to a halt right in front of him. He half raised his arms as the driver came out pointing an M16A1. Deckard felt his heart drop when he saw that it was Special Agent Meeks with his mask partially askew from having thrown it on so quickly.

"We have orders to shoot all escapees," Meeks told Deckard. "What do you think about that?"

"I think if you had the guts to shoot, you would've done it already," Deckard replied. "Instead you're going to march us right back to the tent. It's just right back there."

"No, I don't think so. Not when I have you dead to rights. Not when I can finally deal justice out properly. You see, I am just about sick to death of watching the bad guys walk on technicalities and I'm sure you have your excuses ready and your lawyers all lined up, but you haven't seen what I've seen. You haven't seen the bodies and the walking dead…and the blood! An hour ago, I was at Kingston. You don't know what it's like there. So, no, we aren't going to walk to the tent. We're going to save the American people a long drawn out trial. Now, put the girl down, nice and easy so we can do this in a humane manner."

On his shoulder, Thuy was altogether lifeless and she was like a corpse when he laid her down. "You don't need to do this," Deckard said. His gut went queasy as he took a swift glance around. They were close enough to the command post to see that it was deserted. The skeleton crew was busy chasing down the escapees. It was just the three of them.

"I do, actually," Meeks said quietly. "For all those people out there who will never get justice." He pulled the trigger and even as he did, Deckard was still in denial. He was sure Meeks was just bluffing. He was FBI, he was the law and this…this was straight up murder. The bullet traveled the short distance between them and buried itself deep.

Anna heard the kill shot and a few minutes later, she would walk through the drying blood. She and Eng had gotten the furthest: a half mile through the forest. She had no clue where she was or in which direction she was running; for all she knew, she was running back into the quarantine zone and that would've been just fine with her. Anything was better than the sure death that the tent represented. She paused at the sound of the gun, wondering who had bought it.

She hoped it was Thuy.

Soon enough, she had her own problems as a series of Humvees drove past them. She and Eng hunkered down, their chests working like billows. "Well?" Anna asked Eng. "Aren't you trained for this? *Escape and Evade?*"

"This way," he said cutting to their left. They didn't see the soldier who had been dropped off in the wake of the Humvees and the soldier didn't see them until they were twenty feet away. He immediately opened up with his rifle sending a slew of bullets their way. Luckily for Anna, his aim in his MOPP suit was atrocious. Bullets went everywhere and the sound of the gun in the still forest was like thunder.

"We give up!" Anna screamed at the top of her lungs. She was so loud that Chuck heard her from two hundred yards away as he and Stephanie were being led back to the tent at gunpoint. It made him smirk, however it died away when he saw the blood.

The tent was a glum place when all the prisoners were rounded up. The absence of Deckard and Thuy made the tent seem much larger, not that they could've paced. The prisoners, including Wilson and Burke, who hadn't gotten very far at all, were tied hand and foot with black cord.

"Are you satisfied?" Stephanie spat at Anna.

All things considered, she was satisfied. She had managed to get the very dangerous Tyler out of the tent and the two people who were key in any prosecution against her had been shot trying to escape. "Actually, yes," she answered, wearing a viper's grin. In the back of her mind, she began to wonder how she could get rid of the rest of them, Eng included. If they were all to die, she would be in the free and clear. "Quite satisfied."

Chapter 17

A Photo Opportunity

3:18 p.m.

At about the time Special Agent Meeks was aiming his weapon into Ryan Deckard's chest, General Collins was sipping scalding black coffee in the situation room, thirty feet below the West Wing of the White House. Irritatingly, he wasn't drinking the coffee out of a mug; it was being served out of a teacup. The cup was annoyingly tiny and it had annoying faded humming birds on it. The President explained it was a pattern picked out by Edith Wilson, the second of Woodrow Wilson's First Ladies. This did nothing to stem Collins' annoyance.

"Oh," was all Collins said in response. He had literally a thousand things he had to be doing right then and drinking coffee from a ridiculous teacup just wasn't one of them. Neither was giving a briefing, though this wasn't exactly a briefing, it felt more like a trial. He sat practically alone on one side of a tremendous table. There were women and men on his side but the closest sat four chairs down, afraid they'd be hit by some of the shit that was almost certainly going to be hurled his way when the President exploded on him.

Directly across from Collins sat the President in a sharp, blue suit. The man had the looks of a weathered actor: still handsome but sagging and wrinkled at the edges. On one side of him sat the Vice-President, and on the other was Marty Aleman, his Chief of Staff. And then there were the Secretaries of this cabinet and that, and further down the line were generals and admirals, stiff with medals and self-importance. Political appointees, every one of them, including the military officers.

People always assumed that the military was all about blood and guts and were promoted simply on the virtue of their skill or knowledge and that was true to a certain extent, or at least to a certain rank. Eventually rank becomes political with both parties advancing men and women who align politically.

Collins was looking at a group of handpicked sycophants who would agree to anything the President wanted.

Normally, being around so much brass and so many suits, made him a touch nervous, but he was just too damned tired to be nervous. Besides the questions, were of a tedious nature: Are the infected persons dangerous? Do they represent a danger to the public at large? How contagious are they? Are they really that contagious? Really? Have you seen one with your own eyes?

"Yes Sir, I have seen one of the infected individuals up close and, in fact, I killed it with a pistol I had borrowed from a state trooper. This was after it came at me in a threatening manner, of course. It survived three gunshots to the torso and kept coming as if it hadn't even felt a thing. Hopefully that will put to rest the question of them being dangerous."

"And you killed it with a head shot?" the President asked. It was an odd question, but most of his were. His Chief of Staff had given him a list of questions that only he was allowed to ask and they were not in any particular order. When the briefing was completed, the answers would be edited so that the president would come out in the best light and then the final, much shorter product would be disseminated to the media. Things were moving so quickly that the media was demanding more than low-level aides stuttering and making excuses.

Part of the problem was that the very idea of zombies was just so ludicrous, so undignified that the White House had actually been hoping that the media would find a way to break the story without the military feeding it to them. But then the press had been scooped by Cody Cullin and his YouTube videos. The first had been of the massacre and the next two were grainy night shots of zombie attacks. Ever since then the press had been scrambling to catch up. What they were discovering, such as the glaring errors in readiness of the 42nd and the rumors of a dozen or more massacres, was all negative.

The filmed trial/briefing was Marty Aleman's way of getting in front of the situation by turning the focus on General Collins, and having the President acting as chief prosecutor.

"Can you explain how the situation began and what steps…" The President paused as Marty Aleman whispered into his ear. With a crooked smile, the President began again: "I'm sorry. I'm not used to reading questions from flashcards. Are we sure we can't use teleprompters?"

Marty looked pained by the question. "No. Absolutely not. There can't be a hint of indecision over this. You have to come across tough."

"I never knew flashcards were this difficult," the President joked. He was leader of the free world because he could read a speech off a teleprompter like nobody's business and he was always quick with a joke—hardly the proper qualifications in General Collins view. "What I meant to say was… Can you explain how the situation began and what steps you took to contain the issue as commander of the 42nd Infantry Division?"

Collins cleared his throat before answering. "The situation began at a pharmaceutical research center south east of Poughkeepsie, New York…" He went through a long song and dance. It was forty wasted minutes repeating information that wasn't new to anyone in the room. Next, he spoke about the call-up of the 42nd, its failures and its successes. There were very few of the latter and the initial ones could be chalked up to the timely intervention of Courtney Shaw. Even though her interference had been completely illegal, she had saved Collins at least two hours which had allowed him to scatter a few hundred men around the perimeter. He had no clue how many of them were still alive; not many, he was sure. And yet they had held long enough for him to throw up more fixed lines using the bare bones of skeleton battalions.

At one point, the President stopped him. He glanced down at one of his note cards and said: "I see you've placed the majority of your division along the southern end of the perimeter. Is this where most of the danger lies?"

Most of my division? Collins wanted to ask. He was finding out the hard way that he wasn't really in charge of "his" division. The 42nd had major elements in three different states and thus had three different "commanders in chiefs." On paper, he had just over eleven-thousand men in his division. A third of them were still in Vermont because the Governor hadn't yet called them to service. They were simply on alert.

The Governor of New Jersey had waffled for a few hours, just long enough for the traffic jams in and out of lower New York to fuse into an unbreakable mass of steel and glass. Most of the 50th Combat Brigade was sitting along the side of a dozen crammed highways waiting for the Blackhawks to come and get them. And that was a hell of a mess as well. There was currently a fight on the aviation side of things about who owned what air space in what state. His operations officer, instead of doing his normal duty, was squabbling with three state governments, as well as FEMA and the FFA, and of course, the airlines. It was enough to make a man just walk away from the whole affair.

All of this was detailed in his report, but this was the President of the United States and if he wanted answers to asinine questions, he would get them. "There is danger in allowing a single infected person out of the quarantine zone, but yes, due to the population concentration around New York, I felt that the southern zone had to be given first priority. If you will take a look at the screen you will see the disposition of units..."

"Another question, General," the President said, interrupting. "Your units were in place in record time, were they not?"

"I don't think Guinness keeps these sorts of records," Collins replied, blandly. The President had expected a simple : "Yes", now he blinked in confusion.

194

"Answer the question," the Chief of Staff snapped. He tried to glare at the general, but Collins was like ice and the glare faltered in the face of it. "To make it easier, compare it to the National Guard response to Hurricane Katrina. Go."

Go? Who tells a three star general to go? Collins took a slow deliberate sip of his coffee before answering the canned question. "There are some parallels between this situation and the one that occurred in New Orleans. The greatest difference, at least so far, is that New York Governor Stimpson didn't vacillate when confronted with the issue and made a command decision. This allowed me to get a jump on things, though it may not look like it from an outsider's point of view, we are getting up to speed relatively quickly. The logistics are a nightmare. The majority of the men in my division have to be flown, eleven men at a time in helicopters from up to four hundred miles away in order to be put in place in and around Poughkeepsie."

"It's a miracle of modern logistics," the President said, suddenly.

"Yes," Collins agreed, partially because that's what the Chief of Staff wanted and partially because it was true. Everything he had said was true. Compared to the other governors, Stimpson had acted like a real leader and had made difficult decisions in minutes rather than hours. And the horrible logistical issues were being overcome by screaming, pleading, and the frequent display of weaponry by men with hard faces and harder hearts. Currently, Collins had a hundred and fifty nine Blackhawks either in the air or on the ground being loaded with men or being refueled. His staff at the Command Post were working like madmen trying to leapfrog them over three states to snatch up men and equipment stranded by the traffic jams. By a rather generous reading of the Insurrection Act, the U.S. Army was "lending" another hundred helicopters to the 42nd. They were arriving in dribs and drabs, frequently with empty tanks, making his fuel situation enough to turn his silver hair, white.

The rest of his officers were performing under equally trying circumstances. So precariously was the line being held that the men were being dropped off by the choppers without regard for unit cohesion. In one half mile section just north of West Point, there were squads of a dozen companies holding the line. This made all forms of communications and resupply extremely difficult. The President didn't seem to want to hear about this, however. He began asking questions concerning the massacres: who was to blame? Why weren't the men trained to deal with an anxious population? What precautions were being put into place to keep more of them from occurring?

At this last question, Collins sat stony-faced. Had they not been listening to a thing he had said? He didn't have time to hold training classes on what to do when civilians start shooting you in the face! Of course the only real answer to the President's question was that time would fix the issue for him. A few more hours and there wouldn't be anyone left "alive" in The Zone.

The president began to ask about casualties, making Collins squirm in his chair. He didn't have the numbers on hand. Nobody did since nobody knew who was where. Collins gave a non-answer: "It's hard to say at this point."

This didn't seem to faze the President. "That many?" he demanded, theatrically outraged. Collins blinked in a most owl-like fashion. Hadn't the man heard his answer? Or was this going to be spliced in somehow to make sure everyone knew that the President was as angry as they were? Collins had no clue.

One of the generals, a man with four gleaming stars on his collar, broke in on Collins' thoughts. The general's chest was so decorated with commendations that it was somewhat absurd. He gave a shifty glance to Marty Aleman and said, quickly: "Your eastern border seems wide open."

It wasn't a question. It was a very true statement of fact. Collins wanted to shrug, but one didn't shrug to a four star general when one was only a lieutenant general. And yet what could he say? "The situation north of New

York City warranted an immediate response. We had to stop the flow of refugees out of The Zone before someone infected got through." And so far, they had, miraculously.

"And now?" the general asked, speaking fast before the president could ask another useless question. "We have been monitoring the situation and from all the chatter, it seems men are being diverted to the western and northern perimeters and zero are being allocated in the east. Do I need to remind you just how close Hartford, Connecticut is? If Hartford goes then all of Connecticut goes." He gestured at the map to add to his point.

Collins didn't look. He didn't need to. He knew precisely what the map showed: a few hundred cooks, medics, signalmen, forward observers, and communications specialists holding a line ten miles long; his command post had been stripped of every nonessential man. And Collins didn't need to be reminded what would happen if the disease made it into Hartford. It wasn't just Connecticut that would fall, with no natural barrier, Rhode Island would be overrun in days, and then the entire southern border of Massachusetts would be laid bare.

"We are aware of the situation and I have made this known to Governor Stimpson," was the only way Collins could respond.

The President forgot the stiff white cards long enough to ask: "What was his reply?"

Uh-oh. They had just strayed into dangerous waters. Collins couldn't lie nor could he tap dance around such a direct question. "The Governor said that Connecticut would have to look out for itself. But that was only…"

"That's preposterous!" the President cried. "You get men on that border this instant! There are a million people in the greater Hartford area. They can't be exposed to this…this plague."

"I wish I could obey that order, but I can't," Collins answered.

Marty Aleman was just standing up, thinking that he had to get the briefing back under control when the President lost his cool. The president had never been over-fond of the army or any portion of the vast industrial military complex, something he frequently made clear when he was forced to undergo meetings of this sort. His explosive anger had come to be expected. The old man leapt to his feet and pounded the table with the flat of his hand. "How dare you back talk me? You will do as you're told or I will have you cashiered out of the military and brought up on charges of treason!"

The Secretaries of this cabinet and that were all nodding along, looking ready to kill, however the military men were sitting in various degrees of discomfort. Finally, when the silence in the room became strained, one of the Joint Chiefs of Staff, a four star general named Randal Heider, whom Collins had served under fifteen years previously when they were both with the 1st Infantry Division, spoke up. He had been a sharp, fair-minded officer and it was strange to see the slightly halting manner in which he said to the President: "Uh, sir, General Collins actually can't obey that order. The 42nd is a guard unit."

"So? It's still the army, and he's still a general, and I am still the Commander in Chief. At least the last time I checked I was."

General Heider half-nodded in agreement but also shook his head, so that there was a diagonal movement of his chin. "You are, of course the Commander in Chief, but in this case you aren't exactly commander of the 42nd. Remember, the National Guard is technically under the command of the individual governors of the states in which they are headquartered. If you wish to command the 42nd, you must first federalize it."

"Right," the President replied. He looked to Marty, and asked: "Isn't it about time to federalize the situation? People are dying after all." No one at the table thought it strange that he hadn't asked his Vice President for his opinion. The V. P. owned his position solely because he had been able to carry Missouri for the ticket during the last election. He had absolutely no role beyond that. The two men loathed each other and spoke only when the cameras were rolling *and* when it couldn't be avoided.

"Not yet," Marty replied evenly. The National Guard had barely got moving. Federalizing them wouldn't make them move any faster and it would just add layers of command on an already hectic situation. This meant that there was still too much room for blame in the situation. "We should see how things play out."

Before General Heider had only leaned forward slightly when speaking, never letting his elbows come off the table before him, now he stood. "That may not be the best advice, sir. General Collins' dispositions are dubious at best. The entire eastern side of his perimeter is significantly under-manned. It won't hold up against any test. His northern line isn't much better in spots. If quibbling governors are behind this then it's time someone unified command. General Collins has the man-power available, he just needs the authority to use it."

"I agree," Collins said.

Marty glared at Collins and waved a hand at the general, suggesting that he sit down by the move. "We are handling this. The President will speak to Governor Warner of Connecticut when this meeting concludes."

"I will kick his ass is what I'll do!" the President declared.

Marty tried not to roll his eyes at the outburst. He crowbarred a slimy smile over the grimace on his face and turned to whisper in the President's ear. "She's a woman and remember party unity, Mr. President. It's more important now than ever. It's best not to ruffle feathers. Perhaps we can earmark some funds from the highway bill in order to cover the expense required to call up Warner's forces."

Horace Collins listened to political talk with a pain in his gut. They were worried about how they were going to grease palms while people were dying! And yet what could he do besides resign? As tempting as that was, it would only hurt the situation.

"Now, if we can get back on track?" Marty asked, eventually, gesturing at the cue cards.

Collins waited on the next self-serving question, but instead he received a simple statement from the President and he didn't know what to say or do with it. "Everything that can be done is being done," the President intoned seriously. Collins nodded; though the statement was actually a lie, he didn't think it would be prudent to argue just then.

The President then looked suddenly grave and announced: "This is a grave situation that we're doing everything in our power to come to grips with."

"Uh, yes," Collins said, uncertainly, not knowing if he was supposed to extend his remark or if he was supposed to remark at all.

"The strength of the American people lies in their determination and courage," the President intoned. Collins decided just to nod along like everyone else. Then the President asked: "What's being done to help those stricken with this dread disease?"

At first Collins continued to nod, thinking the old man was still in cue card mode. It wasn't until someone chuckled quietly that he realized an answer was required. "Oh, yes, the disease," he said, trying to collect himself. He had to search the labyrinth of his mind and think beyond the myriad of troop movements and ammunition rate usages and of course, the thing that had him scared to no end: the dire situation of his fuel supplies, in order to recall the plan put in place ages ago by some moronic officer who hadn't lived in the real world where zombies upset timetables and where American soldiers were being killed by panicked citizens.

He had only glanced at the plan earlier that afternoon during the three minutes he had allowed himself to suck down an MRE. He remembered the MRE more than the detailed *Mass Casualty/Terrorism Induced Bioweapons Release Readiness Plan*. The MRE had peanut butter and jelly and crackers, his favorite. On the other hand, the readiness plan consisted of bullshit and even if it hadn't, there was no way Collins could have implemented it. All of his medical personnel, from his medics to his dental technicians, all the way up to his surgeons, were on the line, toting M16s, trying to keep the crowds of people back. So far, the zombie hordes had not been the main problem. Extending the perimeter had made it so that the slow moving zombies wouldn't be a problem until later that evening.

By then Collins hoped to have enough men in place to stop them, and maybe men enough men to begin the Mass Casualty Readiness Plan.

"Our current focus, Mr. President, is curtailing the spread of the disease. This has been our number one priority. We have 330 million Americans to protect and we will do everything in our power to keep them safe and healthy. The entire compliment of our medical personnel is on scene and working just as hard as the toughest infantryman." There was no lie in that answer, however he omitted that when he had hoofed it to his helicopter an hour before, he had strode past a jumble of medical equipment, probably ten million dollars' worth, piled taller than his head. In the scramble for men, fuel, and ammo, it hadn't been considered a necessity and had been heaved out of the back of a truck on a word.

"We will contain this outbreak," the President read off another cue card. "And we will bring those responsible for this catastrophe to justice."

"Yes," Collins replied, again uncertain if more was required.

Evidently it wasn't. The President nodded suddenly and then smiled, relieved. He stood up and shook Marty's hand, he then went to the next most important Secretary of this cabinet or that and shook that man's hand, before continuing down the line. Marty clapped the old man on the back and General Collins was certain he was going to say: *That's a wrap, everyone*, as if he were a director working on a movie.

Collins had stood when the President rose and was expecting some sort of acknowledgement but he was ignored as the president glad-handed down the line. Even the other military brass kept their distance. Collins was in a no-win situation. Civilians had been killed; it didn't matter that in most cases there had been direct attacks on his men and that in some cases his men had been overrun or slaughtered. It only mattered that the word massacre was showing up more and more in the media. And, if by some miracle, he managed to contain the situation, everyone knew all the credit would be taken by the President or Governor Stimpson.

From across the table Marty raised his eyebrows as if to say: *Are you still here?*

"Why is he being this way?" Collins hissed.

"You mean why is he doing his job?" Marty sneered. "His job is to appear calm and presidential in the face of a terrible event. His job is to make sure the American people feel protected. It's your job to protect them! So, I think it would be really swell if you could go do that." In a snap, Marty turned the sneer into a greased smile and went back to schmoozing.

Collins glanced down at his coffee and the faded hummingbirds. The coffee was cold but he swallowed it in a gulp. When he looked up again he noticed that no one would even cast their eyes in his direction. The only person more ignored than himself was the Vice-President, who got up and left alone. A minute later, Collins followed him out of the room. There was a gaggle of self-important suit types at the elevator, but Collins didn't want to ride up with them. He knew his presence would cause all conversation to cease and that he'd be treated as if he was diseased himself. He took the stairs.

An hour later, the film of the meeting in the Situation Room had been edited to make the President come across as courageous, resourceful, and a true leader. It was then disseminated to every media outlet possible. During the hour-long wait, the President forgot about his promise of ordering the states neighboring New York to call up their guardsmen. He spent the time taking selfies with visiting dignitaries and assuring campaign donors in New York City that there was absolutely nothing to worry about. The Vice-President spent the hour calling his friends in the city, telling them to leave as soon as humanly possible.

Marty worked the phones as if this was an election night. He firmly believed that the army would have no trouble containing the issue. For him it was *fly-over* country. From the lofty view of *his* Lear jet—it was government owned but he treated it as his own personal property—that part of the country always looked so empty, as if no one really lived there. He kept up a steady stream of calls, hoping to expand the power and the budget of FEMA so "This sort of thing can't happen again!" Marty owed favors and turning FEMA into an outreach program of the government would go a long way to paying some of them off. Yes, it would mean another bloated, wasteful bureaucracy, but it also meant jobs for the right people and a slush fund that could be raided when campaign donations ran a little dry.

The Governor of Connecticut, Christine Warner was following the situation just west of her border with a wary eye. She had taken a cue from Vermont and had put her National Guardsman on alert. When she watched the canned footage of the President's meeting, she wasn't fooled, as was almost all of America, into thinking the border was secure. According to a map accompanying the meeting there were "elements" of six different infantry battalions on the border. That was completely true and yet many of these "elements" consisted of a squad or less and frequently the soldiers weren't even in sight of one another.

The Governor was properly nervous. She knew the President and she didn't trust him. In his three years in office, the man had proved to be an expert in only two areas: self-aggrandizement and photo opportunities.

Despite the reassurances of the President, the Governor of the great state of Connecticut buzzed her secretary. "Carla, get me General Arnold, please."

The call-up alert went out rapidly and soon the men were primed and ready for action, unfortunately, there weren't all that many soldiers available. In all of Connecticut, there was but a single National Guard infantry battalion—eight hundred fighting men. This was supplemented by two companies of military police, two more medical companies, and two engineering companies, which excelled in bridging rivers but not in battling zombies. Finally, the force was augmented by four companies of state militia. They were ceremonial only, generally only called upon when a parade was scheduled, in fact, two of the companies were comprised of *Horse Guards* and many of the men showed up to formation with their lances ready!

They assembled quickly and the doors to their armories were flung wide. The Governor of Connecticut had no qualms about using heavy machine guns and even mortars to defend her borders. The men geared up; their trucks and Humvees were fueled and the first companies were ready to leave New London by four that afternoon; exceedingly fast by everyone's estimation and yet by then the first zombies had already crossed the state line.

General Collins' command post had been overrun while the President was flipping through his cue cards and trying to look "presidential" for the cameras an hour before.

Chapter 18

Into the Past

2:18 p.m.

Specialist Melvin Delray, a medic with the 427th Brigade Support Battalion was the first to spot the zombies. He'd been leaning back in his foxhole with his mask tilted back on his head, enjoying the sun on his face, when the first of them made its not-so-grand appearance. At a hundred yards, it looked just like a person. It reminded him of his father, being of about the same age and dressed for golf.

"Ah, shit," Mel-Ray whispered. All his friends called him that and had since he was a boy. The physically closest friend to him just then was PFC Rogers who sat thirty yards away on the lip of his foxhole, doodling in the dirt with a stick. For them, the beginning of the apocalypse had been a dull affair. They had been rushed out to the eastern perimeter hours before, their heads filled with wild imaginings, their bodies weighted down with gear, and their lips beaded with sweat.

At first, it had been terrifying. Their foxholes were spaced a hundred feet apart and in many instances, the soldiers couldn't see their nearest neighbors. All of them had expected great mobs of flesh-eating monsters to appear at any second and there had been a number of random shootings as panicked men fired at birds or shadows. Sometimes this set off a torrent of shooting from the men up and down the line.

But then the hours ticked away and many began to even doubt there were zombies at all.

"Someone got punked, big time," PFC Rogers had said an hour before. He had slipped out of his foxhole to visit Mel-Ray and the two had chatted, neither wearing a mask and both with their MOPP coats opened wide because of the heat. A car's engine had spooked Rogers into thinking their sergeant was coming around for another inspection and he had scurried back to his hole in the ground.

Now, fifteen minutes later, there was a zombie…and another…and more, emerging from the forest across from the line. Mel-Ray slunk down into his foxhole until only his eyes sat above the dirt. He hissed "Rogers!"

"What?" Rogers replied, in a bored voice. The single word was very loud; to Mel-Ray's frightened mind, it almost seemed like he screamed it. Mel-Ray didn't answer, he just pointed.

"Holy shit," Rogers whispered and then slid down into his hole so that Mel-Ray couldn't see him. When he came back up his mask covered his face and his coat was buttoned to the neck. His weapon was at the ready as well.

That seemed like a smart idea and Mel-Ray, his hands shaking like crazy, fumbled his mask on and then gloved and buttoned up. Next, he grabbed up his M16 that had spent the afternoon leaning against the side of the pit, and popped up like a jack-in-the box ready to spray bullets everywhere. The zombies were only halfway across the weed field in front of him; fifty yards away.

Mel-Ray was itching to start shooting. He had never been a marksman and had fired his weapon a total of six times in his two-year career in the National Guard: four times in basic training and then once in each of the successive years. He had barely qualified with the M16 and he had always told himself that he was a medic and a healer, not a dog soldier with more courage than brains.

Now, he was itching to start blasting away, even though, if he were honest with himself, he was scared shitless. The zombies were faster than he expected, charging across the field in an ugly, hunger induced quick-march. And worse than that was there just so many of them! He didn't bother to count them, there were simply too many to put a number to and this was just the first wave. He could see the shadows in the forest shifting and the trees swaying and he could hear the snap of a thousand branches breaking under the steps of a thousand more zombies. He was close to pissing himself.

"Do I pop the smoke?" he asked PFC Rogers. He was louder now and his voice warbled in his fear. The zombies had sensed them, though how he didn't know. It didn't look like they could see. Their eyes were black as tar and looked gummed over, and yet they were undoubtedly heading right for the foxholes.

Rogers was way ahead of him. He held up a smoke grenade with two yellow lines on it; yellow meant *enemy spotted*. He pulled the pin and heaved the grenade at the onrushing zombies. It landed at their feet and began hissing out great plumes of a grey-yellow smoke. For Mel-Ray, the smoke was anticlimactic. What they needed were real grenades!

The zombies were momentarily distracted by the smoke; they paused, turned their heads with their noses in the air as if sniffing and then came on again. "Do we shoot?" Mel-Ray asked. He outranked Rogers and yet he was feeling distinctly "civilian" at the moment. Their orders were to shoot only if fired upon or attacked bodily. Right there with zombies...actual fucking zombies, heading right at him the orders seemed outrageously stupid. He couldn't just sit there and wait until the zombies climbed down into his foxhole with him.

And what good was the foxhole anyhow?

Mel-Ray only then realized that the foxhole wasn't any sort of protection. It would trap him and when the zombies came up they'd bury him alive in it under their disgusting bodies!

"Oh God!" he cried, losing all control. He threw the M16 out of the hole and tried to scramble up after it, only the mask gave him tunnel vision and the rubber gloves were slick. He kept slipping down the side of the hole and with each successive attempt his panic threatened to overflow the tiny dam he had built for it in his mind. He had his back to the monsters and when someone up the line began shooting, he pictured the zombies right on top of him.

A scream broke from his throat as he flailed with his limbs. More by accident than design, his boot caught a root and he pushed himself out of the hole. The black gun was right there inches from his hand when he heard a thump behind him. Foolishly, he looked. One of the faster zombies had charged right up and had fallen into the fox-hole. It was disgusting: black blood or snot drained from every orifice, half its face was eaten away as were the fingers on its left hand. They were nubs with black ends, like little burnt sausages.

With guns beginning to fire all around him, Mel-Ray turned his tunneled vision around to look for the fallen M16, and for a second, it seemed to have disappeared in the tall grass. His heart shot into his throat and again he flailed his limbs about, trying to come upon it by feel. First he found a stick, and then a rock, and then…there it was!

In a rush, he snatched it up and had the safety off and fired off three round bursts even before he had it aimed at anything. Six bullets went into the dirt at his feet before he brought the rifle to bear on the zombie in the pit. His first pull of the trigger sent bullets into the wall of the foxhole, the next three tore out the guts of the zombie and the third skipped over the mound of dirt.

The zombie in the pit shrugged off its crippling wounds and was still trying to get at Mel-Ray, but he wasn't worried about that one anymore. It were the other zombies that were only steps away that had his complete attention. He "aimed" again, meaning he fired from the hip, and of the three bullets fired in the burst, one clipped the elbow of a zombie, which didn't seem to notice. The next burst sent two slugs into the chest of another. It staggered but kept coming.

The next pull of the trigger did nothing at all. Their guard unit still used the old 20 round magazines and Mel-Ray was just realizing why the regular army had fazed them out: he'd run out of ammo after only six seconds.

Mel-Ray's panic roared straight through his body right down to his fingers—they went stiff and unfeeling. Two seconds went by before he found the catch to release the spent magazine. It started to fall and, for just long enough to lose more precious seconds, he remembered his training, the main of which consisted of the idea to never to lose an item of military hardware since the cost would come out of his paycheck. He caught the magazine with his left hand and was trying to fumble it into his chest rig with wooden fingers but, no matter what, it wouldn't slide into the little compartment with the others.

With a cry, that was half frustration and half gut-piercing fear, he threw the magazine away from him and, with the zombies almost within arm's reach, he turned and fled.

It was no Olympic sprint. Weighed down as he was with so much gear, all he could manage was a stumbling trot. He was slowed even more because he was trying to load his gun at the same time. He also ran with his head half-turned back, because he was sure the zombies were right on his tail.

And they were. Dozens and dozens. The line of soldiers had barely slowed them down.

The zombies were relentless. They came on without tiring which was the opposite of Mel-Ray who was sucking in great gasps of air through the micro-filters of the claustrophobia inducing mask. After only a hundred yards, he was lightheaded from lack of oxygen and was beginning to stagger among the leaf-hidden logs and the mossy stones and the muddy ruts that were strewn across the forest floor. A trip and a stumble were followed by a low hanging tree limb snagging his mask and turning it forty degrees on his head, blinding him.

He screeched in fear, a breathless: "Huhayy!"

There was no getting the mask back on correctly, not with a fresh magazine in one hand and the M16 in the other. Without thinking, he tossed aside the full magazine, pulled off the mask, and threw that away as well. The clean, fresh, air sucking into his lungs was glorious and partially revived him, allowing him to keep ahead of the zombies until he burst into the staging area where General Collins had set up his Command Post.

After all the shooting and the smoke and the growling zombies, the Command Post was eerily quiet. When he had first marched through it at noon, there had been at least a hundred men in sight working on all manner of things, but now there were just a few MPs standing guard and some faces peeking nervously from some of the tents. Mel-Ray could hear voices from the tents; murmurs mostly but also sharp voices barking orders.

The closest MP was shaking and had been within a hair of shooting Mel-Ray when he first came rushing up. "What the hell's going on?" he asked in a muffled voice. The MP was garbed properly in his MOPP gear and, for a second, Mel-Ray pitied him.

"Zombies!" Mel-Ray cried.

"How many?" the MP asked in fright.

Del-ray paused long enough to look back. There was no sign of his friend Rogers or any of the other medics who had been placed on the line. There were only zombies emerging from beneath the shadow of the trees.

"A lot," was all he said. Along the edge of the clearing were a few dozen Humvees. He ran to the last in line and jumped in.

Before he could start it, the MP yelled, "Hey! You can't leave. That's desertion!"

"It sure as hell is," Mel-Ray said and punched the starter. He gunned it out of there, driving west until he hit the first black top going north. Without a single break, he drove straight to Canada, thinking he would find a place to hide up in the woods, thinking he would put as much distance between himself and anything that even remotely looked like a zombie.

Chapter 19

An End of Prison Time

3:33 p.m.

Chuck Singleton hadn't been able to feel his hands for the last hour or so. He wasn't really worried, however, at least not for himself. When Stephanie had rolled over and showed him her hands, he had to force a smile onto his lips. Her hands were black. He tried to tell himself that they were just a dark purple and that the unlit tent made them seem black, but he was afraid nonetheless.

"You'll be fine, Darlin." His reassurances had worked right up until the firing commenced. There had been shooting going on all day, however this was much, much closer. A few hundred yards at the most.

"We is fucked," John Burke said. "Them fuck-all zombies are right on top of us."

"Then maybe we should keep quiet," Anna suggested. Both she and Eng hadn't spoken much and every time they had, the others glared. They blamed Eng for starting the entire thing and they blamed her for the deaths of Deckard and Thuy. Anna couldn't understand why they were mad at her. She had simply taken advantage of a situation that, in the end, had prolonged all their lives, except of course Dr. Lee's and her goon of a boyfriend. But wasn't that the way the cookie crumbled?

Burke wanted to ream her a good one, but she was right. Their chances were, as his daddy always said, of two varieties: slim and none. He bit his lip and listened as the sleepy camp came alive.

The officers who had been trying their damnedest to keep the perimeter secure, poured out of their tents to find that the section of the line closest to them had crumbled.

Stouthearted, they put up what resistance they could, but the numbers facing them were too great and gradually they fell back to the line of Humvees.

It was too late for that, however. The undead were thick in the forest, going in every direction, some even curling around to come at the Command Post from behind. They were among the Humvees before anyone knew it. The officers fought their way back to the communication tent where they made a final stand.

All the movement outside the tent was confusing, and Stephanie, who thought the officers were leaving them behind whispered to the others: "We can't let them go. We have to scream or something. If not it'll just be us… alone."

"They won't save us," Anna replied.

"Why not?" Stephanie asked. Her words came out with a begging quality that she didn't notice. She knew if the soldiers left, the zombies would come for them, next. Tied up as they were the idea was literally painful to her. There was a pain in her gut like she was trying to digest glass.

"They just won't," Anna hissed. "I wouldn't come back if I was them and neither would any of you."

"Don't believe that mess of a girl. I would come back for you," Chuck said to Stephanie. "Zombies or no zombies."

Everyone heard and no one doubted it, not even Anna. "Then you'd be the only one," she said. "Now, everyone shut up! We can still get lucky so, unless you've thought up a plan, keep quiet."

Chuck could think of nothing that could get them out of the cords binding them. Like Burke, he had never been one to consider himself a cut above the average where smarts were concerned, but he had a good deal of native wisdom. Enough to know that they were screwed, six ways from Sunday.

The battle outside was hot and the sounds of the guns were loud, and yet the presence of the zombies was greater and their moans and growls muted the gunshots. They were everywhere. Some tripped over the ropes holding up the quarantine tent and others fell into its side. Most picked themselves up and left. Some hung around, sniffing the air, certain, in the pea-sized portion of their brain that was still functioning, that there was clean blood nearby.

Inside the tent, the shadows cast by these strays made them seem monstrously large. The prisoners lay on their sides, not daring to talk or even to move. Except for Dr. Wilson who was praying with his eyes closed. Burke stared in a wide-eyed silence and only the binding kept his hands from shaking in fright. Even Chuck was starting to get nervous. Bound as he was, there was no way he could fight. He was hogtied and helpless; in his mind it was no way to die…but then again, wasting away to a weak little nothing as the cancer ate him up from the inside wasn't all that much better.

So far no one had come up with an idea that was better than Anna's "hope to get lucky" plan and for a while the firefight going on seventy yards away drew almost all the attention from the quarantine tent. It couldn't last and it didn't last. The fear was coming off of the prisoners in waves. The scent of it was in their pores and in their sweat. It attracted the zombies with the keenest senses.

Chuck watched as the silhouette of a hand appeared; it fingers seemed extra-long as if they were seeing the shadow of a tremendous spider descending to touch the fabric of the tent. It started to scratch and paw at the wall of the tent near Burke. The man sat up on the nubs of his skinny ass and tried to inch away, quietly. It wasn't possible. His foot scraped and that small sound caused the zombie to react. It clawed at the tent in a frenzy and when that proved useless, the shadow of its head appeared. Its teeth were sharp indentions as it tried to bite its way in.

"It w-won't be able to get in, w-will it?" Stephanie asked, her normally pale face now so white it seemed to shine in the gloom of the tent. "A person can't bite through a tent, right?"

Anna finally looked to be coming undone. Her lower lip quivered as she said: "That's not a person anymore."

The zombie's teeth appeared through the tent linen just as a Humvee engine roared into life. It was a howling metallic sound that could be heard for miles. Whoever was in it had the RPM meter pegged in the red. Then there was a crash and the sound of tree branches snapping and the engine never quit its scream.

It was a bizarre sound as though someone was trying to make a high-speed getaway with the engine stuck in first gear. Burke turned to Chuck—one good ole boy to another—and gave him a shrug as if to suggest that the Yankees in these parts didn't know their asses from holes in the ground.

Chuck was certain that was true enough, however he had more important things to worry about: the zombie had bitten a hole right through the tent and was pushing its head through the opening. He was growling and snapping his teeth. Chuck had a mind to take care of those teeth. The way he figured it, his size thirteen shit-kickers would de-fang the monster.

The only problem was getting himself over to the hole and aligned properly. It took a great deal of squirming and crawling.

"Wait! You're going to get infected," Stephanie said.

"Who cares?" Anna demanded. "Being infected is a whole lot better than the alternative, don't you think?"

Chuck glanced back at Anna. "Why don't y'all just shut your cake-hole? Everythin' that comes out of your mouth is slime." It didn't matter that she was right, he just didn't want to hear it. He turned back to the hideous face chewing at the tent and raised his boots, but something caught his eye and his strength left him. There were more of the disgusting half-men lurking so close that their shadows were painted on the wall of the tent, ranging all down its side.

"Get away from there, Chuck," Stephanie whispered. The shadows advanced, growing to take up the entire wall and then, a second later, they attacked the heavy cloth. The wall bowed in and a pole snapped loudly to match the sound of the gunfire. Stephanie opened her mouth to scream, but her throat was locked shut as if a bear trap had just closed on her larynx.

Anna screamed loud enough for both of them; it shrilled along the highest octave like a broken reed. She wasn't alone in crying out. Dr. Wilson shrieked: "Jesus Christ!" in something that was half prayer, half exclamation. He tried to roll away from the collapsing wall but was too slow and John Burke collided with him in his desperate need to get away. The two men mashed against each other until Burke steamrolled himself right over the top of the older man.

Chuck, realizing what a useless gesture it would be to kick the one zombie, scrambled back to huddle with the rest at the far end of the tent. He kept squirming until he was right next to Stephanie and then he wiggled on top of her. "Just close your eyes, Darlin' and don't listen to nothin'. Just play dead and y'all will be okay."

"What about you?" she asked, quietly.

A smile cracked his weathered face; it was little more than a line with the edges canted up some. It was the best he could manage with the sound of ripping cloth and the weird snarls and the whimpering of Anna and the quick, mumbling of prayer coming from Dr. Wilson. "You know me," Chuck told her. "I'll be just fine."

There was no way he would be. None of them would be fine; it would be impossible. Even if Chuck managed to shield her with his body, she would be infected. The truth was obvious, it showed in her eyes. They were huge and round, and so blue; the tears in them magnifying everything. "Shh," Chuck said, kissing her. "Turn over and just don't look. This is the way it has to be so…"

He was about to go on, reassuring her with the most ridiculous lies, but then the fabric of the tent right above them tore wide open. Cringing, he crushed himself on her, whispering: "Now! Don't look."

Everybody cringed in anticipation of what was to come. With the tent collapsing, there was nowhere left to go and they could only huddle against each other and pray.

Something grunted behind Chuck and he felt his arms pulled back and then there was a sharp pain in his wrist like glass slashing his flesh. He gritted his teeth against it, expecting more, but then his arms suddenly sprang apart and the fire in his shoulders flared…but he was free! Amazed, he looked up to see a woman standing over him sawing furiously at the bindings around his ankles. Her long black hair swung across her face and yet he still knew her by her slim form and soft golden tan: it was Dr. Lee.

"Much obliged, ma'am," he said.

Chapter 20

Thuy Alive

3:41 p.m.

Chuck rolled off of Stephanie and tried to stand; his body rebelled. He was stiff and numb through the limbs. He ended up falling onto Eng, and after a brief struggle righted himself. "Where's Deckard? Was he shot?"

Thuy grunted as she sawed at the cords holding Stephanie's hands pinned behind her back. Chuck couldn't tell what that meant and said as much. Stephanie's hands sprang apart and Thuy went to her ankles next. "Now's not the time," she hissed, jutting her chin at the zombies clawing and biting their way through the tent. "Cover your face if you can," Thuy suggested.

"Maybe y'all should take your own advice," Chuck said. "Here. Lemme do that for you."

He took the knife and with one strong pull, cut the cord. He then went to Dr. Wilson, who was the next closest…other than Eng, that is. Chuck wasn't sure if he was going to cut the lying, murdering bastard free. In seconds, Wilson and John Burke joined Stephanie; they stood near Dr. Lee at the slit she had made in the tent, rubbing their arms and stamping their feet.

"Them too," Thuy said. "We have time." The mindless zombies were getting hung up in the fabric. They had time, but not a lot.

"That's not really the question," Stephanie said in a whisper. "The question is why we should bother. Those two deserve what's coming to them." Burke nodded in agreement, while Dr. Wilson only shrugged his heavy shoulders and looked away.

"You will do as I say or we'll leave you behind as well," Thuy snapped. "We don't know what the future holds. They may come in handy. But if you wish, Mr. Singleton, you may leave their hands bound."

With a look to Stephanie, who seemed confused, Chuck cut their feet free and hauled each to their feet. He didn't like the idea of letting them live and yet he couldn't stomach letting them get eaten alive. He agreed with Stephanie that Anna and Eng deserved whatever the zombies would do to them, but he knew he wouldn't be able to look himself in the eye if he were to leave them as a snack for the zombies.

"Thank you, Dr. Lee," Anna said. She cleared her throat as the others cast glares her way and said, "So what's the plan?"

Thuy was staring out through the slit in the tent. "We wait until there are fewer zombies near the tent and then we make a break for the forest." It was a terrible plan in Chuck's ears, just one step up from staying there and being eaten. There seemed to be altogether too many zombies running around for it to be feasible.

"Fewer zombies?" Stephanie asked. "How is that going to be possible?"

"Do you hear that Humvee? Deckard is trying to get them to chase him."

Chuck gave a gruff laugh and said: "I knew that boy was still kicking."

"Yes," Thuy said.

It had been very close. Deckard had laid Thuy down in the tall grass and she was still so overcome with guilt that she had found she hadn't been able to move, or more aptly, she didn't try to move. So many deaths, so many thousands of deaths could be traced to her hubris and her vanity. First, she had the temerity to play God and then she had been so in awe of her own intellect that she had discounted even the possibility of sabotage. She had reasoned she would see a plot coming a mile away.

Yet it had happened right under her nose.

And so she had given up and when Tyler was sent out to die—another death to be added to her total—she had been so apathetic she hadn't run with the others. Deckard, who had so much life in him and so much vitality, who was fast and who could have escaped easily, stayed back—for her. Even knowing her guilt, he had stayed for her. He had picked her up, put her on his shoulder and ran after the others, and when he had been forced to put her down in the grass, he had done so with gentle hands. She had decided right then that she wouldn't abandon him either.

She laid prostate between the two men and a few feet above her, Meeks had leveled his rifle at Deckard. Calmly, she had reached up and grabbed the barrel, knowing full well that due to the mask he wore, Meeks wouldn't notice her hand until it was too late. Just as she pulled down on the barrel, Meeks fired and the bullet sped unseen right between Deckard's legs to bury itself in the dirt. Thuy's hand rang with a painful numbness and she let out a little yelp.

Above her, Deckard had launched himself at Meeks and with three heavy blows, knocked his mask off his face and laid him out unconscious with his eyes rolled up in his head and his nose gushing blood like a faucet.

Deckard gave her a grin as he helped her up. "Perfect timing," he told her and then bent to relieve Meeks of everything he possessed of value: the mask, the gun, the extra magazines, a set of handcuffs, a two-way radio, and a six-inch jackknife.

Now, Chuck folded up the same jackknife and held it out to Thuy. "Keep it," she said. The sound of the Humvee's roaring engine was starting to fade in the slightest and so were the sounds of firing from the other tents. In place of the shooting came screams; they sent a shiver up Thuy's spine. "Is everyone ready?" she asked. They were at the point where it didn't matter if the coast was clear. The zombies were squirming through the holes in the tent. They couldn't stay. "Dr. Wilson keep watch over Eng. Mr. Burke you do the same for Anna. Mr. Singleton, take this."

She reached outside the tent and picked up an M16A1. "I assume you know how this weapon operates?"

"Yes ma'am I do. And by the by, ma name's Chuck."

"Alright Chuck, lead the way. Our goal is to lose ourselves in the deep woods. Stephanie, you'll buddy-up with me."

Chuck stepped out and even his calm demeanor was shaken by what he saw. There was a flood of undead coming out of the woods to the west. A look behind showed a thousand or more tearing into the tents of the command post or ripping soldiers to shreds as they screamed in a manner Chuck did not think possible for a grown man to scream. To the south there seemed to be a break between the first wave of undead and a new one surging forward.

He was pushed from behind by Thuy to get him going but the way wasn't exactly clear. Within two steps, he was forced to fire the M16. A man with the shreds of his face hanging from his jawline came stumbling from around the side of the tent. Where his nose and lips and cheeks should've been was a horrible black mask of flies that hummed and buzzed, and when he opened his mouth, more flies flew out.

"Ma God!" Chuck cried, bringing the rifle up. He'd never fired an M16 before and still he put a hole smack dab in the thing's forehead causing the flies to leap up and buzz angrily. He had no time to remark on the zombie's passing, nor even time to watch it fall. There were more of the beasts attracted by the new smell of humans and the sound of the gun. He turned a quarter to his right, lined up the sights on another of "them" and caressed the trigger back. Another slight turn and another shot.

His was the only gun that could be heard now. Among the tents, there was only screams.

"Good enough," Thuy said dragging Chuck by the arm as Stephanie hurried along in their wake and the other rushed out of the tent by twos. "We have to chance them getting close, there just isn't enough ammunition left."

They ran, taking a southern course, trying to cut between the two waves of zombies without drawing too much attention to themselves—which proved impossible. The woods hid them to a degree, but soon they were forced out into the open. They crossed a little field carpeted with bright yellow dandelions and suddenly there was a howl and Chuck expected to see a zombiefied wolf, however the sound was coming from human throats.

The waves of zombies coming from the west were moving in a broken line. They came on in a ragged formation: a dozen here, eighty there, a mob of thirty cutting across their front. Five zombies—two in shredded army uniforms, a tall woman and two teenagers—were in the van, ahead of the rest by fifty yards. There was a reason they were in front of the others: they were whole. Not a single one had a bite mark anywhere visible. Other than the black dripping from their eyes and the unholy sound they were making, they seemed altogether human and they were almost as fast as normal humans, and indeed much faster than humans running with their hands tied behind their backs.

With Eng and Anna slowing the group down, the five beasts quickly began to catch up.

"Don't go wastin' no bullets," Burke said, coming to a stop when it was obvious they were going to be caught. He was huffing and bent over at the waist from the run. They were all tired: three cancer patients, two trussed prisoners, a 56-year-old, and a woman who had spent way too much time with her nose in a book or her eyes glued to a microscope. "We should jes give em' this here China-boy to eat. No offense Doc," he added, suddenly remembering Dr. Lee was Chinese of some sort as well. "Y'all said they might come in handy and this here job is one he seems per-ticularly suited for."

"No," Thuy said. "We will not mistreat the prisoners. Mr. Singleton, if you'll be so kind, please shoot the zombies."

Chuck took a deep breathe, aimed and fired, taking off a good chunk of scalp from the nearest of them. It seemed surprised that it had been shot and fell face first with its eyes flung wide. The next shot was dead center and Burke grunted: "Nice." He then turned away from what looked like target practice for Chuck and said to Thuy: "I'm a thinkin' y'all be coming around right quick on the treatment of the prisoners. Look."

The sound of the shooting had stopped the lead wave of zombies, who were even then turning slowly, realizing there were humans near. The little group was now surrounded on three sides. The zombies were arrayed around them in the shape of a bottle and it was clear the little group would be forced to sprint southward in the hope of making it out of the trap closing in on them. With the prisoners in tow, it didn't look like they had much of a chance.

Thuy only raised an eyebrow at Burke, but did not answer him. "Keep shooting Mr. Singleton. Don't let them get too close."

There was a sparkle of sweat on Dr. Wilson's brown forehead as he spun to see the hundreds of zombies closing in on them. The ones to the east were nearest, but the ones to the west were walking on a downward slope and coming on quicker. Wilson's heart was pounding out a speedy rhythm and he was afraid he wouldn't be able to make the run. "Dr. Lee…he may be right. It may be the only way we can get out of this. I know it's horrible to consider, but we should think about the needs of the many and weigh them against the needs of the guilty."

"Interesting choice of words," Thuy said. "But I think we'll be alright."

"Look!" Stephanie suddenly cried, pointing at a Humvee coming up through the tree line. Deckard danced the nimble machine between the trees and the groups of zombies. Everyone cheered, except Chuck who was too busy concentrating on his aim. His chest had accumulated a gob of phlegm from the run and it was making control of the rifle an uncertain thing. He was embarrassed that it took two bullets a piece to take down the last two zombies closing in on them. He coughed up a wad of grey gunk and spat it on the yellow dandelions just as the Humvee pulled up.

"The cavalry saves the day!" Stephanie gushed as Deckard slid out of the vehicle. Chuck coughed some more ugly out of his lungs but it was her words that sent a stab of jealous pain lancing through him. It must have shone on his face because she gave him a quizzical look. "Come on. I'll sit on your lap," she said, banishing the pain from his cancer-riddled body.

"Lucky dog," Burke griped. There wasn't a lot of room in the four-seat Humvee. The two prisoners were crammed in the cargo area with a third a man: Special Agent Meeks. Deckard had been all for handcuffing him to a tree, but Thuy had thought that akin to murder and so Deckard had been forced to carry him three hundred yards to a little stand of birches that provided enough cover to hide them while they figured out what they were going to do. Their futures hadn't really been up for discussion; Thuy wasn't going to let her last three patients die from exposure to the Com-cells and so she and Deckard had waited, looking for an opportunity to rescue the group.

Now, with equal command, she went and sat in the front passenger seat, relegating John Burke to an uncomfortable position stuck on a lumpy console in the back. He was twisted like a gnome to keep his head from rattling off the roof.

"If you have seat belts, buckle up," Deckard suggested. He stomped the gas and the throaty roar of the engine accompanied a quicker than expected acceleration. Zombies surged at them from all sides but Deckard was a skilled driver and dodged the hummer left and right. The ride was far from smooth as they jounced over fallen trees and thumped into dry rain gullies. More than once Burke cracked his skull on the roof and the trio of prisoners cried out as they were flung about in the back.

Deckard did not slow. There was no telling what lay ahead and speed was his only ally. In minutes, they came on a dirt path that ran north to south. On a whim, he turned south and sped a course parallel to the one he wanted. East was the quickest way out of The Zone…if there was indeed a way out. For half a mile, the ride became smooth as behind them they left a plume of dust in the late afternoon sky.

Then they crested a hill and Deckard stopped the Humvee.

"Are we there yet?" Stephanie joked. She was feeling a sort of giddy relief at having cheated death once again, and then there was the straight-up fact that she was falling for Mr. Charles Singleton. A single thought struck her: *I want to be Mrs. Charles Singleton...before I die.* Her smile faded at the finality of the last three words.

"No," Deckard said. "This is one place we don't want to be."

The dirt road could be seen cutting along the edge of the forest for a few miles. Deckard guessed there were a couple of thousand zombies on the road strung out in long lines—there was no getting through them. With the virility of the disease, he didn't dare try plowing over or through them.

"Everyone, check to see if there's a map," he ordered. No map.

"Maybe we should consider the Hudson River," Thuy suggested. "I'm sure we can pick up a boat somewhere around..."

Burke interrupted: "Then y'all can count me out. In fact, lemme have the gun. I'll take my chances crossin' here."

"Are you insane?" Stephanie asked. "Immune or not, you'll get eaten alive."

"I'll take my chances," he repeated. When she opened her mouth again he stopped her with a raised finger. "Look. I only come this way on account of my little girl come this way. That amba-lance headed east; prolly goin' to Hartford. So that's the way I'm goin'."

"You may take your leave of us, Mr. Burke, but you will do so empty-handed," Thuy stated. "I'm sorry."

Burke made a noise like he was spitting out a gnat that had landed on his tongue. "You don't sound all that sorry. You sound to me like a..."

Deckard swiveled his head around and glared. "I'd be careful if I was you. Now are you getting out or not?"

Without a weapon, Burke had no choice but to stay. Deckard turned the Humvee around and drove back into the slowly settling dust they had just kicked up. They went north for six miles, looking for a way east, but their path was blocked at every turn by the undead. With no choice, they next sped west into the very heart of the quarantined zone.

Chapter 21

Child's Play

4:09 p.m.

"I want a big one," Jaimee Lynn whispered. She was in the basement of an abandoned factory listening to the helicopters whoop-whoop-whoop overhead. They had been constant for the last hour, but what had been constant all day was the growl of her stomach. She had fed five times and yet she was still so hungry. The problem was she could only catch the small and skinny ones.

They were there in the basement with her, staring blankly at the wall. She lined them up, biggest to smallest. They would move only when they heard voices or smelled the clean blood. Or when she told them to. That was key. Even though they were so stupid, they listened to her. She hadn't known what to do with the first one, Misty and at first had considered burying her since she was technically dead and wasn't that what you did with dead people? Jaimee Lynn had a vague recollection of her mother being put in the ground, but that felt like ages ago back before her hunger was all-consuming.

She had not known what to do with the nasty, little zombies she had made—strangely, she didn't consider herself one of *them,* because she could think and plan to a degree—and now she had an idea brewing. She would use them to get a big one. Maybe a teenager or a small woman. There had been a woman who had come by screeching for someone named Jane. Jaimee Lynn had wondered if one of her little zombie pets was Jane, but none of the kid zombies blinked at the name, they had only scrambled at the wall trying to get at the woman, their mouths opening and closing, letting out a God-awful stink.

Misty said: "Misty hun-gee."

Jaimee Lynn didn't notice that Misty had actually used a two-word sentence. She was hungry as well and all she wanted to do was climb the wall and get at the blood, but she knew better. Big people were strong and could hurt you…unless you had a pack of children to sic on them like a bunch of rabid dogs.

"If I use them I can get the woman. I can eat her," she whispered.

Saying those words didn't bother her in any way. It was like back when she had been with her dad and she would say: "Daidy, can I have some mac-un-cheese?" To her it was all the same. Mac-un-cheese and the hot, coppery blood of a woman were equal. She was a growing child and she needed food, badly. It was all she could think about, unless she forced herself to concentrate extra hard, then she could hear ideas sprout up inside her noggin. They weren't genius ideas, not by a long shot.

She planned on going up to street level to lay in wait for the first person to come by. Like a sheepdog, she herded the other little kid zombies up the stairs and out onto the street. They blinked unhappily at the tired grey light filtering down through the clouds. The newest one tried to wander back into the dark of the basement, but Jaimee grabbed her.

"No you don't. You wait right here," she said, shoving the little girl down by a trash can. She wasn't very well hidden, but Jaimee Lynn was already stationing the next child behind a rusted out Volvo.

She started to walk away, but the girl grabbed her and asked: "Eat?"

"Hold on!" Jaimee Lynn scolded. "Stay put and be quiet until one comes by." She assumed they would all know what to do when "one" came by. When the little zombies were in place, Jaimee Lynn looked around for her own hiding spot. She couldn't think of anything better than to than to scrunch down next to Misty in the doorway of the factory.

Jaimee Lynn had no clue how to tell time anymore and generally it was a useless concept. Time consisted of the chunks of her life between feedings. This seemed like an exceptionally long chunk. It took so long for someone to come by that it felt like they were playing hide-n-go seek with no one doing the seeking.

After an agonizingly long time, Jaimee Lynn stood up to make sure the other girls hadn't moved and that was when she saw the car. It was blurry and tiny, far down the street, but as she blinked, it seemed to be getting bigger. She was struck by dual considerations: first her hunger was maddening and she wanted to leap on the car and scratch her way through the windshield to get at whoever was driving, but on the other hand, what if it was a man like the one who had hurt her that morning. He was dim in her mind, but she remembered the pain and the strength of his arms.

The idea of a bigger, stronger creature made her plans for her and she turned to scamper back, however the building had been layered with so much graffiti that everything blended together in crazy colors and illegible swirls. The doors were there, somewhere, camouflaged among all of it. "Misty?" she called out, feeling a touch of fear. It was the fear a child has of being abandoned. It was primal and encoded to such an extent into her brain that even with the disease turning her into a literal monster, the fear of being left behind was still there.

"Yes?" Misty answered. The way she said the word she acted as if she was answering God.

Jaimee Lynn oriented on the word and suddenly the doors came into focus; she hurried to where Misty was squatting, looking dull eyed. "It's a car," Jaimee Lynn explained. Misty answered that by licking her lips.

The car stopped by the doors with its engine rumbling, matching the noise of Jaimee Lynn's stomach. The smell of the human was intoxicating and maddening; it was almost enough to pull her from her hiding place early. By the smell, Jaimee Lynn knew it was a woman in the car and one still in her child-bearing years. She had put on lotion not long before, cocoa butter, and in her hair was a chemical product that had no name in Jaimee Lynn's mind. She had eaten recently: eggs and toast and there was an old gum smell to her that suggested she had stepped in some and that it had hardened on her shoe.

All of these human aromas sought out that part of her brain that demanded food…no, not food…it was blood. She needed the blood and the need drove her out into the open.

The woman's eyes bugged at the sudden appearance of the little girl in the dirty hospital gown, with her feet bare and her eyes wickedly black. "I…I am uh, looking for my daughter," the lady said, speaking across the passenger seat and through the open window. "Her name's Jane and…and are you alright?"

"I'm fine," Jaimee Lynn answered. She stood in the doorway, clutching the metal frame with both hands, hoping to hold herself back. It was too soon. The woman was still in her car. She could get away and Jaimee Lynn's hunger was such a hot pulse in her that she *had* to have blood very soon or she would go crazy.

"Your eyes," the woman said, pointing. "What's with your eyes?"

"Dirty," Jaimee Lynn said. "Jane is here. Jane is in here with us." The little girl pointed at the door that led into the factory. "Come see her."

"Jane's in there?" the woman asked, cautiously. "Jane McPherson? She's six years-old and about four feet tall? A little black girl?"

Was one of the little kid zombies black? It strained Jaimee Lynn's power of recollection to come up with an answer: yes. Maybe even two of them were, but she saw race now even less than she had when she had lived with her daddy. "Yes, we have a black one. Come on in here. Come and see the girl. Don't be afraid." Jaimee Lynn could smell the fear. It was tinged by a revulsion the woman had for her, but there was still fear. It was intoxicating, too much so for the others.

The little kid zombies hopped up out of their hiding spots and charged the car. The woman jerked in surprise and shock; her eyes bugging even larger than before. The other kids weren't nearly as pretty as Jaimee Lynn. They were ugly with their throats torn open, and their faces bitten and their black blood clotted like mud. They rushed the driver's side and tried to climb in through the window. They were stupid and dumb and Jaimee Lynn was furious that they hadn't been able to listen to her, and that they had ruined the plan.

And yet, Jaimee Lynn rushed the car, as well. She was afraid the others would get all the blood and leave her with nothing but a few drops. With Misty right behind her, she ran at the car and dove through the open passenger window, just as the woman hit the gas. The car leapt forward and there was a cruel thump as one of the little kid zombies was run over, and the woman cried out in both fear and pain as another of the pack had its teeth in her wrist.

Jaimee Lynn knew none of this. Her stunted ability to think was gone. Instinct and hunger powered her as she flashed in at the exposed neck. The woman was turned away fretting over her wrist and the beast that clung to it and her neck, from shoulder to ear, was left wide open, its soft brown skin with its icing of cocoa butter was a magnet for Jaimee Lynn who stretched her mouth hideously wide before lunging down.

The woman screamed and the one hand left the wheel in an awkward attempt to pull Jaimee Lynn from her neck. It proved impossible. The little girl had one hand snagged up in the woman's hair and the other was clawing back her face, holding the head at an angle. Her feet were planted, one hard on the dash, the other on the passenger seat. She pushed with her skinny legs, basically pinning the woman in place.

Distantly, Jaimee Lynn felt a clot of hair yanked out of her head and nails rake across the back of her neck. There should have been pain, however there was only the ecstasy of hot blood. It filled her mind beyond anything else. Even when the car crashed into a lamppost, so hard that its tail leapt into the air, Jaimee Lynn could only think about the blood.

In seconds, she had to compete as the others in the pack ran to catch up and scrambled around inside the car to get at the meat. Misty snaked under Jaimee Lynn to get at one of the thick thighs, while, on the other side of her, three of the pack were tearing into the woman's arm, breast and leg. From a high vantage they looked like piglets in a row, suckling.

The woman fought and hollered in a hoarse voice until Jaimee Lynn finally got to the plump artery that ran right up next to the trachea. With every bite, she had come closer and closer to the maddening thump-thump-thump-of the artery and when she did…ahhh, nirvana. Her teeth ceased their ripping and tearing because the blood just came gushing up. She let it flow into her mouth and then when her belly sagged from the meat and the blood, she let it flow across her lips and tongue.

Her need left her with every passing second and she began to feel sleepy. Had she been alone she would have slept, curled up in the corpse, but Misty was far from satisfied and her need had been just as great. When Jaimee Lynn stopped fighting, Misty, with surprising strength, pulled her away and went at the neck. On the other side of the woman another of the pack did the same thing and together, the pair chewed until they were into the trachea and the last of the woman's breath whispered in their ears.

The rest of the pack mutilated the corpse trying to get at the cooling blood and when they had their fill, they slunk back down into the dark beneath the factory.

The crashed car and the corpse sat on the quiet street, and during the last few hours of daylight, a number of people looked in at the wreck and saw the corpse lying still and grim. A few of them took the time to call the police, most didn't bother. The police had lit their cars and warbled the air with their sirens as they cut westward. Every last one of them. The people were left to police themselves.

Connecticut's small force of National Guard, being thrown into the twenty-mile breach as quickly as they arrived, could not hope to take on the thousands of zombies streaming across the border and so the Governor, displaying a keen awareness of the situation, had declared martial law and had drafted into the National Guard every last law enforcement officer in the state.

No one knew if it was legal but no one was challenging the notion either.

So the body of the unknown woman lay there for over a day as the Com-cells multiplied and, according to her specific DNA blueprint, healed her enough for her to crack her eyes. Another half-day went by before she could move. Gradually, she sat up, and about the time the coroner in Hartford opened up a cold storage locker and pulled out the body of Carl McMillan, the man whom Jaimee Lynn had infected, the woman was strong enough and hungry enough to begin feeding.

Chapter 22

In the Land of the Blind

4:12 p.m.

Even with top priority given to his limousine, the streets of DC were so clogged with the rush hour traffic that Collins didn't make it back to his Blackhawk until just after four.

The blades were already spooling up and this combined with the pinched look on his adjunct's face, meant there was trouble, or rather, more trouble. "Is it a break out?" he asked after returning Lieutenant Colonel Victor's salute.

"Yes." The one word reply gripped Collins somewhere below the belt and squeezed until it hurt.

When Victor didn't elaborate, the general demanded: "Well? Where? Is it the *Point?*" A collapse of the line holding West Point would mean that New York City itself was threatened. There was no land to give up in that direction, especially to the south. Every mile south, the population doubled until the ten million-person city was reached.

Victor shook his head. "No sir. It was the eastern line. No one has heard from the command post in the last forty-five minutes. They just…poof went off the air. I sent a recon bird over twenty minutes ago. We don't have stills or the video yet, but the word from the spotter is there isn't anything down there but I.P.s wandering around." I.P.s was the official shortened term for *infected persons.*

"Son of a bitch!" Collins seethed. "Get me a map, right now. And get this bird in the air." A fury over the wasted minutes he'd just spent trying to prop up a useless politician overcame him and he punched the side of the Blackhawk, his fist striking the metal inches from a hole where some disgruntled farmer in the Zone had taken a shot at them.

The commander of the 42nd Infantry Division took his spot in the copter and in a second, Victor had the tactical display on a computer screen that folded open. For over a minute, the general gazed with unseeing eyes at the map. Instead of the computer screen, he saw the faces of the men he had left behind to die: Lieutenant Colonel Runners, the division training officer and resident practical joker. It was a point of pride for Runners to put one over on Collins every time they went to the field on maneuvers. His executive officer, Colonel William Tate, who was also his best friend in and out of the division. Major Henry, the only other Cowboys' fan in the state of New York. He lived down the street from Collins, and during football season, was a regular at his house.

"Shit, what's Leslie going to say?" he whispered, now thinking about Henry's pretty wife, the mother of his three children, one of whom was still in fucking diapers.

"Say again, sir?" the pilot asked through the headset. "What's the destination?"

It took a few blinks for Collins to right his mind and bring him back to the urgent situation at hand. He wanted to say: the White House lawn. Though he had just come from a meeting with him, Collins wanted to get the President alone and scream into his fake-tanned face and demand that the situation be federalized. Given two more divisions, the use of his armor, and a shoot on sight order, he knew he could contain the infected persons easily.

"The command post," he said into the mike and then switched it off. He knew it was a stupid order. It wasn't a power failure that had caused the lack of communication, it was the zombies, and that meant the whole area and anything in it was contaminated, which meant it made no sense to go.

But he had to see for himself.

The pilot exchanged a look with his copilot and then went through his preflight checklist. He was lucky he kept his mouth shut this time. Collins was in no mood for the least insubordination. He turned to Victor. "Who's in charge of the southern zone? I need to talk to him."

"It's Colonel Shackleford of the 27th and it'll be just a minute. When we lost the command post, we lost our entire tactical data link system, severing our ability to communicate with many of the units. We're flying blind so to speak."

Blind, deaf, and dumb was no way to run an army, Collins thought to himself. "Do what you can," he said. The Blackhawk lifted off. It was a sensation he'd never get used to, akin to leaping into the air and not coming down again. It took a second for his stomach to settle back in place. Watching the capitol flash by below helped; it looked entirely normal. There was no sign of panic, there wasn't the steady beat of rifles, or the sweaty, nervous looks of soldiers waiting for the zombies. They were just people down below, going about their lives.

Then they were over the green of Maryland and Victor was in his ear: "Com-line two, sir."

Collins hit the button and the muted whir of the engines was replaced by the static of a radio and the background noise of a battle. In his time, he had heard too many of those to think it was anything else. "Colonel Shackleford, this is General Collins, do you need to attend to your men or can you talk?"

"No sir, what you're hearing is nothing. Just a few I.P.s. We had a hell of a lot more earlier and before that, it was the civilians. I'm sorry to say they did not recognize our legal authority to detain them within The Zone."

"Casualties?"

"Heavy on both sides. We were taking sniper fire all afternoon and they were good. There's a lot of ex-military living up in these hills and they are some good shooters. I'm not making excuses but my boys are fighting with what feels like anchors around their necks. When do you think we'll get permission to relax the ROEs?"

"I'm working on it," Collins said. "Now give me some numbers. I can't go to the Governor with 'heavy' as an estimation of our casualties." There was a pause and Collins waited, feeling his insides crimp up.

"One-hundred and thirteen KIA, two-hundred and eleven wounded."

The crimped feeling grew so tight he couldn't breathe. "One-hundred and thirteen killed?" His head spun. That was two months' worth of deaths in Iraq.

"Yes, sir, it was sporting down here for quite a while. They kept probing and always had more men at the point of attack than we did. What's more, we're tied to the dirt. Our orders don't allow for retreat or attack. It's an unenviable position, but our boys are fighting with great skill. When can we expect reinforcements?"

"You haven't been getting any?" Collins asked.

"We got some cooks and com guys, but no infantrymen. And they've been coming in drips and drabs. I need another two thousand men to hold this line properly."

"I'll, uh, see what I can do." Collins glanced at his tactical display. It was a straight up mess with units so intermingled that it would take hours for someone to figure it out—but he didn't have hours and he didn't have any extra someones hanging around. "What about civilian casualties? Do you have any estimates?"

"According to a few of the pilots who've been around the block for a few years, they say we're looking at fifteen, maybe sixteen hundred."

There was the pain again. It was like someone was cinching down his intestines with barbed wire. Sixteen-hundred dead civilians? They died for what? Because they were trapped in a land of zombies? If that number got out to the media, heads would roll. And that was just the southern border, what of the north? The battle around Kingston had been going on since that morning. How many more were dead on both sides up there?

This was what the President feared would stick to him. Someone would have to be responsible for so many deaths. The President had washed his hands of it and the governor of New York could say he tried his best to limit it by restricting the use of force, but what could Horace Collins say? I was following orders?

A part of him wanted to ask: Were the men adhering to the use of force guidelines? In other words, he wanted to put it on the soldiers. *They* got out of control. *They* didn't follow his orders. *They* were the lawless ones. *They* are the guilty ones.

Collins cleared his throat. "I will see what I can do about reinforcements. You…you keep up the good work." *Of killing civilians*, a nasty voice in his brain added, quietly.

"Sir? One more question. All of our communications with your command post have ceased. Are the rumors true that it was overrun? I don't normally listen to rumors, especially from pilots, but we're hanging out here in the dark. We're tactically blind."

There was that word again: blind. The 42nd Infantry Division was a body flailing around without a head. How was he going to fix this situation? All of his most experienced officers were dead and their millions of dollars' worth of communications gear was sitting out in the middle of the forest probably covered in deadly germs. He would normally transfer his headquarters—which currently consisted of Lieutenant Colonel Victor and himself—to a brigade command, however there was no official CIC with the 27th. Their headquarters personnel were fighting alongside the infantrymen on the line, and their millions of dollars' worth of equipment was lying forgotten alongside highways or tipped into jumbles when moving men and ammo to the front by truck and helicopter had been a priority.

The general was seeing his command disintegrate. "I'm on my way to the command post now and will let you know. Collins out."

He sat shaking his head. Three hundred casualties out of how many? There was no way to know. How many had failed to show up for duty? How many had deserted? How many had been trapped when the lines had been arbitrarily moved back?

A sigh, similar to a death rattle, leaked out of him before he keyed his mike: "Colonel Victor, get me whoever is in charge around Kingston."

It had been a battalion commander, either the 2nd or the 4th, he couldn't remember which, but just before he had left for his meeting with the President, Colonel Montgomery, Brigade Commander of the 50th had decided that since a few hundred of his New Jersey men had been helicoptered in, he should be the one to command the battle. Collins who didn't have time to play: *whose was bigger*, between colonels, had agreed.

Everything being so hectic, he didn't know if the change in command had occurred until Montgomery barked into the phone: "Who is this?"

"General Collins. Give me a situation report."

Montgomery's manner thawed quickly and he gave a report that was depressingly similar to Colonel Shackelford's only with more deaths on both sides. The bright spot was that he was being regularly reinforced by both state troopers and his own soldiers who were being choppered in from New Jersey. What's more, he had held the bridge.

The bad news, other than the deaths of so many men, women, and soldiers was that there had been a flare up behind the lines in a town called Pine Plains. It was fifteen miles due east of Kingston and should have been clean. Out of the blue, a man went crazy and attacked a family of four who had stopped for gas before heading to anywhere else—a favorite destination of most of the population of Pine Plains. Since the YouTube video had aired, the little town had dwindled to almost nothing. There were only three-hundred odd people left when the man started biting people.

Now those three-hundred people were in a quarantine bubble of their own. Some had tried to sneak out, but for the most part they kept themselves locked away, ready to shoot the first thing that knocked on their door.

"It means there's a leak," Collins said. "You need to maintain your portion of the lines better."

"My portion? No disrespect sir, but my entire left wing is in the air. We lost contact with the next unit over about the time we lost contact with *your* headquarters company."

Collins bristled at the suggestion that he was somehow responsible…but then he remembered how he had stripped that area in order to hold the bridge. "Be that as it may, I need you to start extending your lines east."

"To where? Massachusetts?"

"Yes. I don't have the manpower to do anything else." In his mind, he heard himself say: *the people of Massachusetts are just going to have to take care of themselves.* It was annoyingly similar to what Governor Stimpson had said, only Collins didn't have a choice anymore, not until the President either took control or forced the other governors to give up their men to the 42nd Infantry Division.

The President was doing neither of these things. At that moment, he had his most important donor on Skype, because those bigwigs liked the personal touch. "We're doing everything we can Mr. Hemsforth," the President said. "You have nothing to worry about." He wasn't exactly lying. Marty had told him the same thing and that meant it was true for him.

He had yet to make any calls to the governors. They were on his to do list.

A minute later, without any prodding from anyone, the Governor of Massachusetts called up his own National Guard forces. His explicit orders: "They're not to leave the state."

And about the time, Collins' Blackhawk was hovering over the remains of his command post, Rhode Island and its puny force did the same.

Chapter 23

Survivors

4:41 p.m.

The sporty but very cramped Audi took Courtney Shaw, a German Shepherd, and the three soldiers on a tour of the quarantine zone. They drove north and discovered the killing fields south of Kingston where the townsfolk had battled against odds, fighting before and aft. Their bodies and the hundreds of zombie bodies, littered the turned up fields that hadn't yet been sown with the summer crop of corn.

"Don't slow down," PFC Max Fowler said. Not all the zombies were dead; some were just then rising up with glittering black eyes, while many more were crawling over each other to get at them.

They headed west with the insane idea of trying to cross the bridge west of Poughkeepsie, but there were still too many zombies roaming the streets to make the attempt. They headed south along the Hudson River, hoping to find a boat, but there were none and either way, zombies floated. Trying the river looked like a sure death.

But that didn't stop people from trying.

The population of pure blood humans within The Zone was less than one percent of what it had been the day before. Humans, by their actions, their words and their odor attracted zombies like flies to shit. Down below the road, on the banks of the river where the reeds grew high, Courtney could see a small group of humans trying to work a speedboat across the water. It had a good tall hull and a strong motor, however the operator was inept and had fouled the propeller in the partially submerged river grass.

The engine was groaning and kicking out a cloud of blue smoke. Around them pruney and water-logged zombies struggled against the slow current to get at them. There weren't many, however. The group had chosen their launch sight well.

"Maybe we can hitch a ride," Johnny said from the back seat.

"I like the safety of the car," Will replied. "Besides I doubt the army forgot about this river. It's probably strung with wire from end to end."

Max gave a shrug. "Yeah, but look at the other side. I don't see too many zombies."

"Once we get across, we'll be on foot, Max," Will answered with a little whine to his voice. "Think about it, will you? We only have so much ammo. The way we burn through it we couldn't take on more than twenty of them. I don't mean to piss you off, but I…" A sharp bang from the river drew their attention back. There was more smoke enveloping the end of the boat, but the sound of the engine had cut off with the bang.

Courtney looked around, fearing they had been standing still too long. "I think God has decided things for us," she said.

"God!" Will exclaimed, making a noise of dismissal.

She didn't bother saying anything to Will. She had always believed in God but for the last day, a prayer had been on the tip of her tongue and in the back of her mind for every second of every minute. "Either way, we should see if they want to come with us." She looked at Max when she said this; she didn't really trust the other two. Johnny was a little too quick to agree to *anything;* there didn't seem to be much going on upstairs with him. The other one, Will, though tall, sandy-haired and handsome, was also quick eyed and sweaty. He seemed to prefer any idea that was the safest at that particular moment without regard to the future.

"Yeah," Max said. "The more the merrier." He started to get out and Will grabbed his shoulder.

"Hold on, wait. They could be diseased. Did you ever think of that? Or they could be thieves."

"Them?" Max asked with a little laugh. It was hard to believe the six people struggling with the boat were desperadoes. There was an elderly couple who looked to be in their seventies, gimping around, their joints stiff and their arms weak. Another pair were teenagers, a brother and sister. Max could tell by the way they clung to each other, unafraid to appear weak. The last two weren't a couple. One was a striking blonde and the other a geek. Even from sixty feet away his odd mannerisms and even odder look was apparent.

He is going to be a pain, Max thought just looking at him. He shrugged off Will's hand. "It'll be ok. I'll check them out, but if you're nervous you can come too and watch my back."

Since that was slightly less safe than sitting in the car, Will shook his head. Courtney tried not to let her irritation show. "I'll go with you," she said to Max.

Sundance wanted to go racing off and he quivered with anticipation, but Courtney told him to "Heel," and he fetched up against her thigh. They made their way down the embankment; it was slick with mud and the two held onto each other and watched their feet more than anything. When the ground leveled off they looked up to see three weapons pointed their way. The nerd, the old man and the teenage sister were each armed.

"We don't have enough room on this boat, thank you," the nerd said. Even Courtney had assigned him the title of 'nerd'. He was skinny to the point of ill health, was in his late twenties but seemed older, wore glasses that were huge and years out of date, and had what looked to be perpetually greasy hair. "We don't want to swamp it," he added. There was little chance that would happen, Courtney saw. The boat was sturdy and had seating for eight and deck space for another six. There was plenty of room, but it was a moot point, the engine had seized.

"We were hoping you'd come with us, actually," Max said. "I mean, you're not still thinking about using that boat, are you? The engine's busted."

"We could paddle," the nerd replied, his gun still pointing. The other two had lowered their weapons; the old man had stuck a revolver in the pocket of his coat with a shaking hand, while the girl, slim, with long straight brown hair and the dead-white skin common to upstate New Yorkers, sat the butt-end of a shotgun on the ground at her feet.

"Paddle?" Max asked. "Are you sure you want to do that? The river is three or four-hundred yards wide here, and for all you know the water is diseased. With all those zombies in it I don't think I would touch it, not even with a paddle."

"Thanks for your concern, but we got this," the nerd replied.

The blonde woman spoke up: "Benjamin, why are you being such a dick? The man's right. We can't paddle across here, not with such a big boat, and I wouldn't want to try in a smaller one. Maybe we should see where they're going."

Benjamin Olski gave her a stiff smile as if trying to appear less dick-ish. "Cheryl, I got this. Trust me ok? I got you this far and I'll get you to safety but only if you trust me. This guy's a soldier. I'm sorry but after what happened in Happy Valley I don't think we can give him the benefit of the doubt."

"What happened in Happy Valley?" Max asked. When he only received an incredulous look from Benjamin, Max protested: "I wasn't in Happy Valley. I've never been there. We were in some place called Myers Corner. And for sure we didn't…"

"We?" Benjamin demanded. He turned to Cheryl and smiled condescendingly. "There are more of them. Can't you see, we can't trust them? They could be…rapists." This last he said in a whisper that everyone could hear.

"They're not rapists," Courtney said. "I'm proof of that. And I did find them in Myers Corner practically surrounded by zombies. There weren't any dead humans, uh you know what I mean. They didn't kill anyone. But if you want to stay, mister, and try to cross on that boat, go right ahead. If any of you others want to come with us, you're welcome."

"Where are you going?" the teenage girl asked, she was afraid, however the presence of Sundance seemed to calm her. She kept glancing down at him and he would thump his tail happily when she did.

Her brother, standing a few feet back, piped up: "Can we get out of the quarantine zone if we're with the army? You know, can the soldier get us out?"

They all stared at Max for an answer. "Truthfully, I don't know. I doubt it. We had our orders: absolutely no one was allowed to leave The Zone. Not cops or firemen or politicians or anyone. They never said anything about soldiers, but I get the feeling no one meant no one."

"Then what good is he?" Benjamin asked the others.

"I think I want to take my chances with him," Cheryl announced, tossing her blonde hair out of her eyes. "How many other soldiers are with you?" She started to climb down from the boat, but when Max told her there were only two more, she hesitated for a moment and then said: "I guess that's better than nothing." This made Benjamin blink.

The brother and sister gave each other a brief look that communicated all that was needed to be said between them and together they picked their way through the sucking mud at the river's edge to come stand by Courtney. They both greeted Sundance before the two humans. "I'm Alivia and this is Jack," the girl said. He was taller but clearly younger. They were both skittish and wore streaks on their cheeks where tears had cut through a film of dirt, and their eyes never stopped moving.

The old couple didn't want to break ranks with Benjamin, they eyed Max darkly. "I would prefer the river," the woman said. "The zombies aren't that bad and…and they can't get at us. We're too high in the water. We can just float downstream until we're out of The Zone."

"That won't work," Max told her. "The army will have the river blocked somehow. Probably wire and rope." The truth was army engineers had chained thirteen barges end-to-end across a narrow point in the river and had sunk nets to a depth of fifteen feet below them. A dozen, smaller fishing boats worked the waters on The Zone side. The men in the boats, sealed head-to-toe in plastic protective wear, went about the endless and horrific task of pulling the zombies out of the water. They would be harpooned and dragged up on to the deck where a single shot to the head would finish them off. Then they'd be flung in the hold where later they would be fished out with a crane, dumped into a truck, which would trundle them off to the fire pit. The smell from the pit was enough to overpower a man.

"Maybe he's right," the old man said. "We should take our chances with him."

His wife hissed: "They don't give chances, do they?"

"Look," Max said, holding his hands out to them. "I'm sorry about whatever happened to you, but not all soldiers are the same. It's not like the movies, we're not bloodthirsty murderers looking for any opportunity to kill."

Benjamin folded his arms and wore a look of self-righteous accusation. "Is that right? Then why did a whole mess of soldiers start shooting a group of unarmed women and children? That's what happened to their whole family. Soldiers just shot them down like dogs and why? Simply because they wanted to walk down a road. That's what I would call bloodthirsty, and that's why, Cheryl, we can't trust them. Now get over here."

"These aren't those soldiers," Courtney argued. "They're in the same boat...so to speak, as all of us. They're not going to be let out of The Zone, either. They're going to have to sneak out just like the rest of us."

"Or fight their way out," Cheryl said. "You guys got guns. I mean really good guns. If we can get enough of us survivors together we could find a weak spot and blast our way out."

Max grimaced at this idea. "I don't know if I can do that. Those soldiers are just doing their jobs. I don't know if I can kill them so easily." The older couple both threw up their hands in anger and Benjamin looked as though he was on the verge of a tirade, so Max went on, quickly: "Also we don't have the weaponry you think we do. All we have are a few M16s and maybe thirty rounds altogether. It's not enough to try to slug it out with entrenched troops. And what if we did get out? Have you seen all the helicopters? They'd track us easily, call in more troops, and kill us. No, the only way out is to sneak out."

Benjamin and the old couple exchanged looks in a silence that wasn't really silent. In the distance, there was the ever-present pop and crackle of gunfire and closer were the odd howls and moans of the undead. A few of them were slogging up out of the water, their feet sinking into the deep mud at the edge. They were harmlessly trapped and didn't rate more than a flick of Jack's nervous eyes.

"Ok," Benjamin said, giving up.

Together with Benjamin, Max helped the older woman out of the boat and then they went to their cars: Benjamin and Cheryl in her odd Juke, the old couple in a 90s model Cadillac, which was the length of a sailboat, and the brother and sister in a fat, white Ford Windstar, the ultimate family minivan. There was red blood on the sliding back door. "Can someone ride with us?" Alivia asked. There was a begging tone to her voice that struck Max hard.

"Johnny, ride with the kids," he ordered. "Keep them safe."

That proved difficult especially as the girl insisted on driving. After hitting a curb, Johnny asked: "How old are you?"

"Seventeen...almost."

"Oh jeeze," he said miserably. They were traveling down the highway that ran on the east side of the river, looking to get lucky and find another boat or maybe another, better armed group who had an idea about what to do. They weren't lucky. There were zombies everywhere, thankfully not in a huge numbers but in groups of ten, fifteen, twenty. Some strode down the road like they owned it, forcing the little caravan to bounce left and right, or run up on the shoulder. They also haunted the forest and would come surging out into the failing afternoon light.

Johnny was lathered in sweat and had done nothing to protect anyone. He had only held fast to the "Oh Shit!" bar above the door and had licked his lips raw in his fear. The girl wasn't a good driver, but she was better than the last car in the line. After having seen their family murdered, the old couple couldn't bring themselves to trust the soldiers and so they had lingered in the rear, fearing a trap. The husband, Gary Reynolds, whose eyesight was failing him quicker than he could keep up with his prescriptions, had a few near misses with the zombies.

Then the small caravan of cars ran into a traffic jam three miles from where I-9 crossed out of The Zone. The cars were hopelessly locked, bumper to bumper and had been since eight that morning. The line had grown during the afternoon as people had come up on it running on their last fumes only to have their cars die in the deadlock.

It was eerily quiet and still.

On both sides of the highway was a strip of grass, boggy in places from the rain, and then forest, hemming in the black top. The way was completely blocked. Not even the strips of grass were clear; cars filled in every available foot of space. Rules and laws had gone out the window in the mad scramble to leave The Zone, but all for naught, no one had escaped this way.

Courtney stopped a good fifty feet back from the last bumper, her foot ready to come off the brake at the least sign of danger. In the back seat, Sundance growled softly.

"I don't see anything," Max said in reply to the dog. The cars were abandoned and the forest quiet.

"Me neither," Courtney agreed. "It doesn't really matter, we can't get through even if we wanted…" Her lips formed an "O" and her eyes opened wide in alarm as she saw sudden movement in one of the cars about sixty feet up the line. It had been just a flash, but it caught her breath right up in her throat.

"Did you see that?" Max asked, edging his weapon up out of the footwell. "Was it human? I couldn't tell."

"What?" Will demanded. "What was it? I can't see anything back here."

"I don't know what it was," Courtney said. "It could have been a dog, maybe." She was unconvincing, even to herself. It hadn't been a dog. The movement had been too…*sly* seemed like the right word.

"It wasn't a zombie," Max reassured. "It would've attacked us by now. It seemed small, like a kid." He gave Courtney a guilty look. He was a little nervous with the quiet and the dead cars, and he really didn't want to go investigate, but if she suggested they should, he wasn't going to puss out.

Courtney felt the same way. "Maybe we should, I don't know, maybe one of us should go check it out."

"Yeah," Max agreed, trying to hide his reluctance. "Will, let's go do this."

Will was even more reluctant and he cursed, "Mother fucker," before he grabbed his mask and his rifle. The two slid out of the Audi, stiff and nervous. They checked their weapons and then slid on their masks. Suddenly, their world got quieter and their vision was reduced, their periphery shrouded. Max pointed at Will and motioned down one lane of cars and then he motioned down the next lane for himself.

There was no need to tell Will to be careful. He jerked his weapon around, pointing it at anything and everything. When he came to the edge of a car, he would leap forward as if he was trying to catch a zombie in the middle of taking a dump. Max waved to him and when he got his attention, he motioned for the man to calm down. The last thing he wanted was for Will to accidentally shoot a kid.

The two crept down the line of cars and trucks and vans, passing about thirty of them when Max suddenly straightened out of his crouch and let his gun relax in his hands. "I don't see anything," he said to Will. "Let's get out of here." Will agreed and the pair tuned back, but only just then, they both heard a sound. Will thought it was a groan and Max thought it was a whimper. It stopped them in their tracks and they looked at each other over the hood of some rusting Buick.

"It sounds infected, Max."

"It sounds scared to me."

Will's mask turned his curse into a mumble and his gun came up. Again, they began creeping along. They passed the Buick, a Rider rental truck, and two Camrys when they finally found the boy. He was just a blur as he tried to hide himself under a truck.

"Hey, it'll be ok," Max said, coming down to the asphalt and trying to crane his head around to see under the truck. The boy, who was maybe nine, and wearing a white and black striped shirt over jeans, slithered to the front of the truck, making a strange sound. It was either very heavy breathing, probably brought on by the extremes of fear, or it was a mutated form of laughter. Either way it straightened Max out of his crouch.

Again, he glanced over at Will. The big eyes behind the mask told him Will thought he had heard laughter, evil laughter. Max wanted to dismiss the sound as having coming from his own fear-ridden imagination, but then the boy popped up from the other side of the truck and he was grinning, white teeth and black gums. His eyes had the diseased gunk dripping right out of them.

"Oh jeeze," Will murmured, bringing his rifle to sight on the boy. Before he could pull the trigger, the boy dropped down, out of sight. There was a blur as he shot from behind the truck to crouch behind another car. Max's gun was also up and at the ready, however he was no longer as nervous as he had been; it was just a kid and for a zombie he was far from threatening. Max figured he was only recently diseased and probably not much of a danger.

To support this theory, the boy hopped up and in his hand was a rock. Again, not much of a threat since Max was padded in two layers of heavy clothing. The soldier began to draw a bead on the boy when he threw his rock. It was a horrible throw. It traveled in a rainbow arc high over Max's head to bounce off the windshield of the Rider truck.

Will fired his weapon a second too late. The boy had popped back down and the bullet skipped off the hood of the car. Again, he was a fast blur, running along the stalled-out cars hunched over. Will sent a few more bullets his way, but they smacked harmlessly into tires or blasted out windows to no effect. The echoes of the gun rolled down the highway after the boy.

"That was weird," Max said, "and a little unnerving. I don't like how fast he was. Give me a slow zom…"

The honk of a horn startled him and he turned back to the others thinking he would give them a thumbs up to show that they were ok, however they were far from ok. The back of the Rider truck had slid up and out of it poured zombies—real zombies. Adult ones who weren't playing hide and seek, or throwing rocks or any other games. They were coming to feast, and there was an amazing number of them. The Rider truck was like a clown car from a circus. They came stumbling out and there had to be fifty or sixty and all of them were between Max and the safety of the Audi.

A horrible thought hit him: that kid zombie did this. He had set up the trap. It was a horrifying idea, but…but it wasn't possible. Zombies weren't smart enough to do something like this. And yet the boy had, and if he was smart enough to spring this nasty surprise, what else was he capable of?

Max turned back and saw that the trap was more complete than he had realized. There were more vans ahead and their doors were being pulled open by the boy in the striped shirt revealing more zombies. Now they were pinned from the front and the rear.

Will saw this as well and, wasting no time, went tearing off in a dead sprint to the west. It was the worst possible direction to run. The Hudson River was not two-hundred yards away; he was cornering himself. Max tore off his mask and screamed: "Will! No, stop!" The man kept running and didn't look back. A good number of zombies gave chase. They were, for the most part, slow and stumbly because of their many injuries, however, some were faster and by experience, he knew they wouldn't stop. Will would, however. Max gave him a minute before his need for oxygen slowed him to half his speed, but the zombies would just keep on rolling right up to the river's edge. He would be forced into the water and with his two layers, he'd drown or slog along the current, exhausted until the beasts caught him and pulled him under.

It was all very clear in his mind and the panic-inducing vision made Max want to sprint east where there was nothing but forest and where he knew he could run for miles. Max held himself in check, barely. East was a sucker's bet. He would, undoubtedly, get further than Will, but he would still be caught and eaten as he laid there gasping for breath. No, the only way to safety was to use his wits. He had to be smarter than the zombies, especially the adult ones who were falling all over each other trying to push through the very slim spaces between the cars.

He watched for a moment and saw in their actions the key to possibly escaping. They were too eager. As if mad, he ran forward, toward the greatest danger and stopped just at the nose of a semi-truck. Like ants boiling out of a kicked-over anthill, the zombies rushed up the gap between the truck on one side and a line of cars on the other. With zombies hurrying from behind, Max waited as long as he dared, and when the ones in front were fifteen feet away, he pulled the trigger of his M16 three times, killing the first two zombies. The rest fell over the top of them in a great twisted mound of arms and legs and grunting torsos.

He then fled up the other side of the semi-truck, using it to shield him from the sight of the ones in front. The zombies on his tail had a very good view and they were gaining, their eager moans zinging up his nerves, making his chest go fluttery with panic. At the end of the truck, he wanted to turn and attempt the same trick, only there were zombies in front flowing around the obstacle he had created on the other side and he was forced to shoot one almost at point blank range. He ducked to the right around a Jeep but there was another blocking his path.

His M16 came up to fire again, but before he could there was a "crack" sound and the zombie spun partially around. Johnny Osgood was laying down cover fire. A modified version of relief struck Max; Johnny had proven to be the worst shot in the company and a bullet meant for a zombie could very well take out Max instead. Still it was better than being eaten alive.

With a side step, Max slid past the beast and then ducked again to his right, this time hoping to give Johnny a better shot at the zombies coming up from behind.

Johnny fired six times in a row, killing the side mirror of a Lexus, the windshield of an ugly teal Ford Ranger, and a tree stump sixty yards behind Max. He also hit two more zombies, killing neither, but giving Max enough breathing space in order to finish his sprint back to the cars unmolested.

Courtney was already turning the Audi and for a panicked second, Max thought she was going to leave him behind, but after three sharp moves that had Sundance scrambling for a purchase on the leather back seat, she stopped and waved him in. Right in front of her Cheryl's Juke was maneuvering in the same manner only much slower because she was forced to wait on Alivia who had tried to forego a K-turn altogether and had swung around in an arc. The Windstar nearly got hung up in a deep gully that had been cut out of the earth by rain. Its front bumper gouged dirt as it struck and then it bounced up. Courtney could see Johnny Osgood gripping the handle above the door and mouthing what looked like a curse.

Last was the Cadillac. It was just sitting there, idling. The three cars sped past it, Max in the last car, waved frantically for it to *GO*!

Gary hauled the cumbersome vehicle around as the zombies closed in. The car moved ponderously, almost casually, its turning radius measuring in yards, not feet. The old man behind the wheel was pulling it around two handed in a manner more suited for a tugboat. It hit the gully with a dull thump and then stopped, the metal of its body shivering as though it were alive. Still moving deliberately and with agonizing slowness, the old man put the caddy in reverse.

Just then, the first of the dead arrived. It wore blood-covered hospital scrubs; its flesh was an ugly grey, but otherwise unmarked. As a man, it hadn't been pulled apart or bitten to death, he had succumbed to the disease, having been fatally infected trying to help subdue one of the first of the Com-cell patients brought into Saint Francis the day before. He had fed during the night and twice that day, and yet he was still ferociously hungry. With one punch, he obliterated the driver's side window.

The old man hollered and his wife screamed. The Caddy shot backwards, dragging the zombie along with it until it went off the road. It plowed across the shoulder and crashed into the trees beyond. This flung the scrubs-wearing zombie to the ground where he tumbled like a ragdoll. Despite the danger, Gary stared back at it, horrified while his wife beat on his arms and screamed for him to go.

Too late, he put the huge car in gear and began to turn the heavy wheel. More zombies came gibbering and howling up. They smothered the car, attacking windows and doors and even the hood. With the old couple screaming inside, it lurched forward and recrossed the road only to go into the ditch a second time, but it wouldn't move again.

The undead beasts dragged the couple out onto the grass and, like hyenas, began feasting on their still struggling bodies.

Seventy feet away Max watched the situation in horrified amazement. The attack had happened so fast that he was too slow bringing his M16 up to his shoulder. Courtney put a hand out to him. "Don't" she said. "Don't waste the ammo. They're dead no matter what."

He knew this was true and he knew their ammo situation was dangerously low and yet…those were people screaming. A part of him demanded that he do something to save them and, another, perhaps greater part demanded that he run away as fast as he could. The two sides vied within him and then rationalizations began to hurl themselves against his moral foundation until it crumbled.

"You're right," he mumbled a moment later, allowing Courtney's words to act as a cover to his cowardice. "We're too low on ammo. We should go." The screams were making him queasy and he was afraid he could also hear the far off ones of Will dying. He put his elbow up on the door and pretended to rest his head in his hand. Really, he was hiding the fact that he had a finger stuck in one ear to help block out the sounds.

Chapter 24

The Cardboard Fortress

5:40 p.m.

Dr. Thuy Lee saw the three-car procession as it streaked back up I-9. She mistook their urgency for designed purpose and pointed Deckard to follow along after. He took the Humvee diagonally across a farmer's field, crushed a wire fence beneath its huge tires, and bounced up onto the highway.

The great beast of a vehicle had no problem catching up and fell into position behind the Ford Windstar. Fearful eyes stared out at them from its rear window. Thuy smiled and waved, in as friendly a manner as she could contrive, but the fear remained and soon the three cars came to a stop and then guns were pointed their way.

"I should probably go talk to them," Thuy announced. When Deckard began to protest, she explained: "I'm the smallest and thus the least threatening of us."

"Check their eyes," Anna Holloway yelled in a muffled voice from the cargo hold of the Humvee.

"She could be right," Deckard said. "They could be infected. That's blood on that minivan. You can tell by the pattern that it's not mud."

"You can rest assured that I will take all precautions," Thuy replied. Deckard, nodded, his rugged face was turned partially towards her and partially toward the cars. He was anxious for her safety. He cared, she could read it in his dark eyes. It made her feel warm inside and she had to hold herself in check otherwise she would've kissed him. She didn't like the idea of kissing him just then—it would seem like a kiss goodbye. There would be too much finality to it.

"I'll be fine," she told him before opening the door to the Humvee. Stepping out, she smoothed the white blouse she had put on that morning, raked her slim fingers through her raven hair and then began to stride toward the cars.

Behind her, Deckard rolled down his window and eased the M16 from its place along the console. He wanted to be ready.

"Hello," Thuy said to the soldier crouched next to the minivan. "I'm unarmed. You have nothing to fear from me." He didn't seem afraid, only wary, however the two teenagers with him were petrified and hid low in their seats.

"What do you want?" a greasy-haired man asked, belligerently. It was Benjamin Olski. He had a curl to his lip and an angry cast to his features. Despite the gun in his hands, Thuy stepped closer to inspect him. His eyes were clear.

She relaxed slightly. "We want to get out of the quarantined area, the same as you," she explained. "We've traveled up and down the eastern perimeter, but there are simply too many infected persons to cross in that direction. The south has too many trigger-happy soldiers; no offense," she added nodding to the other soldier who had come walking up. His name tag read: *Fowler* and his eyes were clear as well.

"Do you have soldiers with you?" he asked, giving a glance at the Humvee.

Thuy shook her head. "No. Unfortunately the area in which we were located was overrun a couple of hours ago and the soldiers there were all killed. We just managed to escape with the Humvee."

"Just managed?" Benjamin asked, incredulously. He turned to the others and declared: "She's probably diseased right now. Everyone knows you can't get too close to the zombies and not catch the disease. It's in the air all around them."

"That is speculation. How the pathogen is transmitted from a human vector has not been determined as of yet, though I would not rule out the possibility of airborne transference in an optimum setting, I am strongly leaning toward a blood borne route as the most likely of the choices presented." The greasy man paused at this, trying to work out exactly what she'd said. While he did, Thuy turned to Fowler. "Tell me, do you know of a way out of The Zone? You're a soldier, I'm sure you know the egress points."

He shook his head, his eyebrows drooping and his face down. There was an aura of grief around him. Even his voice held pain: "No, there aren't any. Once you're in The Zone, you're stuck. The Army won't let you out. Man, I think we're fucked."

"Don't be like that," one of the women in the group told him. She had mop of brown hair on her head that was in need of a brush and her clothes were disheveled and mud splattered. Her entire aspect was one of exhaustion, except her eyes, which were still bright.

"I'm not being like anything," he replied. "What else would you call it besides being fucked? We've tried to get out north, south, and west. They've tried the east. There's nowhere else to go."

"How do we know she's telling the truth?" Benjamin asked, cutting his eyes to Thuy as if to catch her reacting in some other way than puzzlement.

"Why would she lie?" the woman demanded. "You're being paranoid, Benjamin."

"I'm not lying," Thuy said. "Though Mr. Fowler may be correct in his assessment of our situation. With night coming, I don't think we'll make it out tonight. I don't think we should try."

"Wait! Stop," Benjamin said. "What's this 'we' business? We don't know you. We don't know anything about you. We don't even know if you're diseased, despite what you said."

"I know her," the woman with the bushy hair said. "You're Dr. Lee, aren't you?"

Thuy gazed at her, certain that they had never met, so how did she know Thuy's name? The woman didn't have the usual academic air of a scientist, which meant it was doubtful that she knew Thuy by her professional reputation. Few 'normal' people read scientific journals so it was also unlikely she knew Thuy by her published works. And since Thuy wasn't current with social networking of any sort, the woman couldn't have known her face through that means.

This left two options: she was involved in some sort investigative work; perhaps she was a spy like Anna or Eng. However, her attire and her hairstyle suggested she was a local and that left only one way in which she could have known Thuy, and that was by her voice.

"And I know you," Thuy said. "You're Courtney Shaw, the state trooper dispatcher that I spoke to on a number of occasions yesterday."

Courtney grinned. "Yes. I'm so happy that you got out of Walton. Surprised but happy. With the fire, I figured no one had gotten out of there alive."

"It was a near thing," Thuy acknowledged.

For some reason, Benjamin looked upset. "You two know each other? That's rather convenient, don't you think?"

"It is, rather," Thuy agreed. "Since we are not exactly strangers it will allows us an opportunity to integrate our two groups without hesitation or suspicion…at least without unfounded suspicion."

Courtney stifled a laugh as Benjamin floundered in the face of Thuy's logic and cool demeanor. Thuy pretended not to notice. She waved to the Humvee and out came Deckard, Burke, Wilson, Stephanie and Chuck. Introductions were made and that included Sundance who gave a sniff and a tail wag to each in approval. The dog then went to the Humvee where he went about the edges with his nose working overtime and his tiny brain puzzled. He could smell the three people in the back but he couldn't understand why they were there.

The two groups eyed each other in a stiff, formal silence; the soldiers made Thuy's group uncomfortable and Benjamin annoyed everyone as he sneered. He seemed especially putout that Chuck smirked into the face of the sneer.

"So how do you two know each other?" Max asked. Courtney's explanation, augmented on occasion by Thuy, did nothing to ease the tension.

"You did this?" Johnny asked Thuy. "You made the zombies?"

Although Thuy was the smallest person in the group, she somehow managed to look down her nose at the soldier. "I did nothing wrong. My Com-cells, had they not been sabotaged, would've been a cure for cancer. The people who 'made the zombies', as you put it, are in the back of the Humvee."

This spiked everyone's curiosity and Deckard was pressured into opening the back to reveal the handcuffed criminals. Eleven people and one dog stood staring into the cargo area at the three individuals. Eng was a block of ice as he stared back emotionlessly, while Meeks glared and said: "You're all accessories to kidnapping." No one knew what to say to that; they were in the quarantined zone and as far as anyone could tell laws were no longer applicable. They had all been kidnapped, in essence, by the government, and sentenced to death. Each of them had witnessed murder on a vast scale and some had killed what had been humans only the day before. It made the concept of law, alien.

Each had been altered by the sudden calamitous change in their lives. Their inner beings had been reset to a point in their evolution where, as human animals, they could accept death on a daily basis and move on with the demands of surviving, because they had come to understand fully that their time on earth was fleeting as hell.

Anna Holloway understood this completely on a conscious level, which was why she could plot the deaths of everyone around her without feeling the least squirm in her soul. "My hands hurt," she said with a little whimper. "I think they might be suffering from necrosis. That's when the flesh begins to rot from lack of circulation. You can untie me. I don't plan on running. Where would I run to?"

She saw that Benjamin had been hooked by her performance just as surely as if she had a rod and reel. Johnny was equally snagged and even Courtney felt the tug of the elemental cry of mercy that ran beneath Anna's words.

Deckard shut the hatch with a heavy thump and a sour smile. "So, we can't make it out tonight? Is that the general consensus? If so, we need to find somewhere safe to hole up in until morning."

"Nowhere is safe," Alivia said. She was on her knees clutching Sundance in a two-armed embrace. For some reason, he made her feel safer than the men with guns did. "And you can't hide from the zombies. They can sniff you out. I know. I saw it happen to my family and our neighbors."

"It's true," her brother Jack agreed, nodding his head. "I saw it too. And doors won't stop them. The zombies are too strong. They just keep bashing until the wood breaks. Either that or they get you through the windows. Windows are even easier, and it doesn't matter if they cut themselves. They keep coming."

"I know somewhere safe," Courtney said. "Or I should say, safer than a normal house. My trooper station. The windows are a special treated glass and are at least an inch thick. They may even be bullet proof."

The group began to show some signs of excitement at this, but Thuy doused it by asking: "If it's so impregnable, why did you leave?" Everyone became immediately suspicious.

"Because of what happened at Walton," Courtney admitted. "That was a sturdy building and it didn't seem to matter how many troopers we sent in, they all died. I left the station because I was afraid to put my trust in glass and brick, but now I don't have a choice. We can't drive around all night and we can't get out of The Zone, so that only leaves us with hunkering down. And we won't be alone either. Before I left, my lieutenant was recalling all the troopers he could in order to make a stand. There could be forty or fifty men there."

This was the deciding factor.

Courtney led the way in the Audi. She drove at a dangerous speed. The failing light made spotting and dodging the many zombies in the road a difficult thing, however she feared the full night more than she had feared anything in her life. It was childish but it also went along with the evolutionary reset; the night held terrors of the unknown.

Just as twilight was beginning to erode, and the stars were clear as white pinpricks, she pulled into the parking lot of the trooper station. There were lights blazing and Courtney could see a few of her friends moving about behind the glass, but it was eerily quiet and the shadows around the building were intense: anything could be out there only a few feet away.

She slid out of the Audi and called Sundance to heel. In her hand was the Glock. Around her, the others were slipping up close, their eyes staring all around and their weapons at the ready. There was fear in the air, pervading each breath.

Thuy, Deckard, and Chuck were the only ones who seemed unaffected by it. "I believe you might have oversold us on the safety of this building," Thuy said. "For one, it's only a single story. That doesn't allow us any room to maneuver in case one of the doors or windows is breached. And for two, I highly doubt there are forty police officers in that building."

Courtney couldn't answer to the first point since it was logically sound, however, there was no way Thuy could have known how many troopers were inside. "The building is larger on the inside. The troopers could be resting in the holding pens for all we know."

"Look at the parking lot," Thuy said, gesturing with one hand. "There are only seven cruisers so unless the other troopers caught a bus here, I suspect that, at most, there are fourteen men in there and I would wager good money that the number is a lot less. I bring this up only so that the group can decide whether this facility is properly suited to our needs."

"I don't think we have much of a choice," Max said. "We're here, it's dark, and the building looks secure enough. I say we go in."

"Your first two points are neither here nor there," Thuy said, dismissively. "Only your third point makes sense, and yes, I would agree that the building does look secure, but are there other buildings that are more so? A bank for instance might be one. I do not wish to be argumentative, I only want to make other options available to be voted on."

"We don't have time to vote," Benjamin said. Other than Alivia and Jack, he was the most nervous and his eyes sped about with panicked speed. "We should just go in before it's too late."

"No," growled Deckard. "You aren't our leader. I say we vote. Do we pick this place or do we go on and try to find a better spot? All in favor of staying raise your hands." Eight hands went up while only three remained down.

"Excellent," Meeks said, when he saw the vote. "You're going to get what's coming to you. Kidnapping, assaulting a federal officer, conspiracy to…"

Deckard grabbed him by the lapel. "Shut up," he snapped. "Burke, watch the girl. Chuck watch Eng. You, Fowler, watch our back and Mrs. Shaw, lead the way."

"It's Ms Shaw, really, and you all can call me Courtney." Her eyes slid from Deckard's and lingered on Max when she said this. She then went around to the front door of the building and after fishing out her keys, she let them in. "Hello? Lieutenant Pemberton? Renee?"

She had expected to be greeted like *The Prodigal Son* returning, instead Pemberton held a gun on her. "Don't come any closer, Courtney. Let me see your eyes." She opened them as wide as possible and he squinted to see if she was infected. Next, he had every member of the group come forward and do the same thing.

Meeks started in as soon as he was dragged forward by Deckard. "I'm an FBI agent and I am being held against my will."

"Is that so?" Pemberton replied. He looked far from concerned and dismissed the man without another look. He was most curious over Courtney. "Why'd you come back? Too many zombies or too many soldiers?"

"Zombies," Courtney replied. "Out east there was this long grey wave of them. I bet there were at least twenty thousand of them. There was no getting through in that direction."

"Heading east?" Pemberton asked, mostly talking to himself. "Would it be wrong if I said: good? I'm sorry but it's been weird since you left. We've seen bands of them for the last few hours. They're almost always in groups of a hundred or more. Thankfully they haven't come sniffing too close."

"That will change if you don't take certain precautions," Thuy told him. She began ticking off instructions: "Your windows should be covered in dark cloth or cardboard. Basically anything to reduce the amount of light that escapes. This will be made easier when we institute a strict light and sound policy. Next, you'll have to treat every…"

Pemberton interrupted: "Who are you?" He turned to Courtney and asked virtually the same question: "Who is this?"

"This is Dr. Thuy Lee from the Walton facility. She's an expert on the zombies."

Thuy grimaced at the odd compliment. "I'm not an expert on the infected persons and I highly doubt there is anyone who can make an honest claim of being an expert. That being said, simple commonsense procedures should increase our chances of remaining secure in this facility. The infected persons seem to have retained some of their faculties and thus we should minimize such things as light, noise, movement…"

"And smell," Jack added.

"Yes," Thuy said. "Showers should be taken, clothes washed and we should douse the doors and windows with either bleach or ammonia. Food stores and ammunition should be inventoried and all available containers should be filled with fresh water. There's no telling how long the water will remain on."

Pemberton's mouth came open. He was not used to being ordered around in his own station. As he failed to make a noise and only stood blinking, Thuy continued: "Mr. Deckard will be in charge of securing the facility. When it comes to the defense of the building, everyone will listen to him. That is not an option. Mr. Fowler, if you will be so kind as to begin the job of cataloging our weapon situation. Lieutenant Pemberton, will you please take charge of the prisoners."

"Who are you?" he asked again

Thuy gave him a smile, withholding the normal combination of annoyance and condescension she reserved for people who, having not listened to the first response, asked the same question twice. Pemberton's situation allowed for some leeway. "I am Dr. Thuy Lee. I am the lead researcher at the Walton Facility…or, since it burned down, I was the lead researcher. These people," she paused to gesture at the thirteen others, "are survivors of, for want of a better word, the *holocaust* we've found ourselves in. Though I don't assume expert status, our collective wisdom and experience constitutes such and our advice should be acted upon without question or delay."

"I suppose I can see to these three," Pemberton replied. Thuy was not wrong in guessing that his knowledge of the zombies, other than spying on the roving bands of undead from the safety of the station, was almost entirely secondhand.

He stepped forward and Meeks hissed like a snake: "They started this. They are responsible for the deaths of thousands. You should be arresting them. You're obligated to do so, damn it."

"Aw, shut the hell up," Burke said, in an angry drawl. "They're the good guys, dip-shit. And asides, there ain't no law left in The Zone. You, me, all of us, are under a fuck-all death sentence for the crime of being in the wrong place at the wrong time, so maybe you should shut your hole."

Meeks ground his teeth but remained quiet, while next to him Eng shot an eyebrow up. "If there aren't laws any more, you should let Anna and I go. All we care about is survival and we'd be more help unrestrained. It's not like we'd run away. And even if we did, why would any of you care?"

"How 'bout y'all do me a favor," Burke answered, "and go fuck yourselves."

"Mr. Burke!" Thuy said, sharply, in admonishment. When he shrugged and grinned, she took that as an apology and then addressed Eng with an air about her that suggested she was looking upon a lesser form of life. "Laws may be in a state of suspension, however common sense is still in force. Lieutenant Pemberton, if you can see them to a cell."

Pemberton seemed relieved to be following orders instead of giving them and with Burke and Johnny Osgood's help, he escorted the prisoners away. The moment they left, everyone looked back at Thuy. Happily, she assumed command—it was a pet peeve of hers to have to submit to the authority of someone she deemed less intelligent than she was—this constituted the majority of the population.

"Ms. Shaw, I will need a count of everyone in this station. I want names, occupations and any abilities or specialties they may possess. Ms. Glowitz and Dr. Wilson, if you would accompany her, I'd like an evaluation of their physical and mental states. You understand what to look for?"

"Yeah," Stephanie answered.

The group broke up, hurrying to their assigned jobs. Chuck went with Deckard and that just left the two teens, Cheryl and Benjamin.

"What can we do?" Alivia asked.

Thuy had a task that she would normally assign to the two adults, however Cheryl had the vacuous good looks of a girl who had been adorable her entire life. She came across as someone who had never had to rely too strenuously on her intellect, while Benjamin had a slimy, unctuous feel to him. His eyes were those of a pervert's. While Thuy spoke they roved up and down her body, hungrily and she could tell that he was only half listening; the greater part of his mind was on something else, something lecherous, she guessed.

That left the two teens. They had survived when so many adults had died. There had to be a reason; luck only got someone so far.

"There is something I need from you two," she said to Alivia and Jack. "I need you to find a room set aside from the others. We need a place to quarantine any more incoming survivors. During the early stages, the disease acts in an insidious manner and out of necessity we have to keep newcomers from intermingling until we know for certain they are disease free."

"I bet they have an interrogation room," Jack said. "Like with a two-way mirror. We can use it to keep an eye on them."

"Go find it," Thuy instructed them. To Cheryl and Benjamin she said: "Let's go see the rest of the station."

It wasn't much of a building. A squat central block made up the administration and communication areas; one wing held the cells and three different interrogation rooms, while the other held individual offices and the armory. They found the seven dispatchers and the five state troopers who hadn't dared an attempt to break out of The Zone, sitting together in the break room in the main part of the building.

They were a quiet group, dispirited and afraid. After they had been given a basic check-up by Dr. Wilson, Thuy directed them to start covering the windows and shutting down any extraneous light sources. She then had them bleach the frames of the doors before barricading them. Soon, she had the station as fortified and prepared as it could be.

Then came the waiting.

Time became a heavy load on their shoulders and it passed with dreadful slowness. Most of them drowsed but couldn't sleep with the fear building up. Around nine,

Deckard set the first watch and then confided in Thuy: "I'd like to be able to talk to the outside world. It feels like we're all alone here."

The dispatchers had turned off their radios long before. All that had come over the airwaves had been screams, or the frightened whispers of troopers begging for backup as they were slowly engulfed by the hordes. A number of people had used the frequencies to announce their suicides. The radios had been off for hours.

Despite her exhaustion, Courtney flipped through the channels, and as she did, her brows clouded over. "What the hell? Renee, get over here. Try to find an open net."

"What is it?" Deckard asked. "Static?" He'd had a sinking feeling in him that had grown as the day progressed. It coalesced around what he figured would be the inevitable solution to the problem of the zombies: nuclear weapons. A heavy dose of radiation would wipe out the Com-cells and every zombie in The Zone.

"No, not static," Courtney said, her eyes slightly out of focus. "It's the radio channels. I've never heard them so full. It's like there's a thousand conversations going on. It's mayhem."

Chapter 25

The Connecticut Zone

6:51 p.m.

General Collins was living within the mayhem. It felt like a river with a current so strong that it simply swept him along; no matter how he fought back, he was powerless against it.

His command and control of the perimeter was almost nonexistent. The radios were all but useless. Every frequency was jammed with soldiers squawking like birds. Privates were trying to contact their sergeants, demanding more food and ammo and reinforcements. Sergeants were trying to find their men who were scattered without rhyme or reason along a perimeter of a hundred and twenty miles. Half the officers were trying to find their NCOs, while the other half were leading stray bands of men—there were conflicting orders coming from every direction and so much chatter that it was impossible to tell who was who.

With his headquarters company wiped out, General Collins had only his Blackhawk and Lieutenant Colonel Victor to rein in his division. He went back to staring at his tactical display, not knowing how he was going to untangle the mess in front of him. The worst of it was Colonel Montgomery's 50th brigade. Even with the two-hundred helicopters constantly in motion, he had men and equipment strung from Kingston to the Jersey shore.

And yet, somehow he was holding the northern section of The Zone against thousands. Part of that was due to the fact that he had been reinforced by Governor Stimpson. That had been an odd meeting for Collins. Stimpson's trademark tan looked to have faded overnight and he couldn't seem to stop smiling even when Collins had given him an update on his appalling number of casualties. He just went on smiling, his very white teeth showing more and more, as if the politician in him had sprung a glitch.

After Collins had begged, practically with his hands clasped together, Stimpson had taken a cue from the Connecticut governor and had militarized every law enforcement officer in the state and sent them flying to The Zone. This had added to the complexity of the situation since no one knew to whose command they belonged and for how long they were expected to remain and where they were going to get ammo for the myriad of weapons they had brought with them. Montgomery had the idea of using them as a reserve force, but as evening fell, the fighting heated up and he was forced to throw them into the line piecemeal.

On the west side, with the Hudson River acting as a deterrent, things were quiet enough for Collins to begin moving men from there to reinforce the north and south lines.

On the eastern side, things were simply too far gone. The governors of Vermont, Massachusetts, and Connecticut had halted their men at the border and had made it clear that since Stimpson had basically thrown them to the wolves by not protecting that area, they would not send in any forces to participate in joint operations. Each would protect their own citizens only.

There was a lull on that front that wouldn't last. Recon photos showed a great wave of undead slowly but surely baring down on the men crouching behind their improvised fortifications. Connecticut would be hit first and they were the most vulnerable.

All told, five thousand National Guardsmen were rushing into position. Unfortunately, fewer than eight hundred were infantrymen. Augmenting this force was a smattering of companies including the four hundred members of the state's ceremonial militia and a thousand police officers armed with pistols and shotguns.

Collins thought their lines would crumble under the first onslaught. He directed his Blackhawk to the Connecticut border at full speed. It was a thirty minute flight and during that time, he was forced to listen as the FEMA director made pie-in-the-sky estimations of the Agency's ability to mobilize and how they would have the first supplies rolling by morning. Collins wanted to ask how that was possible since four states had closed their borders and Pennsylvania would surely follow suit shortly.

Everyone in the northeast was on the verge of panic. In the face of an unprecedented media blackout, the President's canned responses to softball questions had not been convincing and now a good portion of the thirty million people in the New York area were packing up and heading south. No one knew where they would all go, but that wasn't Collins' problem. His problem was that he had to listen to the FEMA director for another minute.

Lieutenant Colonel Victor gave him an excuse to hang up: "You have another call."

"Listen Rebecca, I've got to go. You know your agency better than I do. Use your best judgments." He didn't know if what he had said was true. She was a political appointee and had never run even a hotdog stand on her own.

The next call wasn't any better. "This is FBI director Ron Gallarti. I need to talk to you concerning certain individuals…"

"Just one moment," Collins interrupted. With a glare and holding a hand over the mike, Collins punched his assistant in the arm. "Why, in God's name, would you put this guy on the phone with me?"

Though Collins was in his early sixties, he was still a big man and his knuckles seemed to have hardened with age. Lieutenant Colonel Victor's arm went dead from the blow. He tried not to let it show how much the punch had hurt. "You've been dodging his calls for three hours now. From what I hear, he's influential with the President. Maybe you can use that."

"For your sake, I hope so," Collins said, and then released the mike. "Yes, Director, what can I do for you?"

"First I need you to answer my calls. You're not the only one who's busy around here. And second, I need the suspects that you have detained. Doctors Lee, Holloway, and Eng. Two are believed to be foreign nationals who are responsible for this act of terrorism and the third is, at the very least, an accessory."

Collins had no clue what the man was talking about and as much as he wanted to apprehend whoever had created the zombies, he didn't have time to play detective. "We have a couple of hundred people who have escaped from the quarantine zone penned up on the football field at West Point. You are welcome to them once it's been deemed they are healthy. Now, I have to go…"

Director Gallarti interrupted: "No. These people are being held at your command post."

"Then you won't have to worry about a trial. My command post was overrun hours ago. Everyone was killed. Now, since I can't be of any further use, I have work to do."

He hung up and was about to apologize for hitting Victor when his assistant pointed at the computer. "You have three more calls in the pipe. This one may be important, it's the Director of the CDC."

As the woman had less actual knowledge of the Infected Persons than Collins, the call wasn't important and yet it was necessary. "We're sending a fourth team by chopper. They should arrive any minute," she told him

"A fourth team?" Collins couldn't recall the first team that had been sent, though he vaguely remembered a few people in blue bubble suits hanging around one of the tents at the command post.

The CDC Director's voice grew sad. "Yes, two yesterday and one today. They were supposed to have gone to your command post but we haven't heard from them at all. We're worried something happened to them, so we are sending this crew to your headquarters."

"In Troy?" Collins asked with little hope in his voice. The first crew undoubtedly died alongside his men and if the second crew had gone to the command post, they were as good as dead also.

"No, your field headquarters. I have the map coordinates as just outside the town of Poughquag. Is that right?"

Collins put the heels of his palms hard into his eyes before answering: "No, damn it. That was overrun. You need to call your men back, do you hear me?"

"I can't," the Director replied in a high voice. It sounded to Collins like she was about to puke. "Cell service is down and the radios are a mess. Can you do something from your end?"

"Me? I..." Collins broke off looking at his display. His was the closest Blackhawk to Poughquag, however a detour there would mean he wouldn't arrive in time to help with the battle at the Connecticut border. There was no telling what sort of shape the citizen-soldiers were in and just at the moment, they were far more important. "I can send another helicopter after them. It's the best I can do."

Perhaps because she didn't realize the distances involved, the CDC Director gushed out a: "Thank You."

When he could hang up gracefully, he asked Victor: "Scare up a bird and a few soldiers and send them to Poughquag. We have a CDC crew to rescue."

"That's in The Zone. You know that."

Collins knew it and he knew that because of the fuel situation and the distances, the closest Blackhawk was forty minutes away. They would be long dead by then. "Make sure they go in full MOPP gear. And don't have them dally. If the CDC crew isn't within a hundred yards of the command post, they are to pull up stakes and get out of there." Once the order was given, he had to turn his mind away.

He ignored the other two phone calls and stared down at the black beneath the gunship. There were no lights. There seemed to be no life. Then far ahead, he saw lights like white stars on the black background of the earth. The pilot headed right for them. It was the command post for the Connecticut National Guard. The chopper hovered in the air as the pilot searched for a clear area to land. All

272

available space was taken up by army vehicles of every conceivable nature, including a few ugly old *Gamma-goats*.

There were even four Strykers and three of the boxy M113 armored personnel carriers. Collins almost sighed in relief at the sight of them. A site was found for the Black-hawk and once it was set down, Collins and Victor huffed it down the road to where a number of tents had been set up. "Where's your commanding officer?" he asked of the first soldier he came to.

"In one of them," the soldier said and pointed toward the tents.

"No shit," Collins said, and then strode past the man. He didn't have time to ream anyone out. The first tent was a makeshift armory and a mob of soldiers and policemen were trying to get in. The second was a med-tent where, already, a number of men were inside complaining of mal-adies to keep them off the line. These men needed reaming out more than the last but again he left in a huff. The fourth tent in line was the Battalion CP. It was crowded with fourteen men.

Victor announced him: "Tent! Ah-ten-hut!"

The men were slow getting to their feet. Most were curious, but a few were angry that some over-decorated ass-hat had come to make the convoluted and dangerous situation more so. Collins understood all too well and, had this been an exercise, he would've done his smiling thing, and asked a few questions and left, but this was real and he had been living it for twenty hours and in a way, he'd been living it for twenty five years.

"At ease," he said. "Who's the officer in charge?"

A small man of about thirty stepped forward and snapped to attention. "I'm Lieutenant Colonel O'Brian of the 1st battalion, 102nd Infantry, assigned to the 87th Infantry Combat Brigade."

"And that makes you mine," Collins said. When O'Brian opened his mouth, Collins sneered it shut. "I know your orders, son. You are not to leave the state, but you are still under my command."

"Yes, sir," O'Brian answered, visibly upset. Again, Collins understood; it was rare for a Lieutenant Colonel to have independent command and any officer worth his salt craved the opportunity. "Let me show you my dispositions."

A large computer monitor sat on a folding desk; its screen was taken up by an enlarged map of western Connecticut. Problems jumped out right away, but Collins refrained from saying anything until he had taken in every detail. "14th CST? What is that?"

"Civil Support Team," O'Brian answered. "It's a team of experts who advise the civilian authorities concerning WMD threats."

Collins kept his shoulders from slumping by the slimmest of margins—more non-infantry soldiers. Almost the entire Connecticut National Guard was made up of them and the interesting thing was, not a single one was under his actual command. Legally, he could only command the men of the infantry battalion because they were attached to the 87th, but not the MPs and the medics and the CSTs, however he didn't have time for legalities.

"Ok, I see what you did, holding the center with your infantry companies and, yes I see the east-west highway is important, but your other forces may not hold, in fact they will not hold. Look at this line from Mount Algo to the Massachusetts border all you have there are two companies of medics and a few hundred policemen."

"It's the least populated part of the state, sir."

"It won't stay that way for long, son. When a thousand IPs come up against policemen with pistols they are going to run right over them and your flank will be turned, just like that." He snapped his fingers in O'Brian's face. "Here's how we're going to do this: you will break up the infantry battalion, right down to squad level. You will then attach two squads to each of the other companies to stiffen their spines, so to speak."

Since the idea was unorthodox and would require a ton of work in a short amount of time, the assembled officers eyed each other with little shakes of their heads. Some even began whispering to each other, something that had General Collins growling: "Shut your mouths. You can bitch later. Right now, I'm not done. We will also pull back all the men you have on the east side of this long lake. We will situate them both north and especially south to protect the approach to Danbury. It will strategically shorten our lines and allow…What?"

O'Brian had been shaking his head and wore a pained look on his face. "The Governor has strictly ordered that the entire border be defended."

Collins' hands went to fists and he was again within an ace of hitting a fellow officer, something he shouldn't have done earlier. He forced himself to turn away from O'Brian and stare dat the map—it was hard to imagine so many men hunkered down so uselessly. "I was wondering why you had all these men all the way down south where they weren't doing anything. I thought you were an idiot."

"No sir, I'm not."

"Good, then you can answer this question: Has the Governor allowed you to prepare fallback positions, just in case the lines don't hold?"

"Yes sir. We have them along these lines…"

Collins smacked his hands together loudly. "Excellent! Then we will pull back the great majority of our forces as I had earlier suggested and we will move all the men out of the south, except of course *Whiskey, X-ray, Yankee*, and *Zulu* companies of the 1st Battalion. They will take over holding the perimeter in these areas."

O'Brian's eyes were wide and there was an uncertain smile on his lips. "There isn't a *Whiskey, X-ray, Yankee*, or *Zulu* company in the 1st Battalion."

"There is now. I've just formed them. Each company will be comprised of two men. They are to watch over whatever main roads that are around there. The men in the south will be safe enough but the men of Zulu company will be stationed on this east-west road and they will be up against zombies sometime in the next hour. They will defend the border with two shots each and then they are to retreat to our premade lines. Now, since there are no questions," he paused to glare, suggesting there had better not be anyone questioning his order. "I need you men to get moving. You have a lot of work to do."

Someone whispered: "Fuuuck." Other than that, they stepped lively.

"Colonel O'Brian. I don't want to get in your way, so I am going to borrow a few of your men and tour the lines. I want to evaluate the state of their readiness."

Collins, with Lieutenant Colonel Victor by his side, went out to where the men waited in the dark. They were strung out in one long, thin line. Where the land was flat and open, there were forty or more yards between the anxious young men. It was worse in the forest where only ten yards would be between them, however with the trees and the dark, their visibility was down to nothing.

The men smoked with shaking hands and whispered to each other, their fear obvious in the high pitch of their voices…and these were the infantrymen! Further on, he came across an eighteen-year-old mechanic who had been pulled from the motor pool and had a rifle thrust into his hands. They heard him before they saw him. He was on the verge of hyperventilating.

"It's going to be ok, soldier," Collins said, though he knew it wouldn't be. The dark was so thick that he hadn't seen the man until he was only a few paces away. What would it be like trying to make headshots under these conditions? Nearly impossible.

"Is it happening?" the mechanic asked. "Is it now?"

Collins squatted down near the edge of the man's foxhole. "No. It'll be another hour or so. Maybe longer. We're going to pull you back a few more miles to shorten the lines. It'll mean there'll be more of you, closer together. And we're going to try to get you some light." He turned to Victor and whispered: "Make a note. I need flares, about a million of them. Also concertina wire, grenades and claymores."

"I'll do my best." Victor appeared skeptical that he would be able to get anything at all. "It's the communications, sir and the fact that every armorer and every logistics officer in the 42nd is somewhere on the line."

After a glance down at the mechanic, Collins said: "We'll do our best."

Trying wasn't good enough. The pair of them, along with a few conscripted soldiers who had been trying to get away from the line by claiming one illness or another, took over half of the 1st Battalion's communication gear. They began to fight their way across the radio-riddled airwaves and time and again, Collins seethed into the mike: "Stay off the fucking net!" as he found people chatting or whining or blubbering uselessly.

His mind strayed to Courtney Shaw as his aggravation reached a peak and he wondered if there was any way to get her help. She had a knack for cutting through the bull and getting what was needed. On a whim, he started to flip through the channels saying: "Courtney Shaw? I'd like to speak to Courtney Shaw."

Eventually a woman's voice said: "Yes? Who is this?"

"General Collins. I need your help."

Her voice was a little thing when she answered: "I think I need your help more."

Chapter 26

Nuanced Murder

7:14 p.m.

Deckard put out a black-gloved hand to the doorknob. In his other hand, was the Glock he had borrowed from Courtney. The front of its barrel was silver with duct tape, holding an empty water bottle in place over the bore. Across his face was a blue surgical mask.

"This isn't right," he whispered and then took a breath to steel himself. He was about to commit murder or something so very close that only nuance kept them separated.

Thuy's ideas to protect the station had held for a good hour and they would've held for longer but people had come and with them came zombies. Not a lot at first and they were stymied by the hot, stinging smell of bleach, but more came at the sound of the shouting.

There had been three men who had come running up out of the dark, their breath rushing in and out noisily, and their eyes wide and fearful. "Let us in," they demanded in whispers, tapping on the door as loud as they dared. No one in the station wanted to open the doors. Each felt bad about not letting the men in, but their fear was too great, even when they knew it was wrong.

"We'll do the right thing," Thuy had said, heading for the door. She barely looked convinced by her own words and yet no one had the guts to second-guess her. Always prudently cautious, Thuy had the men inspected first. Deckard had cracked the door and shone a flashlight into their faces; one had shielded his eyes. They were very dark. "I'm Mexican for God's sake," he had pleaded. "This is always the color of my eyes."

Thuy inspected him as well and she had the same doubt as Deckard. They should have listened to the doubt instead of the man's pleas. The three were placed in one questioning room and that was a mistake as well. Thuy hadn't wanted to contaminate all three rooms if it turned out they were infected.

Now, Deckard unlocked the door and stepped in, confronted by three men instead of one. With the zombies milling about outside he couldn't afford to fire the gun more than once. The makeshift silencer would last for a single shot and then it would get exponentially louder with each shot.

"What the fuck, man?" the Mexican said. His eyes were obviously darker now and his mood volcanic. Yet he wasn't so far gone that he failed to recognize the gun. "What the fuck? You gonna kill me? For what? What did I do?"

So far, he had done nothing but grow too loud. He had screamed to be freed and had beaten upon the windows, and for that, he had to die.

"You know what," Deckard said. "I'm sorry."

The Mexican shook his head. "No way. You ain't no law and I didn't do nothing wrong." He slammed his hand down on the table. "I am fucking innocent! Tell them, Bobby. Tell them I'm one of the good guys. I saved your life, man." The Mexican had been sitting on one side of the table but now he got up and advanced on the other two newcomers with his hands out, supposedly in peace, however, there was a smear of black on the side of his finger where he'd rubbed his eyes. It was like handing them poison.

"Stop," Deckard ordered, the gun leveled. "Just step back away from them."

"Why should I? You are going to kill me anyways, why can't I say goodbye to my friends?"

The wicked gleam in his eyes showed both a burning hate and the ice of revenge. There was no getting around it, now; he was going to purposefully infect his friends. Deckard hesitated at the ugly act before him: he had come into the room with the one job of killing this man. Everyone knew it had to be done and yet no one had volunteered. The nuance between murder and putting this man down like a rabid dog was hard to grasp since he was still talking and walking and generally looking like a human.

"Maybe you should come at me," Deckard suggested. It would make pulling the trigger easier, it would be self-defense.

Hissing, the man said: "No. They did this to me. Out there, they plotted to turn me into one of them. Don't even try to deny it! Bobby I know you were trying to get rid of me and you're still trying. You got me infected, somehow. Admit it! You may be acting innocent now but I know. I know!"

He was loud now, screaming the last word; loud enough to be heard through the walls.

"I didn't do anything to you," Bobby answered. "Neither of us did, so…so just stay back." Both men hurried around the table toward Deckard. He shoved them away with his free hand.

"Go stand in the corner," he ordered.

"Well what are you waiting for?" the Mexican asked. There were only five feet separating them. "You're here to murder me. Go on and…" In the middle of his sentence, he rushed Deckard. It was mildly surprising and he took two steps before Deckard put a hole in his head.

Before the man had even hit the floor, Deckard had swiveled the gun toward the other two men. "Go through that door and into the room across the hall." His voice was slow and even and very cool. Killing the Mexican hadn't been his first morally grey killing. In fact it had been a lot less grey than some, but that had been years ago. "If you try to run, I will put a bullet into your back without hesitation."

The men weren't going to run. They had big eyes, which they kept on Deckard even as they went to the door, and their feet were leaden. They stumbled into each other and it was a relief for them when they finally made it to the next questioning room and were shut inside. The relief was short lived. A heavy crash vibrated along the walls. Zombies were outside the main door.

After a last glance down at the body, Deckard went out into the hall and saw Thuy hurrying up. "They heard," she said.

"How many?"

"It's hard to tell. Eight or nine. It's not many so we're lucky in that regard." She paused and gave him a sick smile before she glanced over his shoulder. "Is it all done?"

"Yeah. We have to get rid of the body, though. We can't take any chances; the germs might continue to grow, right?"

"Normally I would say that was unlikely, however the fungal agent may continue to proliferate and then there'd be spores…You're right. It's best not to take any chances. I would…" Another heavy thud stopped her words. That hadn't been the door. It had been one of the windows being hammered on.

"Don't worry," Deckard told her, giving her arm a gentle squeeze. "The glass is thick. I'll take care of this. You go back and see if Courtney has managed to get us some help."

Deckard rounded up PFC Max Fowler and, once he was dressed in his MOPP gear, the two of them hefted the body to the back door. Johnny Osgood, in a mask and gloves, had his M16 at the ready. "Don't shoot unless you absolutely have to," Deckard told him.

Johnny pulled the door open and then crushed himself against the wall as the two men hurried out into the dark. Between them, the body was heavy, ungainly and they could only make do with a straddled waddle. It was chilling, stepping away from the safety of the building. The night had been crafted out of shadows, which all seemed to come alive, with sudden movement. With their masks blurring the shadows, Deckard and Max couldn't tell if what they were seeing was real and although they had told themselves they were going to take the body to the edge of the parking lot, twenty steps was all either of them would dare to take. They dropped the body which made an ugly, wet, thunk on the asphalt, and then they were sprinting for the door.

Max found himself seemingly running straight into the barrel of Johnny's gun and he cringed a little hoping the man wasn't going to shoot; his aim while in his mask was notorious. But he did shoot and Max's body twitched in one large convulsion as the flash practically blinded him. He stumbled into Deckard, who grabbed him by the shoulder and lifted him off his feet. Johnny fired again within inches of Max's ear and the gun was thunder and yet he could still hear the slapping sound of many feet rushing up from out of the darkness. They were behind him and coming fast.

Someone screamed, Johnny probably, and then he was being shoved through the door by Deckard, and everything was bright and warm and safe. It was the difference between night and day, life and death. Deckard didn't pause to savor the moment, the zombies were so close. He turned and hauled Johnny inside with one hand and with the other, he shut the door right in the face of a swarm of undead. In seconds their hammering hands were added to the din. The building was being assaulted on three sides now.

"Bleach me," Deckard ordered Johnny. Next to the door, they had stationed one bucket of bleach and one of water. With a heavy brush, Johnny scrubbed the two men down. As he was being cleaned, Deckard blew out a sigh of relief and grinned. "I was all set to tear you a new one," he said to Johnny. "I thought you were being trigger happy, but that was closer than I thought."

Johnny didn't grin back. His eyes were haunted. "They were right on you and there were a lot of them. I mean a heck of a lot. We can't go out there again no matter what. We're trapped, man. We are fucking trapped."

"Settle down," Deckard growled. "There isn't any reason to get freaked out just yet. You two watch this door. I'm going to see if we're going to be getting some back up." Before going to the call station, he made a quick tour

282

of the building: the front door was mobbed and shaking under the weight of the blows, the prison cells were quiet. Eng appeared asleep, while Meeks and Anna talked in a low voice. Plotting, Deckard figured.

He then slunk up to the window that was being pounded on. It was in the office wing and he found Chuck and Stephanie sitting in the dark with their knees touching, holding guns at the ready, pointing at the window. "It was the light that attracted them, Mr. Deckard," Stephanie said in a tiny whisper. "We hadn't covered the window completely and some light shone out. It was probably like a beacon to them."

"And it's good now?"

Chuck shrugged. "Ain't no real way to tell unless someone goes out there. Buuut, I reckon it's all good. Those beasties will get bored soon and mosey on." Deckard saw he was trying his best to show an outward calm. Maybe for Stephanie's sake, maybe for his own, Deckard couldn't tell, however he did see in Chuck's eyes that he wasn't nearly so calm as he let on. They both knew something would give: one of the doors, or more likely the glass, and when it did there was really nowhere to go.

Against his better judgment, he inspected the cardboard and the coverings of re-purposed carpet over the window. It was seamless. Then he pulled back the edge of it far enough to inspect the junctions where the glass abutted the wall. There were cracks forming at the corners. They looked like crystalline cobwebs and beyond them were the vile creatures who'd made them. Their numbers were growing with every minute.

He forced a smile onto his face and said: "Just in case, let's find the key to this door." He gave the door a gentle tap; the smile wanted to come crashing down as he heard the hollow thump, but he forced it to stay in place. "It'll slow them down some. Also could you two do me a favor and make sure you have masks."

"We have them," Stephanie held up a pair of surgical masks.

Deckard left with the smile still held in place, however it dropped the second he stepped into the hall. He scowled his way to the call station and was surprised to see all the operators at their stations. "What's going on?" he asked Thuy, hoping they were coordinating a rescue effort, and in truth they were, just not for themselves.

"They're being useful," she answered. That seemed like a good thing but her lips were tight, suggesting otherwise. "Some are trying to unravel the communications mess that the army finds itself in and others are trying to track down different supplies for them: flares and night vision equipment, that sort of thing."

"And what about us? What kind of help can we expect?"

"None," Thuy said in a little voice. "We are in The Zone and, according to some general, no power on earth can get us out."

"That's bullshit," Deckard snapped. He stormed over to where Courtney sat speaking into her headset. He was surprised to hear her lying to whoever was on the radio.

"Yes, this is direct from Governor Stimpson's office. Yes…no, I'm his Chief of Staff. Yes…no, this doesn't fly in the face of your orders. We have been in contact with Governor Allen and he has okayed this. Yes, because it is being considered a rescue operation. Sir, we don't have time to argue. The lives of hundreds of people are on the line and we're just talking flares, and yes the goggles, that's right. Look sir, we have a plane on the tarmac even now. Yes, at Andrews. You just need to give the order. A verbal would do for now and we can follow that up with… great, thank you sir."

She hung up and began running a finger down the pages of a book that seemed comprised solely of columns of numbers. "Yes?" she asked, without looking up.

"We need help," Deckard stated. "Us. Right now."

"Yeah and so do five thousand National Guardsmen."

Deckard took the book and closed it on her finger. "You don't understand. The window in Pemberton's office is cracking and when it goes, there is only a very thin door between us and them and their numbers are growing. So you had better consider using that radio to help us before we have a houseful of zombies."

"I tried already," Courtney answered, her voice now as hollow as the office door. She had begged General Collins to the point of embarrassing herself and he had remained adamant and stoically calm: *I can't and I won't. Rescues have been tried in The Zone and they have all failed. I just lost a helicopter with all on board trying to rescue a CDC crew and another came back with an infected individual. I want you to know, Courtney that I would send out my own Blackhawk if I could, but somethings are beyond my power. I can't risk the lives of the other three hundred million people in this country.*

She had replied with a faint: *I understand.*

"You tried? That's not good enough," Deckard said. "Here you are pretending to be the Chief of Staff to the Governor, why don't you do that again in order to help us?"

"Because there is no helping us," she answered. Courtney had been up for two straight days and now her exhaustion was making her apathetic. "The army won't help us. No one will help us. We can help others, however, and I plan on doing that until….until…you know." She flipped open the book and was about to start searching for the next call on her list when Deckard grabbed it up. He was going to throw it across the room when an odd sound, almost like a gong being struck, echoed throughout the building. This was followed a moment later by Stephanie backing out of the room she'd been in. She had an M16 pointed toward the sound.

"Fix this!" Deckard bellowed, not at Courtney, but at Thuy.

"What am I supposed to do?" she yelled after him. Even though he heard her, he didn't look back.

He ran to where Stephanie was standing. She was shaking so badly that the gun jittered in her hand. The *gong* sound came again. He knew what the sound was and it didn't make sense. It was the sound of someone throwing a heavy rock at the glass. But these were zombies. The two concepts did not go hand in hand, and he was still standing there in puzzlement when Chuck, Burke, and Pemberton came hurrying up; the lieutenant with a set of keys. "What the hell is that?" Pemberton asked. Everyone knew what the sound was and yet no one bothered to answer him.

"I heard voices," Stephanie said, her voice as jittery as the gun in her hands. "They were right on the other side of the window. They were talking." She jumped as the window *gonged* again.

They were talking? The first thing Deckard thought of was Von Braun. He had somehow retained enough of his mind to talk and to work the elevators. It had made him ten times more dangerous than the average zombie. A locked door wouldn't stop someone like him. "Ok, we have to abandon this side of the building. The window will go soon and this door just won't hold. But before we go, I need all the desks and cabinets and whatever is in these offices pulled out and moved into the main part of the building." There was another door that led to the main section. He hoped to barricade it so that when that door failed as well, and he knew it would, they'd be able to gain more time for whatever plan Thuy was concocting.

He had boundless faith in her intelligence.

She, on the other hand, knew her limitations, not the least which was the lack of anything useful to work with. They had weapons, enough for each to shoulder a rifle or a pistol, and they had enough ammo to kill a thousand of the infected persons, just so long as no one missed, and they had enough cars and enough gas to drive in circles for an hour…but they had no way to get to the vehicles without a major battle and, if they could get to them, they had nowhere to go that was any safer than the building they were currently in.

"We need helicopters, Courtney, enough for thirty one people…"

"Thirty one plus Sundance," Courtney said, interrupting.

Thuy tried to smile away the interruption. "Yes, and Sundance. But how do we do this? Can you speak for the Governor again?"

"I've tried. I've even contacted individual pilots and they won't do it unless given a direct order from their commanding officer, and yes I've tried going to him, but he won't allow it without a direct order from General Collins."

"Ok what about…" Thuy paused as the window finally shattered. Everyone glanced up and from the other wing a few of the state troopers came running. "See what Deckard needs," she ordered them. She then turned back to Courtney. "What about tanks? The army has them in abundance, correct?"

"Yes, but they aren't allowed to use them, and they're not allowed to come into The Zone either."

Thuy's patience was wearing not just thin, it was on the sheer side of see-through. Down the hall came crashes of a louder nature as if the zombies were actually inside the building. She guessed that they were. "Fine, let me talk to General Collins." Courtney opened her mouth to try to dissuade her, but saw that there wasn't anything that could change the doctor's mind. She dialed up the frequency and handed over the headset.

"Courtney, do you have my flares yet?" Collins asked right away. "Things are getting dicey out here."

"And they're getting extra dicey over here, sir," Thuy answered right back. "But to answer your question, I do have your flares available, and I can have planes over your positions in forty minutes." Courtney began waving her hands franticly as if to say that wasn't possible. Thuy turned her back on the woman. "However if my demands aren't met you won't see a single candle."

"Who is this?" Collins demanded. "This is a restricted net."

"My name is Dr. Thuy Lee. I am the creator of the Com-cells. I am with Courtney Shaw and a number of other people, including John Burke, a man who happens to be immune to the disease and whose blood may be worth a thousand helicopters. As well, I have here the two individuals who were responsible for sabotaging my work. It is imperative that they be interrogated. We are currently under attack and are in need of immediate rescue."

Collins was quiet for a time before saying: "I'm sorry but I can't. The risks to the general public are far too great. We just can't let anyone out of The Zone."

"We would of course, submit to a voluntary quarantine period outside The Zone. We would be of no danger." This wasn't even close to being true and she knew it. There was no telling how many things could go wrong—the list was nearly endless.

"No, now put me on with Courtney."

"You are declining America's best chance at understanding and perhaps controlling the disease. That seems like an ill-conceived answer, however, let me sweeten the pot. I will deliver the flares on station in thirty minutes if you say yes, and if you don't, I'll fold this shop up. Your communications will go straight to hell and you won't have anything to see by. When your lines crumble, I believe that will present a greater danger to America than we ever could."

Collins pounded the desk in front of him. "Listen, lady that is not how these things work. There are lives at…" he blinked suddenly as the radio transmission suddenly cut out. "Hey! Lady? Courtney?" There was nothing but static coming through. "Son of a bitch!"

He hopped up and stepped out of the C&C tent and stared west where the night crackled and banged with gunfire and the sky lit with hot white light here, and there, as flares were popped over the lines. They had flares, but not many, not nearly enough to last the night. They had even fewer night vision devices; it was the bane of being a National Guard unit, they were constantly using old equipment and, because of the lack of funds, when things broke down, they were rarely replaced.

"Fuck," Collins whispered, as an explosion lit up the night. He headed back into the tent and keyed the radio: "Ok let's make a deal, but I have stipulations of my own."

Chapter 27

The Line has Fallen

8:40 p.m.

The mechanic's name was Cori Deebs. He had floated through high school as directionless as a butterfly and only graduated by the skin of his teeth. After high school, his prospects of finding a career or a path through life seemed just as unlikely, so, along with a friend, he joined the National Guard. There were many perks and not much responsibility: one weekend a month and two weeks in the summer.

As he had only been in the unit for six months, he had not yet had to do his two weeks. Everyone said it was fun and, as of the day before, he had looked forward to it. But that was back when it was light out and people weren't trying to eat his face off. Just then, sitting in the second ditch he'd dug that night he swore he was going to quit just as soon as they let him. A strong part of him wanted to just up and sneak away in the dark, only there were rumors flowing along the line that "they" were shooting deserters.

With guns going off left and right, front and back, he firmly believed it.

"What the fuck am I doing here?" he whispered.

In the hole with him was Specialist Jerome Evermore, a soldier who had been distinctly unhappy going on maneuvers once a year—he wanted to do it year round and if had not been for the fact that he had a very cush job as a buyer's assistant in a sporting goods store he would have joined the regular army long before.

"Pissing yourself," he said in answer to Cori's rhetorical whine. "You gotta grow a pair." Jerome had sweaty palms and his back was drenched, but he was more excited than anything else. He told himself that he was built for combat; it was why he had practically begged to be an infantryman.

"Easy for you to say," Cori hissed. He had been relieved when the lines had been pulled back and consolidated, but he wasn't exactly happy with his Rambo-wannabe partner.

Jerome shrugged. He was sitting hunkered down behind a M249 light machine gun with one two-hundred round belt in the feeder and another sitting in a can just to his left. He wanted more, however, a five-ton truck toting about a million such rounds had broken down outside New Haven and hadn't been seen since. Jerome had many snide remarks about the abilities of the battalion's mechanics.

"At least we know enough to bring extra batteries," Cori shot back, referencing the night vision goggles perched uselessly on the top of Jerome's helmet. The batteries had died two hours before and there had only been a few spares left, either that or people had hoarded them— no one wanted to be without when the shit hit the fan, which was right where Jerome found himself. Lucky for him he had the *Hammer of the Gods* which was what he had named his machine gun.

"How do we know that's true?" Jerome asked. "That five-ton might have had a battery issue, as far as we know. So don't go…" A sudden barrage of gunfire off to their right clamped his lips shut. It seemed to go on and on. Then came screams.

They were bloodcurdling. Cori felt his stomach tumble over on itself and his bowels turn to water. He was quite sure he was going to shit himself right there.

"I should do something," Jerome said, taking the extra ammo and wrapping it across his shoulders.

"What?" Cori cried. He grabbed Jerome with fear-driven strength, pinning him back to the side of the foxhole. "You can't leave. That's abandoning your post or going AWOL. You can't."

Jerome threw Cori off of him. "Keep your hands off me you fuckin' pussy. There are men dying over there and all we've been doing is sitting here wasting our time." Cori, in his fear grabbed Jerome's feet as he was leaving the hole, causing him to trip and go face first in the dirt. Cursing, Jerome scrambled around for his gear and then, after flipping Cori off, began to pick his way through the forest, but just then, there was a roar of engines that came blasting through the woods. A pair of Humvees mounting . 50 caliber machine guns raced by traveling along the dirt path that linked the foxholes.

Seconds later the heavy thum-thum-thum of the .50 cals erupted like chained thunder. The firing went on for a full minute, during which time, Jerome stood transfixed by the sound. There was so much power to it that he felt a rush of adrenaline shoot through his system. Unfortunately, it was short-lived. The guns stopped and the two hummers roared off to another location to fight another battle.

"Son of a bitch!" Jerome seethed. "This is your fault, you dick."

"I saved you," Cori answered, petulantly.

"What? That's the dumbest thing in the world." Jerome pouted as he slid back into the foxhole.

Cori kept his distance at the far end of the hole. "I saved you twice. Once from getting an Article 15 for leaving your post and another from getting run over. Those hummers would've squished you with how fast they were going."

Jerome made a sound of dismissal and then set both elbows on the edge of the hole, looking like a first grader who had just been sent to the principal's office. He sat like this, brooding and pissy, for over half an hour when there came another storm of fire.

"Don't," Cori said.

"It's a hundred yards away. You'll be fine, and don't you even think about touching me. I will break that ugly face of yours, I swear."

He looked like he meant it and so Cori remained on his side of the four foot long trench. "What about waiting on the hummers?" It was a begging sort of question. The hummers could be heard miles away, their .50 cals sounding soft and echoey with the distance. Jerome snorted in answer to the question and lifted first his gun and then himself out of the hole.

"You'll be fine, Cori. You got Smitty and Bill right there by that tree and over there are a couple of state troopers. I bet they shot a lot of people in their time." He hitched the M249's strap over his shoulder and said as he jogged away: "Wish me luck."

Jerome felt as though he needed it. He'd been craving combat ever since he was six-years-old when he had watched the events of 9/11 play out on his TV. From that day on, he had wanted to bring the *Hammer of the Gods* down on the enemies of America, both foreign and domestic. He had never figured "domestic" would mean zombies, but he was more of a beggar than a chooser at this point and he would take what he could get when it came to combat.

Decked out as he was in his normal BDUs with the thick MOPP gear over it, and with the two-hundred rounds slung across him and the bulk of the twenty-five pound machine gun cradled in his arms, and his mask thumping against his leg and his chest rig and his canteen and miniature bible, and everything else a soldier carried, he could barely make jogging speed. He was huffing and puffing up the trail with sweat trickling from under his helmet. Still, he was determined to get into the action and he ran the distance of two football fields in a minute and a half.

The sound of battle drew him on. It was a desperate affair. Hundreds of undead came streaming through the woods rushing up with frightening, hungry eagerness at a point in the lines guarded by a handful of men. They fired their weapons and screamed for help. The soldiers and police in the neighboring foxholes sometimes sent one of their number for help and sometimes they didn't come back. All told, thirteen men lit up the night in flashes as they shot at the barely visible zombies.

Flares could have made a difference, but there were so few of them left that the squad leader radioing for help had been told to: "Hold on, you're on the list."

Jerome waddled through the trees until he came to a point between two foxholes that sat twenty yards apart. There was a downed tree that stood between him and the horde; he plunked the M249 down on it, flicked off the safety and began firing at anything that moved. In the dark, lit only by the blinking lights of the guns, there was no telling friend from foe. And yet he felt safe in his assumptions of what he was shooting at since he had positioned himself parallel to the other soldiers.

It seemed unlikely that one would be in front of him but, after firing for a minute and cutting down thirty or more zombies, one managed to get within a few feet of him. Like the rest, Jerome gave it a quarter-second squeeze and sent eight bullets ripping into its chest. It was thrown back by the force, hitting a tree so hard that it looked as though its head came off. Something round came rolling down a little incline toward Jerome.

It was a soldier's helmet and thankfully, there wasn't a head inside it. "What the fuck?" he cried, staring first at the helmet and then at the ugly shadows advancing toward him relentlessly. A sudden reluctance held his trigger finger from its job. Who was out there? Seemingly, from all around him, both front and back were human sounds: curses and yells, screams: some of pain, some from men giving orders. Jerome began to worry that in the dark he'd been turned around and was now firing the wrong way!

"Hey you guys!" he yelled, adding to the din and confusion of battle. "Which way are we supposed to…"

His words were cut off as a brilliant light lit the sky above them—the last of the flares burst into life and hung like a great star in the night sky. Jerome squinted against the glare and saw the zombies properly for the first time. Among them were a few soldiers, their faces chewed off and their uniforms shredded. They were as horrible as the rest.

Jerome's finger went back to work. He leaned into his gun and the heat of it was appalling, and amazing and fantastic, all at once. There was almost no time to consider what a wonderful weapon he held. Zombies were all over the foxhole to his left. He swiveled the gun to the side and mowed them down, sending fountains of black blood into the air; it came down like rain.

Then to the right were more screams; these were desperate and charged with elemental fear. He swung the M249 back around and commenced to chop the zombies down. There was no time to worry about headshots. The only thing that mattered was saving the men in the holes. At some point in the fighting, his weapon jammed; he cleared it without thinking. Seconds later the first of his ammo belts went dry. Like an automaton, he changed out the belt for the fresh one and then went on firing.

With sixteen bullets left, he ran out of targets.

"Wow," he whispered when the noise of the shooting finally died away and the men began to look up with the realization that they had survived. A few had flashlights and they began to shine them around at the mangled corpses that lay in heaps. Many of the bodies still moved and some of the men began taking single shots to finish them off.

Jerome couldn't waste the ammo for such things and he knew he had to get back to Cori. A part of him was sure that the soldier had shit himself when he had left. But first, he went to the foxhole on his left and looked down at the two men he had saved. One was a deputy sheriff who had been using a shotgun to try to hold back the hordes, and the other was a combat engineer who had built his foxhole with a slide rule in mind. It was an exact rectangle. The two men were covered in the black blood, but no one seemed to care.

"That was quite a fight," Jerome said.

"Was that you working the SAW?" the engineer asked. When Jerome nodded, he held out a hand for him to shake, but Jerome didn't like the look of the blood on it and fiddled with his gun, pretending not to see it. The engineer didn't seem to notice. He left the hand out as he babbled: "You really saved our bacon. I thought for sure we'd be killed. I mean…I mean they were all around us and my stupid gun kept jamming and John here with his shotgun had to reload, like every five seconds. It was a real mess, man. And then you opened up with your SAW and I swear I almost cried." He grinned up at Jerome and the deputy grinned as well.

Jerome soaked it in and would've stayed to hear more of the adulation that he felt he deserved, because after all, hadn't he been a hero? Hadn't he taken the bulls by the horns and laid that fucker out? But an approaching hummer cut in on it. He had to get back to Cori and he had to find more ammo for his weapon. They weren't out of the woods yet…or so he hoped. He liked battle just as much as he thought he would.

"Look, I've got to get going. You two have a good night."

"Hey wait," the deputy called after him. "What's your name? I want to know who I'm going to be buying a drink for when this is all done."

"Jerome Evermore," was all he said. Had there been a sunset in the direction he was going he would have moseyed right on out of there feeling like the hero he was. Instead, there was only the black of night but he still felt his exit a good one.

Feeling pride swell like a sunburst in his chest he went up to the trail and then headed back to his hole and his place in the line. When he got there, he found it deserted. He shook his head, thinking that Cori had chickened out, but then he noticed that the dirt from the hole was in back. It wasn't their hole. Jerome had decided to mound the dirt from his hole ten feet in front as an added measure to slow the zombies down.

This must have been Smitty and Bill's hole. They were from one of the MP companies and he hadn't known either of them before that night. Although they had seemed like stand-up guys, they had taken off. "Or were out there taking a dump in the woods," he whispered. "Hey, Smitty? Bill?" He called into the dark. Nothing.

"Pussies," he muttered and then went to the next hole in line and found Cori messing in the bottom of the hole.

"It's deep enough," Jerome said. "Hey, you were wrong about…"

Cori looked back, but it wasn't Cori in the hole. Even in the dark, Jerome could tell it was a zombie. Cori was what it was eating. "Da-fuck," Jerome said in a small voice as he stepped back. The zombie tried to scramble out of the hole after him and Jerome shot it. He hadn't even been consciously aware of what his hands were doing.

The bullet took out its right eye, vaporizing it before tumbling into its black brain. It slithered back into the hole. Jerome stepped up to the edge and looked in to find Cori looking at him as blood gurgled up from a gaping wound at his neck. He tried to say something but this only caused the blood to bubble.

Though he couldn't speak, his eyes said everything. They accused him of desertion, of being AWOL, of leaving his buddy to die.

"They needed me more," Jerome told him. "That whole section of the line would've…" he had been pointing back the way he had come but then movement caught his eye. There were more zombies around him, a lot more. Thirty or forty were converging right on him. Again, his hands worked their magic and the M249 swung up. He fired in shorter bursts now, conserving his ammo, doing in two or three rounds what he had been doing with seven or eight.

Even while his hands worked, he saw Cori out of the corner of his mouth, pleading something with silent lips. Was he asking to be rescued or put out of his misery? Or maybe he had a note for a loved one in his pocket? None of that mattered. Jerome wasn't going back in that hole for all the money or glory on earth. He slowly backed away until he heard the snap of twigs behind him.

There was relief at first but then he turned and saw that it was another zombie. How did it get back there?

They should've only been coming from a single direction! *The line has fallen.* The thought just bloomed in his mind, taking it over completely. The line has fallen! They had lost. They were surrounded, overrun, dead.

With the last of his bullets, he blasted out the face of the zombie…and then he was running for his life. His gear weighed him down and caught on trees and brushes. The *Hammer of the Gods* was the first to go; without bullets, it was useless. He let it fall. Next to go was his helmet which wouldn't stay properly even on his head. It would slip in front of his eyes turning him blind, making the panic turn him crazy. It hit with a thud and a second later, it was tripped over by the onrushing zombies who were nearly as fast as he was.

The mask went next, then his chest rig, and then his MOPP coat. Now he was faster and he blundered through the forest until he was on the trail that the Humvees had used. He stopped long enough to look both ways. No headlights were in view but there were others on the path. The ones sprinting were the humans—there were not many of them. He ran, angling towards the closest soldier. Jerome was almost up to him, when the man went down with a garbled scream.

"Shit! My ankle, my ankle…"

Jerome barely slowed. The hero in him was dead. There were no more visions of parades or medals in his mind anymore. Stopping to help the injured soldier would only get them both killed. This wasn't Nazi Germany or Iraq where the distance to safety was measured in yards. If he stopped for that soldier, it could be miles before they found safety. And he was already winded.

These were the excuses he used as he treated the fallen soldier as dead already and shied away. In seconds, there was the sound of firing in Jerome's wake and then screams.

"That was the right thing to do," he gasped. "Anyone would've left him." Saying the words didn't seem to help with the sick feeling in his gut that had hit him the second the soldier had fallen. It persisted right up until he came up on a two-lane black top, and then he felt a bizarre sense of relief as if the road represented some sort of safety. He stood on it for ten seconds turning his head back and forth and praying with all his might that a Humvee or a truck or anything would come by.

Another scream, this one off to his right, had him running again. He ran up a treed hill on the other side of the road and had made it halfway to the top when he heard a Humvee barreling up the road. Without hesitation, he turned and charged back down, waving his arms and screaming.

He made it to the road just ahead of both the hummer and the wave of zombies. "Stop!" he screamed with the last of his breath. In his pounding heart, he knew that if it didn't stop he'd be killed; there was no more strength in him to run. With that in mind, he stepped into the Humvee's path. There was a screech of tires and Jerome found himself screwing his eyes closed and grimacing, expecting to be crushed under the machine, only he wasn't, though it was a near thing. Pebbles sprayed across his boots and the heat of the engine washed over him, but the metal grill stopped just short.

Jerome reached out a shaking hand and touched the hood as if to confirm that it was real and then he went around to the passenger side of the vehicle, always keeping his hands on it so as to keep it from simply evaporating back into the night. A window rolled down and a soldier was there. It seemed that he was talking however, no sound came out.

"The line has fallen!" Jerome screamed into his face. "They're everywhere! They're…" Just then, the gunner standing in the turret started lighting up the night with the . 50 cal. The sound was deafening and again the man in the passenger seat started moving his lips and gesticulating madly. When Jerome only stood there trying to puzzle out the motions of the man's lips, the man grabbed him and yanked him close.

"Get in!" he screamed into Jerome's face before thrusting him toward the next door.

The sound of the gun muted the second he jumped into the hummer and he was able to hear his own words: "The line is fallen."

"Shut up!" the man in the passenger seat yelled. He then flicked on a radio on the console. "Delta is crumbling. The line is ruptured in at least three spots. We can't hold any longer."

Chapter 28

Brittle Lines

9:16 p.m.

Seven miles away, General Collins heard the words as clear as a bell. They stung. The line was failing. The men were being reduced to fear-filled children in the face of the horde. He didn't blame them. These weren't other men they were fighting, men who knew reason and fear, these were monsters in league with the night and they didn't need their teeth to kill. A simple touch would do the trick.

This was what was causing his men to turn tail so easily.

"Pull them back," he said. He spoke with one of his liver-spotted hands resting across his eyes, feeling a weariness ache his bones. "Charlie and Echo will have to pull back as well. We can't leave them hanging like that."

There were a number of 'Yes sirs,' but Collins wasn't listening. He stood up—as far as he could in the cramped Command and Control Humvee—and went to the door to look up at the night sky. "Where are you? Damn it, where are you?" Dr. Lee's supposed miracle was late and without it, his lines would continue to disintegrate under the constant grinding attack. And with the miracle? Maybe they could hold on…maybe.

A ripple of confused gunfire erupted directly west of him. Every caliber he could think of was being shot. It was a strange and desperate sound, something he was becoming all too familiar with. His men would fire like mad for a few minutes and then run.

How far this time, he wondered? The new battalion command post was seven miles back from the lines and it still seemed too close.

Again, he glanced up at the sky. Except for the stars, it was all sorts of empty. "Please," he whispered in prayer, before ducking back in. "Someone give me an ETA on those birds."

"We can't, sir," a lieutenant answered. "Our aviation company is on the line, fighting. I have a link with...let's see...forty-six Blackhawks and six Chinooks only two of those are grounded for repairs. The rest of the Blackhawks are under brigade level control."

"Yeah, that's great, but I wasn't asking about *our* birds," General Collins said as more gunfire sounded.

The same lieutenant made a sound of annoyance in his throat. "We can't talk to them either, not by radio at least. I can put a call into Otis if you want. It might take some time since they're probably busy too."

Collins shook his head. Phone calls now would eat up too much time. The birds would either get there or not, and his men would either die horribly or not.

Six miles away the Humvee Jerome Evermore was in, came to a stop. They were north of Danbury where the woods were beginning to thin and little gentlemen farms sat looking expensive and deserted.

"Everyone out," the driver barked. There were six men crammed in the vehicle and three more on top. Another Hummer pulled up behind theirs and an equal number of men tumbled out, each looking about with wide eyes. Although there hadn't been a single shell fired, they were shell-shocked and none strayed far from the Humvees.

"All right," one of the soldiers said in a strident voice. He seemed unnecessarily loud as if the thunder of the .50 cal in his ear for so long had turned him old. "I need you men to spread out. You see that barn?" He pointed and everyone squinted at a building a few hundred yards away. It was only a smear of white in the dark. "I need the last man situated there. The rest of you fill in to this position."

No one moved.

The barn seemed far away, and worse, whoever was stuck sitting in a hole in front of it would have no cover on their flank. Zombies could just curl up around him and take him from front and back.

Jerome looked down at his boots; they were scuffed from the day's adventures and he was just thinking that they would need a coat of polish before the next drill weekend, when the man who had been speaking—his rank, if he had any was lost in the dark—tapped him on the shoulder.

"You. I want you to anchor the line."

"I—I would, I swear but I don't even have a weapon." He spread his arms to show everyone that he wasn't just being a coward, though if any one asked where it was he didn't know what he'd say. Every excuse that came to mind sounded like a shit-ton's worth of cowardice.

The soldier in charge turned to the next man: "You, step up. It'll be fine. We're going to fill in the line from there on." The man whose shoulder had been slapped let his jaw drop and he looked around hoping to see some John Wayne hero-type step forward to claim his spot, but all the men there had seen the horror and they too looked down at their shoes or the grass or perhaps they toed a rock. None believed the promise that more men were coming.

Each man was then picked to take a spot and they left, most with a deep breath and a stony look suggesting they were ready to fight. Jerome watched them go with an increasing sense of relief until the man in charge turned to him. "Here you go."

Jerome cocked his head like a quizzical dog. "Uh, here you go, what?" The second after he said this he noticed that the man was holding something out for him to take. It was a holstered pistol. "Oh…Uh, you want me to…uh take that?"

He was trying to rein in the urge to add: You want me to fight zombies with a goddamned pistol? The idea was astounding to a man who had seen them up close. "Look, I would, but…"

302

"Good," the soldier said, shoving the weapon into Jerome's hands. "You're the anchor on this end of the line. Hold it as long as you can. I promise, we're rounding up more men."

A second later, the Humvees were spitting dirt and roaring off into the night. Jerome squatted down next to a sap-dribbled pine tree with a string of curses whining out of his mouth in a high whisper. Forty feet away someone else was making the same noises and Jerome shushed him, afraid that he would attract attention. He could barely remember the big, manly feeling he'd had not too long before when he had killed so many of the fiends.

Now, he knew only a heart-pounding fear. It grew in his ears and his hands shook. The night seemed to grow darker and darker and then there came sounds from the woods in front of him: the snap of branches, the crunch of leaves, the thump and skitter of rocks being kicked, and of course, the heavy ragged breathing of the zombies.

Belatedly, he checked the pistol: a nine-millimeter Beretta. He counted his ammo and summed up the frightfully low number of forty-six rounds for the gun. Forty-six wouldn't last him ten minutes in battle, but then the accusing face of Cori Deebs came to him complete with all the blood and the bubbles and the pain. It made Jerome rethink the number.

He had forty-five bullets to work with. He would save one as a last resort.

With the sounds picking up, he feared he wasn't far from that moment. Sound traveled far in the night and it was some minutes before he saw the first shadows coming steadily on in a long wave. By then his fear had him almost hyperventilating, and he wasn't the only one on the line feeling it.

A man fifty yards to his right, hissed: "Oh fuck!" and shot his rifle. Other men fired as well, but Jerome couldn't. He couldn't waste one of his forty-five bullets shooting at shadows. With his puny gun, he'd have to wait until they were close…painfully close, and with the dark he feared to take a shot from further than ten feet. He clicked back the hammer as the other guns roared.

But then there was screaming from in front of them. "Hey! Stop shooting, damn it! We're human."

"Why didn't you say so?" the man closest to Jerome asked.

The men in front grumbled and one answered: "Jeeze, we didn't even know anyone was there. Now don't shoot, we're coming up."

"Wait, hold on!" someone cried. "How do we know you aren't infected? How do we know you weren't in The Zone and are trying to bust out?"

There was a general cry of indignation and a sharp-voiced man came walking up, fearlessly. "Look jack-wads. We're from the 643rd MP Company from right here in fucking Connecticut. Anyone want to check my ID? You're welcome to."

"No," the reply came.

"Good, now where is the end of the line? We'll fill in from there." As they were more of a line segment, the man, a sergeant by the name of Segal posted seven men on the far end and eight on the nearer one next to Jerome.

He was almost mewling with gratitude, but the feeling didn't last long. The zombies were coming again. No one doubted it this time and once again, someone whined: "Oh fuck." Most everyone agreed with the statement.

Sergeant Segal did not. "At ease that shit!" he barked.

Men cringed at how loud the sergeant was being and one had the temerity to say: "Shush or they'll hear."

"Let them hear," he yelled back, his booming voice reaching to both ends of the line. "We need to stop cowering in fear and running at the first contact. Listen, boys, Connecticut is only so big and if you keep running you're going to run out of state real quick." The sounds in the forest grew and came on faster. Segal flicked on a flashlight and pointed it outward. "We need to man up, right this second. We need to put a halt to this or our families will be the ones to suffer. Now makes some noise! Louder!

Get mean and get nasty and we just might get out of this alive."

Jerome felt a stirring reminiscent of when he had been wielding his M249 and mowing the fuckers down. He gripped his pistol tighter and gritted his teeth. "Fuck yeah!" he snarled.

"Fuck yeah is right," Segal declared. "Now let's make some noise. Let's bring them right to us and wipe them out."

The first part of the plan was the easier of the two. The men cried out in a yankeefied version of the rebel yell and the zombies came on. In a minute, the firing began and once again, Jerome with his pistol was forced to wait, but not long. Soon the black-eyed terrors came stumbling out of the woods with their mouths gaping and their clawed hands reaching.

With his rediscovered bravado intact, he waited until the first was eight steps away before firing. For a fraction of a second, the light blinded him and by the time he blinked his night-sight back there was another of them charging. At six paces, he put a hole in the thing's forehead dead center. Again, the flash was like a strobe, limiting his vision so that it felt as though he was taking extra-slow blinks.

Four paces: and something horrible and mangled, something that looked like it had pulled itself out of a plane crash came closing in from his right. Another shot and another ugly thudding sound. The night was now a solid inky wall of blackness out of which creatures from hell strode. One monster had its head hanging by some tendons and a xylophone of creaking vertebrae. It took two shots to bring the thing down.

Another was without arms. It waved stubs.

Most came at him with chunks missing, fingers gone, jaws torn practically off and the skin of their cheeks split to the ear. Jerome's bravado began to fade, replaced by a crazy, mindless panic. Involuntarily he took two steps back and then a third.

"Hold the line!" roared Sergeant Segal. "Stand your ground."

It felt as though Segal was talking only to Jerome and with a feeling of guilt, his boots planted themselves as three of the things came at him. The last went down at his feet making a gurgling noise. There were more and they never stopped coming. A man began screaming: "Help! Shit, it's got me, it's got me."

Others wavered, their hearts quailing. The fight was a nightmare and, up until Dr. Lee's miracle occurred, only Sergeant Segal and his booming voice held them in place. Nothing else on earth could have. The old adage that a man fought for his buddy in the next hole didn't have any bearing on this fight. The dark made it seem like each man was fighting his own war, and if he did happen to catch the twinkle of a muzzle flash it wasn't fired from a friend's gun. They were strangers surrounded by more strangers… and all of them were surrounded by death.

But then the miracle came in the form of a tremendous white bird that spat out a series of mini-novas as it banked over the battlefield. Each of the novas was bright enough to turn night into day. Jerome could finally see what was coming to eat him—the numbers were terrifying and yet he was able to fight the urge to run. Finally, he could assess the danger. He even saw that off to his right were a series of trees that had fallen during some long ago storm. They would make an excellent barricade.

He blasted out the useless brains of the closest zombie and then jogged the twenty feet and took a position behind the trees. The zombies came at him and got tangled in the branches or were brought to a standstill by the belly-high trunks. Calmly, he shot them down.

His gun clicked empty just as the flares descended into the trees.

"Oh please come back," he whispered, his head canted upward as his hands went through the motions of reloading. The sound of the twin engines on the Coast Guard HC 144-A Ocean Sentry burrrred away, and for a time, he stared after the twinkling lights, but then the fiends came and he fought in the dark but always with an ear out.

A few minutes later, the plane was back and more flares were ejected and the men cheered and smiled as they fought.

The plane was far from its usual Atlantic haunts where its eleven-hour flight time and its two-thousand mile range made it ideal as a search and rescue craft. General Collins was embarrassed that no one but Dr. Lee had thought to contact the Coast Guard and ask for assistance. They were technically a part of Homeland Security and his mind had been on the purely military side of the question.

General Collins went limp with relief when he saw the large white planes whisking over the lines. "Oh, thank God," he said. After a brief chuckle that was mostly relief, he barked out: "Get someone, anyone in contact with the Coast Guard. I don't care how you do it, but we need to be able to talk those birds and direct them as if they were ours."

The general then radioed Courtney Shaw. "The Coast Guard is here. Tell me, where are we on the second part of our deal?" He thumbed off the mike to listen, what came back to him was the rattle of small arms fire and screams. "Courtney!" he bellowed into the mike. The others in the Humvee lifted their eyebrows and shot each other glances, each thinking that Courtney was likely the general's mistress.

They weren't far off the mark. In the last day he had begun to think of her as, if not a daughter exactly, then maybe a favorite niece, and it had stung his heart when he told her that rescue was off the table, but then Doctor Lee had offered something Collins had been in desperate need of: a way to light the battlefield, a way to give his men a fighting chance, and that had put rescue back on the table again.

It meant he was going against a direct order from the President, and a separate one from the Governor and, of course, common sense, which told him that absolutely nothing should come out of The Zone, alive or dead. But he had relented, though not without a stipulation of his own, one that he was not sure was worth it.

A voice on the radio screamed something about a door that "wasn't going to last" and then the line went dead in his hands. For over a minute he sat with his ear to the headphones, his face was that of a carven statue; the lines in it were deep with worry and his brows were heavy with grief.

"Hold on Courtney," he whispered. He then turned to one of the three lieutenants in the cramped confines of the Humvee. "I need two Blackhawks, right now. Divert the first two that aren't carrying anything essential to a…"

The lieutenant didn't look up from his console. "They're all carrying essentials." He pointed at his screen. "We've got seventeen of them transferring fuel, another twelve are bringing up ammo. These ones near Kingston are moving troops. Most of the rest are overloaded with everything from water to concertina wire. All except these parked south of the Point. Six are down for repairs and the rest are out of fuel, in fact, most of the birds that are in the air are low to very low on fuel. The rest are being controlled at the brigade level and lower. I can try to get in contact with them but communications are still fucked… sorry sir."

Collins ignored the curse words; he'd been cursing practically nonstop all night. "Well, how soon can you get me two?"

He stared again at the screen and spoke low under his breath. Collins caught only mumbled numbers. Finally, the lieutenant looked up, his face had an unhealthy glow from the light of the computer; it made the young man look Collins' age. "Fifty minutes…maybe an hour," he said.

Chapter 29

The Boy with the Striped Shirt

9:43 p.m.

General Collins' bargain was simple in concept, nearly impossible under the circumstances and within the time allotted. All Courtney had to do was convince the Governor of New York of two things: One to ignore the Rules of Engagement laid down by the President, and allow his men the ability to shoot on sight, something they were doing anyway, and two, Collins wanted the use of his entire arsenal.

Basically, he was asking for Stimpson to grow a pair and take some: "Damned personal responsibility for the state he was the governor of."

"And you'll get us some helicopters?" Courtney had asked. "We need them right away."

There had been a long pause, which had Thuy and Courtney glancing at each other, nervously, and then the general had agreed: "Just as soon as I can."

That had been back when life was simple, back when there was only the one breach in the building. The office window had shattered into a thousand worthless diamonds and then, minutes later, the door was attacked. Pounding fists drummed at it and the walls shook.

Doctor Lee had stood there, her face a porcelain mask, showing an outward calm that she didn't feel. She had turned to Courtney, saying: "The Coast Guard has a multitude of flares of all sorts. They also have the means of delivery so the general won't have to divert any airpower he is currently using. Call them before you try the Governor."

She had done just that. It had proved to be the simplest task she had performed in a week. The Coast Guard Air Station on Cape Cod had been preparing and waiting for exactly that sort of call; within minutes planes were wheels up and heading west at full throttle.

The next call, to Governor Stimpson went nowhere. Her name seemed to be flagged and her first attempt at faking her way past the myriad of secretaries failed because just as she was affecting the bored voice of a "fellow personal assistant"—she was finding out the hard way that secretaries hated to be called secretaries—another loud gonging sound caused all the women in the call center to cry out as if in misery; another window was being attacked.

"I'll have to call you right back," she said, as Deckard ran up and began shouting orders.

"I need two men over here, now! The rest of you keep hauling out the furniture. And ladies, if you don't mind, shut the hell up. The zombies still have to get through the doors and they'll be harder to break down than the windows."

That seemed like an obvious lie to Deckard, but the women quieted and went back to work, doing what they could to untangle the communications mess that the 42nd Infantry Division found itself in. He knew the doors wouldn't hold. Whatever evil creature was wielding the stone would probably put two and two together and see that the same stone that broke glass could hammer off a doorknob almost as quickly. When that happened, the halls would flood with the undead.

Only that didn't seem to be happening. The stone-wielding zombie went from window to window breaking them so that soon every office had been invaded and all the office doors were being subject to a relentless attack.

"Ok, let's pull back," Deckard said when the men who had been guarding the doors started to look around in fear. At his orders, the office wing was basically abandoned. Only Deckard, Chuck, Burke and Max Fowler remained standing behind a barricade of desks at the end of the hall. At their backs was a heavier fire door that led into the center of the building, where the others were guarding the doors to the outside, working the phones, or sitting pensively, waiting without much hope for a rescue.

Chuck practiced dropping magazines out of the bottom of his M16 and slapping in a new one as fast as he could. It kept his mind occupied. The sound of the zombies pounding and pounding had gained in volume so much that it seemed to be taking over his thinking. When he felt he had perfected the art of reloading he glanced around at the nervous faces of the others. "You fellas should go on and get inside. Me and 'Ol John here will guard," he said. At this, Burke gave Chuck a quick look, one that was easy to read: *Why the hell are you volunteering me for this shit.* But he didn't say anything, he just rubbed the scruff on his cheek with the ragged nails of one hand. The scruff might have been only a few days old but Deckard figured he would look much the same if it had been a month.

Chuck went on: "I don't got long for this world neither way and John's immune. You two should ju…" One of the doors down the hall splintered, sending shards of wood flying. He swallowed loudly and began again: "As I was sayin' y'all should get on inside."

"The other areas are holding firm," Deckard said. "So there's no need for you to be a hero, Chuck. And you too, Burke."

"I ain't no hero," Burke replied. "I'm jes tryin' to stay alive. Just cuz I'm immune don't mean I can't get my face ate off. I swear that's what I hate most about them, they like to eat faces. That's just about the grossest..." The door down the hall staggered and then sagged in the middle and now grey arms could be seen reaching out, scrabbling at the carpet. Suddenly the desks in front of them didn't look like much of a barrier and Burke felt exposed with only a few pieces of flimsy office furniture between him and who knew how many thousands of zombies trying to bash their way in.

Deckard brought up his weapon and sighted down the length and then made a noise in his throat. "It doesn't need to be this dark. I think the zombies know we're here already, and if not, when we start shooting…" he didn't need to finish his sentence. They all knew that it would be like a tremendous dinner bell ringing and they would come flocking to the feast.

He sent Burke to switch on the lights in the building. It was better to fight in the light and it would chase away some of the fear that was obvious on some of their faces.

Chuck was the best at hiding his fear. Max Fowler, who stood next to Deckard seemed to have the driest tongue on the planet. He kept licking his lips but they would never go moist, not even enough to put a shine on them. He tried to laugh as he said to Chuck: "He's right, there's no need to be a hero, but if you want to be last inside, be my guest—ha-ha."

Now a head and torso dragged itself through the gap in the door, leaving long peels of dead flesh on the shards and a smear of black blood on the carpet.

"Who wants to take the first shot?" Deckard asked.

With a grunt, Chuck raised the M16 to his shoulder. "I'm still getting used to this thang. It looks mean, but it's so light that it makes me a tad nervous that it won't do the job." He was quiet for a moment and then Bam! He fired and his aim proved to be a hair too high; the zombie lost a good chunk of its scalp, but it didn't notice and went on squirming in the breach.

"Hmm," Chuck murmured, squinting at the zombie. "I swear that bullet just jumped up some." He aimed lower and the second shot holed the creature's forehead dead center. "Careful boys, there's a rise to these guns."

Deckard opened his mouth but before he could say anything there was a new sound that was even more frightening than the sound of the eight doors in the hallway coming apart, and the moans of the undead growing louder and louder.

They all turned toward the admin area where a huge banging noise filtered through the cracks of the door. Burke asked: "What is that? A fuck-all sledgehammer?"

"Sounds like two," Deckard said. Each loud bang added to his burden of stress. He felt the stress more than the fear. It hunched his shoulders and made the muscles of his face grow tighter and tighter. "You three stay here. Just keep knocking them down until you feel it's appropriate to retreat."

He left them just as another door came apart and a zombie fell into the hallway. Burke killed it with a single shot.

There were eighteen people in the admin area and not one was moving. Conversations had ceased and satellite phones were ignored. Breathlessly, they stood listening to the crashes. The sound was coming from the incarceration wing. Deckard pointed to three of the state troopers. "You three come with me. If you have masks get them." Deckard only had a blue surgical mask, while some of the troopers had more elaborate, protective masks.

While the men scrambled to put their masks on, Deckard went to the door, but Thuy beat him to it. She came marching up fast with a pistol in her hand. It seemed very large compared to her delicate fingers. "Where do you think you're going?" he asked, very much ready to play the man card and demand that she stay back.

"If that door is about to fail, we're going to have to move the prisoners," she explained and reached for the door handle.

He grabbed her wrist in a soft grip, and whispered: "Be careful in there. Don't trust any of them."

She gave him a smile. It was a small thing that barely showed her white teeth but it was a sweet one to him. It cracked the tense look she'd been wearing all day and it almost made him smile in return. The huge metallic banging was practically a guarantee that a smile wouldn't replace the scowl that he wore.

"I'll be careful, that goes without saying," she whispered. "But...but I'm glad you did say it. I'm glad you're here with me."

His hand left her wrist and slid up her arm. He pulled her close, and despite the banging and the symphony of moans that filled the air to such a degree that it made a few of the women dribble tears constantly, Deckard leaned in and kissed her. It was gentle and way too brief.

The troopers came up and their presence ended it and when it did, Thuy's face twisted back into its tense sharpness, which she hid behind a blue surgical mask. She reached up and pulled Deckard's mask down over his nose and mouth, just as she had done the day before and, just like then, he felt the same electricity at her touch.

Finally, he smiled. Thuy could tell by the new lines at the corner of his eyes. "Alright," was all he could think to say to her. He opened the door and glanced into the incarceration wing. The short hall consisted of the three questioning rooms on the left and a single door on the right that led to the holding cells. At the end of the hall was an emergency exit that rattled and shook under the thundering blows. It wasn't fists denting the door. It was something else, something heavy and hard.

There were two troopers standing halfway down the hall. They held their pistols out but looked ready to bolt. One was Lieutenant Pemberton, he glanced back and Deckard would describe the odd look he wore as "grateful."

"The door isn't going to hold," Pemberton said. "What the fuck are we going to do?"

Deckard didn't trust the wild eyes of the man. They were too unpredictable. "Here's what you're going to do. You're going to leave this to us. I want you to go into the cells with Dr. Lee and move the prisoners to the storeroom. The rest of us..." Deckard paused. He didn't know what they were going to do, really. Waiting for the door to come down didn't seem like much of a plan. "...Uh, we'll get ready."

"Get ready for what?" the trooper who had been with Pemberton asked. He was aglaze with sweat despite the air conditioning that made the building feel like an autumn evening.

"We'll go on the offensive," Deckard declared. "If they have sledge hammers we can't just sit here waiting. So the plan is to kill those fuckers out there and grab up the hammers or whatever it is they have. Any questions?"

"Whoa, hold on," one of the other troopers said. "We don't even know what we're dealing with. There could be hundreds of them out there."

Deckard opened his mouth to speak but just then Thuy and Pemberton, with guns leveled escorted Anna, Eng, and Meeks out of the holding area. When they were safely out of earshot, he said: "There are going to be hundreds of them out there. You can count on it. That's why we shoot fast and accurately. Don't hesitate, don't miss, and we'll be good."

This brought on mumbles but as no one else had a better plan, they went to checking their weapons and gear. Deckard waited until Thuy and Pemberton returned to get the two men who'd been with the Mexican he had killed. He gave them both a long look, checking their eyes and their gums. They seemed clean, but no one knew if that would last.

When they were gone, the men put their masks in place. Breathing through a mask, even the surgical ones wasn't the easiest, but the way these men breathed it sounded like they were panting. Deckard was sure at least one of them would run away, but none did.

The men edged forward towards the door as if they thought it was a time bomb that was only a tick away from exploding and when they were within three feet, Deckard stopped them. He pointed at one of the troopers who held only a pistol. "Put that away. You'll come last and grab the sledgehammers. Got it? Good. You, Driscoll, follow me on my left and Brady on my right. Don't hesitate with those shotguns. Blast anything that moves and then step back."

He then turned to the other two men who had M16s. "You two come in right behind them. Don't worry so much about headshots. Just keep blasting them. Knock them down, knock them back, I don't care. I want our total time out there to be twenty seconds at the most so that means we're going to pop out, start shooting, grab the hammers and get back in. Any questions?"

There were none. There was only fear and men trying their best not to show it.

Deckard took a long, deep breath and then kicked at the bar across the emergency door. It was labeled with a warning: *Alarm Will Sound*, and it did. A ringing was added to the already noisy station, and then a second later, gunshots punctuated the air as well.

It was not a sledgehammer being used on the doors as he had hoped. He thought he was going to pop out to find a couple of Von Braun types, zombies who were still able to think to a degree. He figured he would put a couple of rounds through their brains and that would end the major danger facing the station. Instead, he found himself face to face with a pair of 'regular' dumb zombies and they weren't wielding tools, either, at least not in the traditional sense. Someone, or something had duct-taped heavy rocks to their hands and they were using these to batter down the door.

This was far worse than sledgehammers; it was far more diabolical.

Before the zombies could truly understand what was happening, Deckard fired twice in quick succession; a cloud of black blood misted the air and the beasts fell. He then swiveled the gun toward the gathered horde but did not shoot; he needed to find who had done this, he needed to find the zombie with a spark of intelligence in its eyes and he needed to kill it, fast.

The zombies howled and charged, while behind Deckard the troopers tried to surge forward in accordance with the plan. Caught between the two, Deckard was forced to shoot. As fast as he could, he pulled the trigger on his M16 as he roared out: "No! Back inside. Everyone get back inside!" The troopers were slow to listen and for ten horrible, long seconds, Deckard was alone, facing down a mob of undead.

Those in front were raked by his bullets and went down, while those behind stumbled over their bodies. They got so close that he could smell the putrid stink of their gaping mouths as they fell at his feet. Finally, a hand pulled him back inside and the door was shut on the monstrous faces.

"What the hell happened?" one of the troopers demanded. He was breathing heavily although he hadn't done much of anything but press forward a few feet and then scramble back the same distance.

Deckard's mind was too jumbled to answer just then. It felt untethered from reality and all he could think was to order one of the men: "Check me for blood." A few black spots were quickly bleached and scrubbed and all the while, the troopers waited for an explanation as to why he had aborted the plan. When he finally told them, most didn't understand the worry in his eyes.

"But you killed the two with the rocks," one man said, relieved. "We should be safe now."

"No, we aren't safe. Somebody taped those rocks to those zombies. Whoever it was had to have been in that crowd somewhere." A part of him had expected to see the charred corpse of Eric Von Braun among the mob of undead, but he wasn't one of their number, and worse, Deckard hadn't seen the slightest hint of intelligence in any of their faces.

"If we don't find him and kill him, I think we can expect to see a lot more zombies with rocks tied to their hands and our doors will come down that much faster." That was the best-case scenario. What would happen if the 'smart' zombie remembered how to make fire?

"So how do we do this?" someone asked. "Do we make a foray out there? Do we go on the attack?"

"What about roof access?" another wondered. "We could pop the main guy from up there."

The roof wasn't a bad idea. Deckard put two men on watch at the door and then went to hunt down Pemberton to ask about the roof access and to see if he had any ideas.

The lieutenant was shaken by the news of smart zombies and sat staring at something just beyond his nose that no one else could see. "No...no, there isn't a way to get to the roof from inside. There's a ladder out back but who would be stupid enough to use it? Not me, that's for damned sure. No way, not me."

"What about video feed?" Thuy asked. She had been waiting for the outcome of the battle and had been confused at how brief it had been. She had given Deckard's hand a squeeze when he quick-marched into the admin area, and now she kept close to him, making sure that their arms touched. She didn't want to admit it, but she was terrified and felt the need to be close. This wasn't difficult as everyone had crowded around to hear what had happened. They had been cheered when the hellacious banging stopped, but now they were even more depressed: the news of smart zombies had been coupled with the increased sound of shooting from the office wing where Chuck, Burke and Max Fowler were being flooded by zombies coming through every door.

On Thuy's other side was Stephanie who was biting her lip in worry over Chuck. Thuy squeezed her hand in an attempt to calm her.

"I see there are cameras positioned everywhere," Thuy said, "And I assume there are more outside and that they are still operating. We can use them to pinpoint the "smart" zombies and find a way to destroy them. The obvious question: how do we see the feed from the cameras?"

"Courtney can show you; she knows how," Pemberton answered. Courtney was still trying to get in touch with the Governor and so it was up to Renee who brought the video feed up on her computer. The depression in the station grew as they saw that every door but one was being mobbed by zombies. In some places, they were a hundred deep.

"Where is this door?" Thuy asked.

"The loading dock," two of the dispatchers answered in unison.

"It's empty," Pemberton gasped. "We can escape that way."

Deckard grunted and said: "I highly doubt it. There are too many in front by the cars, which means you'll be traveling on foot in Indian country. That's equal to suicide. Everyone is safer inside until the helicopters get here."

"If they get here," Benjamin muttered, loud enough for everyone to hear. He figured they wouldn't listen to him, since they hadn't listened to him all night. He hadn't liked the way he was once again being treated as a nerd by pretty much everyone. Who were they to judge? They didn't know him. They didn't know he had heroically saved Cheryl from her Ex and they didn't know how he had kept her safe that entire day. He was as good as any of them…except for, maybe Deckard, who had bulging arms and the hard look of a man who has seen his share of action. Benjamin especially didn't like how Cheryl was looking at him—like she had never seen a man before.

"The helicopters will come, I trust Courtney. She's very resourceful," Thuy said as she clicked the screen away from the empty loading dock door. She clicked through the screens before settling on the one that showed the emergency door that led out of the incarceration wing.

At first, all that could be seen was a wide-angle view of zombies pounding on the doors, but then they could see something starting to shove them back. "That's a boy," Thuy said, in a whisper. A boy of maybe eight or nine, wearing a striped shirt that Max Fowler would've recognized was pushing the zombies back…and they were obeying him!

"How is that possible?" Stephanie asked. "Why aren't they attacking him?"

Thuy could barely take her eyes off the screen. She mumbled: "It's a fair guess to say he's infected. Interesting. Very interesting. Is he partially immune just as Jaimee

Lynn Burke was? Or is he under the influence of an opiate or narcotic? Or maybe…"

Her train of thought was derailed as the boy pushed away the last of the zombies. He then left the screen and Thuy had a sudden hot flash strike her. "Deckard! Is there any one left in the incarceration wing? Get them out of there…"

He was already running. With fear lending him even more strength, he threw open the door that led into the hall and screamed: "Get out of there! Something's going to happen." On edge already, the two troopers ran just as the emergency door crashed inwards and the Audi that Courtney had driven that day came barreling inside with a sound like an explosion.

Behind the car came a flood of diseased bodies. Deckard ignored them. He emptied the magazine of his M16 into the windshield; there had been something in the car. Perhaps it was the boy. With only time to slap in one fresh magazine and fire a few more rounds, he aimed this time at the hood of the car, wanting to put it out of commission.

As he fired, hands grabbed him from behind and pulled him into the admin section.

The door was a heavy one and the lock very sturdy, still it was with a sinking feeling that he slammed the door shut and rammed the bolt home. They were running out of room to survive.

Chapter 30

To The Hill

10:12 p.m.

Despite his age, General Collins climbed up on the boxy communications Humvee and stood on its roof gazing west. It was an intriguing sight, seeing the flares suddenly pop into life and drop from the heavens like shooting stars falling in slow motion. He wished he could remain just an observer, but judging by the planes and helicopters banking all over the sky, and the endless chatter of small arms fire, there were at least a dozen battles going on.

Like a teenager, he slid down the front of the windshield, hopped off the vehicle and landed in the grass, easily. He went to the next Humvee over, the "Operations" Humvee. When they had moved the sight of the command post, there hadn't been time to put the tents up and now they were operating out of specifically designed communications and control Humvees. They were highly mobile but cramped as hell. Four men were inside, hunched over computer screens while another five men were outside kneeling over a map that was spread out on the ground.

"What's the situation?" Collins asked.

Lieutenant Colonel O'Brian didn't glance up. "Even with the flares, we're fucked...sir. That first wave crumpled our lines on a ten-mile front and we're just starting to find our men. Some retreated straight east to the second line, but most scattered in any direction but west."

A captain pointed at a spot on the map and said: "In some places we've managed to collect enough men to make a stand, but in others, like at this town of Burrnel, we have a handful only."

"How's morale?" Collins asked. Morale was almost always the difference between winning and losing and had been since the beginning of warfare. Collins frequently quoted Napoleon to subordinates and one of his favorite lines was: "Morale is to the physical as three is to one." Another, further emphasizing the point was: "Moral force rather than numbers, decides victory." Then again, Collins knew that if he had another fully equipped division to shore up his ranks, it would also decide victory.

"It's as high as can be expected," O'Brian answered. "I have no doubt that the flares are helping, but that won't last. The men have light to fight by, but pretty soon that same light will show how fucked they really are. We need more men and I've already used up my reserve force. All I have left is my headquarters company." The men around him looked suddenly uncomfortable as though Collins might send them off to fight zombies any minute, even though it was the dead of night.

"No, don't send them in, no matter what you do," Collins said, much to the relief of officers. "It'll just make matters worse, trust me."

"Then what do I do?" the colonel asked, earnestly. "With every step back my command is becoming more and more isolated from one another and the gaps widen, meaning *they* are getting through. It wouldn't shock me if some came walking up right this moment."

This had a chilling effect on everyone, Collins included. They all paused to look to the west where the lights in the sky were bright but the shadows below were deep and seemed to be moving.

Crouching in those deep shadows, Specialist Jerome Evermore was numb straight up. He was down to his last four bullets and the woods were quite literally crawling with the dead. One of them might go down, but that didn't necessarily mean it was out of the fight. In the dark his shots were never sure; at one point—when he had twenty three bullets left—one went down right in front of the log palisade he'd taken cover behind. Figuring it was dead, he went on shooting the others when, after a minute, he felt something grab his boot. He screamed in a way that he wasn't proud of, and would never admit. He was so freaked that he nearly shot his own foot off while killing the zombie.

There were two other "crawlers" in his tree-lined fort. The sight of them had given him the shakes which continued as his bullets dwindled.

When he shot the fourth to last bullet, he decided he had reached the point where he could honorably retreat. "I'm out!" he yelled. "I'm out of ammo." He was backing out of the little fort when he heard something to his right, moving fast; he was within an inch of proving himself a liar by almost killing Sergeant Segal with his pistol as he came jogging up. "Oh jeeze, you scared the crap out of me," Jerome hissed.

Segal didn't seem to care. "Here's a mag," was all he said.

It was a magazine of 5.56 ammo used for one of the M16 variants. Jerome pushed it back, saying: "All I have is a Beretta. So I'll fall back to the next dedicated line and…"

"We don't have a fallback position yet." Segal looked at the pistol as if he had never seen such a thing. "Where's your weapon, soldier?" His growl was full of accusation. He even went so far as to glance around on the ground as if he suspected Jerome of having thrown his weapon away. Jerome had, but that had been almost an hour before while running for his life.

"This is all I have," Jerome insisted, holding the Beretta out. Surprisingly, Segal took it and then to Jerome's disappointment he handed over his own weapon, an M4. Not only that he pulled two more magazines from his chest rig and pressed them into Jerome's hands.

In a booming voice, Segal called out: "We will hold this line! There will be no running and we will fight to the last bullet." He added this last after he had dropped the clip out of the butt of the Beretta and saw the three remaining slugs gleaming up at him. "Get on the line," he said, unkindly.

"I wasn't going to run," Jerome said, defensively. "I was just down to my last…"

"Save your breath for someone who cares. When I come back down the line, your ass had better be right here."

Segal left Jerome steaming mad. Sure, he had run before, but that was only when he was out of ammo. "And no one else had to fight with just a pistol," he groused, walking back to the downed trees. Two zombies were struggling to cross them; he shot them both from a range of four feet.

More zombies came. It seemed a never-ending stream of them. The line failed not long after Segal left Jerome. Although he was in a good position, what with the trees, the men at the far end of the line were flanked and had to run. They all fell back, but without the steely-eyed sergeant. He had walked away down the line and no one heard from him again. The same was true for a lot of the men. They didn't desert, they either died outright or were turned. The survivors fell back to a farm where they took refuge behind a line of low fences called stiles. These held up the beasts and made them excellent targets, but ammo was running short and they had to fire from up close. When the fence finally failed and the zombies bulled through, Jerome led the shrinking group to the next farm.

They had lost all contact with the men on either side and their flanks were always "up in the air" meaning they were easily surrounded. Jerome asked for volunteers and posted the first two who raised their hands out alone on the wings. It was a dangerous mission and, after they fell back for the third time only one returned. The men ran again and when they stopped at a line of barbed wire, they were bent over at the waist, too tired to be afraid. How long they fought, no one knew. The night seemed to go on forever and the zombies just kept coming, endlessly and they never tired.

"Where are we?" Jerome asked of the little group. There were perhaps thirty of them left and he had no idea how many they had started with or how many had died.

The numbers kept changing as stragglers joined them and others went down screaming under piles of the undead.

In reply to his question, all he received were shrugs. Jerome looked around for the next place where they could make a stand. A hill off to their east would do. It had a sharp face, which would slow up the beasts some.

It also slowed the men…and women heading up it. A soldier next to him tripped and cursed in a high voice. It was only then that Jerome realized that almost a quarter of the group was made up of females. "Well fuck me," he whispered to himself. From that point on he held his shoulders a little straighter and tried not to wheeze so much. It wasn't easy. It felt like he was running a marathon in full battle dress and boots. Even the relatively light M4 was weighing his arms down.

They trudged up the long slope and behind them, the zombies followed relentlessly after. Some were close, only forty or fifty yards back. This vanguard of the undead drove the survivors faster up the hill. Finally, Jerome stopped and pointed for the others to continue. He would kill the closest ones and then hurry to catch up, but as his breathing slackened and the others left him he was able to hear what sounded like the hum of a motor. It was coming from up the hill. Motors meant humans!

With fresh legs, he forgot the trailing zombies and jogged upward, passing the soldiers who were gusting wind in and out. Soon he topped the hill and saw a circle of Humvees. Now, he was even more worn out than the others, and could only point with an arm that he could barely keep aloft. The others saw and some went down on their knees thanking God while others struggled forward.

Jerome understood. Since the moment his M249 had gone dry, he hadn't thought he was going to live to see the sunrise. He had fought, and he had run, all with a certain dread weighing him down, but now there were trucks and Humvees and people. He could hear them in the darkness.

"Wait," he said to the soldiers who were heading for the tents. "We have to form a line here." At their looks, he added: "It'll be ok. I'll get reinforcements and extra ammo.

We'll be able to fight properly." He would also need flares. They seemed far from where the planes were dropping the flares in the west. "Spread out. Don't let any of those things get past you."

He hoped to God that this was an infantry company, but he began to doubt it when nobody challenged him. Heading for a little knot of people he asked: "Who's in charge around here?"

An older man, tall and grey, with three stars on his collar, said: "I'm Lieutenant General Collins, and you are?"

Jerome should've been too tired to care that he was so close to the Commanding Officer of the 42nd, but all he could think of was the M249 he had thrown away, and the protective mask he had jettisoned to lighten his load, and the helmet that he had kicked away because it hadn't stayed in place. He saw Collins looking him up and down and for some reason he was sure, the general knew all of this.

"I'm...I'm, uh, Specialist Jerome Evermore, sir." He knew he wasn't supposed to salute when they were in the field but the hand really wanted to come up. He was able to stop it in mid-salute so that it looked like he was about to karate chop Collins.

The general only raised an eyebrow. "Is there some reason you're not on the line, son?" Jerome's presence was setting alarm bells off in Collins' head. The young man stank of fear, sweat, and battle. His eyes were those of a cat's when it was caught in mid-hunt by something bigger than itself. He looked just as capable of running as of fighting and Collins saw that his mental state could only be described as brittle. That Jerome had deserted his post was a certainty in Collins' mind right up until gunfire started popping off, not fifty yards away.

"What the hell?" Lieutenant Colonel O'Brian asked, in sudden worry. He glanced Jerome's way and saw him fully in his ragged state for the first time. "Who is that shooting? What unit are you with?"

"We're not really a unit. Those are just soldiers and some medics and I think some aviation guys. We just formed up when the line collapsed. We formed a second defensive perimeter but it didn't last. Ever since then, we've been fighting nonstop in a long retreat. Do you guys…Sorry, I mean do you have any ammunition, sir? We're down to our last magazines and there's a butt-load of gray meat heading our way."

Collins started to run to the edge of the hill, but stopped and barked to O'Brian: "Get him some ammo and get every available man over here."

"I don't think that's the right order, sir," O'Brian said, causing Collins' eyes to grow furious. "We should fall back and prepare a better spot to fight from."

"Where? Hartford?" Collins asked with sarcastic acid dripping from his tongue. He pointed east at the lights of the city. "That's only twenty miles away. We don't have a fucking inch of room to spare. If we can stop them here then we damn well better stop them here! I need every spare soldier to get their asses up on that ridge!"

The general jogged to the line of the hill and stared down at the advancing zombies. There were thousands of them. They were like a biblical plague. "I need my damned artillery!" he raged up at the night sky.

"Artillery wouldn't do you much good…sir," O'Brian said, again slow enough on the accompanying "sir" to be disrespectful. "All of my artillery men are out there some-where. Guns won't do you much good without their opera-tors."

Collins was within a whisker of punching O'Brian in the face. He reined it in…somewhat. He brought his hand down on the colonel's shoulder with excessive force, and gripped the muscle there in a hard grip. The smile on his face was evil, but with a touch of pretend friendship to it. "You know what's also useless? You are Lieutenant Colonel O'Brian. Your insubordination is actionable, how-ever I need every man, even a back-talking son of a bitch like you. I'm tired of you undermining me at every turn, so from this point on I want you to take up a rifle and defend this hill."

O'Brian took a step back and his eyes were fierce, as if he was going to punch Collins, and now it was his turn to rein it in. He was also just able to. Sneering, he said: "You want to take responsibility for fucking this up, too? Go right ahead, have fun."

He stormed away and Collins whispered: "Good riddance." Louder, he yelled to the soldiers on the hill: "There will be no more falling back. There will be no more retreat. This is where we draw the line and this is where we make our stand! Your friends and loved ones are counting on us to stop these creatures right here and right now."

"Who the fuck are you?" someone demanded from out of the dark.

This brought a laugh from the general. He could imagine the pain, fear and stress these soldiers had endured, and now they were being told they couldn't run from a flesh-eating horde? "I'm your Commanding Officer and those Humvees back there represent my command post. It's not moving. When I say we cannot run any further, I fucking mean it! Running at this point means surrender. It means we've lost the state, possibly the country and maybe even all of humanity. So we're going to fight. We're going to shred those motherfuckers like pulled pork. We're going to stop them here and now!"

He grinned again when the rag-tag group of tired men and women let out a raucous curse-laden cheer. Their guns began to fire and Collins jogged back to the command post where he was greeted by the stunned looks of the officers. He began barking orders: "I need the miniguns pulled off my Blackhawk, and that goes for every chopper that puts down here. Next, I want those Strykers and Hummers that were sent out recalled from whatever they're doing. I need them to keep a lane open for the retreating men. Next I want the Humvees we have here moved to the edge of the hill."

"But these aren't weapons platforms, sir," a captain said, explaining the obvious. "We don't have guns. We only have computers and comm gear."

"No shit, son," Collins shot back. "But they do have headlights and until we can redirect some of those Coast Guard birds in this direction we're going to help our boys fight. Now get your asses moving."

The hummers and ammo trucks were brought up to the line and in the glare of the high beams, the soldiers saw their peril more clearly than they ever had. They were just a handful compared to what might have been two thousand or more of the undead. Panic rippled along the lines and it grew worse when Lieutenant Colonel O'Brian was seen throwing down his M4 and running. He wasn't deserting; he ran to the field where the general's helicopter sat. Two men, the pilot and Lieutenant Colonel Victor, were trying to disconnect the cumbersome, electric Miniguns from the side of the craft. O'Brian saw there was no time for it.

"Get this bird in the air!" he ordered. "I need your guns on targets in two minutes or there won't be a line left."

The pilot knew he'd be disobeying Collins' direct orders and he paused, but only for a second. "Ok, but I need you to work the other gun. I sent my crew to the line." With a colonel in each door, the pilot, only a captain, lifted off, going just high enough to clear the roofs of the hummers. He brought the bird to hover twenty feet above the slope of the hill where the concentration of zombies was the heaviest. "Remember, short bursts. Don't burn through the ammo. If you're not careful this will be a one minute ride."

"Go lower!" Victor yelled into the mike. "The angle sucks." He had been firing on a downward trajectory and it seemed like a waste that missed shots went into the dirt.

The pilot dropped the bird so that it hovered a few feet off the ground and now Victor and O'Brian opened up. The heavy rounds zipped out at head height blasting apart the zombies to the great cheers of the men and women on the line. Gradually the pilot worked the Blackhawk in a circle, laying out 360 degrees of death. All too soon, the miniguns went dry and the copter went to re-load—the one problem being that reloading meant a trip back to the airbase outside of Albany. The men were once again on their own.

General Collins had watched the scene with one ear to his satellite phone; Courtney couldn't be reached and worse, neither could Governor Stimpson who was, sup-posedly on the phone with the President. "Probably look-ing to fire me," he said to himself. "Which is just fine with me. I need the sleep." He glanced over at the comm unit: he had thirteen calls waiting for him and a battle to run. The calls would have to wait.

Chapter 31

The Escape

10:40 p.m.

"Governor Stimpson, please. Hold for the President, please," she said, her tone was well beyond the point of being snooty. It basically brooked no argument whatsoever and Stimpson's secretary who was well beyond the point of dealing with another dignitary's assistant, even the President's, only grunted out: "One second."

Stimpson was on the line a moment later and he was altogether breathless. "Listen, sir, you have to take this mess off my hands. I've got seventy-eight lawsuits from this morning's incident alone. I've got reporters crawling all over the place looking to lay blame, and you know what the *New York Times* is doing? They're blackmailing me. They just sent me tomorrow's cover with a note that read: *Now do you want to talk?* The fucking picture is of me with my finger and thumb cocked like it was a gun and it looks I'm pointing at those dead bodies from that fucking YouTube video. They're trying to pin this on me, sir. I tried to tell them that it was the army but they're going with this commander-in-chief business, which is completely unfair. It's killing me is what it is. My poll numbers are dropping like a rock!"

There was a long pause and Stimpson said: "Mr. President?"

Courtney Shaw cleared her throat, amazed and dumbfounded that these were Stimpson's main concerns when talking to the President. Shouldn't he be worried about the people who were trapped in The Zone? Or the people out there dying or those already dead? "This isn't the President. This is Courtney Shaw. I had to talk to you and this was the only way, I'm sorry. Your secretaries are tough to get around, and..."

She could feel Stimpson's wrath through the phone line and she was sure he was within a second of hanging up. Quickly, she added: "General Collins asked me to call you."

His voice was ice. "That's a lie as well, isn't it?"

"No, sir."

"I think it is. You see I have a direct line to him. If he wants to talk, all he has to do is pick up the phone. Now, I think you have gone too far this time, Courtney. I'm a busy man and I can't be bothered with pranks. Don't take it personally but you will be receiving a call from the State Bureau of Investigations. Have a nice day."

"Let them call," she said hurriedly before he could hang up. "They can come and arrest me if they want. I'm at the trooper station on highway 54. But if they come, they better come with about a thousand men."

Stimpson was slow to reply. "That's in The Zone, isn't it? Ah, Courtney, I'm sorry, but there's nothing I can do. I can't allow anyone out. It's for the safety of the rest of the state. You understand, don't you?"

He was back in politician mode and his voice was soothing and for a second she really did understand. In fact, she felt a slight bit sorry for him that he was forced to make such a hard decision. But it was for just that second and then she blinked away the spell. "Right, I get that, but I'm not calling for me. I really am calling for General Collins. His men are in big trouble and they need you to step up. They..."

The door to the office wing slammed open and Max Fowler backed out of it, firing his M16. Seconds later, he was followed by John Burke and Chuck Singleton. Chuck smashed his shoulder against the metal door while Burke worked the lock. They then began to heave the displaced office furniture against it to bolster the meager defenses. This door was the weakest point now. It wasn't nearly as sturdy as the one that led to the incarceration wing or the heavy glass ones in front.

Deckard and Thuy came to help, while a few of the others stood around and watched. There wasn't much more anyone could do besides wait for the inevitable. Except for Courtney that is, she could do something. "Like I was saying…"

"Was that gunfire?" Stimpson asked in a quiet voice. "Are you ok?"

"For now…for the minute. Listen, Governor, I need a favor. Well, really it's the general who needs a favor, but don't think of it as a favor to him. Think of it as a favor to your men. You are the Commander in Chief. Those are your men out there fighting and without you they don't stand a chance."

Stimpson was slower to reply and there was a caginess to his answer. "From what I gather my lines are fine, all except in the east and those aren't really my lines are they? Connecticut and Massachusetts are dealing with that sector, so maybe you should talk to them."

"I will if I have time," Courtney said, raising her voice. The zombies were assaulting the door from the office wing and it was loud in her ear. "But you aren't as secure as you think. Remember last night? Remember how we thought we had a handle on this thing time and again?"

"Yes, but the lines are holding. I've seen the aerial reports, the main grouping of infected persons is headed east. They're not my problem anymore."

"Maybe they're not your problem tonight, but they will boomerang. If Collins can't stop them before they hit Hartford then instead of dealing with a hundred thousand zombies, he'll be dealing with a million. With what he has now he won't be able to stop them. They'll flood into Rhode Island and where do you think they'll go from there?"

"Massachusetts?"

"You're right, a lot of them will, but not all. Some will come back this way. Maybe only a quarter of them, maybe ten percent, but how many will there be by then? Five million? Ten? If ten million zombies boomerang to

New York, what chance do you have? Listen to me, Governor. You have the chance to help stop this now."

"The feds will step in before any of that happens. They have to. They…"

A new sound came. It was almost as loud as when the zombies were hammering the doors with rocks. Deckard ordered a man to take his place and then he and two others advanced toward the front of the building. Courtney's lip began to jabber up against the mike. They were running out of time.

"Yes, they will take over," she said, "and you'll be the man history blames. They'll say you did nothing to stop it when you could have. You better believe that's how the President will play it, because that's how he's playing it now. He's going to wait for you to make the hard choices because he can't and he'll blame you if you don't."

"But the voters…you don't get it, Courtney. They already blame me for what happened this morning with that massacre. What do you think will happen if I authorize more force? That's what you're looking for isn't it? You want me to let the general have his tanks and his gunships and his jets. The people won't stand for that."

"That was this morning. Pretty soon they'll be begging for it and in the meantime, Collins isn't looking to harm New Yorkers. He needs the weapons platforms for Connecticut. He needs you to allow New York troops to operate outside the state line. He has permission from the Governor of Connecticut for this and one signature from you will make all the difference. You'll be absolved from the actions they take. You can be decisive without taking a risk."

Again, there was quiet as Stimpson thought through his options. "I'll need to talk this over with my staff."

A gun shot from the front of the building stiffened Courtney's resolve. "No! There's no time. You have to decide right now. Think about it! These aren't people anymore. They're not voters. Please, there is only upside to this."

He breathed out: "Fine. What's he need?"

As Courtney let out a sigh of relief, Deckard waited at the front door of the station, with his mask down across his nose and mouth. There had been more of the rock-handed zombies and they had put three head-sized holes in the thick glass of the front doors. These doors hadn't been designed to be bulletproof but they were close and still they were coming apart under the relentless attack.

Another zombie with its hands covered in duct tape was pushed through the crowd by the boy in the striped shirt. He was the evilest thing Deckard had ever seen. The way he grinned hungrily, and the way his eyes were black and hating but in a gleeful manner, made Deckard's skin crawl. The boy had power over the other zombies. They were unthinking and usually relied either on hunger or hate to drive them but they accepted his guidance without question. Luckily, it seemed their ability to comprehend was extremely limited. They knew to bash and little else.

Deckard stuck the barrel of his M16 through one of the holes in the door and tried to kill the boy. The angle he had to shoot the little bastard was bad; it was too high, and the bullets thudded with an ugly sound into the zombies just behind him. Then he was gone again, hiding in the pack of ghouls that surged forward. Deckard fired through the holes trying to get at the one with the rocks tied to its hands, but couldn't find the right angle and had to wait until it made its first hole in the glass at which point he plugged it straight away through the eye.

Unmasked and unafraid, Burke came into the foyer, pushing past the two troopers who had shied back from the proximity of the beasts. "Y'all look like ya need some hep," he said, genially. "It's like a game of whack-a-mole. Y'all ever play that?" John had many times. He used to take Jaimee Lynn down to the Nickel-A-Play and whack all sorts of moles with her.

Deckard couldn't remember ever playing the game, but he understood the analogy. Hands were constantly grabbing at the holes and ripping at them and when they did, he would step up and shoot whatever beast was just on the outside of the hole. There was diseased black blood running down the inner wall of the door and sprays of it on the outer. After only a few minutes, there was no way to look out.

"This is getting ugly," Deckard said, pausing to reload the M16. He eyed one of the troopers who had a Glock in his sweaty hands. "Step up, will you? The pistol is a little better for this kind of work. Don't worry. We'll bleach you down when you're done." A question came to mind: who would bleach the last man in the foyer when the door finally caved? No answer came to that, probably because at that point no one would be worried about germs.

He had the other trooper give him and his weapon a scrub down making his eyes water with the chemical stench. When he was clean, he went into the lobby and stepped around the backup barricade Dr. Wilson was constructing from what was left of the furniture. He had the two teens along with a dead-tired looking Stephanie Glowitz helping him.

"Maybe you should take a break," he suggested to her. "I can get one of the state troopers to take your place."

She shook her head but began coughing, making a wet sound. The two teens backed away, fearing that she might have the zombie disease. Dr. Wilson put a hand on their backs to steady them. "Don't worry. She doesn't have the sickness you're afraid of. She's sick with something else. Please, Stephanie. Go take a seat. Why don't you guard the prisoners and send me one of those two in the back. They haven't done anything all evening as far as I know."

They all knew to whom he was referring.

Cheryl had stayed as far from any action as humanly possible, which meant she was generally far from anything that could be considered work. Thuy had volunteered her to watch over the prisoners, mainly because she figured that, cuffed as they were, they weren't going to be a danger, and it wasn't like they were going to run away. Thuy also chose Benjamin because it was clear that he wasn't going to leave her side no matter what. He was as bad as Sundance who sat next to Courtney Shaw and wouldn't budge. In the dog, it was endearing; in the human, it was skeevy.

"There won't be a helicopter," Eng said, suddenly, and to no one in particular. The prisoners were sitting on the bare floor of a storeroom that sat just off the loading dock door. No one had spoken much. Anna had tried to nap, laying her head on Meeks' lap. He hadn't said no to this but not because of a sexual reason. She seemed to have had a rough time of it. Her hand was mangled and swollen, her face was bruised and cut in places. Supposedly, she'd had a part in the tragedy that had befallen them, but Meeks had a hard time believing it.

The two men who had come in with the now dead Mexican had been shunned by the others and sat as far from the rest as possible. One was named Bob and the other, Allen. They glanced at each other and then at Eng. "What are you talking about?" Bob asked.

"Just that there won't be a helicopter. Where will it land? You heard them, there's no roof access. That means we'll have to go out there. We'd have to fight our way through a mob of zombies."

"Not if we take the back door," Benjamin said, jerking his thumb toward the loading dock. "There aren't any zombies out there."

Eng smirked at this. "No zombies and you're still sitting here? Wow."

Cheryl's dull eyes sparked at this. "What do you mean, wow? Are you saying we should go out there? That's idiotic when there is a helicopter coming."

"Oh, you are so young and naive," Eng said, shaking his head, wearing a rueful smile. Anna gave him a sharp look that no one saw but him. There had been a question in the look and he answered, warning her to keep quiet with the tiniest shake of his head. "You don't know these people like I do. Lying is second nature to them just as backstabbing is. You should ask them how they managed to get out of Walton when so many others died or were infected. You better believe it that if there is a helicopter, I won't be on it and neither will Anna. We know the truth and they can't let that get out."

"Well, that sucks for you," Benjamin replied in his usual abrasive fashion.

"It sucks for you as well," Eng said, easily as if he hadn't heard the pettiness in the man's voice. "Even if there is a helicopter coming, do you think you'll be on it? *They* take care of their own inner circle of friends, which I can tell you're not a part of. Besides how many people are here? Thirty, forty? And how many will fit on a helicopter?"

"Eleven, I think," Meeks answered. His face was suddenly the color of curdled milk.

"Maybe they'll make a second trip?" Cheryl suggested.

"Will we last that long?" Eng asked. "There's no way. You can hear them coming through the doors." They all paused and sure enough, the banging and the shooting intensified. "If I was you, I'd hightail it out of here as fast as you could. I'd rather run or try to make it to the cars than just sit here waiting until you're left behind."

Benjamin and Cheryl shared a look. "What do you think?" Cheryl asked, her face close to Benjamin's as if she was sharing a secret.

"Wait here," he said and then slipped out the door. He tiptoed down the hall to the call station and saw the fear on everyone's faces. He saw the barricades that were being set up inside the lobby area and he heard the crash of rocks on metal and on glass. What he didn't hear was the thrum of helicopters. They were minutes from death and where were the helicopters? One look at Dr. Lee and her oh-so-superior eyes and Benjamin turned back to where he had left Cheryl.

"We're getting out of here," he said, breathlessly to her, pulling her to her feet. "The doors aren't going to hold. The zombies are almost through and there's no sign of a helicopter."

She made a whining sound in her throat as she nodded. Cheryl had a measly .38 and she wasn't even comfortable with that small of a weapon. Benjamin had a shot-gun that held three shells in the chamber. He had felt tough with it when the Lieutenant Pemberton had given it to him, now he was starting to second-guess the weapon. Three shots wasn't much, not compared to the thirty in an M16. He had been thinking for some time that they had cheated him and now with the seed planted in his head that once again he was only a nerd in their eyes, a second-class citi-zen, he was sure the gun wasn't top of the line.

But it would have to do.

They started for the door and Anna pushed herself up. "Hey! What about us? You can't just leave us."

"I think I can," Benjamin said.

"I'll scream," she warned. "You won't get too far if I do."

He brought the shotgun up to his shoulder and walked right up to her so that the fat bore of the gun was shoved into her throat. "I'll kill you if you do," he whispered. "I'll say you were trying to escape. I'll kill all of you." His eyes displayed the panic in him and Anna saw she had made the wrong play.

"Ok, Ben. I won't scream. Just take it easy."

"Easy-peasey," he replied and then backed away with the gun still pointed at her. He walked into the wall, checked behind him and then backed out of the room.

Cheryl was dancing from foot to foot, her face was screwed up in fear, making her ugly. "I don't know about this, Ben. Maybe they'll let us on the helicopter." She was actually thinking that maybe they would let *her* on the he-licopter, but she didn't know for sure. Normally, because of her looks she would've been a shoe-in for the first ride out, only things were all sorts of weird. She had tried to break away from Benjamin's clinging grasp when they had first arrived at the station, but the cops had acted strange. They had kept to themselves and spoke only in whispers. She guessed that they had done something, or perhaps many somethings evil.

The other men weren't all that open to her advances, either. Deckard and Chuck had their eyes on other girls,

Dr. Wilson was old, Burke was sick, Max was married and Johnny Osgood was weak and she didn't trust him. This just left Benjamin, and now she felt she was stuck with him. So far, at least, he had done his job; he had kept her safe. She was sure he would give up his life for hers. There wasn't a chance in hell she would ever return the favor.

"We don't have a choice," Benjamin told her as he tugged her to the door. "This could be our only chance and I don't want to bet my life on the kindness of those strangers. We'll just make a run for the Juke and find a better place. Remember what that Asian chick said about hiding in a bank? It isn't a bad idea. No one's getting in a bank. Now, get your keys out." As she dug in her pocket, he leaned his ear to the door. Up from the cool metal came the vibrations shaking the building. They hummed down his ear canal and right into his soul. The station wasn't going to last. It made opening the door into the unknown that much easier—that and the fact there wasn't a whisper coming from the other side of the door.

"Let's go," he said, taking Cheryl's hand and holding the shotgun in the other—there was no way he'd be able to shoot the weapon like this, one handed, but he thought he looked cool. Luckily for him, there wasn't anything to shoot. The back of the building was dark to the point they couldn't see the woods twenty yards away. To their right was a green garbage dumpster; to their left a short wall that led to the single reinforced loading door that was in the down position and locked with a heavy Yale padlock. In front of them was a ramp that led to a back street.

They went down it hand in hand—his was wet with sweat, as was his face and hair. Under his arms were dark crescents that were spreading quickly. Cheryl was chilled and she shook. Half her attention was on Benjamin; she was worried he would just run away at the slightest hint of danger, and there were many hints. The back of the station might have been free of the zombies, but there were things moving in the trees. Branches snapped and leaves crackled. They could hear ugly moans that weren't human.

"This way," Benjamin said in voice so high that he sounded as if someone had his balls in a vice. His contorted face expressed something similar. He pulled her along, hurrying for the side of the building, stopping just shy of the corner. He actually thought it was a secret that he was petrified with fear, even though he was almost hyperventilating. "W-we j-just have t-to get around the next s-side of the b-building and we'll be in the clear."

Finally, he decided it was time to let go of her hand, only his fingers were confused by the concept and they tangled momentarily until they both snatched their hands back. He took the shotgun in a tight grip. "Ok, here we g-go. No matter what you d-do, don't drop the keys. Girls always drop the keys in the movies."

"I'm not going to drop them," Cheryl replied, angrily. "I'm not an idiot."

He gave her a look that suggested he didn't quite believe her. With a final shaking breath, he went around the corner, leading with the shotgun. What he saw caused him to stop short and when Cheryl bumped into him, he nearly pulled the trigger.

On the east side of the building there was a tall tree that grew not far from the station. It had long, dipping branches that were constantly in need of pruning and during the afternoons, they threw down a soft shade over the building. Now it was psychedelically shadowed beneath the tree. There was no wind, but the shadows moved and swayed...and moaned. There were zombies beneath the tree, a strange line of them. They stood shoulder to shoulder but didn't advance.

Benjamin didn't stop to question why. Foolishly, he assumed the beasts couldn't see in the dark. Why else would they just stand there? With this erroneous thought guiding him, he pointed to the forest, because what was darker than that? Cheryl shook her head and mouthed the word: 'No.' For her the forest was just too frightening.

"They can't see in the dark," Benjamin whispered in her ear. "Let's go." She was resolved not to do something as stupid as going into the forest at night, however a little thing caused her to hesitate; Benjamin's breath smelled of decay and onions. It was ghastly. She'd been smelling it all day, but when he coated her with it directly like that, her face squinched up and she waved a hand—but she didn't say 'No" to his plan, and worse, he was already creeping away from the building.

Cheryl had to hurry to catch up. The .38 in her hand was shaking as she had it pointing toward the forest. She reached out with her free hand to grab the back of Benjamin's shirt; a part of her thought that he would run away from her if she didn't hold on.

For his part, he hid behind the shotgun, holding it far out in front of himself, not bolstering it against his shoulder as he should have. It was as if he didn't trust the night or his eyes, or he feared that there might be invisible creatures just in front of him that he would be able uncover with the tip of the gun.

The forest immediately at hand was loose in their vision; the trees were not straight and proper as they were in the light. They were amorphous in their structure, seeming to grow or shrink depending on the movement of one's eyes. Thirty feet from the forest, halfway between the abstract nature of the forest and the literal concrete of man, Cheryl stopped and pulled back on Benjamin's shirt, untucking it and gagging him at the collar.

"Something moved," she hissed. "Right there."

"It was just your eyes playing tricks on you," Benjamin replied. "You're being hysterical." He started edging forward and despite his words, he shied away from the area to which she had had pointed. At twenty feet away, she pulled on his shirt again. There was no need for whispering this time because the movement had been accompanied by a grunt and a snort, and Benjamin couldn't chalk that up to an over-excited woman.

The pair froze as a dim shape materialized in the dark. It was a zombie, tall and gruesome. It had only one arm left to it and even that wasn't completely whole. It reached for the pair, straining, but not moving forward. Another one was just next to it and it too was reaching with the tips of its fingers curling and uncurling in desire. And it too was held back by an invisible force.

Only when Benjamin shifted to his right, in the direction of the loading dock, did he see the ropes around their necks. Someone had tethered the zombies in place. There were more of them along the wood line. Benjamin and Cheryl slowly backed away confused and more frightened than if the beasts had simply charged them. They had no clue what was going on, however they both knew on a gut level that there was something sinister about the way the zombies were roped in place. It felt like a trap had been set but neither of the pair was keen enough to realize that it had been sprung already.

They backed away with guns pointed out at the forest and it wasn't until a grunt sounded behind them that they turned. Now, zombies were charging from around the other side of the building cutting off all escape. They were strange, silent zombies that ate up the distance between them and their victims, quickly.

Benjamin felt his bowels turn to water and with a scream on his lips, he fled, leaving Cheryl who had frozen in fear. She managed one shot with her pistol before they were on her, grunting and making a noise that sounded like: "Mmmph," over and over. She screamed a note that was similar to a train's whistle: high, long and piercing.

Her one-time hero didn't get very far. When he had turned to run away, he saw the entirety of the trap. The forest was lined with tethered zombies as was other side of the building. The whole perimeter was probably surrounded by the horrible creatures all caught up by the neck. They probably formed a solid wall. The thought caused him to hesitate, which caused him to die. Near silent zombies rushed him. He fired the shotgun and the recoil was so great that it nearly leapt out of his slack hands. His grip was much firmer with the second shot and he turned a zombie's head into mulch with it. His third was equally as effective, taking down another.

But then he was out of ammo and they were on him with their rending claws. His screams joined Cheryl's as claws pinned him while others scratched at his face and arms…but where were the teeth? He wasn't being bitten! His screams were more out of terror than pain. It was a few seconds before his panicked mind recognized the duct tape covering the zombie's mouths. It made no sense until the boy in the striped shirt came up. His mouth was free of the tape and Benjamin saw the wickedness in the grin.

He also saw the hunger there, and soon he felt it as well. The boy wanted Benjamin's blood all for himself and had contrived to make it so. Benjamin's death was slow— the boy had small teeth. They were like a rat's: gnawing and gnawing, and then there came the slurping and the erotic panting. Benjamin took twenty-two minutes to die and all the while Cheryl fought against the zombies holding her down. They were relentless in their desire to eat her but they could not get past the duct tape. She was battered by their fists and lost an eye to their claws, but she was very much alive and conscious when the boy waddled up with a belly ballooned by Benjamin's blood.

"Mine," he whispered as he knelt over his feast.

Chapter 32

Anna's Victory

10:58 p.m.

With all the shooting inside the building and all the pounding from the outside, Benjamin and Cheryl's screams went unheard, however the fact that they weren't at their posts guarding the prisoners was remarked upon when Eng slipped out of the store room looking for a way to get his cuffs off. He figured there'd be keys to the cuffs in practically every desk drawer.

He never had the chance to find out. One of the dispatchers came hurrying out of the women's room and practically ran right into him. The two stared at each other and then the woman said: "I'm gonna tell." Eng shrugged as best he could with his hands cinched behind his back. As the woman scurried off, presumably to "tell" he looked around at the situation.

It wasn't good.

The gaping holes in the front door were being slowly widened with each passing minute and now huge cracks connected them. It was only a matter of time before they came crashing down from the weight of the beasts pressing on them. The door that led to the office wing was already bent on its hinges and now Chuck and PFC Max Fowler were taking turns shooting through the gap. It was slowing the zombies but not stopping them. The hallway of the incarceration wing was jammed with the undead. They were so densely packed that they could hardly swing their arms enough to pound the door. The door was safe, but the exit was blocked completely.

Not only were the people in the station trapped, the trap was closing in on them.

Eng went back to the storeroom. "We're screwed," he announced, and then described what he'd seen.

Minutes later, Deckard came back, holding his M16 at the ready. "Where'd your guards go?" he asked.

"They did what any smart person would have, they ran away," Anna answered. She paused, swallowed loudly, and then asked: "How bad are we screwed? I mean is there any chance of a rescue?"

"Slim," was all Deckard could honestly say. "We're hoping for a couple of Blackhawks to get here before the doors come down. You say they ran away? Out the back, I'm guessing." She nodded, trying her best to be agreeable. He gave them a hard look, which melted away with the stress he was under. "Stay here, please, for your own sakes. Some of us are…a little wired right now. You might get hurt."

"What's he mean by that?" Allen asked as Deckard left the room. "We didn't do anything wrong." They were all nodding but jumped as Deckard opened the loading dock door. Cheryl was just about dead and still her screams cut the night like a razor.

Meeks looked like he was about to be sick. He was imagining that it was himself out there. Eng smirked at this and said: "And that's how you thin the herd." Meeks snarled something about revenge, making Eng shake his head. "You should be thanking me. You heard Deckard: a couple of Blackhawks. According to my count, there were thirty-one people and a dog in this station. Now there are only twenty-nine, and the dog. Your chances of getting on one of those choppers just went up. You're welcome."

"You knew they were going to die out there," Meeks accused.

"I didn't know, actually," Eng answered. "But truthfully, I didn't care." They paused their conversation as the door to the loading dock closed and Deckard walked by. His face was drawn down and the lines produced aged him by ten years. He had crept out to the edge of the building and had seen the horde of beasts crowding over the two

346

bodies and he had seen the others straining at their leashes in the tree line.

There were hundreds.

In a flash he saw the trap for what it was; it made him want to gag. This was a step up from rocks tied to hands. This was diabolical. This was planned evil. This was why he knew he was going to die sometime in the next half hour. He hadn't been lying when he had told the prisoners there was only a slim chance of being rescued, and now, seeing this trap, he would say their chances were even lower.

With that dark thought in mind, he went to where the dispatchers were working. Under orders from General Collins, they were trying to find where many important, but abandoned items belonging to the National Guard were. During the scramble for men to hold the line, equipment such as guns, ammo, fuel, water, and even batteries, had been left behind, either in trucks on the side of the road or in warehouses. They were also making lists of men: who was where and under what command. Two of the ladies were trying to keep track of the helicopters that were constantly whipping by overhead. It was their job to coordinate between the aviation side and the supply side of the army. Deckard knew there were supposed to be specifically trained soldiers doing this, but where they were, he didn't know.

The women worked with one eye on their computer screens and with the other on the doors that were minutes from coming down. They spoke in a high-pitched jabber and took many tiny sips of air instead of normal breaths. Deckard wouldn't be surprised to learn that a few of them had wet themselves in their fear; if he had known, he would have understood.

He sidled up to Courtney, trying not to let on that he was as scared as they were. "Where are we on the choppers? You gave Collins everything he asked for, he's not going to screw us is he?" She started to shrug, but he turned her chair around to face him. Next to her, Sundance gave a growl of warning and showed some teeth. Deckard glared right back and said: "I need an honest answer."

"He'll come through," she answered. "I just don't know when. Jenny is working the choppers, you can ask her."

Jenny didn't look up from her computer as she said: "Fifteen minutes give or take...but they've been saying that for the last hour, so I don't really know. I don't even know where they are."

"Then stop what you're doing and find those choppers!" Deckard snapped. "I want them here in fifteen minutes like they promised. The rest of you prepare yourselves to either get on those choppers or to fight. As of this moment, you're done working for Collins. You're working for me now."

"What we're doing is very important," Courtney said. She had tears in her eyes; she didn't think the Blackhawks would get there in time to save them and she wanted her last moments to be in helping the situation and not spent cowering in the corner crying. "This will save lives and besides, stopping now won't get those choppers here any faster."

A grimace crossed over Deckard's features. He was bristling, ready to either snap out a harsh reply or pull the trigger on his M16 and put a hole in each of the computers. Thuy appeared at his elbow. As usual, he calmed when in her presence and as usual, she had a grasp of the entire conversation even though there was no way she could have heard it all. She inferred what she hadn't heard from their expressions, and by the way they held themselves.

"Courtney, we will proceed from this point as if the deadline for our rescue is set in stone," Thuy said, confidently. "Have the other operators make preparations to abandon their positions. Back up the files that need to be saved and then have them inform their contacts among the various National Guard units that they will be out of the loop for a minimum of one hour. Deckard, you will do the same thing with the personnel here. Prepare them to make a quick and possibly bloody exit from this building."

Bloody exit…those words went deep into him, echoing down to the crevice where he hid his fear. It bloomed like poison.

Perhaps she saw. Thuy put a soft hand on his arm. "We'll make it out, right?" she asked.

You will, he thought to himself. "Yes, without question," he said. Inside he crushed down on his fear, pushing it back down into its crevice. He even managed to give her a smile. It would be his last smile of the day.

The second he left her, the smile morphed into a scowl. He wore it as he began to round up the people who weren't currently fighting, bringing them to sit in the call station, which was the geographic center of the building. The prisoners were also brought forward to sit slightly apart from the others. Bob and Allen, the two men who had come in with the dead Mexican sat at the edge of the room. So far, their eyes were clear, but no one trusted them.

"M-Me and Allan sh-should be armed," Bob said in a light stutter that went hand-in-hand with the sound of the guns blasting away. "And we shouldn't have to wear these stupid cuffs. We didn't do anything and besides we can fight. You have to let us fight, at least for our survival. It would be inhumane if you didn't."

Thuy cast an eye Deckard's way suggesting that she thought they were correct, but before he could say anything, another of the prisoners spoke up. "And what about us?" Meeks asked. "The least you can do is uncuff us. I don't know about them, but I am innocent. I was wholly within the law. You may not like it and I'm sorry it went down the way it did, but this…you can't do this. You can't leave us cuffed and unarmed, and pretend that you're the good guys."

"Uncuff them, but no weapons yet," Thuy ordered.

Deckard handed his M16 to Dr. Wilson, knowing it would be dangerous to bring it among the five prisoners. "Cover me," he said to the doctor.

Wilson chuckled. "Aren't you being a little melodramatic?"

"No," Deckard replied. He wasn't blind to the desperation in their eyes. And he hadn't forgotten that two of the five were mass murderers and that Meeks had been willing to kill in cold blood. Deckard ordered the five to face the wall. When they did, he went to Anna first. She was the smallest and with her mangled left hand, she was physically the least dangerous. When she tried to turn around after the cuffs were off, he pressed her face against the wall.

"Not yet. Not until I say so." She smiled as if to say there were no hard feelings, but she couldn't hide the cold look in her eyes. He went next to Allen and then to Bob. Next, he went to Meeks. One cuff was off when two different screams lit the air.

One was Burke who yelled: "They're in! The door is down! Everyone get ready."

The other was Jenny who whooped: "The Blackhawks are almost here! I just got in touch with the pilots, we have two inbound in ten minutes."

Meeks spun suddenly. He was smaller than Deckard and fast as a snake. He was also a trained FBI agent and knew a dozen ways to break the grip of a bigger man. Deckard was trained as well and, more significantly, he had been trained to a higher standard than what was mass-produced in Quantico. The spin didn't catch him unprepared. A quick step back gave him room and then he leapt up and in, surprising Meeks and catching him square in the diaphragm with his full weight driving in behind his right knee.

Meeks went down gasping for air as Deckard stepped back, his eyes flicking to Eng, whom he suspected of being the most dangerous of them. Eng smirked in appreciation of the move and said: "My cuffs? I'll be good. I promise."

"No, not yet." He strode to Wilson and took back his M16 and then glanced to the front where Burke, Johnny Osgood, Lieutenant Pemberton and two of his troopers were killing the zombies piling in through the collapsed front door. For the moment, the flying lead was holding the beasts back. At the door to the office wing, Chuck was pointing for Max to join the fight at the front of the lobby, and in the call center, the women were pulling memory sticks from their computers and rushing to join the group waiting to leave. The situation was, for the moment, under control.

It was a short moment.

Deckard had to get to the front of the building. He could see the zombies blasting through the broken doors and the sound of gunfire was thunderous. He jerked a thumb toward the prisoners and was just yelling to Wilson: "Watch them closely," when Anna made her move.

The vial of Com-cells had sat in her bra all this time and now she fished it out. Calmly, she stepped behind Allan and took a hold of his collar. "Whatever you do, don't move," she said to him. Louder, she called out to Thuy: "Dr. Lee! Do you recognize this?"

Thuy's dark eyes went wide as she recognized the vial. "How? I mean…that's not possi…" Her words faltered as her mind struggled to come to grips with what she was seeing and what it meant. She wanted to tell herself that Anna was bluffing, that the world was full of vials if one knew where to look…however Anna's vial had a black top with a band of gold around it—the same ones they had used strictly for the Com-cell trials. They were exceedingly rare outside of a research lab; and in the hilly forests of the lower Catskills it would have been impossible to come across one.

Logically, this meant Anna had to have picked it up in Walton, and this begged the question: if there *weren't* Com-cells in it, why would she have bothered to steal it? There was just one answer: she wouldn't have.

The only conclusion Thuy could reach was that she had stolen it sometime before or during the trial, probably to give to the company she was spying for…and now she was threatening to release the Com-cells in a room crowded with people. Thuy glanced around; of the twenty-nine people trapped in the station, twenty-three of them were in the immediate vicinity and of those, only three were currently masked.

"No one move!" Thuy commanded. The people weren't stupid. They saw the vial and they knew where Anna had worked; they had frozen in place even before Thuy had spoken. "What do you want?" Thuy asked.

"I don't want to kill anyone, but I will if I have to," Anna said. She held the vial up, ready to hurl it if need be. "I just want to get out of here, the same as all of you."

With zombies already in the building and now this, Thuy could feel her heart begin to jitter. It was a struggle to force her words to come out smoothly. "I already planned on taking you with us. I swear that is the truth."

"Sure, if there is enough room, right? That's a big if, Thuy. Those helicopters fit eleven people. According to my math there's going to be a few of us who are shit out of luck."

"They'll take more," Thuy said, though if this was true, she didn't know. She had just assumed they would.

Anna shook her head. "I'm not taking the chance. And besides, even if you were going to take us with you, weren't you planning on having me jailed?" Thuy could only nod. There was no sense lying so obviously. "That's not going to happen. What is going to happen is that the five of us prisoners are going out on the first chopper that lands. We'll take five hostages with us. The rest of you can go on the second chopper."

The simple math before Thuy was appalling. Nineteen people on one Blackhawk? Her heart was skipping erratically now. She took a breath to steel herself before saying: "That's unacceptable. Deckard, shoot her."

This made Anna laugh. She cocked her arm ready to wiz the vial. "If that gun moves everyone in this room will get a good coating of Com-cells in their purest form. Try me, Thuy. I would much rather get shot by your lap dog than turn into one of those things out there and I'd also much rather get shot than be left behind and eaten alive, and I would much rather get shot than be the scapegoat for this entire mess. So go ahead and raise that gun, Deckard and see if I'm bluffing."

The gun in his hand felt like it weighed a hundred pounds. He knew she wasn't bluffing. Slowly, he took his right hand away from the trigger housing and held it up. She beamed at him. "Here's how this is going to work. Everyone will turn around. The five of us will each take one weapon and a hostage. The rest of you will face away until the chopper lands and then *sayonara* and good luck to you."

Thuy stood like marble: stiff, cold, brittle, beautiful. Behind her, heedless of the hostage drama playing out, men were cutting down the zombies who were now at the barrier of furniture. There was no more time for bargaining, but the number nineteen kept swimming through her mind. "Take two more hostages and we have a deal," she tried.

"No. You're going to have to figure out who you want to sacrifice." Anna's smug face was full of glee as she added, "I doubt it'll be you who volunteers to stay behind."

"That's where you're wrong, Anna. I will be the last to leave this building." Thuy took a shaky breath and doomed herself by saying: "Everyone turn around. Whoever is chosen as a hostage, go quietly and without fuss. Anna will not kill you unless she has a reason to. Isn't that right?"

"Of course," Anna said around a smile of victory.

Chapter 33

Revenge of the Damned

11:22 p.m.

The mechanic, Cori Deebs hadn't died in the foxhole after Jerome left him. He had shoved his fist up into the hole in his neck where the zombie had chewed right to his jugular and then he had rolled over, letting his weight apply the needed pressure to stop the bleeding. More than the pain, fear had his waking mind in an iron grip and he would have blubbered or cried out with every branch snapping in the forest, and every moan from a passing zombie, but thankfully, he had fallen unconscious from blood loss.

In the hour he lay there, the Com-cells worked their magic. When the Coast Guard planes, punching flares out into the sky, woke him, he was no longer afraid. He was angry. He was stone-cold fucking furious that he'd been left behind by Jerome and abandoned by the entire army. And he was angry over the lights searing his eyes. He squinted and threw an arm over his face when the planes roared overhead.

"Mother fuckers!" he seethed, growing angrier with every pass.

When he was able to, he stood. He went light-headed and had to grab the side of the hole to keep from falling. The world spun before his eyes, but not only did he remain standing, he was also able to climb out of his foxhole dragging his M16 behind him. Hate drove him beyond the normal physical limits of his body. Hate propelled his legs and made him ignore the pain—not the pain in his neck, he barely felt that, but the pain in his head. Every step felt like someone was stabbing his brain with a barbecue fork.

But even that was nothing compared to the all-consuming hate. As he walked, he planned what he would do when he found Jerome…oh, the things he would do to him! At first he mapped out all the horrid and torturous things he would do, however gradually, he came to realize that what he really wanted to do was to eat Jerome. Slowly, of course so that when the hot, fresh blood, pumped into his mouth, Jerome would still be alive and he would be screaming.

"Mmmm," Cori murmured, picturing it. Unbeknownst to him, he was feeling something new: lust. This corrupt lust had a component of sexuality to it, a small component to be sure as the rest was the purest evil. Cori wanted to cause pain with every fiber of his body.

Picturing it, he ate up the miles walking with growing eagerness to the sound of the guns. Above, the night sky had grown dark, as the Coast Guard had slowly shifted their flights eastward. As Cori trudged along there were others in the dark with him. Among them were half-mad soldiers with black eyes, their blood steeped in Com-cells and turning septic. Both Cori and the pure zombies ignored them. If one got too close, Cori would sneer and clutch his weapon closer to his chest.

At this point, Cori wasn't exactly sure how to work the M16. In the hour he had been plodding along, it had become a puzzle, just like math or remembering what his mom looked like. Things were becoming distinctly hazy in his mind. They were murky but clearly so. His boots were a fine example. He could see the laces and he knew he should have been able to tie them but for the life of him, he wouldn't have been able to even if someone had put a gun to his head.

And the canteen sloshing at his hip. The sound of it was maddening. Somewhere along the line, he had pulled it out and stared at it. The lid was supposed to come off, he knew that, only how did it come off? How did it go? Was there a button? A lever? A switch? He bit at the top, gouging grooves in the plastic with his teeth and still it wouldn't budge. His thirst became over-powering, driving his feet faster and faster.

When next he thought about the canteen, it was gone. It had been in his hand, then somehow it had disappeared. His thirst raged through him; it was all he could think about besides the anger, of course. He was furious and thirsty and so in need of clean blood that he wanted to scream in frustration. The sound coming from his wounded throat was a poor substitute for the real thing.

He drew in a deep breath for a proper scream, only just then a helicopter flew by. From its side door what looked like a line of fire blazed. Bark and splinters from the trees all around Cori flew up into the air while the ground puffed dirt and grew small holes with amazing rapidity. Next to him, a stinking woman in the ragged remains of pink pajamas came apart, spraying him with black blood and greying flesh.

Belatedly, he came to the conclusion: *I'm being shot at!*

Now his fury was uncontained. It was a wild beast within him and only his subconscious mind was left to control his body. Up came the M16.

The Blackhawk was like a shadow painted on the night's sky. It had come charging up to unload its compliment of soldiers but because there was no dedicated ground control for the command post's LZ, and there were two other copters trying to land, the pilot was forced to pull back. The pilot was in no rush and couldn't believe he was in any real danger. With his door gunners blasting at the target-rich environment, he kept the bird hovering twenty feet over the tree line with its nose pointed toward the landing zone.

Cori emptied a full thirty round clip into the Blackhawk. Most of the bullets tinked harmlessly off its metal hide. One bullet rapped off the door gunner's helmet, sounding and feeling as though someone had come up behind him and had given his helmet a hearty smack with a ballpeen hammer. Another skipped off the glass next to the copilot's right ear. He gave a jerk of shock and stared at the mark it had made on the bullet resistant glass. "What the hell?" he exclaimed loudly.

The pilot leaned over to see what had riled his friend and was struck by flying lead just at the corner of his right eye. The last bullet to leave Cori's weapon had taken a path through the air that could only have been guided by the evil intentions of the devil. It sizzled through the open side door, passed beneath the gunner's left ear as he started in surprise from his helmet having been hit. The bullet then blazed between a passenger seat and the frame of the gunship, a space three inches wide, before hitting the pilot who was out of position to be protected by his reinforced chair.

He was not killed by the bullet, nor was he killed by the subsequent crash. He was killed when the zombies ate him, trapped in his chair and screaming deliciously.

Helicopters, far more than planes, are delicate instruments. When the bullet blasted off the bone at the corner of his eye, the pilot spasmed, yanking back hard on the cyclic, the joystick-like controller that sat between his knees. Immediately, the gunship pitched back, its nose begging for the sky.

The co-pilot turned from the window to see the pilot shooting blood in an arc onto the instrument panel. Then as the Blackhawk canted back, he stared at his instruments in confusion. He lost three seconds and by that time, the tail rudder was dipping amongst the trees. There was a loud "crack" and then the Blackhawk began spinning in its pitch. It looked like a monstrous ballerina up on its toes, pirouetting in the night. There was no coming back from this. The copilot shoved the cyclic down, but just then, the pilot still fighting to do his job and save his craft, did the same and together they slewed the great machine straight into the ground.

The zombies rushed forward in a mass, they swarmed the smoking wreckage and ate their fill of the fourteen men on board who were too stunned or injured to defend themselves. Cori, driven by his maddening hunger hurried to the crash site but was too late. There was a bank of zombies fifty deep as he got to the wreckage. Grunting with the effort, he threw aside those in front, one by one, but, by the time he got to the feast, the blood was cooling and the hearts that sent it pulsing in that slow erotic way were now all stopped. The interior of the Blackhawk was a scene straight out of hell: blood, both black and red covered every inch of it. There were pieces and parts of humans everywhere and the remaining bodies were so badly mauled that most of them appeared to have been turned inside out. Their empty skins hung limp off the chairs like dirty clothes flung about a college dorm.

"Mother fucker," Cori growled. His stomach growled louder. There was a splash of red on the door and he took his finger to it—cold. It made him want to gag.

He cursed again and then his eyes fell on another black rifle. He grabbed it without checking to see if it was loaded. Such things were simply beyond him now. The gun killed things, that's all he knew. Along with a thousand others, he turned from the Blackhawk and again headed for the hated lights.

The crash of the helicopter went unremarked upon by the soldiers fighting a quarter mile away on the hill's edge. They saw it twist ugly in the sky, saw the flash as it struck the earth and heard the odd, rubber warble of a three-hundred-pound metal blade flying through the air after it had snapped off the machine, but they had other things to worry about, chiefly ten thousand monsters trying to kill them. The great din and rumble of gunfire, as well as the lights from the Humvees and trucks acted as beacons, drawing every zombie from miles around. They came stumbling from all directions of the compass save for due east where a corridor of freedom led to a straight shot to the city of Hartford and her million citizens.

With a horrible death swarming up in the thousands toward them, the men and women on the hill displayed a courage unequalled on any battlefield. With grim determination, they struggled against the terrific odds and fought until they were ankle deep in hot brass from the spent rounds of their weapons. Yet courage alone was no guarantee of victory especially when their flanks were turned and they could see the undead closing in to cut them off. It made it nearly impossible to concentrate on the ones in front.

"On the right!" yelled Lieutenant Colonel O'Brian. "We got them on our right. Give me volunteers to shore up our flank. You, you, you," he said, picking men all around Jerome Evermore, leaving him feeling extremely lonely and friendless though he hadn't known any of the men who had been around him. Just then, he had the first inkling of worry creeping in over the soldier's bravado that he had wrapped himself in ever since General Collins had given his short "rah-rah" speech earlier.

He worried because he knew this was how all the other lines had fallen; they had been too few to hurl back the zombies.

Taking a deep breath, he began firing again, but not a second later, his M4 made a metallic "chunk" sound, indicating it had run dry. His practiced hands slapped a new magazine in place. There were only three more on the ground next to him; he could shoot through that in minutes.

"Ammo!" he cried. He wasn't the only one. Up and down the line the cry came at short intervals. A woman came huffing up, pulling behind her a child's red wagon filled with full thirty round magazines. She handed him four and then looked around; the nearest fighter was fifteen feet away. "What happened to everyone?" She had wide eyes and the magazines had clinked together when she had handed them over. She was afraid the men were deserting, Jerome guessed. She was afraid she would come back with more ammo and there would be no one left but the zombies.

"Extending the line," he answered, trying to sound nonchalant; had this been a man he would've only grunted as a reply. Instead, he added: "Don't worry, it'll be alright." He could only hope it would be. A pair of deadheads were struggling up the slope. He took another breath and made to show off by knocking these two down the hill to add to the other forty he had already killed. But then his breath cut short. Two, he could handle. Ten, he could handle if they didn't come all at once.

Beyond the pair was what looked like a battalion of them. It was hard to see in the dark and at first, it looked as if the land was swaying like the sea, but it was a mass of zombies marching in close order. A few thousand of them.

"I'm going to need more ammo," he whispered, feeling the saliva turn to dust in his mouth.

"I can give you two more and that's if you promise not to tell any…" As she spoke, Jerome reached over and pulled the wagon over, spilling all the magazines into a sliding steel heap. "Hey! These aren't just for you," she cried.

He grabbed her hand as she started to pick them up again. "Stop! Look." He pointed with his rifle at the tremendous moving shadow. "I'm going to need help. Tell the general. Tell him I'm going to need help right away. Tell him to send anything he has." She was already backing away, her fear well beyond the big-eyed stage, now. Jerome pulled her close to him and yelled in her face: "Don't you fucking run away! Go tell the general right now."

"Yes. Ok." Her name was Cindy Austen and she was a medic—the most useless MOS on the battlefield that day. If a soldier was wounded by a zombie then he was shit out of luck, and if they were shot by friendly fire then they kept on fighting in place. Where else could they go? The surgeons were all on the lines like everyone else. The cry of *Medic!* had not been heard on the hilltop that night and Austen wouldn't have come running if she had heard it; ammo bearer was a far more important job right then.

She ran for the Command and Control Humvee and Jerome watched her until she was at its open door. He then turned and at a range of thirteen feet, sent the two deadheads flopping backwards. They rolled like bowling pins all the way to the bottom of the hill to fetch up against the others. Very quickly, they were trampled under thousands of feet as the shadow advanced, moving onto the hill.

Austen found Collins staring with red eyes at a computer screen. He and his small staff had been working feverishly and without rest, racing to concentrate troops on the hilltop before his second command post of the day was overwhelmed. Tired soldiers, retreating from the sundered lines, were implored to hurry to rejoin the others with Collins hinting strongly that if they didn't, they would be trapped in The Zone forever. This got them moving beyond the point of exhaustion and kept them barely in front of the zombies chasing after. Despite being weighed down with their gear, some of the men had road marched twelve miles in two hours. Those who fell behind were eaten, their screams causing the survivors to choke on their tears as they pressed on until the point of collapse.

As they came straggling up, Collins sent them onto the line as fast as he could, extending the perimeter over and over again. The zombies continually overlapped his flanks, bending them back until the line became "U" shaped with only a few hundred yards separating the sides. He was in danger of being surrounded and cut off.

"Sir!" Austen cried. "There…there are zombies coming."

This wasn't exactly helpful information, they had been coming nonstop all day. Too tired to raise his voice at the asinine statement, he calmly asked: "Where's the problem, Austen?"

She pointed straight west, the one area of the line he expected to be the easiest to hold because of the steepness of the hill. Normally, he might have blown her off; she was just a private, after all, however he had seen her running ammo. She had to have seen every part of the line as well as her share of the zombies. A few wouldn't have had her this rattled.

"How many?" he asked.

She shook her head. "I don't know. A thousand? Maybe more. It's the biggest horde I've seen."

"Get back to work; we're going to need all the ammo you can carry." He turned from her and asked: "Captain Dell, what's our reserve situation?"

"Just us, sir," he said, waving an arm at the men around the Humvees. "The northern line was almost flanked again. It's downhill on that side and they flow like water."

"Shit," Collins swore under his breath. After his earlier experience he was loathe to lose even a single man from the headquarters company, but a thousand of them? A thousand zombies at any point in the line would rupture it with ease. "Here's what you're going to do, get your ass to the edge of the hill and get me an estimate of the numbers there. And you had better run. Hendry! Where are the damned Apaches?"

"Anyone's best guess, sir. We can't use satellite phones to connect with helicopter pilots and I don't know what frequencies they're on. They aren't normally part of our force structure, sorry, sir."

"What about Courtney Shaw? Any word on her?" He had sent the first Blackhawk to her location 90 minutes before. By all reckoning, it should have been back.

"None. No one is picking up."

Collins's teeth gritted at this and he bit back another curse. "What about…"

Captain Dell rushed inside, cutting him off. "We have to retreat! There's too many of them. A thousand, easily, bearing right down on the front of the hill."

"There will be no retreat," Collins replied, evenly. A retreat would mean the collapse of the lines, his men would be crushed from three sides and only a very fortunate few would escape. Once again, he was forced to use poorly trained and equipped weekend warriors. He had only this smattering of men and women from the headquarters company to stand in the breach. There were maybe twenty of them in and around the various Humvees. Most were over forty, a few were straight up fat, and one was six months pregnant; she looked like she was smuggling a soccer ball under her shirt. But at least she had shown up, not everyone had.

"*We* have to fight," he said, smacking one hand into the other. "Get your weapons and get out on the line. All of you, except you," he said to the pregnant woman. "You will be in charge of communications. Get the Governor of Connecticut on the phone. Tell her the center will not hold. She is to fortify her cities as best as she can. Then call the Joint Chiefs of Staff. Tell them that I will resign effective at midnight if the situation is not federalized by the President."

The Humvee was quiet for a span of three seconds and then Collins roared: "Well? What is everyone waiting for? Get moving!" The soldiers went in every direction, grabbing up M16s that were in many cases as old as they were. A few attempted to put on their masks. "No masks," ordered Collins. So far, every soldier had complained bitterly about the masks, all saying it was preferable to risk exposure rather than greatly increasing the chance of being eaten alive because of poor shooting.

They dropped the masks and then began checking their ammo situation. They were being too slow. "Everyone out!" Collins yelled. He too picked up a rifle. He supposed it was the pregnant soldier's and he hoped to God she wouldn't have a need for it. Just in case, he handed over his Beretta and said the same sexist thing Jerome had earlier. "It'll be alright."

She looked at the gun and turned green. "No thank you, sir. I can't." She touched her belly.

"Sure, I understand," he said, though he didn't at all. There was no time to argue, however and he rushed out into the fight. He could do nothing more as commander. He had secured his lines north, south and west of Poughkeepsie, and he had done all he could in the east…meaning he had failed.

"Not going to dwell on that now," he said as he went to the line of battle. It reminded him of the old paintings that hung on the walls of West Point. Men lined up shoulder to shoulder facing an enemy only yards away. He had never understood the courage needed to stare down the muzzles of your enemies' guns at such range, and yet there he was, finding a gap to stand in. The mass of creatures before him was enough to take his breath away.

He struggled for air and then said: "Let's see if I remember how to do this," before shouldering his borrowed rifle.

Just as he was about to fire, someone asked: "Finally deciding to join the fight?" It was Lieutenant Colonel O'Brian wearing a smug look, but one tinged with respect. He hadn't expected Collins to come out of his Humvee.

"I was just waiting until it got sporting out here." Collins fired three times into the mob rushing up the hill. Two were proper shots; the third only skipped off the top of a skull. The M16 was a light weapon and the recoil wasn't bad and yet he felt it right down into the joint of his sixty three-year-old shoulder.

"At this distance you'll want to aim a little lower, sir," O'Brian said. He shot six times in a row—four were definite kills. "You see?"

"Yeah, thanks. I've got a job for you, O'Brian. We need to shorten our lines and close them up. The northern line extends too far. Our only chance is if we shift some men to this spot and then use the rest to button up."

The ramifications of the order were obvious; a twitch zipped the corner of O'Brian's eye. They were going to be surrounded and cut off. They were going to die on the hill. "Gonna be like Dien Bien Phu," he said, referencing the famous siege that ended the French involvement in Vietnam.

"No," Collins replied. "More like Ia Drang. I plan to walk out of here."

O'Brian took a moment and then smirked. "Yes, sir. You're probably right. It's the only way." He left on the run and Collins shook his head at the retreating form, wondering how he had made it to the rank of Lieutenant Colonel. He was competent, but conceited as hell and always on the edge of insubordination.

A scream brought him around. A female soldier was struggling to clear her jammed weapon as zombies came closer and closer to the lip of the hill. Half a dozen men rushed to her aid, blasting the undead beasts back. Those in front fell, spurting black blood; they rolled into those behind causing a temporary lull. Four of the men ran back to their points in the thin line. The other two tried to help the woman with her weapon while she wept in a spasm of fear, her chest hitching and heaving.

"That only takes one man," Collins barked. "I want to hear communication, people. If they're getting too close say something before it gets to be a problem." He turned back to his little spot and saw that even a moment lost was detrimental. The zombies were ten feet away now. He aimed at their chins and fired—perfect. He burned through his magazine and gained a breather.

"Ammo!" he cried, joining a chorus of others.

The soldier next to him paused his shooting and handed him one of his remaining magazines. It was Jerome Evermore. "Here you go, sir. It's always nice to see an officer finally pulling his weight."

Collins took the magazine, slapped it home and asked: "What do they put in the water around here? All of you Connecticut boys act like you've never heard of the word insubordination." He said this with a smile and the soldier laughed.

But only for a moment. The zombies were pressing close again and they had to concentrate on not missing their targets. Their ammo situation was getting scary low and the numbers of zombies appeared endless. It was especially bad when the Coast Guard would roar overhead dropping their flares, then the entire hill was lit and the masses of undead were fully on display as they wriggled and crawled over their finally-dead brothers.

Some of the soldiers couldn't take the sight. They backed away from the edge of the hill, on the verge of running. "Stand your ground!" Collins yelled. "We are surrounded. There is nowhere to run, so stay and fight."

This didn't have the effect he had expected, not only did those who were backing away continue to do so, others also started to. "I said, stand your ground! That is an order." In the dark, he was just an old man in a uniform— he could've been the world's oldest private for all they knew. They left, running to who knew where.

When they were gone, there were gaping holes and the remaining men shifted over and now that they weren't shoulder to shoulder, the courage to stand in the face of the oncoming beasts was even greater than before. Even Collins began to feel it: the horrible odor, the hungry, anxious moans, and the gruesome visage of so many of them, made it difficult to aim into their hideous faces.

But he did. Just like the other soldiers, he stood his ground and fired his weapon until his shoulder went numb, of course, there was a great deal of pain up to that point but there was no getting around it. And still they came on and on. Austen, the ammo girl pulled her wagon up, dumped a handful of magazines and left again, rattling her red wagon on to the next soldier in line. Time lost all meaning and five minutes felt like forever.

He found himself worrying. Where was O'Brian with the reinforcements? Where were the Apaches that Stimpson had finally allowed to cross his borders? An Apache gun ship, just one, would help tremendously. And where was Courtney? He had been a fool not to divert a couple of Blackhawks long before, but that begged the question: when could he have? Every flight that night had been make or break. Every one of them necessary in some crucial manner.

As he was worrying, his weapon stopped working when he squeezed the trigger; he was out of ammo again. That was another fear: would the ammo last?

Slowly, his old man's hands went through the motion of reloading. There was pain in his hands, especially in his knuckles. It had been growing for years now, but the cold night and the rough treatment firing the gun had made it worse. He fumbled the magazine and it dropped into the dirt. Bending over and there was another pain. It lanced up from the small of his back.

Who was he kidding? He was no soldier, not anymore. He was less of a soldier than the middle-aged men and women he had denigrated as "weekend" warriors.

When he got the magazine in place and sent the bolt home, the zombies were right there. It was the same up and down the line. "Bugger me," he said, and then fired his weapon, raking it back and forth. There was no time for aiming. There was barely time for pulling the trigger. They toppled left and right and he stepped forward, driving them back.

And then there was one wearing mottled, green clothes. He stood right at the edge of the hill and just as Collins pulled the trigger, he realized this was a soldier and he was going to kill him His finger tightened down, automatically. Then to his great relief, nothing happened. He was out of ammo again, but this time it was ok.

"Oh, God, I almost shot you," he said, wondering where the soldier had come from.

The soldier answered by looking up. His eyes were wet and black and there was just enough left of Cori Deebs to know to pull the trigger of his own weapon. He didn't aim, but as he was four feet away, he didn't need to.

The bullet was more stunning than painful. It struck the wind from Collins and took his strength. He sat down, or rather plopped down and then Cori was on him in a second, grinning the horrid black grin of the damned.

Chapter 34

And Then She was Gone

11:33 p.m.

Thuy faced the wall, but couldn't help peeking over her shoulder, thinking that one of the five hostage takers would come to collect her. Eng had said: "Get the small ones, they'll be easier to handle." She was the smallest, even smaller than Alivia the teenage girl. Eng had relieved Deckard of his M16, and then took the Glock Thuy had stuffed in her front pocket. He went to Alivia, twisted a hand into her long hair and pressed the pistol to her temple.

She started to whimper; he whispered into her ear: "You should count yourself lucky, you just might make it out of this alive, but only if you keep your head about you."

Anna took a Glock from one of the state troopers and then went to the girl's brother, Jack. She didn't threaten him with the gun, but instead she stuck it in the pocket of her coat. For a weapon she held the vial of Com-cells at the ready.

Meeks took the dispatcher, Renee, hostage, and Bob took Jenny. This left just Allan who didn't look like he wanted to be part of the hostage taking, and yet he kept glancing to the front of the building where the zombies were crawling over each other to get inside. He went to Stephanie, but Anna said: "No, not her, she's sick. She'll slow us down."

Allan actually apologized to Stephanie before going to Courtney who was manning the radio. "Choose someone else. I'm not going," she said. He waved his gun at

368

her, ineffectually. She only shook her head, keeping her eyes locked on her computer screen.

One of the other dispatchers, a woman who clung to the wall as if gravity had flipped 90 degrees, raised her hand. "I'll go." Her voice trembled as did the hand in the air.

"Me too," another woman said, speaking quickly and shooting her hand up, also.

"No, that's not fair," another of the dispatchers said, when Allan hurried to quasi-threaten the first woman with his gun. "He should get to choose." The other dispatchers agreed; they were all desperate to get on the first helicopter. The gunfire from the front of the building was growing in intensity as the zombies pressed forward and now that Chuck had turned his gun away from the office wing, that door was being bent, alarmingly. There was little time left for any of them.

Allan looking lost, waved his gun around, but after another glance to the front where the zombies were now dropping all over the barricade of furniture, he grabbed the first woman roughly by the collar even though she was more than willing to go, and shoved her to stand with the others.

"I want to know how you plan to get out," Deckard asked. "When the helicopters come, you still have to get by the zombies and the back door isn't as safe as you think. It's a trap back there and there's no room for a helicopter to put down."

"They're going out through the front door," Courtney answered, when Eng and Anna didn't say anything but only looked at each other with lifted shoulders. "In three minutes, the first of the Blackhawks will be here. It'll clear the front door with its guns and then you'll board. They know about the hostage situation and they're willing to drop you off anywhere within thirty miles. They don't have fuel to go any further."

Eng let out a pent-up breath. He had feared the zombies, but he was also afraid that he would have to wrest control of a military gunship. In China, American heli-copters had an evil reputation and were universally feared.

Deckard had a completely different response. "What the hell, Courtney? Whose side are you on?"

Without looking up from her computer, she answered: "I'm on the side of seeing as many people as possible get out of this alive."

This shamed Deckard into dropping his angry look to the floor. "Keep doing what you're doing," Thuy told Courtney. "It's the right thing." Deckard grunted in agreement.

During the next three minutes, they all became clock-watchers. It seemed the hands of the clock had gained weight and it became a tremendous effort for each second to journey on to the next. Everyone, except the fighters up front, stood, sweating or crying or whimpering, and in nearly every case, praying. Even Sundance was pensive. Taking a cue from the others, he whined and whimpered as much as any of them.

Only Deckard could be considered calm, although he was only outwardly so. Inside he was a bundle of springs. He was running scenarios through his mind, setting para-meters and evaluating risk. He was sure that in the next few minutes there would be a number of opportunities to free the hostages. Of the hostage takers, only Anna and Eng truly had it within them to kill innocent people. Bob and Allan certainly wouldn't be able to do it. Meeks was somewhat of a mystery. What would he do if Deckard went after Anna's gun? She had foolishly left it hanging out of her pocket where anyone with even a little speed could snatch it.

Deckard planned to grab it from her and shoot Eng. There was a fifty-fifty chance that Alivia would be killed and, sad as it was, those were good odds in Deckard's mind. There was a 99% chance that whoever remained behind when the helicopters left would die a much worse death. He also figured that there was a twenty percent chance that Anna would release the Com-cells. It would mean her own death and he hoped that she loved herself too much to commit suicide. However, he could not rely on hope. He had speed, and he would use it.

Anna had proved herself smart and capable and yet she wasn't trained. There had been many instances in the last two days in which she had been physically slow to react. He was counting on that again. He ran over the simple steps in his mind: snatch the gun from Anna, shoot Eng with it in the next second and then turn back to Anna and grab the hand holding the vial. All perfectly possible—except what would Meeks do? During this time, Deckard would be defenseless and Meeks could kill him with little effort. But would he? Would his anger prevail or his common sense? It could go either way.

That was the dilemma he was facing.

Thuy solved the mental problem by reaching out and taking his large callused hand in hers. He shook his head in a short arc, just a tiny movement. She shook hers right back. 'Don't,' she mouthed. His lips pursed in anger for a second, but then relaxed as he realized she had somehow read his mind. This spoke to him. There was a connection between the two and had been since the first time he had seen her walk into Stephen Kipling's office.

On that first occasion, Deckard remembered, he had watched Thuy as she had sat among the other scientists. Before anyone had spoken, he had known it was she who had discovered the cure for cancer simply by the set of her eyes and the way her chin was tilted up in the slightest. At the time he had felt psychic, now he knew it was more than that.

It had been love at first sight. From that day to this, his feelings for her hadn't changed a hair and the connection between them was just as strong. She knew he wanted to try something and she probably knew exactly what and likely knew the odds of success better than he did. He wanted to fight her on this and she knew that, too. She took his hand and pressed it to her lips.

They remained in that position, looking into each other's eyes, until Courtney yelled over the din of the gunfire: "The first copter is here! Get back from the door!"

Everyone cringed away and for a full second and a half Deckard could have plucked the Glock from Anna's pocket and shot Eng. Thuy kept a good grip on his hand and then the second and a half was gone and the whup-whup-whup- of the rotors came and then the roar of engines. "Get down!" screamed Courtney and then she yelled into the radio: "Go! Go! Go!"

A second later, the air shook as the Blackhawk's miniguns opened up, shredding the zombies in the front of the building. The door gunner had never used his weapon with such savagery before. In the glare of the spotlights, heads exploded, arms were shot away, leaving only bleeding stumps, while intestines ran like wet rope. Blood fountained everywhere, coating everything in a black shine. The gunner began to feel sick to his stomach and he was afraid he was going to barf into his mask.

He didn't have time to be sick.

The zombies turned from the building and came charging at the helicopter. "Slow turn, 180 degrees," the pilot said through his earpiece. Gracefully for such a big machine, the Blackhawk turned in the air giving both gunners a chance to clear the craft in a full arc. "Prepare to receive passengers," the pilot said, in that easy drawl all pilots seemed to use. "Do not try to interfere with the hostages."

Inside the building, the barrage of bullets had been terrifying. The front doors were blasted away and the zombies clustered there had been literally eviscerated. Even the barricade of furniture was gone, having exploded outward in a rain of shrapnel. Everyone was stunned, except Courtney who had hidden beneath her desk and had stuffed her hands over her ears.

She was the first up. "I need group one to go. Get up! Come on there's no time."

Eng jumped to his feet, pulling Alivia along with him. "Everyone get in a tight group," he ordered. "And keep your guns ready. If they try something, use your hostages as a shield and don't be afraid to kill them."

He began heading for the door, holding Alivia in front of him. Anna went next, keeping very close to Eng. Then Bob and Allen with their hostages. They apologized to the others as they went. Finally Meeks went, walking backwards, awkwardly. There was a gap between him and Allan, and Chuck, just realizing what was happening stepped in between.

"No, Mr. Singleton," Thuy said. "It'll end in bloodshed and it won't help us." Reluctantly, Chuck stepped back and glared into Meeks' face as he passed.

Once outside, Meeks was blinded by the spotlight and the hundred mile per hour wind caused by the wash of the blades whipping by overhead. In his hand, Renee trembled and kept stumbling over the body parts that carpeted the earth. They squished and slid out from beneath their feet, making walking treacherous. Falling would mean getting covered in the black, zombie blood and even with masks, it would very likely mean getting the disease.

No one fell, but their feet were slimed black and they tracked it into the helicopter. No one wanted to touch a thing. Eng was forced to, however when one of the door gunners pointed to a headset and then pointed to his mouth and mimicked talking. With the sound of the engines blocking out even thought, the headsets were the only way to communicate.

"Where to?" the pilot asked. His drawl was now tainted with anger and wasn't nearly so easy going. He hated what he was being forced to do.

Eng had no idea where he wanted to go other than out of the quarantine zone…and to some place he could dip his feet in a vat of bleach. A hospital came to mind right away, but those always had armed guards. "A grocery store," he said. There would be plenty of bleach there and people with cars. He would figure out the rest as he went. "You will drop us off and leave. And know this, calling the police will only get people killed."

"You don't have to worry about the police too much," the pilot said. "As far as I know there are no more police left. They're all fighting the dead-heads or have run off."

"Even better," Eng murmured. With no police left it would be nothing to clean himself up, change clothes, kill Anna and the others, and then ghost away. He almost laughed, delighted and relieved.

In the station, Thuy started moving the second Meeks left the building. She dropped Deckard's hand and began issuing orders: "Everyone get your masks on, and glove up. There are extra gloves in a box by the ladies room. Grab at least two pairs to be safe. Deckard, Mr. Singleton, do what you can about re-barricading the door. Wilson and Stephanie, take stock of our ammo and gun situation."

As they hurried to carry out the orders, Thuy spun once, slowly, taking in the havoc and the possibilities and the danger. She then hurried over to Courtney who was wearing a pained expression. "How long until the next helicopter arrives?" Thuy asked.

The pain seemed to deepen. "Ten minutes. They had to stop and pick up a few stranded soldiers."

"How many soldiers?" Thuy asked, dreading the answer.

"Six," Courtney answered so quietly that Thuy barely heard. Still the words struck her like a kick in the guts.

"Six? Really? That's...that's too..." Thuy had to pause and swallow hard in order to collect herself. "Call them back this instant. I need to know how many of us they'll take."

As Courtney did, Thuy looked around at the nineteen of them and worried over who would be forced to stay behind. She knew that if she had to, she would stay and that meant that Deckard would likely as well. It also made sense that Chuck and Stephanie would remain—they would be dead from cancer in a couple of months anyway. That was the easy four; of the rest, who would she choose if she had to?

She would not choose Burke, if he was truly immune, his blood would be needed for study. And not Wilson, either. He was a doctor after all. And not Courtney; she was still young and pretty, but so too were the pair of soldiers and some of the state troopers, and the...

"Twelve," Courtney said, interrupting the knot Thuy was finding impossible to unravel. "Only twelve."

Again, Thuy experienced the feeling of being kicked. "That's unacceptable," she said, rubbing her stomach where her emotional state was having physical effects. "Ask them what their weight capacity is? Tell them we don't need seats, we'll stack one on top of the other if we have to."

Courtney relayed the question. The answer was dismaying: "Twenty-six hundred pounds internally of which fifteen hundred pounds is already accounted for. But he said he thinks the chopper can take an additional eleven hundred. So that's twenty-two hundred pounds we can use."

Thuy turned back to the group and tried to judge their weight. Unfortunately, Eng had taken all of the smallest people. Thuy was absolutely tiny, however the next smallest person left in the station was Courtney at a hundred and twenty pounds and then Stephanie at a hundred and twenty-seven. From there the weights began to shoot up. The remaining dispatchers ranged from plump to chubby, while the soldiers and troopers were all taller than average and broad in the shoulders. Deckard was the strongest of the men and Wilson the heaviest with his balloon of a gut. Even skinny Burke and lean Chuck Singleton were up over one-seventy.

She had twenty-two hundred pounds to work with. She calculated an average weight of one hundred and sixty pounds; that meant fourteen could go and five would die.

"I need your attention!" Thuy called out. When everyone looked over, she took a breath and said plainly: "There's not enough room on the helicopter for everyone. Five of us will have to stay." She meant to say more but her strength left her as almost everyone began to whisper and look around, each deathly afraid of being one of the five left behind. Only two of them remained silent.

Deckard stood like a statue, his eyes on Thuy; he was reading her just as she was reading him. He would stay and was pissed that she thought she would as well. The other person was Chuck who nodded and then raised his hand.

John Burke scowled and then looked pained and then scowled some more. "I would, but I got me a little girl I gots to find. Y'all understand, right."

"I have a child, too," one of the dispatcher's declared, her face a vision of misery. There came a louder murmuring over this. Those without children started to become angry, thinking this was the one criterion that would keep a person safe.

Thuy raised her hand to quiet them. "Everyone shut up. I'm looking for volunteers. We have one in Mr. Singleton. I am another. And…"

"My ass you are," Deckard snarled. He strode over to her and put her hand down, pinning it to her side. She didn't try to stop him. He could have bent her into pretzel if he wished. "I will stay but you can't," he said. He turned to the others: "I need three more volunteers."

"She just volunteered," one of the troopers said. "You only need two."

"She volunteered out of guilt," Deckard said, sneering at the man, "Because she thinks she had something to do with this. But she didn't do anything wrong, and if there's anyone who can find a cure for this it will be her. She's getting on that helicopter."

"You can't make me," she said in a whisper.

His eyes blazed. "That may have been the only stupid thing I've ever heard you say." He dug in his pockets and showed her the handcuffs he had taken off Anna. She started to splutter out a protest but before she could get a coherent word out she was cuffed with her hands in front of her. He then clamped a hand over her mouth. "Now I need three more volunteers."

Stephanie Glowitz stepped forward. She took tiny steps to come to stand next to Deckard, Chuck said under his breath, "Oh damn." He didn't try to stop her, they both knew they were doomed. He took her hands and kissed her lightly on the mouth.

"Two more," Deckard said. "And you don't have to worry about volunteering," he said to the trooper who had made a fuss about Thuy not being allowed to volunteer. "I don't need any cowards staying because I plan on making it out and I won't have you dragging me down. Now, come on, two more."

Max Fowler raised his hand and stepped over. Deckard clapped him hard on the back and Chuck gave him a nod. Stephanie couldn't acknowledge him. She could do nothing but fall into Chuck's chest. She was so afraid she didn't know if she could stand. A part of her felt like fainting and she really wanted to. She wanted to black out and forget any of this was happening, but she fought against it. She knew Chuck would carry her if she fell and she wasn't going to burden him with her weakness.

Now, heads hung low and people toed the floor, refusing to look up. An uncomfortable silence dipped over them that was broken only by the sound of the zombies reforming their ranks and heading toward the smell of fresh blood. "You have to take me," Thuy said in a mumble. Deckard's hand had never been hard on her lips, he loved them too much to bruise them.

"You know I can't," he whispered in her ear. "I mean that. You know me. You know my heart or at least I hope you do. I can't watch you die, not when I can keep you safe so easily."

He was right, she knew his heart and that was why she wanted to stay. Never in her life had she had such a connection. Who knew it could hurt so bad? "What happened to making it out?"

There had never much of a chance and now that Stephanie was with them it dropped even further, the cancer had made her frail and weak. To make matters worse, Dr. Wilson cleared his throat and raised his hand. "I'll do it. If Thuy's not going, somebody has to be the brains of the outfit."

Deckard smiled at him but inwardly he felt his heart sink. He had been hoping for Fowler's buddy Osgood to volunteer or at least one of the troopers. Now he had an over-weight fifty something who couldn't shoot for shit, on his team.

"I guess this is it," Deckard said. "Fowler and Chuck, make sure we each have one of the M16s and also plenty of ammo. I want to be re…"

Courtney interrupted him. "They'll be here in three minutes." Everyone glanced to the front where the first of the zombies were coming in through the shattered remnants of the main doors, sliding in the entrails of their brothers. Dozens more were behind these. Courtney flipped off her computer and then came up to Fowler with Sundance right at her hip as always. She gestured to the dog and asked: "Bring him back to me will you?" He nodded but his throat had seized up. They were twenty miles from the nearest border and still had no way to cross. It was pitch black outside where the dead always had the advantage over the living. Just then, he was scared of the dark like he hadn't been since he was a child.

"Thanks." Courtney looked like she wanted to say more but her lips trembled and she turned her face away.

Of the five who were to remain, Chuck was the least afraid, at least for himself. In truth, he was furious at how cowardly the other men had been. He was very near to cursing those leaving, but he feared Stephanie would see the anger as doubt that they wouldn't be able to make it out of The Zone…and she would be right. There was no way. He didn't even think they would make it to the woods and that meant he would have to kill her.

He knew how it would go: they would run outside and become surrounded by the monsters. They would fight until it became obvious they were just putting off the inevitable and then he would kill her with a shot to the back of the head and then he would kill himself just as he had been planning on for months now. Thinking about this, he felt the fury inside him flip on its tail and he was suddenly sad. "It'll be ok," he said to Stephanie. She was clinging to him, shaking all over.

The sound of rotors slapping the air came to them. Thuy turned to Deckard. She had to yell to be heard. "Uncuff me!"

"No," he said. He fished out the key to the cuffs and tossed them to Burke. "Make sure she gets on that chopper. Throw her in if you have to."

Burke advanced on Thuy and she screamed: "No! Get away from me, Burke." She looked like a wild thing all of a sudden and he stepped back with his hands up. She then turned on Deckard and with that same wildness, snarled: "I love you. You know that, damn it. Now, promise me you'll make it. Promise me!"

She wanted to be lied to, they both knew it.

"I promise."

For some reason she laughed at this, but it was a broken sound because she also cried. "Will you kiss me, now?" She was afraid that she wouldn't have time to be kissed good-bye if they waited even a minute. The rotors were louder and the miniguns had opened up, ripping the night with what seemed like one endless explosion, and the engines of the Blackhawk were a lion's roar.

Deckard took her shoulders in his heavy hands and pulled her close. "It'll be alright," he lied again and then kissed her deeply. It was all warmth and softness until a hand grabbed Thuy and pulled. It was Burke. The Blackhawk was on the ground and the survivors were rushing out the door. She said something but the wind from the rotors tore the words away. He yelled: "I love you!" but Burke had turned her and was pulling her through the wrecked station where the howling of the machine drowned everything out.

And then she was gone.

Chapter 35

Midnight and Death

Courtney Shaw had seen the kiss and, despite her fear and exhaustion, she had felt jealousy slip into her heart like an assassin's dagger. When she had said goodbye to Max Fowler, she had wanted him to kiss her, only he was married. Though he hadn't once mentioned his wife in the few hours they had together, she had seen the ring and she had seen how he had held himself in reserve around her out of loyalty to his wife.

She had wanted that kiss, not because she loved him, but because he was a man. A real man who had fought for her and beside her and he had volunteered to die so that others could live, so that she could live. She felt she owed him something, as if he deserved for someone to touch him one last time, to show they cared. To show that he wasn't dying for a bunch of cowardly ingrates.

But those seconds had slipped away and then the chopper was there. Sundance had tried to come with her and had barked loud enough to be heard, but Max had a hold of him and she could only wave until she was at the side of the Blackhawk as the minigun deafened her. Hands pulled her up into it and she was crushed into the others, squished so she could barely see anything.

It seemed like only a second later that they lifted off. She tried to wave again but as she watched, the door from the office wing finally gave way and the horrible beasts flooded into the lobby, blocking out all sight of the five who had remained behind.

Next to her, Thuy saw this as well. She opened her mouth to scream but nothing could be heard and then her knees buckled and she would have fallen but some un-known soldier caught her. She cried, with her head hanging, looking like a porcelain doll that had been broken by sheer sadness.

The ride in the Blackhawk was cold and loud. The second day of the ordeal had become a memory at the stroke of midnight but no one knew and no one cared. The survivors took turns washing their shoes and lower legs in the bleach that some of the troopers had brought with them from the station. The rest was poured on the interior decking. Burke, who had washed Thuy's feet, unlocked her and then tossed the cuffs away into the dark. Courtney saw him mouth: *I'm sorry*, but Thuy didn't see.

Five minutes from the landing zone a whispering began—actually it was one person yelling into the ear of the person next to them, although when Courtney heard she had to have it repeated twice by Burke. She yelled back: "It's a hot LZ? What's that mean?"

It meant they were going to be landing in an area under attack. From the air it looked worse than at ground level. The undead were everywhere, surging across the fields and farms in numbers that were beyond belief.

"Don't land here!" people started yelling. They pounded on the walls of the Blackhawk, but it was no use. The pilot paused over the hilltop to let his gunners burn away the last of their ammo and then he thumped down in the grass behind a line of trucks. Immediately, people were there pulling them off the chopper and stuffing weapons into their hands.

"To the front go! Go, go, go."

"Where's General Collins?" Courtney demanded of the man.

"At the front. Now go before it's too late." He pushed her in the direction of the hill's edge.

With Thuy next to her looking grim but ridiculous, with an M16 in her hands, they went to the hill where men were firing at point blank range into the masses of undead. With little choice, the soldiers, the troopers, the dispatchers and the one remaining scientist hurried to take their places in the line. The effect was immediate. The black-eyed beasts were mowed down with little thought for aiming. For a few minutes, the zombies were halted as a wall of bodies was built up that had to be crawled over.

During that short breather, they were resupplied. While Thuy spent a moment figuring out how to work the rifle beyond the simplest: point and shoot, Courtney went in search of General Collins. She asked everyone: "Have you seen the General?"

Only a young woman, who was staggering with exhaustion and pulling a little red wagon, could answer. She pointed to a spot off to Thuy's right. "He was right there, but I don't know where he's gone to now."

The shooting started up again on the other side of the hill and the battle sounded fierce, but Courtney ignored it. She had a sinking feeling as she approached the piles of bodies where the girl had pointed. There were many of them contorted in death. They were all dark things, evil things. She couldn't make out their faces until a plane flew overhead spitting flares out its port side. Under the blinking glare of the harsh light, she edged forward holding the M16 out in front of her, as though it were a spear instead of a gun.

She was ready to kill; a strange feeling.

But what was there was dying already. It was an old man. In his hand was a pistol and there was black blood sprayed across his neck and chin and the body of a soldier lying over his legs. Strangely, his eyes were still the purest blue. "Are you one of them?" she asked.

"I will be if you don't kill me," he said in a raspy voice. "Just pull the trigger, child."

The voice was different, tired, weak, and close to death…or close to an eternal life as a vile creature. The words, however were his. "General Collins, is that you?"

"No," he whispered, sudden tears coming out of his eyes. "Private Collins. I've demoted myself. I've…I've failed my men and my nation. Go on, please. Kill me. It'll be for the best."

Courtney shook her head, side to side, rapidly, her own tears forming. This wasn't how she had expected to meet this man. She had thought they would share a beer one day and laugh at the craziness of the last couple of days. She dropped to her knees next to him. "I won't do it, because you didn't fail. The line has held, sir. It bent, but it didn't…" She choked on her words.

"That's nice of you to say, but I hear the truth. I hear the screams." There were screams but suddenly they didn't sound like they were of pain anymore. Courtney looked around, wondering what was going on and then she saw the fruition of her work in the sky. They had finally made it.

"You're wrong, sir. You've won. Those are shouts of joy. Look, you asked for the cavalry and they're here." She pulled him to a sitting position so he could see the twinkling lights. Four abreast, in a long line they came flying out of the west. Courtney had known about the Apache gunships. She had begged and begged for them to hurry, not knowing if there would be anyone left alive when they finally showed.

As they watched, the Apaches came swooping in, their 30mm nose-mounted chain guns spitting death. Each flight engaged the zombies at treetop level, first with their chain guns and when those spun, smoking and empty, they unloaded their Hydra rockets into the masses. On the hill, the soldiers cheered and danced as the undead were torn apart by the explosions.

Among the Apaches came more Blackhawks loaded with men and equipment. They set down for seconds at a time and then were off again, their door gunners blasting away. It wasn't as smooth an operation as it could have been and Courtney was thinking that she could now pull her girls back so they could do the job they were in no way trained to do and yet had done all day.

"We did it, Courtney," Collins said, smiling, now.

She was surprised to be recognized. "How'd you know it was me?"

"Who else could've pulled this off?" He laughed, interspersed with a wet cough. It only lasted a few seconds before he sobered up. "Thank you for everything, but now...it's time. I can feel it inside me. It's hateful and evil." She was about to ask: *Time for what?* when it dawned on her, he wanted her to kill him. Suddenly she remembered the gun she had laid down next to him.

"Maybe we can get a medic or a…"

"No, there's no cure and I don't want to become one of them. But if you can't do it, I understand. Just find someone, please. The pain is…is bad."

She reached for the gun, but now it grew heavy and she couldn't lift it into position. Her hands and her heart were too weak to kill this man. "I don't think I can…no, that's not the truth. I don't want to. I would never want to hurt you, ever."

A shadow suddenly appeared over the two. It was a small shadow, the smallest on the hill. "I can do it," Thuy said, a hard note to her voice. Her face, twisted with emotion was equally hard. "I'll kill you, but only if you give the order to find Deckard and the rest of them. That's the deal. If they live, you can die. All you have to…"

Courtney hopped up quick and pushed her back away from the general. "No!" she hissed in sudden savagery. "We won't use him like that. Thuy, listen to me, I'll do what I can for Deckard, but I won't let him suffer any longer. If you won't kill him then I will."

Thuy was quiet for a moment and the hard look in her eyes faded. "You're...you're right. I'm sorry. I can do it. Maybe you should turn away, Ms Shaw."

Courtney was about to when she remembered how she hadn't kissed Fowler goodbye and how she had regretted it. "One second," she said and then knelt again and laid her lips on Collins' forehead and her tears dropped to mingle with his. "It'll be okay," she lied just like everyone else. And then stood.

She was twelve very long steps away when Thuy fired. The sound was a jolt even though she knew it was coming. She jumped and then whimpered and drew a sleeve across her eyes because they were wet and miserable. Men stared at her, which she found infuriating. "Margret! April!" she called to two of the closest dispatchers. "Go find the others. We have work to do."

Epilogue

After Midnight

The Governor of the great state of Connecticut sat at her great desk, twenty square feet of gleaming wood, and felt like a small person. Although the hilltop had not been overrun and the majority of the zombies blasted into goo, she was still under the impression that her western border had fallen and that thousands of zombies were advancing across the state in one great sweep.

She felt small because her first impulse was to figure out how she could get all the food and weapons she could find, grab a boat and sail as far away as she could. After a few deep breaths, she came to her senses and began making calls. The first was to the Mayor of Hartford, whose office was all three blocks away.

"Should we evacuate?" the mayor had asked. "I have some plans in place that are sup…"

"No," the Governor said, calmly. "Massachusetts has closed their border and is arming it as we speak. I'm sure Rhode Island will do the same when they hear the news. This is crazy, but I think our only choice is to turn our cities into fortresses until the Army shows up."

"What? Yeah, that is crazy."

"No, what's crazy is evacuating our cities and filling our state with three million nomads going from place to place looking for safety when there is none. I think we need to create those safe zones in place. So…so I want you to declare martial law in your city. Use your citizens to dig ditches or moats. Have them create walls out of cars or buses or trucks; anything that will stop the zombies. I will coordinate from here, and Ron, if you have any connections in Washington, start begging for favors."

The Mayor of Hartford hung up, putting the phone slowly, almost gently into its cradle and the thought of running crossed his mind as well. Reluctantly, he stayed at his own, far less grand desk, and started making calls. With the police fighting in the west he had very few resources left to begin creating a new defensive perimeter around the city. Calls went out for firefighters, garbage men, even schoolteachers.

Television stations were contacted with carefully prepared speeches, the gist of which was: there was nowhere to run so you might as well stay and help. Although it was after midnight, the vast majority of the citizens were awake and afraid, waiting on news of what was happening in the western part of the state. A large portion of those awake were all packed up and ready to jump in their cars and get the hell out of Dodge, and a lot of them did just that. They heard the news saying to stay and they were the fastest out the door.

There really was nowhere to go. Massachusetts had armed men at every crossing. They downed trees, dug deep ditches, and strung barbed wire stolen from nearby farms. The other cities in Connecticut were also preparing defenses and were quick to turn away people from the outside. Eventually, after driving half the night they returned the way they came and began to help as well.

The western line defending Hartford was set up at the Farmington River—it wasn't much of a river, but it was the best they had. Brush was cleared, cars were pushed end to end at every crossing, and fencing and wiring of all sorts was strung down its entire length. On the east side of the city, they used the Connecticut River as a defensive line; it was a much bigger river than the Farmington. North and south, they chose the widest roads they could as the edge of their lines and began the laborious process of hemming themselves in from all angles.

And all the while, the small zombie pack in the middle of the city continued to grow. Jaimee Lynn Burke's appetite was never satiated for long. Thirty minutes after gorging herself until a burp would bring up a gout of blood along with it, she was hungry again. It was an eternally, gnawing, evil hunger. It made her feverish and shaky and it was hard to concentrate on her traps.

By midnight, the humans around the factory had become skittish. The cat was no longer working. For half the evening Jaimee would give the cat, a checkered one with a bushy tail, a good squeeze and it would screech out a loud, sad meow. It would only take a few of these squeezes before someone would show up. They had eaten three people that way and Jaimee's blonde hair was stiff with old blood. It stuck up everywhere.

But now the cat wasn't working.

She gave it a really big squeeze and it only made a sound like a toad farting. "This thing's no good," she said, tossing the cat to the side where it just laid with its pink tongue sticking out. Jaimee racked her addled brains trying to come up with a replacement for the cat. She thought of a dog, but they had big teeth. And she thought of a goat but there was none around. And that was all the animals she could remember. It wasn't until one of the new kid zombies started whining loudly for more blood that she had her inspiration.

Thirty minutes later, she was in a small park. After setting her little fiends around the edges of it where there was shrubberies, Jaimee Lynn screamed out, "Help me. I hurt my leg! Oh, it hurts so bad."

She blubbered on for a while until she heard someone coming. It was a lady with a flashlight, which stung Jaimee's eyes when the beam struck her flush. Jaimee Lynn hid from the light behind a slide. The lady asked her, "Are you ok?"

"I don't know, can you check my leg. I think it's all busted up from falling off..." she looked up at the swingset but the name of the contraption wouldn't come to her. "From up there somewhere."

The lady leaned in close and shone her light down on Jaimee's leg. The lady smelled so good. Yes, there was the blood pumping through her veins, but she also smelled of cinnamon. The two went together so well that Jaimee's stomach growled like a man's.

"Are you cut?" the woman asked. "There's a lot of blood all over your leg…and your dress? And…and it's in your hair."

The woman had long dreads and a sweet brown face that looked soft as cream cheese and Jaimee Lynn wondered if it would leave a mark if she just touched it gently. But there was no gentle left in Jaimee Lynn. She stuck her fingers in the dreads and launched herself at the sweet face and yes, it was as soft under her teeth as she had reckoned it would be.

The pack heard the scream and came racing to get their fill of blood before it became cold and before the woman's wonderful heart would stop beating. They knew that wonderful heart wouldn't last, just as they knew that it wouldn't stay quiet for long. Just like theirs had, it would start again and the woman would come alive again. Just like the rest.

The End of Day Two

Author's Note

Thank you for reading The Apocalypse Crusade, War of the Undead Day Two. I sincerely hope that you enjoyed it. If so, I'd like to ask a favor: the review is the most practical and inexpensive form of advertisement an independent author has available in order to get his work known. If you could put a kind review on Amazon and your Facebook page, I would greatly appreciate it.

Peter Meredith

P.S. Yes there IS a day three. The Apocalypse Crusade War of the Undead Day Three

Chapter 1 The Hunger for Life

1–2:06 a.m.
Hartford, Connecticut

Jaimee Lynn remembered her name, at least her first name, and she had a firm image of her father's face. She also knew she was from a place called Arkan-na-sas or Arkarassis or something like that, and at the very edge of her memory where everything was quickly becoming grey fog, she recalled the part she had fought for in the school play when she had been in the fourth grade.

She had played a tea cup, and there had been rainbow streamers hanging from the rafters, and there had been a mean boy who had pinched her bottom in front of everyone and had thought that was so funny that he had pointed at her and got his friends to laugh along.

But how long ago that was, she had no idea. It seemed like maybe it had been two years since the fourth grade, but it might have been ten. Numbers were somewhat of a mystery to her, while time consisted of either "now" or "before."

A lot had happened "before," and it was all a blur. There had been a funeral with her mama in a box, and a hospital that burned up and there had been a cat that had got all stiff and wouldn't meow or nothing. And there had been an ambulance with lights that turned the night dizzy, making everything two different colors: red then white, red then white.

And there had been blood. A shiver ran up her back at the thought of the blood. It was always so agreeably hot. She loved it hot. When it was cold it, it tasted like soup that had been left out to congeal and it made her stomach go icky. Jaimee Lynn would never drink cold blood. Never ever never…unless she had to. Unless there wasn't none other.

Thankfully there was lots and lots of blood around, nice and hot and clean. There was blood in the people who were in all the houses and buildings. She was in a city full of houses and buildings, but she had no idea what the name of the city was. Arkanasas maybe? She didn't know and she hadn't spent a moment caring.

All she really cared about was blood, hot and coppery. She cared even though she wasn't hungry yet and wouldn't be for a few hours. Her belly pushed out the front of the white gown she wore as if she had a baby growing inside of her stick-thin body. It was a blood-baby if it was a baby at all. Her belly sloshed liquid when she rolled over.

She was full and sleepy and her eyes were heavy and her brain was addled. Her limbs seemed far away; maybe ten feet away or maybe nineteen. She didn't know and she didn't care. She was too sleepy to care about inches and miles and all that.

What she really wanted at that moment of fullness and contentment was to be cuddled. Even before that school play about the tea cup and the rainbows, and maybe even before the ambulance with its lights, she remembered being cuddled.

It must have been a thousand years ago, back before that rotten boy had pinched her. It was long ago and that was for sure, and it had been her mother who had done the cuddling. Her mother had been the color of gold, like wheat or a sunrise. And she had been soft.

Jaimee Lynn thought nothing could ever be so soft and yet there was a brown woman with thick yarn for hair, laying not three feet away. She lay sprawled out with most of her insides spilled out on the ground. She was growing cold, but for the moment she was warmer than the grass where the *pack* lay in knots like cats in a sunbeam.

The pack were Jaimee Lynn's children, sort of. They were ugly. Some were missing parts and pieces. One little girl was missing most of her hair. It had been ripped out in great chunks and her head looked like pinkish hamburger, except where the bone showed through and that was white as chalk. It was ugly and she was ugly.

There was another boy who was missing his leg from the knee down. He moved around like some sort of pale spider on two hands and the one remaining foot. He was surprisingly quick.

One kid didn't have a face and Jaimee Lynn didn't know if it was a boy or a girl, though it didn't matter all that much to her. She wasn't going to play with it no matter what it was. *They* were different. The other kids were all gross and stupid and couldn't even speak except for a few words like "hungy" or "mama," and everyone knew that even little babies could say those words.

Jaimee Lynn looked down her nose at them as they slept. The blood made them slow, like ol' hounds and they wouldn't budge for a few hours. They wouldn't roll over or scratch themselves or nothing. They would sleep like rocks. It was dangerous to sit out like that, though Jaimee Lynn couldn't remember why.

Remembering was hard, especially when she was full and sleepy. She was full but cold and all she could think was that the brown woman had soft, soft cheeks and that she was still warm. There was steam lifting up from her guts. Jaimee could smell the heat. It was a coppery sort of smell. She crawled to the woman and snuggled up into those warm guts, pulling a flap of skin around her like a blanket.

It was almost perfect, and she felt a bit like a baby herself, especially as she pulled the woman's arm around her, taking her soft brown hand in her small white one. She brought the hand to her face, put the thumb in her mouth, bit down savagely and then fell asleep, sucking gently on that thumb, drinking sips of blood like a baby would from a bottle.

Fictional works by Peter Meredith:

29838359R00217

Printed in Great Britain
by Amazon